Also by Allison Brennan

The Third to Die
Tell No Lies

Look for Allison Brennan's next novel
The Wrong Victim
available soon from MIRA.

THE
SORORITY
MURDER

ALLISON
BRENNAN

mira

Recycling programs
for this product may
not exist in your area.

ISBN-13: 978-0-7783-1168-3

The Sorority Murder

Copyright © 2021 by Allison Brennan

This edition published by arrangement with Harlequin Books S.A.

For questions and comments about the quality of this book, please contact us
at CustomerService@Harlequin.com.

Mira
22 Adelaide St. West, 41st Floor
Toronto, Ontario M5H 4E3, Canada
www.Harlequin.com

Printed in U.S.A.

Tim and Barbara Simonsma
Good people and good friends.

THE SORORITY MURDER

One

Three Years Ago
Friday, April 10

Candace Swain forced a smile as she walked out of her dorm room.

Smiling was the last thing she wanted to do, but Candace had an image to uphold.

She was going to be late for the Sigma Rho Spring Fling—the last big party before the end-of-year crunch. Studying for finals, capstones and senior projects, stress and more stress, and—for some of them—graduation.

The mild April weather was perfect for an outdoor gathering. Candace had led the sorority's social-events committee with setup, and they'd included heat lamps along the perimeter. The Mountain View dorm—which housed all campus sororities, each with their own wing—was on the northeast corner of campus, adjacent to the football field. The Spring Fling was held on the large lawn that framed the north entrance, where they had the most room. It was open to all students for a five-dollar admission, and was one of the biggest moneymakers for the sorority, more than covering its cost. Any profit was donated to one of several charities. Candace had fought for—and won—giving the profits to a rescue mission that helped people get back on their feet. She volunteered weekly for Sunrise Center, and it had changed how she viewed herself and her future. She now planned to be a nurse in the inner city, working for a clinic or public hospital, where people deserved quality health care, even if they were struggling. She even considered specializing in drug and alcohol issues, which were unfortunately prevalent among the homeless community.

She used to think of her volunteerism as penance for her failings. She wasn't religious but had had enough preaching from her devout grandmother to have absorbed things like guilt, penance, sacrifice. Now, she looked forward to Tuesdays when she gave six hours of her time to those who were far worse off than she. It reminded her to be grateful for what she had, that things could be worse.

Candace exited through the north doors and stood at the top of the short flight of stairs that led to the main lawn. Though still early in the evening, the party was already hopping. Music played from all corners of the yard, the din of voices and laughter mingling with a popular song. In the dusk, the towering mountains to the north were etched in fading light. She breathed deeply. She loved everything about Flagstaff. The green mountains filled with pine and juniper. The crisp, fresh air. The sense of community and belonging felt so natural here, something she'd never had growing up in Colorado Springs. With graduation on the horizon, she had been feeling a sense of loss, knowing she was going to miss this special place.

She wasn't close to her parents, who divorced right before she started high school and still fought as much as they did when they were married. She desperately missed her younger sister, Chrissy, a freshman at the University of South Carolina. She'd wanted Chrissy to come here for college, but Chrissy was a champion swimmer and had received a full scholarship to study practically a world away. Candace had no plans to return to Colorado Springs, but she didn't know if she wanted to follow her sister to the East Coast or head down to Phoenix where they had some of the best job opportunities for what she wanted to do.

Vicky Ryan, a first year student who had aspirations of leadership, ran up to her.

"That weirdo is back," Vicky said quietly. "Near the west steps. Just loitering there, freaking people out. Should I call campus police?"

Candace frowned. The man Vicky was referring to was Joseph, and he wasn't really a *weirdo*. He was an alcoholic, and mostly homeless, who sometimes wandered onto campus and wouldn't accept the help he had been repeatedly offered. He wasn't violent, just confused, and sometimes got lost in his own head, largely from how alcohol had messed with his mind and body. But his problems understandably made her sorority sisters uncomfortable. He'd twice been caught urinating against the wall outside their dorm; both times, he'd been cited by campus police. He wasn't supposed to be on campus at all anymore, and Candace knew they'd arrest him if he was caught.

"I'll take care of it," Candace said and made her way around the edge of the party.

She found Joseph on the narrow grassy knoll that separated the football field from the dorms. A small group of students approached her, but one in their group turned toward the grass, likely to confront Joseph.

Candace walked faster, caught up with the student, and smiled brightly. "I got this."

"It's okay," he said. "I'll handle him."

"I said *I* will take care of this. I know him. But thank you anyway."

Mr. Macho didn't want to walk away, yet Candace stood firm. She didn't want anyone to harass Joseph, and she knew he would listen to her. While he wasn't violent, he could be belligerent, and being confronted by a jerk wanting to impress his girlfriend was a surefire way to trigger Joseph and have him dig in his heels. It would only lead to an arrest, and that wasn't going to help him in the long run.

The group walked off, grumbling; Candace ignored them. She approached Joseph cautiously, so as not to startle him. "Joseph, it's Candace," she said. "Remember me? From Sunrise Center?"

He turned slowly at the sound of her voice. A tall man, nearly six foot four, he could intimidate people. But he was also skinny and hunched over from years of walking the streets and looking down, rummaging through garbage, with his hangdog face, ragged salt-and-pepper beard, and watery blue eyes. He was the kind of guy her grandmother would have called a *bum*—dressed in multiple layers of dirty, mismatched clothes, and smelling of dirt and stale beer. He looked about sixty, but she knew that he was only in his forties. She'd heard he'd been living along Route 66 for the better part of ten years. The people who ran Sunrise Center didn't know much about his personal life, only that when he was sober (which was rare), he would talk about home being east, at the "end of the line." But no one knew if that meant Chicago or any of the stops in between.

Candace wanted to know more about his story, how he came to be in these circumstances, why he wouldn't—or couldn't—accept help. Many of the homeless who came to Sunrise for shelter or food would talk to her freely. But not Joseph. When she'd pried once, he disappeared for a while, so she stopped asking. She would rather him be safe than riding the rails.

"Candace," he said slowly after several moments.

"You can't be here, Joseph. The campus police told you that. Don't you remember?"

He didn't say anything or acknowledge that he understood what she said.

"Would you like me to take you over to Sunrise Center? You can get a hot meal there, maybe a cot for the night."

Again, silence. He turned away from her but didn't leave.

She *really* didn't want to call campus police, but if she didn't do something, someone else would.

"Is there a reason you are here?" she asked.

"Leave me alone," he said.

"I will, but you have to leave. Otherwise someone is going to call the police." *If they haven't already.*

He abruptly turned toward her, staggered on the slope of the lawn. His sudden movement startled her; she stepped back.

"No cops!" he shouted.

"You have to leave, Joseph," she said, emphatic. Her heart pounded in her chest, not so much from fear but uncertainty. "Please go."

Again, he turned abruptly, this time staggering toward the stadium fence. She held her breath, watching him. He almost ran into the fence, put his arms out to stop himself, then just stood there. A minute later, he shuffled along the field perimeter, shoulders hunched, without looking back.

She breathed easier, relieved that he was heading off campus. She would talk to the director of Sunrise on Tuesday, when she went in to volunteer. Joseph couldn't keep coming here, but she didn't really want to call the authorities on him. He needed help, not more trouble, and definitely not incarceration.

Candace was about to return to the party when she heard someone call her name. She turned and saw one of her former tutoring students, Lucas Vega, running toward her. She didn't want to talk to Lucas tonight. How many times did she have to tell him to leave her alone?

She stopped anyway and waited.

"Candace," he said, catching his breath. "Thanks."

"What do you want?" she snapped, crossing her arms over her chest.

"I'm sorry."

"Sorry," she said bluntly.

"I didn't mean to upset you the other day. I *am* sorry about that."

She blinked. He sounded so sincere. And truth be told, something he'd said to her a few days earlier made her think long and hard about herself, her life, and the time she'd spent as a student at Northern Arizona University.

A lie for a good reason is still a lie.

Lucas and his wide-eyed, good-natured innocence, his innocuous questions had *her* feeling guilty for no reason. He had picked up on that. And pushed.

No reason? *Ha.* Plenty of reasons. All these doubts and worries she'd been having this semester, the sleepless nights, all came from something she'd done as a freshman that she now had good reason to regret. But what could she do about it? What would come of the truth now?

Maybe there was no good reason to lie.

"All right," she said. "Thank you." It was easier to forgive Lucas than to hold on to this anger. None of what happened was Lucas's fault.

"So will you tutor me again, for finals?"

"No. Afraid not." She could forgive him for prying, but she really needed first to forgive herself. And she didn't know if she could do that with Lucas around, reminding her of her failures and mistakes. He didn't even know what she'd done, but seeing him now was like reliving the past, and her chest tightened. "I'm sorry, but I have too much studying of my own, too many tests. And I'm not working at the writing lab anymore."

Because of you.

Was that even fair? Was it because of Lucas…or because of her own guilt?

He was disappointed, but that wasn't her problem.

"Okay, I understand," he said.

"Besides, you're smart. You'll be fine."

He shrugged. "Thanks."

"Uh, you want to come to the party?" She gestured over her shoulder. They could hear the music from where they stood. "I'll get you a pass. Won't even cost you the five bucks."

He shook his head. "I'm fine. I'm not really one for parties. But thanks anyway."

He turned to leave.

"Lucas," she said. He looked at her over his shoulder. "I'm really sorry."

Then she left him there, waiting for something she couldn't give him.

It took Candace several minutes before she could work up the courage to return to the party. An idea she'd been thinking about for the last few months was now fully developed, as if something inside clicked after her brief conversation with Lucas. Everything shifted into place, and she knew what she needed to do; it was the only thing she *could* do.

No one was going to like her decision.

When she realized she no longer cared what anyone thought, a burden lifted from her heart. She was certain then that she was doing the right thing.

Everyone at the party was asking for Candace, and Vicky had become worried when her friend and mentor hadn't returned after thirty minutes. She sought out Taylor James, the Sigma Rho president, and told her about the homeless guy. "I don't know where Candace is," she said. "I should have just called campus police."

"Candace says he's harmless," Taylor said, frowning. "Sometimes she's so naive. I'll go look for her."

"Thanks. The party is great by the way. Everyone seems to be having fun. How does it compare to previous years?" This was the first party Vicky had helped put together for the sorority, so she was eager to know how well she'd done.

"As good or better," Taylor said with a wide smile.

Vicky tried not to gloat as she practically floated over to her friends chatting near one of the heat lamps. It wasn't cold, but the warmth of the heat lamp and the glow from the string lights added terrific ambience to the place.

"Oh my God, Vicky, this is a blast," her roommate, Nicole Bergamo, said. Nicole was a half-Black, half-Italian math major who could have easily been a model she was so tall and stunning. "*Everyone* is talking about how great it is."

Vicky smiled, talked for a bit, then moved around, being social, doing all the things that she'd seen Sigma Rho board members do. Hundreds of people were dancing, talking, mingling, eating, drinking, playing games. Mostly, they were having *fun*, which was the whole purpose. When the new Sigma Rho advisor, Rachel Wagner, told her it was the best Sigma Rho party she'd been to *ever*, Vicky thought she'd never come down from cloud nine.

"I agree," said the gorgeous woman who was with Rachel. "I'm Kimberly Foster, by the way," she introduced herself. "I'm a sorority alum, and I'm so happy I came up this weekend. You've done a fantastic job. Rachel said you're part of the social-events committee. Isn't Candace leading the committee? I haven't seen her yet."

"Yes, she's around," Vicky said. "This is all her vision. We just implemented it."

"I *love* Candace. Oh! I see her over there."

Vicky looked to where Kimberly was gesturing. Candace was talking in a small group.

"I'm going to catch up with her," Kimberly said. "Nice to meet you, Vicky."

The two women walked away, and Vicky continued her rounds. She was having a blast as her worries that the party might flop were replaced with pride and satisfaction over its success.

Hours later it was midnight, and per city ordinance—because their dorm bordered a public street—they had to cut off the music. That put a damper on things, but it was fine with Vicky—she was exhausted after working all day prepping and all night making sure everything was running smoothly. She was a little miffed that Candace was hardly there: Vicky had only caught a glimpse of her twice. But whatever, she'd seemed preoccupied, and that would have been a party downer.

Vicky ran into the dorm to get extra trash bags—they had to clean up tonight so wild animals wouldn't get into the garbage and create a bigger mess in the morning. She came back out and heard voices arguing near where the DJ had been set up. He'd already packed up and left. She couldn't hear exactly what was being said. It seemed like a quiet, intense exchange between Taylor and Candace though Rachel and her guest Kimberly were there, too. Everyone, especially Taylor, seemed angry.

About sixty people were still milling around, mostly Sigma Rho sisters helping with the cleanup. Nicole came up to Vicky and said, "What are Candace and Taylor fighting about?"

"I don't know. It's probably nothing."

"It's not nothing," Nicole said. "I heard Taylor call Candace a *selfish bitch*."

"Ouch. Well, Rachel is there. She'll mediate."

But Rachel looked angry as well; it seemed that Candace was on one side, and the other three women were yelling at her.

"You're wrong!" Candace screamed, and Vicky jumped. She glanced at Nicole, who looked perplexed as well. Vicky handed her a garbage bag, and they both started picking up trash. She didn't want anyone to think she was eavesdropping.

But she was. As she inched closer to the group, she heard Kimberly say, "Let's talk about this tomorrow, okay? When everyone has had a good night's sleep and we can all think more clearly."

"I *am* thinking clearly," Candace said. "I'm done. Just… done."

She left, walked right past Vicky without even seeing her. There were tears in Candace's eyes, and Vicky didn't know if she was angry or upset, but probably both. Vicky thought about going after her to make sure she was okay, then felt a hand on her shoulder.

She jumped, then laughed nervously when she saw Rachel. Taylor and Kim had walked away in the other direction.

"Sorry. You startled me."

"I'm sorry you had to witness that," Rachel said.

"I didn't, really. Just saw that Taylor and Candace were arguing about something. I didn't want to intrude."

"It's going to be fine. Just a little disagreement that Candace took personally."

"About the party?" Vicky asked, her insecurities rising that she'd messed up something.

"Oh, no, the party was perfect. Don't worry about that."

Relieved, she said, "Maybe I should go talk to Candace."

"No, let her be. I've known her since she was a freshman and took my Intro to Bio class. She has a big heart, and sometimes you can't help everyone."

Now Vicky understood, or thought she did. Taylor had been the most vocal about the creepy homeless guy hanging around the dorms, and she'd been the one who'd called campus police last time, after Candace said not to.

"Let me help," Rachel said and took a garbage bag from Vicky's stash.

Rachel chatted with Vicky, who felt lucky to be able to spend so much one-on-one time with her sorority advisor. Rachel was so smart, an associate professor at just thirty-two, an alum of the University of Arizona Sigma Rho chapter. Plus she had such interesting stories to share. By the time they were done with the cleanup—it didn't take long with so many people working together—Vicky had forgotten all about the argument between Candace and Taylor.

It was the last time anyone saw Candace alive.

Two

Lucas Vega didn't go out to eat often because he didn't have a lot of extra cash, but he owed Lizzy Choi big-time for all the extra hours she'd put in helping him with his senior capstone project—a podcast called *The Sorority Murder*.

"I told you, you owe me nothing," Lizzy said. "This helps me, too. I'll have to put together a capstone myself next year, and I've learned so much more about audio engineering even in the short time we've been doing this."

Lizzy was in the Engineering and Technology Department and one of the smartest people Lucas knew. He was a forensics major and knew he wouldn't have been able to pull off this podcast without her, as he'd told her more than once.

"Humor me, okay?" he said and bit into a fry. McCarthy's had the best burger and fries in town, but that wasn't the only reason Lucas wanted to come to this place. "Do you think I should be worried that we've only had those two callers? And no other leads?"

"No," she said. "It's a new program, and we've only aired two episodes. Give it time."

"Time is one thing I don't have," he said, sipping his beer.

"It's not only about you solving the cold-case murder, right? Because that's an incredibly high bar. You're doing this for your capstone, so it's the paper you write after the podcast finishes airing that you're going to be graded on. What you learned from researching the cold case, whether a podcast can help—or not—in solving the case, all that stuff. And if no one calls in, so what? That tells you something right there, doesn't it?"

He shrugged and nodded at the same time. "I know you're right."

"But you want to solve the crime, too. I get it." She stole one of his french fries and leaned over, said quietly, "Isn't it the next episode where you're going to drop the bomb that Candace wasn't killed at the lake?"

Lucas shot a glance around the pub, to make sure no one heard Lizzy. The music was loud enough to cover their conversation, but he couldn't take a chance. They were at a high top against the window, but a large table in the middle was filled with sorority girls. He couldn't be certain one or more of them weren't from Sigma Rho.

"You think that revelation will prompt listeners to call in?" Lucas asked. "Even more than the last episode where I presented evidence that Candace was alive for the week after she initially went missing?"

"Well, yeah, because no one knows it. I mean, publicly. It's going to hit hard, and yeah, people will call, even if only to speculate."

Lucas had loosely scripted out each of the eight episodes, but only the first four were in detail because the others he had planned to develop further after he gathered more information—from callers that hadn't yet manifested themselves. Someone knew where Candace was that first week she was missing, he was positive. And he'd hoped that once he got that break, other clues and episodes would fall into place. If no one called in to crowdsource good information or viable clues, he could still run with some prerecorded interviews, but they'd be half as interesting.

His first episode was basic: Who was Candace Swain, and why should listeners care about her murder? He documented Candace's childhood, her time on campus, even scored an interview with her younger sister, Chrissy, a senior at the University of South Carolina. He also had a clip from the director of Sunrise Center, where Candace had volunteered weekly for three years: it underscored her commitment to helping others. He had other interviews recorded to interject throughout the eight episodes. The only person who refused to talk to him was Steven Young, the Flagstaff detective in charge of the original investigation three years ago. Lucas only had a letter from the public information officer that gave the status of the investigation—open, inactive. At least the campus-police community relations officer had talked to Lucas and given him a lot of great background information on how Candace's missing-person case had been handled. But ultimately, once the campus cops turned the case over to Flagstaff PD, they were no longer involved and thus could provide nothing new to Lucas's podcast.

At the end of the first episode, Lucas revealed that Candace Swain had disappeared after a Sigma Rho party she'd helped organize, and wasn't seen again until her body was found the following weekend in the lake on the Hope Centennial Golf Course.

The second episode focused on the basics of the missing-person investigation. Lucas revealed that Candace was thought to have been alive during most of the time she was missing. Per the autopsy, she was killed a week *after* her disappearance. He'd made a request on air during the last episode that if anyone could remember having seen Candace between the party and the time when her body was found, to call that detail in. With that critical new intel, he might be able to further piece together those missing days and solve her murder.

But only two callers had responded, and they hadn't given their names. While they sounded authentic, he wondered if someone was playing a game with him and making things up. He couldn't tell for sure, and that bothered him.

"Knock it off, Lucas," Lizzy said. "You're just feeling sorry for yourself. You've done a great job laying out Candace's life and how the police handle missing persons on campus—and even how they changed some of their procedures after Candace disappeared. You are doing a public service, you know? Like a PSA or something, because you're telling people how to report an incident, that it's better to be embarrassed than have a friend or roommate hurt or worse. That's common sense to me and you, but some people are dense."

He appreciated her pep talk. "Maybe you're right. Once people know her body was moved, they might start thinking more."

"And aren't you going to ask that friend of your department advisor for help?"

"Professor Clarkson wants me to. He says maybe I need to ask different kinds of questions to entice listeners to call in. And I was thinking, maybe having a conversation with an expert would be more engaging than just my talking, you know?"

"That's a great idea," Lizzy said with a wide smile.

Former US Marshal Regan Merritt, a graduate of NAU, was scheduled to be a guest lecturer the following afternoon. Lucas's advisor was also the department chair. He offered to arrange a meeting for the three of them so Lucas could pitch his podcast, then ask Regan if he could interview her live on air. He could easily adapt his planned third episode to fit that format, and having an expert on with him when he provided his evidence that Candace's body had been moved would give his statement more weight. He was just a forensics major; Merritt was a former US Marshal.

"See? Now you have a direction." She reached out and squeezed his hand. "You got this, Lucas."

He warmed at Lizzy's touch, but she'd given no indication that she'd be receptive to being more than friends. They'd met when she was a freshman, he was a sophomore, in an advanced-math class he was required to take for his major. They'd been friends ever since. Back then, he'd been hung up on his high-school girlfriend who broke up with him right before they went off to different colleges. He was still kind of pining over his ex a year later. Maybe he had given off those unavailable vibes. Or maybe Lizzy just wasn't attracted to him. He was an average guy. Smart, but not super smart like Lizzy. Whatever, he was grateful for her help and friendship.

"You ready to go?" he asked.

"You still have more fries."

"Eat them," he said.

She did and said, "Stop looking at that table."

"What table?"

"The sorority table."

"I'm not."

"Are too."

"The blonde keeps looking over here, and she looks angry," he said.

"Maybe she has the hots for you, and you're with another girl."

He laughed, actually laughed out loud, because the idea of that was hilarious.

Lizzy ate the last fry. "*Now* I'm ready to go."

Vicky Ryan, the current president of Sigma Rho, finally relaxed now that the student podcaster was gone. "What's wrong?" Nicole, her best friend, asked.

"You didn't recognize him? That was Lucas Vega, the jerk who's running that podcast about Candace Swain's murder."

Nicole looked around, trying to catch a glimpse. "Really?"

"He's gone."

"I thought he did great," Nicole said. "I mean, he said nice things and even had an interview with her sister. If the family is supporting him, why shouldn't we?"

For someone as smart as Nicole, her roommate could be naive. Vicky once had been just as naive herself, but she had grown up real fast over the last three years.

"I don't trust him. Just little things—like asking why we, the sorority, didn't call in the missing-person report earlier. We told the police everything at the time—we didn't *know* she was missing. She often spent the weekend with one of her boyfriends, and she was twenty-one. And he talked about the fight between Candace and Taylor as if it was a big deal, when it was practically nothing."

"So he's a bit sensational. What do you expect? I'm

just happy that he didn't harp on the fact that she was juggling two boyfriends, like the reporter who first covered her murder."

Vicky remembered the news coverage after Candace had been killed. The local crime reporter had a big headline about Candace's love life, which was totally inappropriate and irrelevant. You had to read the entire story to realize that the police had determined neither of the men in Candace's life were involved in her murder. Vicky hadn't known Candace super well, but she remembered that she wasn't *that* into her love life. It wasn't like dating two guys was unusual these days, anyway.

Vicky glanced over at the bar, but Richie Traverton wasn't working tonight. He'd been one of the two guys that Candace had been seeing three years ago, and he was super cute, but Vicky only knew him in passing. He wasn't a student, and she thought she'd heard that he had another girlfriend now or something. Was that why the podcaster was here? To talk to Richie? Would Richie even go on that stupid show? Vicky hoped not: it would just make everything worse and further divide the sorority.

"Earth to Vicky," Nicole said.

"Sorry. Thinking."

"I think *you* should go on it," Nicole said. "Drive the narrative. I think we should have agreed to help when he first came to the council. We need a voice."

"No. It wouldn't be a good look for the sorority, and Lucas refused to share any details about the show in advance. We can't go into something like this blind."

"Maybe, but I think he would have been open to negotiation."

At the beginning of the spring semester, Lucas had spoken to their sorority council—Vicky was president, Nicole was secretary—and told them he was doing his capstone project on Candace Swain's murder. They asked questions. He wouldn't answer. He said that he was still formulating his outline and wanted to interview Vicky as president, Rachel Wagner the sorority advisor, and former president Taylor James, who had been arguing with Candace the night she disappeared. But he wouldn't share his questions in advance. All he said was that he had known Candace because she had tutored him in English, and he wanted to use the podcast as a way to encourage listeners to share what they knew about her last days, in the hopes of solving her murder.

"The police have her murder in the inactive file," Vicky told Nicole. "It's not closed, but they have a suspect."

The police suspected Joseph Abernathy at the time, the creepy drunk guy who Candace was far too nice to. Vicky was positive he killed her. Who else could it be? He was belligerent and had come around campus all the time even after he'd been removed by the police. And he disappeared the day Candace's body was found. He killed her and skipped town. It made sense, and usually the most obvious answer was the right answer. If the police thought he did it, then they must have good reason to believe he was guilty.

Their advisor had questions for Lucas, the board had questions, and Lucas said he wasn't prepared to go into detail. They voted unanimously not to be interviewed, and that was it.

But the whole thing left a foul taste in her mouth. She had an image to protect—her image and her future career, her sisters, and the sorority as a whole. Some of her sisters had disagreed with the board, thought they should have participated, and Nicole started listening to them. The division was upsetting, because before this they had been unified.

Lucas Vega's podcast had become a *major* thorn in her side, and Vicky couldn't wait until he was done with it.

Three

Being back at Northern Arizona University to present a guest lecture was odd enough, but walking into Henry Clarkson's office was even more unsettling. Regan Merritt had only been in the office of the Criminology and Criminal Justice Department chair a half dozen times. It would have been a large office if there weren't so many towering shelves, overflowing with books and papers. The antique desk was twice the size of a normal desk, with a glass top to protect the old wood. The last time she'd been here was when she asked Henry for a recommendation letter for the US Marshal's office, fourteen years ago. Not much had changed—except it seemed he had more books.

The trim, sixty-two-year-old professor, dwarfed by his stately leather chair, poured himself a Scotch, neat, then gestured toward her with an empty glass. "I imagine you enjoy Macallan from time to time, just like your father. It's nearly five o'clock."

"You're a bad influence, Henry," Regan said but took the offered drink, nonetheless. He poured her two fingers—

more than enough—and she held it as she sat in his guest chair. She angled the chair so she could see the door, an instinct she doubted she'd lose after nearly fourteen years as a US Marshal.

"It may be against the rules to have alcohol in my office, but no one has turned me in yet." He slid over a coaster—a tile with the emblem of Coconino County that looked like it had been bought from a souvenir shop off Route 66. "I would very much like you to teach a seminar here."

"I don't want to teach," she said.

"You have a commanding presence. Very few students were on their phones today."

"The lecture was optional. They wanted to be there."

She'd guest lectured on careers in law enforcement, with an emphasis on the US Marshals Service. Though she'd walked away from her job last fall, she still thought it was one of the best law-enforcement jobs to have—and one of the hardest to get into.

When one of the students had asked why she'd left, she didn't respond. It was no one's business. Henry didn't know the entire story, either, and she doubted her father would have shared the details, even though her former professor and father had become friends.

"You're knowledgeable, articulate, young. I'm not asking you to be a full-time professor—"

She laughed; she couldn't help herself. The idea of spending hours every week in a classroom was akin to torture. She was smart yet detested school. Not because she was incapable or bullied or opposed to learning but because she greatly preferred being outdoors than being trapped in a room.

"I'm well aware of your kinetic personality, Marshal."

"I'm not a marshal anymore, Henry."

"Your father is no longer the sheriff, but most people address him as such."

With Henry, sometimes there was no winning.

"I'm happy to speak, on occasion—once a semester, maybe—guest lecture like I did today. But I'm not generally interested in shaping young minds or grading papers. But thank you anyway."

"I'm going to ask again."

She smiled, sipped her drink. "Of course you are. The answer will still be no."

Regan saw movement in the hallway outside the door. Classes were on the first floor, staff offices on the second. Because of his position in the CCJ department, Henry was afforded the largest, quietest office at the end of the hall. He never closed his door.

A student stood in the doorway about to knock when he saw Regan. He was skinny, about five foot nine—same height as Regan—with dark hair that curled at his collar. Dark eyes, naturally tan skin, dressed in an NAU Lumberjack sweatshirt and jeans, like half the students on campus. His most distinguishing feature was his bright green Converse high-tops. And because of the Day-Glo shoes, Regan recognized that he'd been at her lecture that afternoon.

"Lucas! Come in." Henry spoke before the kid said anything.

Henry was unsurprised at the interruption, which immediately made Regan suspicious.

"Regan, Lucas is one of my top students. A CCJ and biology dual major."

"Forensics," Regan said. She'd been a CCJ and psychology dual major because she had considered criminal profiling and had even thought about becoming a psychiatrist. Time and money—and the fact that the thought of years of medical school made her hyperventilate—had her ending her academic career with two degrees in four years and no regrets.

"I'm hoping to get in with Phoenix PD," Lucas said, his scratchy voice showing his nerves. He cleared his throat. "They have an awesome lab, but mostly, that's where my family is. My older brother is going through the police academy now. My mom's a nurse, my sisters are still in high school. I really enjoyed your presentation today."

"Thank you."

"Lucas has developed one of the most interesting capstone projects I've seen in my two decades teaching here," Henry said. "He's hosting a podcast about an unsolved campus murder that happened a few years ago. Lucas, please, sit down. Join us."

Lucas sat in the other guest chair, the one still facing the desk. He had surprisingly good posture—maybe because of his short stature. Too often Regan saw kids who had perpetually slumped, misaligned shoulders because they carried heavy backpacks on one side for years.

"Tell Regan about your podcast. *The Sorority Murder.* Isn't that a provocative title?"

"It is," Regan concurred. "Is this about that nursing student who was killed three years back? My dad talked about it once or twice."

Lucas nodded. "Candace Swain—a nursing student with Sigma Rho sorority—was found dead in the lake at the Hope Centennial Golf Course. While the police had a suspect, a transient who was seen on campus several times in the weeks leading up to her disappearance, they never found him. According to a witness, he was seen jumping on a freight car shortly after her body was found."

Regan remembered a few details about the case. "What's the purpose of your podcast?" she asked.

"Well, there's a lot of oddities about the case that I want to explore, but mostly I want to retrace her steps, from her disappearance until her death."

Lucas leaned forward, clearly excited about his project. "Candace went missing shortly after midnight on a Friday right after the Sigma Rho Spring Fling ended. Her body was found Sunday morning—*over a week later*," he emphasized. "No one has come forward to say they had seen her, talked to her, anything.

"The police know that Candace was friendly with a transient, Joseph Abernathy, through her volunteer work. Several witnesses said Candace confronted him the night she disappeared. My theory is that the police had it in their heads that Abernathy was guilty, and they didn't fully look at other options. There was some circumstantial evidence against Abernathy, and his disappearance is suspicious. But I've done a lot of research over the last few months, and I'm positive something else happened."

"What do you think happened?"

"I don't know," he said. "Just not what the police think." He took a deep breath. "I'm really getting ahead of myself. Here are the facts. Candace disappeared after the party. She was seen arguing with another sorority sister and walked off, upset. She wasn't reported missing until Monday night. Her roommate had gone home that weekend and assumed when she returned late Sunday that Candace was with her boyfriend, so she didn't worry about her until later. The campus police found Candace's vehicle in the parking structure on Tuesday morning. They called her family, her friends, and then notified Flagstaff PD on Wednesday morning. At that point it would seem she'd been missing for five days.

"Flagstaff PD retraced campus-police steps—talking to her friends, her family. Candace was romantically involved with two men, a student and a bartender. They were both interviewed. Police also went to Sunrise Center, where Candace regularly volunteered, to talk to Abernathy, but he hadn't been seen by staff for more than a week. This apparently wasn't unusual because he only slept at the shelter when it was cold, though they were surprised he hadn't come in for a meal. There had been previous complaints about Abernathy from business owners, so the police knew who he was and issued a BOLO.

"No progress was made until Candace's body was found Sunday morning by the maintenance crew at Hope Centennial Golf Course."

"And because it's a golf course, people were there on Saturday but no one saw a body," Regan guessed. "Could her body have been weighed down? Perhaps rising to the surface after a week?"

"That was, I believe, the assumption, except that the autopsy report revealed that Candace was killed between ten o'clock Saturday night and one o'clock Sunday morning," Lucas said. "No signs of long-term restraint, sexual assault, or malnourishment were present—nothing to indicate that she had been held captive. A rock was used to weigh her down, but it wasn't tied on well, and she surfaced. The autopsy was clear. Candace was strangled, but that wasn't what killed her. She drowned."

"Perhaps," Regan offered, "she was strangled to unconsciousness, and the killer thought she was dead and pushed her into the lake."

"That's a theory. Except she didn't drown in that lake."

"Now you have me intrigued." She took another sip of her Scotch. "How do you know this?"

"I interned at the morgue last summer as part of my degree program. I read the reports. The water from her lungs was highly chlorinated. I talked to the maintenance crew at Hope Centennial. They don't chlorinate their water because they stock fish to keep the eco-balance. But just to check, I took samples of the water, and it's nowhere close to being a match."

It was definitely an interesting fact, but there could be other explanations. "No court would accept water samples three years apart. Too many other factors could change the outcome."

"That may be true, but it doesn't discount the fact that Candace drowned in heavily chlorinated water. My problem with the entire police investigation is that they fixated on Abernathy and, I believe, excluded all other possibilities. Abernathy was known to be belligerent, but not violent. *Maybe* he could have killed her. He was an alcoholic. He might not even know or remember what he did. But then how did he transport her to the lake? He didn't have a car. Was he strong enough? Possibly. Evidence from the autopsy indicates that Candace was dragged postmortem. I tried to talk to the police, but they just gave me the standard media line—the case is open, inactive, pending new evidence."

"And you're looking for new evidence," Regan concluded.

"Witnesses. Someone must have seen Candace during the time she was missing. She didn't disappear into thin air, even though she wasn't seen in the sorority, didn't attend any classes, and didn't have her car or phone with her. So where was she? I'm using the podcast to...well, I guess you could say to crowdsource the information. By going over the facts that we know, encouraging people to search their memories. One of my problems is that the sorority doesn't want to be involved."

"What about her family?"

"I interviewed her sister, Chrissy Swain, and aired part of the interview on the first episode of the podcast, a short snippet on the second, and I have more to share. Her parents weren't responsive. Chrissy says they're still grieving, but I had the sense that Chrissy is the one who cares the most and her parents were using grief as an excuse. She wants to help, but she's in South Carolina."

"Why are you doing this? Why pick *this* cold case?"

He hesitated, just a second too long, and Regan wondered if he was going to tell her the entire truth. He'd been so forthcoming up until now. "I was interested in Candace's murder mostly because I kinda knew her. She worked in the writing lab when I was a freshman and helped me get through English comp. She was a senior nursing student. We talked about some of the classes she took that I was going to have to take for bio, and so, you know, I was as surprised as anyone when she was killed."

"What else?" Because there was more.

He hesitated again, then rubbed a hand over his face. "I saw her that night," he said with a sigh. "Outside the party. I saw her talking to the homeless guy, Abernathy. She convinced him to leave. I learned later, through the media reports, that he'd been banned from the campus and that Candace didn't want to call the police on him. I saw him walk away."

"Did you talk to the police?"

"I didn't know that I should have. I didn't know she was missing, and I only heard through the grapevine that she was killed, but none of the details. It wasn't until weeks later that I heard about the theory that Abernathy had killed her and jumped on a train to escape."

"It's plausible."

"Could he have kept her captive for a week? She was a healthy young woman. She had no drugs in her system, no physical signs of captivity. I don't see it. Her phone was found in her dorm room. Who leaves without their phone?"

"You mean, who leaves *willingly* without their phone?"

"Right," he said.

"Are you reaching the right audience?" she asked. "I would imagine that most people who were at that party have graduated and are no longer in town."

He conceded that might be an issue. "Still, there are others like me who were freshmen then and are still on or near campus. They may not have thought about the case or even realized it's still open. Professors. Staff. The show is broadcast live from the campus studio and reaches Flagstaff city limits and part of the county. It's also streamed on our website and then archived as a podcast, and anyone can listen through podcast apps. Another student, Lizzy Choi, is helping me. She knows everything about the campus radio station and is acting as my producer. We're hoping to grow our audience through word of mouth. The first two episodes aired last week. I'm running the next one tomorrow night, at eight. I'd like to interview you on air. After listening to you today, I think you'll be able to shed light on criminal procedure and help me frame questions, maybe even spur more call-ins."

Regan looked from Lucas to Henry. "This was your idea."

"It was Lucas's idea when he heard you were coming to lecture on campus. I thought it was a good one and told him so."

"I was a US Marshal, Lucas. We don't run murder investigations. We primarily transport prisoners, protect witnesses and courthouses, and find wanted felons. We run the WitSec program. I don't know how I can be of any help."

"But you *do* look for missing persons," Lucas pushed. His whole body leaned forward, as if physically urging her to commit. "I want to get the word out about this unsolved case right here in our backyard but worry that I'm not asking the right questions. Those days she was missing could be critical. Don't you think the killer should face justice? Isn't that why you went into law enforcement at some point? To help right wrongs?"

Her reasons for being a marshal, she thought, were simple: law enforcement was in her blood. Her father had been a cop, then elected sheriff; her oldest brother was a deputy in Maricopa County; her grandfather had been a US Forest Ranger.

But the reason she had chosen the Marshals Service was complicated. Partly ego, partly to do something different from the rest of her family, partly to escape Flagstaff. She loved her hometown—hiking, skiing, kayaking, camping— there was no more beautiful place in the country than northern Arizona. The staggeringly tall mountains, the deep Grand Canyon, the rivers for kayaking, the land for hunting, the clean air and down-to-earth people. But it could also be claustrophobic. Being a Merritt in a long line of service-oriented Merritts, you always had to be on your best behavior.

Yet here she was, back home for a while, wanting to make changes in her life and licking her raw wounds… wounds she doubted would ever heal.

After Regan provided no answer to Lucas's question, Henry filled in the awkward silence.

"Regan, what if I make a suggestion?" he said. "Listen to the first two podcast episodes. See if your curiosity is piqued.

If so, lending your expertise would help Lucas in his project. One evening, one interview—it might help steer the direction of the case. Because I must admit, I *have* been curious about where Candace Swain was before she died, as well as who killed her. Was it a crime of opportunity? Passion? Revenge?"

"You read too many mysteries," Regan said, grateful that he'd lightened the mood.

"She was a student here, after all. Her unknown whereabouts was an outlier in the case at the time, one the police never sufficiently explained."

"Now you're sounding like a lawyer," she said with a slight smile. "You know the police don't always share the information they have, especially with the public." Yet Henry was right: the case *was* more than a little intriguing. She'd always been a sucker for cold cases. Some of her most memorable evenings growing up were spent talking to her dad and older brother about unusual crimes and missing persons, trying to come up with ideas about what happened. She wondered if Henry knew about that. It wouldn't surprise her if her dad had told him, or if he just remembered her inquisitive nature from college.

"No promises," she said, "but I'll listen. Do you have a number where I can reach you tomorrow?"

Lucas pulled a page out of a college-ruled notebook and scribbled his name, phone number, email, and the name and URL of the podcast. "I live in an apartment off campus, the other side of downtown. We record here at the campus radio station, a studio in the communications building. Lizzy handles all the equipment and stuff, and the idea was that she would screen callers—but we've only had two. We have numbers—people are listening. Not a huge number live, not yet, but we've had several hundred downloads. If you would, maybe come thirty minutes before we go on?

Then I can run through the program, answer any questions you have, get you comfortable."

"I said no promises." She finished her drink and put the glass on the Coconino County coaster. She'd *said* she wasn't committed, but she had a lot of questions. She'd never been able to let questions like this go. A cold case? Here, at NAU? There was a lot of mystery surrounding Candace Swain's murder.

"Henry, thank you for everything. Surprisingly, I enjoyed lecturing today."

"And the class…?" he asked hopefully.

She just laughed.

"Lucas, I'll let you know either way, okay?"

"Thank you. I really appreciate your time."

Lucas watched Regan Merritt leave Professor Clarkson's office. He put his head in his hands. "I didn't do that right. I was all over the place, trying to convince her to help."

"You did just fine, Lucas. Just fine."

He stared quizzically at his advisor. Had he been part of a different conversation? "I should have told her more, about the police reports, the argument that night, how no one in the sorority will talk to me, about—"

"You told her enough to interest her. The rest she's going to learn in the first two episodes. She's going to do it."

"Really? You think?"

"I'll bet a bottle of Macallan."

"I'm broke, so I'll just take your word for it." He hoped his professor was right, because he feared—like he'd told Lizzy last night—that no one would call in with clues and he'd never find out what really happened to Candace Swain.

Four

When there is no place to go, you go home.

Regan was grateful that her childhood home in Flagstaff, west of the city limits off Naval Observatory Road, hadn't changed much over the years: the wide, eastern-facing covered porch where beautiful sunrises could be viewed; the clearing to the south where her dad and older brother had put in a brick barbecue and firepit, where they'd had more family-and-friend gatherings than she could count. It looked unused—remnants of her youth, because her dad lived alone.

The house had been in her family since her grandfather built a two-room A-frame with a loft more than seventy years ago. He'd added on, each room a testament to his attention to detail and carpentry skills he'd inherited from his own father. It was a good house, a mostly happy house. Built largely from pine and stone that had been locally harvested, the house had grown over the years, and shortly after she was born, the second of four kids, her grandfather gave it to her father.

"You have a growing family. You need the roots."

When her grandfather wasn't working—he worked near

every day until he died—he lived in the small two-room apartment above the barn. He died when Regan was ten, and she still missed his ornery wisdom.

And now, home was a refuge as she tried to figure out what to do with the rest of her life.

Regan had seen every facet of human life and death during her years as a marshal, but one thing surprised her: even when people had an awful childhood—even when their parents were physically or emotionally abusive—they almost always went home when they hit bottom. Four out of five times, they showed up exactly where Regan expected, and she took them into custody. Usually without incident.

Sometimes in a body bag.

She'd had a comfortable childhood. Parents who sometimes argued but who'd loved each other. Siblings who got along. They weren't rich, but they never wanted for anything. Her dad was a deputy, then became sheriff; her mother was a nurse. They were comfortable, not fancy. The tragedy of her mother's cancer when Regan was in high school had left a sorrowful mark on an otherwise idyllic, middle-class upbringing.

If anything, her family name demanded community service. No sitting around binge-watching TV. If you slept past six, you had better be sick. Chores were done without expectation of an allowance. Regan grew up believing—still believed—that you did what was necessary in the house because you were part of the family.

Her granddad, who'd patrolled the Kaibab National Forest until he was forced into retirement—and died only months later—had often said, "God made us stewards of the earth, which means more than taking care of what's yours. Give more than you expect to receive, and be thankful for every day you draw breath in our beautiful country."

She knew from her dad that her granddad wasn't the easiest man to live with, though she'd always enjoyed spending time with him. He'd expected a lot from his three boys but doted on his grandchildren to the point of spoiling them. Her dad, John, and her uncle Theo—named after her granddad's idol, Theodore Roosevelt—were close, and both had done well in life. Back in the early eighties, on the day he turned eighteen years old, her uncle George had moved to Los Angeles, got involved with drugs, and was in and out of jail for stupid crap. If her dad had a blind spot, it was his little brother. Yet George never came home. Maybe he hadn't hit rock bottom. Maybe he hadn't lost all hope.

For Regan, when her life was destroyed, there was no place she wanted to be except home. Her dad had welcomed her with open arms and without question. Even though they hadn't always seen eye to eye, her dad loved her unconditionally; he was her rock. He grieved, too, but she refused to talk to anyone about her son, Chase, because there was nothing to say.

Chase was dead.

He would never see his eleventh birthday.

In three weeks her son should have been celebrating with family and friends, eating his favorite ice-cream cake and going to the opening game of the Washington Nationals, his favorite baseball team, as he'd done every year since he was five. Even if opening day didn't fall on his actual birthday, it was the only thing he wanted to do. It had become a tradition.

She pushed the looming day firmly to the back of her mind. She could not think about everything she had lost. Not now.

When she walked into the house, she found a note from her dad that said he'd left to help a neighbor with their well and wouldn't be home for dinner. She didn't particularly like to cook, so she made herself a cold roast-beef sandwich with extra horseradish and sat down in the breakfast nook that her dad and brother had expanded to include not only more space but a window seat that Regan's little sister used to spend hours reading in. They rarely ate in the dining room, only used it for their large Thanksgiving gathering.

The kitchen bled into the great room. This grand, open space was where she and her siblings spent most of their time growing up. The worn sectional sofa had since been replaced by two leather couches, but Dad had reupholstered his favorite chair and still sat in it every night. The small television they rarely watched had been replaced with a bigger wall-mounted model after John had retired. He only watched sports and local news, though on occasion Regan could entice him to watch a classic Western.

There was comfort here. Family pictures taken over the years, photos of beloved pets—the golden retriever they'd had during most of Regan's childhood, the yellow Lab who'd joined the family her senior year. Photos of her dad's horses, which he'd sold to a neighbor after Bri left home because he didn't have the time to care for them. She missed horseback riding with her sister and dad—it was one thing she'd enjoyed that her brothers hadn't.

She'd noticed as soon as she moved back home last fall that her dad had taken down her wedding picture. She didn't know if he removed it months ago when she told him she and Grant were getting a divorce, or when she told him that she'd resigned from the US Marshals Service and asked if she could come home until she figured out what to do.

There were, of course, many pictures of Chase, John's first grandchild, along with photos of JT's two young girls. A recent picture of her and Chase caught her eye. Even among the hundreds of photographs mounted on the great-room walls, her eye always gravitated to it. They'd come to visit her dad the Christmas break before Chase was killed. They'd gone skiing at the Snowbowl atop the San Francisco peaks. Chase's face was red from the cold and exertion, but his green eyes lit up with joy. She was grinning, and now remembered how free she'd felt that week. How happy she'd been to share so much with her boy. Like her, he loved the outdoors. He took to skiing like a fish to water, and she'd been so proud of how, when he fell down, he got right back up.

Chase was her kid, through and through. She'd never settled for failure. She worked at something until she mastered it. Chase did the same.

Today, she didn't know how to get back up.

She averted her eyes for fear of being lost in the past. Finished her sandwich and washed her plate. She then sat in the living room and pulled out her phone to listen to Lucas Vega's podcast.

It would keep her mind off—well, everything, for an hour or two.

Before she hit Play, her dad walked in.

"I brought you peach cobbler," he said. "Jeff insisted."

"I'll eat it later."

"You should have joined us. Jeff cooks better than any-one in our family."

"I don't know about that. You can barbecue a mean steak, Dad. And your venison stew is the bomb."

"True." He put the cobbler in the kitchen and sat in his favorite chair, across from where Regan sat curled on the sofa, her feet tucked under her butt. "How was your presentation this afternoon?"

"Good. The students seemed interested. They had intelligent questions. After, I went up to Henry's office. He said to say hi." Her dad and Henry Clarkson had become friendly over the years. They'd met on campus when Regan was a student, and being from the same generation and loosely in the same field, they'd started playing golf on occasion. They didn't see eye to eye on everything—Henry had been a criminal-defense lawyer in his day, and her dad was a strict law-and-order guy—but their arguments were good-natured. Her dad had guest-lectured for Henry multiple times.

"Our last two standing golf dates were rained out, but it looks like this Sunday is going to be clear."

"Cold, but clear. That's what the meteorologist says."

"You don't agree?"

"Ask me Saturday morning." It could be bright and sunny one day and a storm could brew over the San Francisco peaks overnight and dump inches of water on them in a matter of hours. The local weather was wrong far too often for her to ever trust a forecast more than twenty-four hours in advance.

"Join us. You used to be wicked on the course."

"Not this time." She enjoyed golfing occasionally but much preferred more rigorous sports. "Jessie and I are going hiking in Sedona on Saturday, and knowing Jessie, I'll need Sunday to recoup. Humphreys is still covered in snow, and I'm not in the mood to pull out my snow boots." Humphreys Peak, the highest point in Arizona, was one of her favorite hikes. It was ten miles, and at the top on a clear day you could see the Grand Canyon. It wasn't an easy trail and was best to tackle in the late spring or summer.

Jessie Nez had been her best friend since forever. She worked for the Arizona Game and Fish Department. If Regan's naturalist granddad were still alive, he would have loved her, but he died the year before Jessie moved with her mom to Flagstaff from the Navajo reservation.

"I would love to go up there again, but I don't think my knee would tolerate it," her dad said. He'd had knee-replacement surgery shortly after he retired. He'd had problems for years, but her dad never did anything about it, much to her frustration.

"What do you remember about the Candace Swain murder investigation?" she asked.

"Swain—the college student, body found at the public golf course?"

"Yes."

"Not much. Flagstaff PD handled the investigation, and I'd already retired." He thought a moment. "Strangled, drowned in a lake, if I recall. I remember them looking for a transient, a homeless guy who had been hanging around the sorority. He disappeared around the same time they found her body."

"One of Henry's students has a podcast. He's retracing Swain's steps, trying to find out exactly where she was after she disappeared and before her body was found."

Her dad frowned. "I forgot about that aspect of the case. I assumed that she died shortly after she disappeared."

"According to Lucas—the kid who's running this project— no one knows where Candace was or what she was doing for more than a week prior to her murder. He wants to interview me on his podcast, but I made no promises—other than to listen to the first two episodes and see what he has and if it's interesting. Want to listen with me?"

"Sure, it's not too late." Her dad put his feet up on the ottoman and leaned back.

She glanced at the clock. It was eight thirty. *Too late* by her dad's standard was ten o'clock. He was the poster child for the *Early to bed, early to rise* philosophy.

Regan took out her earbuds and turned up the volume on her phone. Living in the mountains didn't make for speedy internet, even in the twenty-first century, so she'd downloaded the two recordings earlier.

Music, sort of a contemporary combination of *The X-Files* and *America's Most Wanted* with a jazzy beat, filtered in.

Lucas's voice was smooth, as if he had some experience with radio, even though he sounded nervous at the beginning. As he went on, he gained confidence, and his voice reflected that.

"My name is Lucas Vega, and I'm the host of *The Sorority Murder,* a podcast about the cold-case homicide of NAU nursing student Candace Swain.

"*The Sorority Murder* is an eight-episode program that airs twice weekly, live, on Tuesdays and Fridays. I am asking anyone who has information about the case to call in and share." He gave a phone number. "Tonight, I'm going to tell you about Candace and what we know about the night she disappeared from the Sigma Rho Spring Fling party three years ago."

Lucas quickly ran through the victim's background. Candace grew up in Colorado Springs, the older of two girls. She had a strained relationship with her parents after they divorced when she was fourteen but was very close to her younger sister, now a senior at the University of South Carolina.

"Chrissy Swain remembers her sister as the first person to help a friend, the first person to volunteer at school," Lucas said.

A female voice came on. "Candy was special. Candy—

she hated when anyone else called her that name, but she let me."

John leaned forward and muttered, "Smart move to interview the sister."

"We grew up in a typical house with typical divorced parents," Chrissy said. "It bothered Candy more than me, maybe because she was older, I don't know. We were both close to our grandma, and we spent a lot of time at her house, especially when our parents started dating other people. That was…well, weird, to be honest. Candy came to every one of my swim meets, and after she went to college she often came back for the weekend if I had a big competition. She would drive me all over before I got my license, even though she was popular and always had dates or things to do. She played soccer, and she was a cheerleader, and she got invited to every party, but if I needed to be picked up after a late practice, she was there for me. I miss her."

Lucas said, "Candace had been a straight-A student in high school and received an academic scholarship to NAU, where she studied to be a nurse. Chrissy said she was excited about her new career. Because of her volunteer work at Sunrise Center, a homeless shelter and food kitchen in downtown Flagstaff, Candace wanted to work in a clinic in an underprivileged area, focusing on people who'd slipped through the cracks."

Chrissy said, "Candy was about helping people. That's all she wanted to do."

Lucas discussed how Candace joined the Sigma Rho sorority because of the large percentage of women there majoring in STEM. She quickly moved up the sisterhood ranks, becoming a general-council member her second year, the secretary her third year, and vice president her fourth year. She also served as liaison to the Greek Council, tutored at the writing center, maintained a 3.7 GPA over her first seven semesters, and volunteered every Tuesday at Sunrise Center.

"I reached out to the director, Willa March, who knew Candace during that time."

"Candace was our most reliable and dedicated volunteer," Willa—by her voice, older—said. "We are a low-overhead organization that relies on volunteers and donations for much of what we do. She served food, talked to our guests as people, not problems. She assisted our volunteer doctor in our weekly clinic. Her murder hit us all hard. The world is poorer without Candace in it."

Lucas said, "Candace Swain had everything going for her. Education, a commitment to public service, family, friends. She was on the verge of graduation when she disappeared shortly after midnight as the Sigma Rho Spring Fling was winding down.

"No one realized Candace was missing, until her roommate, Annie, called campus police late Monday afternoon."

Regan half expected audio of Annie at that point, but instead, Lucas continued.

"According to the police report, the last person who spoke to Candace was her fellow sorority sister Taylor James. Several people reported that Candace and Taylor had been arguing, but according to Taylor, they were having 'a stupid disagreement' and it wasn't an 'actual argument.' She said to police, and I quote, 'Candace got angry and stormed off. She did that sometimes when she was losing an argument, but she never held grudges. Neither do I. I expected to see her later.'

"Taylor and a small group of people she was with were the last to see Candace alive as the Spring Fling was breaking up. Just over a week later, on the morning of Sunday,

April 19, Candace's body was found in Hope Springs Lake, a man-made lake in the middle of Hope Centennial Golf Course."

John said, "Over a week? That's a long time."

Regan concurred. "It's the primary reason I agreed to listen to the podcast and consider going on his program. According to Lucas, she was dead less than twenty-four hours. That should be easy information to verify."

"Hmm."

Her dad was thinking. He was one of the smartest cops she knew.

Chrissy's voice came back. "My mom called me Tuesday. She said not to worry, it was likely a misunderstanding, but Candace left campus Friday night and hadn't returned. She asked if Candy had called me. She hadn't."

Lucas said, "When Annie returned to campus late Sunday night, she didn't think twice about Candace not being in the room because she often stayed out late or over with a boyfriend. It wasn't until Monday afternoon when Annie came back from class and tried to call her roommate that she found her phone in their dorm room, on the charger, with dozens of missed calls. That is when she called NAUPD, the campus police."

Regan thought that Lucas did a decent job recounting the initial missing-person investigation, from Annie's growing concern to contacting campus police to the delayed call to Flagstaff PD when campus police determined she hadn't returned home—something that often happened in the college experience.

"According to campus records, Candace's student card key—the card that is used to enter the dorms or use the meal plan—was used to enter the Mountain View dorm at 12:20 a.m. Saturday morning, consistent with witness statements that Candace left the party after midnight. Her card key was used once more—Sunday night at 11:10 p.m. According to the police, no one saw her enter the building or leave after. A thorough search of the building yielded no additional information or signs of foul play. There are no security cameras inside dorms or on the side entrance where she entered—the entrance closest to the parking garage. The police have never suggested why she might have returned or when she left again. Her card key has never been found.

"Once Flagstaff PD were notified on Wednesday morning," Lucas continued, "they focused their investigation on friends, family, and boyfriends of Candace Swain. Witnesses indicated that Candace had been seeing two different men, one a student and one who worked downtown as a bartender. Both were publicly cleared by the police in her disappearance."

Good to know, Regan thought, but she would want to read the reports.

You haven't even decided whether to get involved.

Except maybe she always knew she would.

Lucas explored every public theory of Candace's disappearance, from being overwhelmed with her finals to a possible accident to foul play.

Chrissy said, "Candy would never, never, *never* disappear. Not without telling someone. Not without telling *me*. We were close. We talked every week. I…I blame myself. I should have known something was wrong when she didn't call me on Sunday. I had a meet and didn't get back to my dorm until late and just didn't think about it… I keep thinking if I reached out, if I had talked to her, this wouldn't have happened."

Lucas said, "No one has come forward stating that they

saw Candace after the Spring Fling party. Her car was found in the Mountain View parking garage, dedicated parking for the sororities, on Tuesday morning—but no one could verify how long it had been there. She didn't go to any classes, she didn't volunteer at Sunrise Center, and she didn't contact anyone—at least, no one has come forward. The missing-person investigation became a homicide investigation on Sunday, April 19, when Candace's body was found in Hope Springs Lake."

Lucas continued. "The Spring Fling is the last time anyone saw Candace alive. Were you there? Call in and tell me. Did you see Candace? What was her disposition? Did you see her leaving? Was she with anyone?"

John interrupted. "Those are all questions the police would have asked."

"Shh," Regan whispered.

"According to media reports that came out the week Candace was missing," Lucas said, "the police were looking for a homeless transient named Joseph Abernathy because of accusations by the sorority—not just Sigma Rho, but several other sororities that shared the Mountain View dorms—that Abernathy had been hanging around the dorm harassing the women and making them uncomfortable. According to the NAUPD crime reports, campus police removed an unnamed homeless man twice, once for loitering and once for public urination.

"If you were at the party, did you see Mr. Abernathy or anyone who fits his description? He is described in the press as an 'unkempt forty-eight-year-old transient with long graying dark hair and untrimmed beard.' He is six feet four inches tall and approximately one hundred eighty pounds."

Lucas paused, as if waiting to take a call, but there was

no call, and he continued. "Taylor James, the Sigma Rho president, told police that Candace had confronted Joseph Abernathy outside the dorm at the beginning of the party and asked him to leave. According to Taylor, their later argument was in part about whether they should have called the police on him. Adam Carroll, the community relations officer for NAUPD, explains what students should do in these situations."

A male voice came on. "Our department recommends that if anyone on campus makes you uncomfortable, to call the office or use one of the blue-light emergency phones that have a direct line to our dispatch. One of the strengths of NAU is that we are an open campus in the middle of town, and we welcome community members to share our resources and trails and to attend our concerts and sporting events. But this can also become a drawback because some people don't obey the rules. It is better to be safe and contact us than try and deal with a potentially violent individual on your own."

Lucas said, "Officer Carroll also confirmed, because NAUPD makes all reports public, that there had been multiple complaints about Mr. Abernathy, and after the last time he was removed, he was told he would be arrested if he returned.

"We need your help to retrace Candace Swain's steps. She disappeared Friday night, just after midnight, at the Spring Fling party three years ago. She was last seen talking to Taylor James when she walked off, apparently angry. Did you see her that night? Did you see Candace at any time in the days before her body was found? Did you see her Sunday night, late, in the dorms when her card key was used? Call in and share what you know."

Chrissy's voice came back on. "I just want to know what

happened to my sister. I want to know who killed her. I want to know *why*."

Lucas said, "If we can re-create Candace Swain's steps, we might just solve the Sorority Murder."

Five

"What do you think?" Regan asked her dad when the first episode ended.

"I think he's playing Hardy Boys and is going to ruffle a lot of feathers for no reason." John rose from his seat and stretched.

"It is a cold case," Regan reminded him. "Three years. Maybe some feathers need to be ruffled."

Her dad grunted. He didn't agree or disagree with her, he wanted more information. But he was curious. Just like she was.

"Nightcap?" he asked.

"Sure." As her dad walked behind his small bar and pulled out a bottle of Jack Daniel's, she asked, "You didn't hear about this last week when he aired the first episode?"

She remembered when her dad and her older brother had built the bar between the kitchen and the family room. It had ended up being a central gathering place when the family got together.

"No one mentioned it to me, and I don't think I've listened to a podcast in my life."

"He told me earlier today that he has evidence she didn't

drown in the lake. I'm surprised he didn't share that on his podcast."

"He has evidence? That he didn't turn over to police?"

She shook her head. "He read the autopsy report, and because he's a forensics student, he understood that the water in her lungs was heavily chlorinated. The lake is not."

"Then, the police know that and are investigating accordingly."

"Maybe."

Her father handed her the JD over ice. "Maybe. You know how these things work."

"After three years it seems the police are stuck. Maybe this podcast can jump-start the investigation and solve Candace's murder, give closure to the family. Her sister is cooperating."

Her dad didn't comment. He wouldn't be easily swayed, but he was a fair man.

"Ready for the cobbler? It's good," he said.

"I can get it."

"No, go ahead, start the next episode, I'll dish you up a bowl."

He sounded like he wasn't interested, but she knew her dad well enough to know if he didn't want to do something, he wouldn't do it. He just wasn't ready to admit the case intrigued him.

She started the second episode. After the music, Lucas gave a brief summary of the first episode and reminded his listeners that the podcast was live and if anyone had information about the case, and in particular Candace's whereabouts during the days she had been missing, they were encouraged to call in. He gave the studio number, his website, and his email.

"Remember," he said, "Candace was missing for over a

week—but she was alive. We know this from the autopsy report, which indicates that she was murdered between ten in the evening and one in the morning the Saturday night *before* her body was found in the lake. Where was she all that time? Someone knows. Even if you only saw her in passing, anything you know will help us piece together her last days, and maybe together, we can solve this horrific crime."

Her father settled back into his chair after handing Regan a bowl of cobbler. It was amazing, just like he said. He was having a bowl himself.

On the podcast, Lucas talked about how the missing-person case was handled before it turned into a murder investigation. He frequently paused, likely hoping for a call—but still no calls came in.

Lucas was right about one thing: the delay in reporting first to campus police, then to Flagstaff police, was problematic. Officer Carroll came on to explain how missing persons were handled by NAUPD. "There is no one standard protocol because each case is unique, but the first thing we do, in the absence of any indication of foul play, is to call the individual's family, contact their friends both on campus and at home, and talk to their professors. Usually when a student is reported missing, it's because they didn't check in with someone when they were expected. Ninety-nine times out of a hundred, the individual is fine. But it is better to be embarrassed than to have something happen and no one look for you.

"For Candace Swain, we alerted all local law enforcement Wednesday, after we first contacted family and close friends, just in case she was with one of them and not really missing. We reached out to her parents and talked to the girls at the sorority and her professors. Her vehicle was on

campus, which led us to believe that she may have walked
off or called a ride. We checked with her off-campus boyfriend, the app-based rideshare companies, and taxis with
the assistance of Flagstaff PD. Once we exhausted standard avenues, Flagstaff PD took over the investigation."

Lucas said, "No one came forward to tell authorities that
they saw Candace, which is unusual. Where was she? Did
she leave town? Why? If you know anything about Candace Swain's whereabouts during the time she was missing,
please call in. Together, we can put together a time frame
and re-create her final days."

He paused. "My producer, Lizzy Choi, has a call holding
for us. The caller wishes to remain anonymous."

He sounded very excited as he took the call.

"Hi, caller. You're on the air live with Lucas Vega. You
told Lizzy, my producer, that you think you saw Candace
on Sunday afternoon, after the party. Can you explain?"

"Well, I really don't know, but you said even if I *think*
I saw her, to call in." The caller was female, sounded nervous.

"That's right."

"And I went to your website and saw a picture of Candace and a picture of her car, and that's when I thought
maybe I had really seen her."

"Great. When and where?"

"I, um, I'm only going by my memory, which is three
years old. I only remember the day because I was driving back to campus on April 12 from Las Vegas, where
my family lives. It was my sister's sixteenth birthday that
weekend, so I went home Friday, drove back Sunday afternoon. I stopped in Kingman for gas, then drove through
Starbucks. I saw Candace Swain. Or I think I did. The only
reason I noticed was because she was in a blue VW con-

vertible Bug, and I loved the color. Then when I saw an NAU sticker on the window, I did a double take because, you know, I was a student. She was sitting in the driver's seat in the parking lot of Starbucks. I think she might have been on the phone, but I just looked for a second. Maybe I'm wrong, but I really think it was her because of the car."

"Could you tell if she was upset? Happy? Angry?"

"No. I mean, I wouldn't have even remembered it if I didn't remember the car."

"Just to clarify, this was the Sunday after the Spring Fling."

"Yes. The twelfth. Like I said, my sister's birthday was the eleventh, so I know I got the day right."

"Are you still a student at NAU?"

She laughed. "Yeah—fifth year. But I finally have enough credits to graduate."

"And you didn't say anything to her, didn't hear what she was saying?"

"I was in my car at the drive-through. I just saw her as I was driving away. And I'm only thinking it was her because it looked like her—blonde, really pretty—and her car is distinctive."

"Thank you for calling in." He ended the call and said, "Kingman, Arizona. Two hours west of campus. If Candace was in Kingman Sunday afternoon, why? Was she visiting someone? Driving through, like our caller had been? Was she on her way back *to* campus or coming *from* campus? Who else might have seen her or her car?

"If our caller is accurate about the timing of her sighting, this means that Candace took her car from campus on Friday night and returned sometime Sunday evening. We know from NAUPD that her card key was used to enter the dorm at 11:10 p.m., though no one has come forward to say they saw her. When did she leave again? There are no cameras in the lot and parking is by permit, so there's no tracking of when people come and go. They *assumed* that Candace's car had been there all weekend because they had no witnesses who said otherwise. Did they even ask? If you know something and are worried, I will keep your confidence. Call or email me." He recited his contact information again.

"The police issued a BOLO—or Be on the Lookout—for Joseph Abernathy as a person of interest," Lucas said. He reminded listeners about Abernathy's history. "A witness saw Abernathy hopping a train on Sunday morning—the morning that Candace's body was found. Did you see Abernathy on or off campus?"

He rambled a bit, clearly expecting another call. He then went through the rest of the missing-person investigation, but it was a lot of repetition.

"We have a call," Lucas said, trying not to sound excited. "Caller, you're on with Lucas Vega. Do you have information about where Candace may have been the week she was missing?"

"No, but I know Joseph. I mean, I knew him." The voice was male, older.

"How did you know Joseph?"

"I had a rough couple of months back then. Sunrise took me in. Lost my job and my house. My wife had died of cancer, and I had all these bills, and I was grieving and self-medicating. It was a fu—bad time," he quickly corrected himself.

"I'm sorry to hear that," Lucas said.

"Joseph was a serious alcoholic. Half the time you couldn't have a conversation with him. But when he was half-sober, he was a nice guy. He just couldn't stop. Didn't want to stop. But I don't think he did what the police think he did. He wasn't a bad guy, just broken."

"Did you see him that week?"

"I saw him sleeping down by the train tracks one night. I was doing community service. It was a way for me to give something back while I got clean. Cleaning up the roadways and stuff. And he was sleeping at a homeless encampment, just a place near the tracks. There's a creek that goes through the area, maybe a hundred yards away. Trees and shelter and maybe five or six tents. Out of sight. It's not there anymore, but three years ago it was. And Joseph was there, sleeping under a tree. I tried to convince him to come back to the shelter, but he told me to leave him alone. So I did."

"Do you remember what day?"

"No, it was during the week, that's all I know."

"Did you tell the police about it?"

"I told Willa, the director. I assume she told the police. They came by a couple of times to talk to her, look for Joseph."

"Did you know Candace?"

"Not really. I knew who she was. She always said hello and smiled when she served food. She was very nice."

"And that was the last time you saw Joseph."

"Yeah. I think something bad happened to him."

"Why do you say that?"

"Because he always came back. That's what Willa said. He might leave for a few weeks, a month or two, but he'd come back, like a homing pigeon, she said. But he was sick with the drink, you know. He could have died in the middle of nowhere, and who would know?"

Lucas thanked the caller, talked a bit about the police search for Abernathy, then concluded the episode.

"On Tuesday, I'm going to outline exactly what happened to Candace. We know that she was strangled, but she died by drowning. Her body was found in the Hope Springs Lake in the middle of the public golf course. The security cameras at the entrance weren't triggered, but there are other ways to get to the lake. Did she die in the lake? Or was she killed elsewhere? I have evidence that suggests the latter."

The podcast was over, music filtered in, and Regan turned off the app.

"What do you think, Dad?"

John mumbled, "He should have talked to Detective Young."

"Do you know Young?"

"No."

John Merritt, as the elected sheriff of Coconino County, had sometimes butted heads with local police departments. Generally, though, he'd had a good working relationship with almost everyone, directly or indirectly, and generally deferred to the local jurisdiction.

"In my experience," she said, "a police detective isn't going to give a college student the time of day. Young probably sent him to the media officer or told him to put in a FOIA request." The Freedom of Information Act gave the public access to most information in criminal investigations, but there were some limits, especially in an open case.

"I guess the kid's onto something," her dad said. "I heard the transient theory and assumed that they had evidence to back it up. They still could. If they think Abernathy is involved, they likely have a good reason. He probably rides the rails—it's surprisingly common. Remember that guy who raped and killed four women about ten, twelve years ago? He was living near the railroad tracks, hopped on one day, and if someone hadn't seen him jumping cars, he may have disappeared forever. And the Route 66 murders? That hobo killed for money and booze across three states, using the rail system to disappear until he was finally caught."

"No one says *hobo* anymore, Dad," she said.

He waved away her comment. "I don't like this kid's amateur tactics, and I'm pretty sure the police know a lot more than they're saying. One thing about investigations, they are dependent on the questions you ask and *who* you ask. People lie to cops—sometimes intentionally, sometimes by omission. No doubt they looked seriously at the two boyfriends. If she had two, could she have had a third that she didn't tell anyone about? And I'm not buying into the swimming-pool theory, not yet. The police have the same forensic reports, and they would have tested the water at the time."

"What if they didn't?" she asked.

"Most do the work and put in the time."

"Sometimes we make assumptions and don't realize it. Reports can be lost or misread."

John grunted. "Not going there. Not without evidence that there's a problem. Maybe you should talk to Young, see what he has to say."

"Maybe I will. So you don't think I should do the interview with Lucas?" Regan said.

"I didn't say that. Like I said, I'm intrigued. He asks some good questions. Maybe he'll find the answers. And maybe you can help." Her dad looked at her pointedly. "I know you don't like unsolved murders any more than I do."

Her heart twisted into a knot so tight she didn't know if she could breathe. She didn't want to respond to him by lashing out, saying something she'd later regret.

Her dad didn't apologize or backtrack; she knew he meant it. She knew he wanted her to face Chase's death head-on. It didn't matter that she knew who killed him: there were still a lot of questions—questions she hadn't been able to ask because the shooter was dead.

Instead, she picked up her phone from the coffee table, grabbed her jacket from the back of the couch, the flashlight from the shelf by the door, and left the house for a walk.

From the Missing Journal of Candace Swain

"Everything in your life is a reflection of a choice you have made. If you want a different result, make a different choice."

I stumbled on that quote while scrolling through my Instagram feed, and it stuck with me. For weeks, I couldn't sleep more than a few hours. I couldn't eat more than a few bites. Because as the quote dug deeper into my soul—if I still even have a soul—I realized that I couldn't fix my life. I can't make a different choice. I can't go back in time and say no. I can't go back in time and stand up. Fear? So easy to blame fear. Fear for my life? Maybe. Not my physical life, but my future. Because what life would I have if people knew the truth?

As time marches on, as my choice torments me, I realize that it wasn't fear that drove my decision.

It was selfishness.

Six

As Lucas sat in his bedroom trying to focus on his homework, he kept thinking about his conversation with Regan Merritt. He figured it was fifty-fifty that she would come on his podcast. Maybe sixty-forty: she had seemed interested and hadn't dismissed him flat out like Detective Young. *Jerk.*

He hadn't admitted to her that he was stuck. He hadn't even talked to his advisor about it. On paper, the podcast had seemed like a brilliant way to find out the truth about what happened to the victim. But he hadn't received the feedback like he'd thought he would. He'd been so excited about the caller who saw Candace in Kingman, but then... crickets. No emails, no follow-up calls, no other contributors. Was he asking the wrong questions? Had he structured the show wrong? Should he have led off with his big reveal the Candace didn't drown in the lake?

Lizzy kept telling him to stop second-guessing himself, reminding him that he'd structured the show to end with a cliff-hanger to entice people to talk about the show and tune in next time. The stats from the last episode showed a twenty-percent increase in people livestreaming, and they were getting steady subscribers to the podcast.

Some of the emails bothered him—people accusing him of exploiting Candace's murder. No one in Sigma Rho would talk to him. He'd reached out twice to Annie Johnston, Candace's roommate who was now a pediatric nurse in Phoenix, and she'd ignored him.

While the caller on Friday had been anonymous on air, Lizzy got her name and an email when she first called in. Her name was Abby and she currently lived ten minutes off campus in a large apartment complex near the interstate. A lot of college students lived there because it was cheaper than places closer to campus, and the city bus was free for students. He'd emailed her on Friday, thanking her for her call, and asked if he could ask follow-up questions. She hadn't responded yet.

What if she'd lied? What if someone *was* playing games?

He pushed everything out of his mind and tried again to focus on his homework, but his mind wasn't cooperating. He hadn't been able to concentrate on anything these last few months except the Candace Swain murder.

Lucas had a theory he couldn't share with anyone— not with his advisor and certainly not with Regan Merritt.

If he was right, he would solve two murders. If he was wrong…well, he'd worry about that later.

He didn't think he was wrong.

"Hey, Lucas." His roommate, Troy Thompson, rapped on the wall just inside his open bedroom door.

"Whassup?" he said, tearing himself away from his email.

"Would you mind disappearing for a couple hours? Denise is coming over and…" He winked.

"Sure." Lucas generally didn't mind letting Troy have

the apartment to himself on occasion. They didn't have a lot in common, but flexibility of this sort actually made their friendship work. They'd been roommates for a year and a half now. Lucas was the slight Hispanic scholarship kid from south Phoenix, and Troy the tall Black rich kid from Scottsdale with a dad whose claim to fame was that he pitched three innings in relief in a World Series more than a decade ago and had a 2.40 ERA over an eight-year career. Troy was real people, *buena gente*, as Lucas's *abuela* would say. Lucas liked him, even though Troy only cared about football, girls, and physical training—which was his major. He planned to be a physical trainer in the NFL. Lucas knew next to nothing about football.

But tonight Lucas was in a mood, and Troy must have picked up on it because he said, "Hey, if you don't wanna, that's fine. Denise and I can watch movies and stuff. You're probably studying."

"Nah, it's fine. Really. I'm just tired and frustrated."

"I'm making her dinner, but I already started, so give me two hours?"

Lucas laughed. "I'll get a beer at the pub, be back at eleven?"

"Perfect. Thanks, buddy. And I'll have plenty of leftovers, so feel free to help yourself."

It was just after eight when Lucas left, passing Denise as she was coming up the stairs. She smiled and said hi, cute in her down jacket and jeans. She was the nicest of Troy's long string of girlfriends and seemed to have some staying power. It had been three months already, and Troy was still *enamorado*, as Abuela would say.

Lucas zipped up his jacket. Being early March, there was no more snow on the ground, though higher in the mountains they still had plenty and some people still skied.

Tonight, it was freezing cold, already forty degrees. He missed Phoenix. It got cold there, too, sure, but a person did not have to endure months of twenty-, thirty-degree nights. The first week they were on campus after Christmas break, it had actually been *ten degrees below zero.* Who in the world wanted to live in a town where the temperatures dropped to below zero?

Lucas called Lizzy to see if she wanted to meet him. He should have driven. He had a truck but usually kept it at the apartment because he didn't want to spend money on gas if he didn't have to. But Lizzy didn't answer. Probably had a date or something. She was cute *and* smart. She'd had a boyfriend for two years, but they'd split when he graduated. Lucas was pretty certain she had plenty of friends to hang with, and he was not really fun to be around these days.

He walked down to McCarthy's, where he and Lizzy had dinner the previous night. He liked the place, and not just because Candace's bartender boyfriend worked there. It was comfortable, and though Lucas wasn't into sports, he liked the noise, and when he was alone he could pretend to watch. Baseball wasn't too bad: at least he understood it better than football. It was a popular hangout for older college students as well as locals and was always busy.

Lucas had reached out to Richie Traverton, Candace's boyfriend, via email two months ago when he was putting together his podcast project, asked if he would be willing to make a statement or be interviewed for the show, but Richie never got back to him. There was no reason the bartender would know him, and Lucas hoped to keep it that way.

He ordered a pint and sat at a table for two. He opened his laptop and brought up the outline that Professor Clarkson had approved for his capstone project. The podcast was only part of it. He also had to write a paper on the topic:

methodology, interviews, procedures, outcomes, more. Updating the existing outline with details along the way would make it easier to finish his paper later, when the podcast was over, so he fleshed out several of the points and wrote a timeline about responses and problems he'd encountered.

He really, really hoped he could solve Candace Swain's murder. Otherwise, all his efforts would be for nothing.

Lucas didn't know if Richie killed Candace, though it didn't make sense for a lot of reasons. Mostly, though, Lucas believed in Richie's innocence because Lucas knew more about the police investigation than he let on. He was hesitant to share all the info on his podcast because he wasn't sure about the legality of what he'd done. When working in the medical examiner's office over the summer, Lucas had been able to access all police reports—not just the public ones. Technically, anything written down by a cop could potentially be made public, but anyone interested would have to go through the Freedom of Information Act to legally obtain the information. What Lucas had found still wouldn't have been released that way because Candace Swain's murder case remained an open investigation. But the police had cleared both Traverton and Tyler Diaz, the student Candace sometimes dated. They had solid alibis for the night she was killed *and* the night she disappeared.

But just because Traverton hadn't killed Candace didn't mean he didn't know more about what had happened to her, at least for the time she'd been missing. But if he did know something, wouldn't he have told the police? Wouldn't he *want* to help solve her murder?

Lucas worried he was in over his head. He had thought for certain that after his first episode, he'd have a dozen people calling in, telling him they'd seen Candace, that he'd be able to piece together her last days alive. It didn't happen.

Discoverability was key to a podcast's success. He had stats of how many people had subscribed—just under three hundred people after the first episode, which was good for something he'd only advertised on his social-media pages and through the school's pages. Double after the second episode. He'd posted flyers on every board—attractive flyers, because his roommate was nice enough to let him use his color printer so he didn't have to pay for them. Candace Swain had been popular. Even though she was killed three years ago, wouldn't others be interested in a nursing student's murder that had taken place only a couple miles from campus?

You know why they wouldn't. People don't care about anyone but themselves.

He pushed the thought aside. He had to focus on the here and now, not the past.

He nursed his one beer and nibbled on a side order of nachos while working on his paper, then switched over to research Regan Merritt. He knew some things about her from her talk on campus, and Professor Clarkson had privately shared more when Lucas had approached him about inviting her on the podcast. Lucas knew that her son had recently been killed and she quit the Marshals Service. But it wasn't like he could ask her about it, and he could find very little online.

At quarter to eleven, Lucas closed down his laptop, slung his case over his shoulder, and left the bar. It was even colder than when he'd arrived nearly three hours ago. He wished he'd brought a hat, but even after nearly four years of living here, he hadn't quite adapted to a cold lifestyle and always forgot a hat and gloves.

Now he *really* wished he'd driven.

His phone vibrated as he turned the corner and started up the short hill that led to his apartment complex. He pulled it out and saw that Lizzy was calling.

"Hello," he answered.

"You called and didn't leave a message."

"I was going to McCarthy's and thought you might want to meet me."

"I totally would have. Next time text me, or leave a message."

"I figured you had plans."

"Hardly. You still there?"

"Walking home."

"It's freezing."

"You're telling me."

"Did you hear back from Clarkson's friend? The marshal?"

"Not yet. Crossing fingers and all that."

"I think she'll do it. It's too interesting. I mean, who just disappears for eight days and then shows up freshly dead?"

Lizzy could be blunt, which was one of the things Lucas appreciated about her.

"I hope you're right," he said.

"If she doesn't, who needs her? We had two calls, we'll get more. They'll start steamrolling, or whatever that expression is."

Lucas smiled, told Lizzy he'd see her tomorrow evening, and ended the call.

He heard a car behind him and expected to see lights. When he didn't see them, his sixth sense kicked in, and he knew something felt...off.

He glanced over his shoulder. A boxy car—a Jeep, he thought, though it was hard to tell in the dark—was slowly driving up the hill behind him, lights off. He hoped they weren't drunk. Just to be safe, Lucas moved farther to the right, as far from the street as he could get without falling into the ditch. The Jeep continued up the hill and passed him, lights still off but not driving erratically or doing anything that would prompt Lucas to call the police to report a drunk driver.

Sometimes people were just clueless.

He continued up the hill, turned right, then walked up the stairs to his apartment. It was a nice place, eight units, and the owner–manager Mrs. Levitz lived on the first floor with her four cats. He and Troy fixed a few things for her, and she made them cookies at least once a month and left care packages for them. Her cooking was pretty good. Not as good as his mom's, but better than what he could put together for himself.

Troy and Denise were on the couch watching a movie when he walked in. "Hey," he said before going into his bedroom, not wanting to disturb them.

He sat down and checked the podcast email. A dozen messages basically calling him a jerk.

And then there was one that didn't.

The subject line was can i trust you.

It had been sent through an anonymous address, maybe an email created just to communicate with him, a bunch of numbers and random letters at a Gmail account.

He opened it.

i listened to your podcasts. i almost called in, but i'm in sigma rho, and they would recognize my voice. i saw candace driving like a bat out of hell into mountain view parking. it was around ten at night, two days after the party, sunday night, and she almost hit me. i don't know if that helps you, but i'd get in trouble if i called. call me a concerned sister.

p.s. i'm sure you've figured out that the sorority put a total lid on talking to you. they say they want to protect candace's image, but it's really more the sorority's image they care about. but some of us listen to you, hang on every word, because we want to know what happened to candace as much as you do.

maybe even more.

Seven

Regan met her best friend, Jessie Nez, for breakfast Tuesday morning at Marcy's Grill, a diner that had outlived the original owner by twenty years. Marcy's granddaughter Susan ran the place now, and very little had changed—which suited Regan and everyone else who ate there regularly. She and Jessie had breakfast together at least once a week since Regan came back. Jessie ate here every morning because she hated to cook.

"You look like shit," Jessie said as she sat down, adjusting her heavy utility belt and putting her radio down on the red-checked plastic tabletop.

"No tact, but to the point, I give you that," said Regan. She had arrived early and was already on her third cup of black coffee.

"You'd better not fucking be canceling our hike on me."

"I'm not canceling. Though, I think the weather is going to turn."

"Shit."

Jessie swore as easily as breathing. Regan had never

heard her parents utter a bad word, but Jessie had littered *shit* and *fuck* and *damn* into her speech from the day Regan had first met her in middle school. Jessie, born on the Navajo reservation to a Navajo father and white mother, had moved to Flagstaff with her mom when her parents divorced. Those teenage years had been difficult for Jessie, and she had her own way of coping with it.

She'd run away from home several times. She lived with her father for six months in eighth grade, then realized why her mother divorced him: he was sweet as molasses when he was sober, unpredictable and violent when he was drunk. In high school, she'd once dyed her long black hair bright pink. She later admitted that had been stupid. In college, she cut it off at her ears to get rid of the remnants of pink. Now, she wore it medium-length, which she usually pulled back into a ponytail.

"You look soft," Jessie said. "Are you sure you're going to be able to do this one? It's the most difficult trail in Sedona."

Her comment didn't deserve a response, so Regan ignored it. "I wanted to pick your brain. Do you remember three years ago a sorority girl, Candace Swain, who was found dead at Hope Centennial Golf Course? In the lake."

"Yep."

"You answered quickly."

"I listen to podcasts in my truck. You know how much I can't stand driving, and that seems to be half my job now. I found the one about her death. *The Sorority Murder*. Kid from the college. I didn't think you'd have the patience to sit still and listen to anything."

"I spoke at the Criminology and Criminal Justice school yesterday, and Lucas Vega, the host, asked to interview me."

"No shit. You doing it?"

She nodded. "The case is intriguing, and I think I can help. I'm just concerned about the directions of his questions, so I need to lay down some ground rules. I'm very private."

"Ya think?" Jessie snorted.

The server returned with their food: three eggs over easy, bacon and toast for Regan, a loaded omelet for Jessie. She refilled their coffees and walked away.

"Do you remember the murder?" Regan asked as they ate.

"Sure, it was on my radar—FPD issued a BOLO for Candace Swain, missing person, so it was posted on our board and in my truck. Also a BOLO for some homeless guy, Abernathy—the Vega kid mentioned him. So you're going on the podcast to help? Share your expertise?"

"I don't know how much I can help, but I have some ideas on how he can frame questions and maybe have a better response. Someone knows something. They might not even know what they know." For nearly half of Regan's thirteen years in the Marshals Service, she'd tracked fugitives. She had often been called for cases outside her jurisdiction because she had an uncanny way of getting into the heads of those who didn't want to be found. She also had a knack for getting people to remember details they thought they'd forgotten or never consciously knew. People saw and heard a lot, but remembering those details could be difficult.

The missing days in Candace Swain's calendar intrigued her. It was virtually impossible to stay off the grid for that long unless you planned to. Money, food, shelter. But there was no clear reason this twenty-one-year-old student had any reason to go on the down-low. Regan was drawn to the challenge of helping Lucas re-create Candace's whereabouts.

And she'd been in limbo for too long. Regan had to do something to keep her mind off her son and the man who'd killed him.

"You doing it tonight?" asked Jessie.

"Yes."

"I usually download podcasts for the truck, but I'll listen live tonight."

"If you call in and embarrass me, I will get revenge."

Jessie laughed. "No call-in. Promise." She glanced at her watch and quickly finished her omelet. "I gotta bolt. Someone up on Schultz Pass Road reported a mountain lion near the trailhead. That's getting a little close to population centers, so I'm going track it—if the woman is even right about what she saw. People will see a fucking *deer* and think it's a mountain lion. Twice that's happened to me."

Regan believed it. Both fear and imagination could run wild.

"And then there was the idiot who thought she was *helping* by taking two cubs into her barn. She called in, was worried they'd been abandoned. Like a mama lion is going to abandon them? She was told *twice* to leave the cubs alone, that their mom was out hunting, but she didn't listen. I loved writing her up and fining her the maximum, but those cubs are now in a fucking zoo instead of living their best life." Jessie rolled her eyes. She put a twenty down on the table and got up, grabbing her radio and clipping it to her belt.

"That's too much."

"My treat, you get the tip. Saturday morning, I'm picking you up at six."

"I'll pack the picnic."

"No, I'll pack the food. You never bring enough to eat."

When Jessie left, Regan finished her toast and called Lucas Vega to confirm. He sounded pleased that she'd agreed, then she said, "Let's establish some ground rules beforehand, good?"

"Yeah, sure. Come to the studio at seven, an hour before we go live?"

"I'll be there."

"I got an email last night," Lucas said. "Can I forward it to you? I think it's legit, but she didn't sign it, and the email address is anonymous."

"Sure." She rattled off her personal email.

"Thanks, Regan."

She ended the call, and less than ten seconds later the email came in. Regan read it twice.

One sentence really caught her eye:

they say they want to protect candace's image, but it's really more the sorority's image they care about.

Who did she mean when she said *they*? The sorority as a whole? A group within the sorority? Did someone there know more than they'd told police?

She read the message a third time and determined that the sender was likely a senior—possibly a five-year student— who had been a freshman or sophomore when Candace disappeared. She didn't say that Lucas couldn't read the note on the podcast, just that she wanted to be anonymous. This might give them a jumping-off point tonight.

Regan chatted with Susan for a minute while she paid the bill with the money Jessie left, then she walked out, heading over to her truck. She thought about going home and talking to her dad—she hadn't spoken to him since she'd walked out last night. That hour-long walk in the cold hadn't tempered her anger. She controlled her temper well—had learned to at a young age—but the tension left her with a headache that hadn't dissipated even after four aspirin, coffee, and food.

Not fair maybe, but nothing about life was fair.

She had just clicked the unlock button on her key fob when she heard someone call her name. She turned and almost did a double take.

"Tripp?"

"Regan Merritt, didn't expect to see you, but sure glad I did."

Tripp Garza strode over and gave her a tight hug. She hugged him back. She'd known Tripp practically her entire life—he was her brother JT's best friend since kindergarten.

"I didn't expect to see you. When I got back here in October, Dad said you were still deployed."

"I was, took my papers in January. I gave near half my life to the army."

The last time she'd seen Tripp was when he was best man for JT's wedding. That was eight years ago. Back when she had a husband, and a son, and a job she loved.

"What are you doing now?" she asked.

"Same thing you are," he answered.

She didn't know what to say to that. What did he know? Was he also here to figure out his life?

Tripp added, "I went to see JT a few weeks ago."

He didn't have to say anything else. She had told her brother everything that had happened in Virginia and why she came home. She had expected his complete confidence, but she should have known better. JT and Tripp had been inseparable growing up; she shouldn't be surprised they still shared everything now.

"Well." She cleared her throat. She had nothing to say about it.

Tripp said, "Don't blame JT. I asked."

"So you're home trying to piece together the remnants of your life, too?"

She sounded angry; maybe she was. She didn't want to think about Chase, but he was all she had been thinking about since her dad's comment last night. The pain was still too raw, too fresh, even though he had been killed eight months ago. She feared it would never go away, that she'd live with this constant pressure on her chest, the never-ending grief of losing the most important person in her life.

"Hell, I can't even find the pieces to stitch back together," he said, his tone far lighter than his words. "One day at a time."

She nodded because she understood exactly what he meant. "You staying in town?"

"I'm thinking about taking the GI Bill and going to college. NAU."

She laughed; she couldn't help it. Tripp had barely survived high school, and she couldn't see him in college.

"I know, I know. I don't expect to finish. I just have no fucking idea what to do anymore and thought taking a couple practical classes might help put something together."

"Where are you staying?" Tripp's parents had separated after he enlisted. His dad had remarried and moved to Texas; his mom remarried and moved to Phoenix.

"My grandma is letting me stay in her guest house."

"I didn't know she had a guest house."

"Most people call it a shed, but it has a bathroom. I don't want to put her out, and I'm not really good company these days. I'm getting there. Thanks to your brother." He playfully hit her arm. "It's really good to see you, Regan."

"You, too, Tripp. Don't be a stranger."

Eight

Regan spent the afternoon at the NAU library reading everything she could find about Candace Swain's murder investigation. There wasn't much. In fact, Lucas had covered all of the key public facts on the first two episodes of his show. There was no mention that Candace had not drowned in the lake, no real forensic details outside of the basics. The police had clearly indicated to the media—because they reported heavily about Joseph Abernathy—that he was a person of interest, i.e. a suspect.

A reporter had written an investigative article about individuals who ride the rails. Not only transients took the free, but often dangerous, jump onto freight cars. Young people were increasingly participating in these endeavors, and he'd interviewed two college dropouts who spoke on the condition of anonymity. "Jan" and "Tom" estimated they had ridden more than ten thousand miles on the tracks over the last two years.

"We were able to see most of the country, places most people don't even know about," Jan said. *"We're taking a break but are meeting up with friends later this summer."*

Jan and Tom both know Joseph Abernathy. They once

shared a railcar with him from Flagstaff to Albuquerque a year ago.

"Joseph was quiet, kept to himself. He drank heavily, and when he was sober he had a hard time remembering things. He told a lot of stories, but you didn't know if they were true or not. But he was harmless. He would yell at people sometimes, and you didn't really know why, but he never hurt anyone."

Serious alcoholics didn't always know what they did when they were intoxicated. It was certainly possible to kill and not remember.

There were too many questions, and nothing in any of the official statements gave her anything more to go on. The police felt that Abernathy was their best and most viable suspect, and as her dad had indicated, they could have evidence they kept to themselves.

At quarter to seven, she headed over to the communications building where the recording studios were located. While dorms always required a card key to enter, most buildings were open during class hours, and there were many evening courses around campus. After hours, only a card key could get you in. Fortunately, the communications building was open. Lucas had texted her that he was in room 303, down the hall from the studio.

He had his door open. "You ranked your own office?" she said as she walked in. It was small—barely fit a desk and a chair, with a second chair squeezed in—but it had a door that locked.

"They had the space, and I made a pitch as part of my capstone. There was no room in the criminology building, and this is right down the hall from the studio."

She sat down across from him. He was working on his laptop. There were binders on a shelf next to the desk, and a few crime-related books, plus one on forensics. But there was no clutter; he clearly didn't spend a lot of time in here.

Lucas said, "I really appreciate you doing this with me. I think it'll help."

"Exactly what do you want from me? Yesterday you mentioned interviewing techniques, discussing how the Marshals Service looks for missing people, things like that."

"Yes. But I also think you can help frame my questions in a more productive way. I really expected more people to call in."

"I think your questions are a bit open-ended. For example, after the caller said she saw Candace in Kingman, you asked *who else saw her?* And *why was she there?* You need to invite people in a more direct way. You did it in the first episode when you asked if people were at the party, if they saw Candace. You handled the interview with the caller very well, got as much information from her three-year-old memory as I think anyone could have gotten. The fact that the date was memorable for her because it was the weekend of her sister's birthday tells me that it's an accurate memory. People generally associate memories around such events. Holidays, birthdays, deaths, special occasions. I interviewed a witness once who was credible because he was a football fan and saw the suspect we were looking for, remembering the individual because he was rushed to get home to watch the Super Bowl and the suspect delayed him at the store. Details like that ground the average person."

"Would people get in trouble if they have information but didn't tell the police?"

"Not unless they lied to the police. If the police never

asked someone a question, how would someone know they had answers the police might need?"

"Makes sense."

"Now, I really only have one rule."

"Anything you want. I just appreciate your time."

"No personal questions."

"Okay. And that's it?"

"Yes. I'll let you know if something else comes up."

Regan was going to have to trust him. She didn't have anything to hide, but she was private and planned to keep living that way.

"Tonight I'm going to reveal the fact that Candace didn't drown in the lake."

"How certain are you?"

"One hundred percent," he said with confidence. "I might not know how to run a police investigation, or how to interview witnesses, but I know how to read a lab report. She drowned in a highly chlorinated body of water, most likely a swimming pool. They're a dime a dozen, but it still tells me that someone intentionally moved her body to either cover up the crime or destroy evidence."

"Or both."

"Exactly. I also want to read the email on the air. The fact that Candace was on campus Sunday night gives us another point in the timeline, and that might jolt other memories."

"I agree."

"So I'm going to restructure what I planned, and instead of leading with forensics, I'm going to read the email and then ask you what you, as someone who has found missing persons, would ask."

She agreed. "And your goal?"

"I need people to call. To trust me, to believe in what I'm doing. Three years is a long time, but I think people would remember the last time they saw a person who later died, right? If Candace went back to the sorority late Sunday night, why didn't anyone see her? When did she leave? Maybe they thought it was a different day, maybe they got confused, or maybe the police never asked them. Or someone did see her but never told anyone."

Very valid questions.

"I spent the afternoon at the library reading everything about Candace Swain's murder. I'd like to know what you have. I might be able to help more than directing callers or offering advice."

"You'd be willing to do that?" He sounded surprised.

"Yes. I think Chrissy Swain needs to know what happened to her sister. I've met with survivors before. The year I worked in the courthouse, I sat in on dozens of trials. And the one thing that survivors have in common—other than loss and grief—is a sense of closure once they watch the justice system work. It works more often than not."

"That would be—well, awesome! I mean it. If you have the time."

I have nothing but time. But she didn't say that.

"If you're right, and Joseph Abernathy is not her killer, Candace's killer is still at large."

"I didn't actually say that," he said.

"But you don't think he did it."

Lucas shook his head. "I have doubts. Mostly about how he transported her body and why. If he was in a drunken rage and killed her, would he have the wherewithal to steal or borrow a car and dump her body? And while I know his disappearance is suspicious, I find it hard to believe he could disappear for three years. The police have his name and his picture, and he had a routine. How could a drunk elude authorities for so long?"

"What do you think happened to him?"

"I don't know."

"You think he's dead?"

"I guess I do," he said. "I never thought about it that bluntly, but yeah, it seems the only explanation. A witness saw him jump into a freight car the Sunday Candace's body was found. I'd like to talk to that witness, but the name wasn't in the paper, and I couldn't get the notes from the police report."

"Then, you need to ask the right questions," Regan said. "I can help there. You know a lot about this case, and if Candace's killer is listening, that could put you in danger. I don't want to light the match tonight and walk away. If we push—and especially if we start gathering better information about Candace's missing days—I fear you're putting a target on your back."

He frowned. "I don't know about that."

"I do. You know what the Marshals Service does, right? We don't just track down fugitives and guard federal courthouses. We also protect witnesses. You need to be careful. If you see or hear anything out of the ordinary, call me and I'll come. Is this where you keep all your notes?"

He shook his head. "Some things, but I have a timeline and all important documents at my apartment, off campus." He looked at his phone. "We don't really have time to go over there before the show, but maybe after, if you want."

"That's good for me if it's good for you."

"Yeah. Any help you can give I'd appreciate."

She didn't have anything else to do, and helping Lucas

solve this murder—along with giving Candace's family closure—gave her a purpose.

Which Regan really needed right now.

Nine

Regan had never been inside the campus recording studio before—she'd never had reason to be. While she didn't have a lot of experience with radio or podcasts, the studio appeared state-of-the-art, small but well-appointed. Lucas's partner, Lizzy, was a bundle of energy and came into the room drinking a Red Bull. Cute and petite, Lizzy might have weighed ninety pounds soaking wet.

"We're *so* excited that you agreed to come in," Lizzy said with a grin, revealing deep dimples. "I'm Lucas's producer, I guess you can say. I handle the recording, the live cast, editing, taking calls, the whole nine yards. I even convinced my advisor to give me a credit for the work as part of an independent-study project." She laughed. "Not that I need it, but it's nice to have the points, you know?"

"Slight change of plans," Lucas said. "I'm going to read an email I got last night, and Regan is going to help frame the questions. If we don't get immediate calls, then I'll interview her about missing-persons cases as I planned, and specifically how to handle witnesses. I'm hoping having someone of her caliber in the studio will make people feel more comfortable calling in. But I also want to cut in with the second part of the interview with Chrissy, what she says after I tell her about the forensics report."

"Tugging on heartstrings," Lizzy said.

"Chrissy wants to help," Lucas said. "She knows what I'm trying to do here."

"I was kinda joking. But it *is* emotional for her. That plays on the tape. I'll have it cued up for you, just give me the signal."

Lucas motioned for Regan to follow him into a sound-proof booth. Lizzy was on the other side of thick glass with most of the controls. Lucas had his laptop, plus on the table was a multiline telephone and speaker that went into the producer's booth. Two comfortable chairs were positioned in front of the hanging mic.

"Lizzy had never done this before, but she learned everything practically overnight," he said. "I couldn't do this without her."

"Good friends are hard to come by," Regan said. She thought of Jessie, who would do anything for her. And likewise.

Lucas pulled two semicold water bottles from his backpack, put one in front of her. "I'll introduce you first, ask a bit about US Marshals, then why I asked you to join me, then I'll read the email, okay?" He opened his laptop and turned a page to her. "I'm going to read this by way of introduction. Good?"

She skimmed the brief bio. "Yes, perfect. Slick to mention my dad."

"Yeah, well, anything I can do to command authority, or whatever it is that people are waiting for before they call. And I *know* they're out there."

Lucas and Lizzy tested all the equipment, then she started the countdown. The on-air light came on above the door, which they could see through the booth. Lizzy controlled the music lead-in, then Lucas took over. He gave a brief summary of the last two episodes then said, "With me tonight is NAU alum and former US Marshal Regan Merritt. Regan majored in criminal justice and psychology. She follows a long line of law enforcement—her grandfather was a forest ranger in Kaibab, her father was the elected sheriff of Coconino County for sixteen years before retiring three years ago, and her brother is a deputy sheriff for Maricopa County. The last six of her thirteen years in the Marshals Service she served as part of the Fugitive Apprehension Unit."

He explained what the Marshals Service did, then said, "I planned on asking Regan questions about missing persons and witness recollection, and I will do that later in the episode, but first I want to read an email I received from someone who signed it A Concerned Sister. She chose to come forward after hearing our caller on Friday."

He read the key part of the email, leaving out the comment about the sorority protecting its image.

"I saw Candace driving like a bat out of hell into Mountain View parking. It was around ten at night, two days after the party, Sunday night, and she almost hit me. I don't know if that helps you, but I'd get in trouble if I called."

Lucas paused to let the comment sink in, then he detailed the timeline. "On Friday night, Taylor James and several other people saw Candace Swain leave the party shortly after midnight. She was angry and upset about an argument that witnesses state was critical of her for not calling the police about the presence of Joseph Abernathy on campus.

"On Sunday afternoon, Candace was seen in Kingman, Arizona, by a student, at approximately three o'clock. She was in her blue Volkswagen. On Sunday night around ten p.m., Candace was seen in the same vehicle driving into the Mountain View parking garage, which is dedicated to the sorority dorm. Her card key was used to access the dorm at 11:10 p.m., but no one saw her enter or exit. On Monday afternoon, her phone was found on the charger by her roommate after she couldn't reach Candace. Her vehicle was found in the parking garage on Tuesday morning. There's no indication as to how long it was there.

"According to the autopsy report, Candace was alive and well almost the entire time she was missing—no signs of captivity, malnutrition, or dehydration that might indicate that she had been kept against her will for any length of time. She was killed between ten and one Saturday night, a full week after the party, and her body was found early the next morning, Sunday, in Hope Springs Lake. People rarely disappear into thin air, and I believe there are more people out there who saw Candace. One reason I asked Ms. Merritt to join me this evening is because of her experience interviewing witnesses. Ms. Merritt, after three years do you think that the information from the caller on Friday and the email my podcast received last night are valid? Do you think they remembered the information accurately?"

"Yes. People often attach memories to specific events, and those are more reliable than, for example, a witness to a bank robbery giving an accurate description of a suspect. Because the caller had mentally attached her sister's birthday—a fixed date—to her memory, I would rank the memory as valid."

"And the email?"

"I put some credence on the email. However, I would want to ask the writer follow-up questions. How does she know it was a Sunday night? She says it was at ten o'clock.

That means it was dark. How can she be accurate about the time and day three years later? If it was dark, how could she be certain it was Candace's car? A jolt of fear can etch a memory—such as almost being hit by a car—but if she was angry or fearful, did she mention the event to anyone? Did she see Candace exit the parking garage or enter the dorm? We can assume that she didn't know that Candace was missing—no one reported it until Monday afternoon."

"Is that unusual?"

"No. With an open college campus and an adult student with a vehicle, no one would be suspicious unless she didn't show up when expected."

"That confirms what the community relations officer told me," Lucas said. "People might leave campus for the weekend, not think to tell anyone, come back before classes on Monday."

"Exactly."

Lucas said, "I would ask the Concerned Sister who emailed me to consider Ms. Merritt's questions. How can you be certain of the day? That this wasn't another day before the party? That it was Sunday night? That it was in fact Candace?"

"Yes," Regan said. "But let's assume that she is confident in her memory. One reason I used the bank-robbery example was because fear creates certain stressors, and memories can be clearer—or completely off. If you're scared, you may see a threat as worse than it is or a person as physically more imposing than they are. For example, I once helped investigate a string of bank robberies because a fugitive I was pursuing was involved. The fugitive was five feet ten inches tall and one hundred sixty pounds—not a large man. Virtually every witness identified him as over six feet, and one said he had to be two hundred pounds.

But it was my fugitive, who has a distinctive tattoo on his neck, and that is what ultimately identified him. Yet, of the three witnesses I personally interviewed, no one had the tattoo accurate. One said it was an eagle, one a naked woman, and one a blob of blue ink. It was in fact Pegasus from Greek mythology. They all remembered, however, that it was on the left side of his neck.

"Fear can taint memories, but it can also solidify them. Interviewers need to be careful when drawing out details from a witness. We start with easy-to-confirm facts—time of day a crime occurred, day of the week, the purpose of the witness's visit to that location, things like that. Make the witness comfortable with mundane, easy-to-remember details, and then start asking more specific questions about the event—in fact, asking the same question in different ways can help gain more accurate information. It's also important to keep witnesses apart. There is a very real problem of confirmation bias, when a group of witnesses will agree to something that just isn't accurate."

Regan hoped she wasn't overtalking, but Lucas seemed interested in her comments. He then said, "I am hoping that A Concerned Sister will call in—or email again—with the answers to these questions. Regan, what if someone didn't come forward during the initial investigation, would they get in trouble now if they did speak up?"

"Most likely, no," Regan said. "First, many people didn't even know Candace had been missing, not until her body was found. Second, the police would have questioned those most likely to have answers—the people who last saw her at the party, her roommate who reported her missing, other sorority members, her boyfriends. They would have interviewed the staff at the golf course, and then after collecting and analyzing evidence, if that led them anywhere, they would have expanded the interviews.

"But no one is going to get in trouble because they might not have known they had information. If you're a clerk in a store, and the police come in and ask if you saw someone, show you a picture, and you hadn't see them, you're not going to get in trouble even if they were there. Maybe they were hiding their face. Maybe they didn't stand out in a long line of customers. But if you saw them and lied, and the police found out that you lied, they're going to want to know why. Were you paid to lie? Did you lie because you didn't like the cop asking the questions? Did you have something to do with her disappearance? But if the victim had been there but you were never questioned by the police, you might not even know you had information they needed.

"This is a roundabout way of saying that the evidence is only as good as the questions the police ask—and who they ask. I would suggest your listeners look at their calendars, schedules, social-media posts from the week of April 12 three years ago. It's easy to check your memories, see what you posted, who you were with. What were you doing? Do you recall seeing Candace? If so, when and where? In the age of social media where people document their lives online, it's likely someone saw Candace and just didn't think anything of it."

Lucas asked, "In your experience, knowing what you know about this case—that Candace didn't go to classes, that no one in the sorority saw her, that she left her phone and her car behind—would she be able to avoid detection?"

"In the short term? Yes. Is eight days short-term? I would say probably yes. In the case of a private citizen, not wanted by law enforcement, it's easier to disappear for a few days. Human beings are complex, but they are also predictable. Most people can't go completely off the grid for longer than a week. People need people. They also need shelter, food. It's *possible* to disappear, but it's rare for both psychological and practical reasons."

Lucas said, "Two people have come forward to say that they saw Candace *after* she left the party. Two people who were not interviewed by the police, so the police were unable to fully trace her steps and—maybe—find out what happened to her."

Regan replied, "People lie to the police all the time for a variety of reasons. Sometimes lack of trust in authorities, sometimes because they're hiding something. But unless someone lied to police, if they know something, they should come forward now with confidence that they won't get in trouble. *Someone* killed Candace Swain. Her family deserves to know what happened."

"Someone killed Candace," Lucas repeated. "And someone also moved her body."

He let that sit there for a moment, then said, "As I reported on the first two podcast episodes, Candace Swain was strangled, but her cause of death was by drowning. She was found in Hope Springs Lake on the Hope Centennial Golf Course.

"The autopsy was thorough, and full toxicology screens were taken. This means Candace's body was tested for both legal and illegal drugs, the contents of her stomach were analyzed, as was the water in her lungs. The water she drowned in was highly chlorinated. The golf maintenance staff told me that the lake is not chlorinated. My theory is that Candace drowned in a swimming pool, and her body was dumped in the lake to destroy evidence."

Regan didn't say anything. Lucas motioned to Lizzy

through the window, then said, "Chrissy Swain wants to know what happened to her sister."

Chrissy's voice came through the speakers. "The police told me that Candace drowned. They said her body may have been moved to the lake, and they were investigating all possible scenarios. Then silence. Nothing. I called at first every week and then monthly and...well, it just got to be so frustrating to hear they had no new information. Her boyfriends were cleared, they had alibis, and the police believed that a homeless man killed her, panicked, and just... just *threw* her body in the lake. He disappeared, and they have been looking for him. But after nearly three years, they haven't found him? It makes no sense."

Lucas said, "One theory posited by the local media, and not discounted by the Flagstaff Police Department, is that Candace disappeared for a reason completely unrelated to her murder. What do you think about that theory, Ms. Merritt?"

"I don't have all the information that the police have, but I think it would be unusual—definitely coincidental, if true. She left, but she didn't take her car? It seems odd— unless someone else was with her, someone who hasn't come forward."

Lizzy signaled that there was a caller.

"We have a caller," Lucas said as he pressed a button on the phone. "This is Lucas Vega with Regan Merritt. You have a comment? Did you see Candace?"

"I'm not comfortable giving my name," said a male voice. He sounded like he was trying to disguise his voice by talking soft and low. "Candace wasn't a saint. Maybe you should look into her *other* life. Her lies and manipulation and sneaking around."

The caller hung up.

Lucas seemed surprised. When he didn't immediately speak, Regan said, "It's difficult to take a caller seriously when they drop a bombshell about a double life without providing details or context as to why they believe that a victim might have had secrets. It reeks of slander and sour grapes."

"Still," Lucas said, "is it possible Candace was involved in something unethical or illegal?"

"That is conjecture as well," Regan said. "Nothing in any report indicates that Candace was involved in anything illegal."

"Nothing in the *public* police reports," Lucas countered.

The way the anonymous caller had spoken, the fact that he was male, the bitterness he couldn't hide... Regan suspected he might have been in a relationship with Candace. Richie Traverton? Tyler Diaz? An unknown third boyfriend? Definitely possible.

Maybe the killer.

No, she was fairly certain whoever killed Candace wouldn't call in to the podcast. He'd gotten away with murder for three years. He might not be in town, might not even know about the podcast. If he was listening, the only reason he would call would be if Lucas had stumbled onto something close to the truth and the killer wanted to obfuscate the situation. Still, Regan thought that was unlikely. Someone who thought he was free and clear wasn't going to do anything to rock the boat. And a podcast couldn't arrest them and send them to prison.

He? Why do you assume the killer is a he? Candace lived at a sorority, and the sorority has closed ranks. It could have been one of the girls. The killer could be a she.

But could one girl move her body from a swimming pool to Hope Springs Lake? Maybe...but unlikely.

Maybe more than one person was involved. That could complicate matters.

Regan had a thought. "One thing we haven't discussed is the complexity of living in a sorority. The pressures, the friendships, and former friendships. The friendly rivalries—and not-so-friendly ones."

"Were you in a sorority during your time at NAU?" Lucas asked.

"No, but Greek Life plays a huge part in the lives of people who belong. There are a lot of positives—immediate friends, a sense of belonging, a sense of being special, contacts for the future. For a sorority like Sigma Rho, you have an added sense of togetherness, since the majority of young women were majoring in STEM. There were nursing students, engineers, math majors—all difficult degrees that require extra study."

She saw Lizzy snort on the other side of the glass, and Lucas picked up on it. "I suppose those who aren't math- and science-oriented think they're difficult, but for some people it comes easy."

Regan laughed. "You're right. I wasn't a math person. Barely passed trig, and for my math requirement here I took business economics, the easiest class I could find. My point is that these are students who are likely taking their chosen fields seriously. Sigma Rho isn't a party dorm—and I think we all know who is. What kind of pressures did these young women have that might have contributed to Candace's state of mind when she disappeared?"

"I hadn't thought of that," Lucas admitted. "Maybe someone who knew Candace could share what they know, that might help us get into her head."

Lizzy indicated they had another caller.

Lucas pressed another button. "We have another caller.

This is Lucas Vega with Regan Merritt. Would you like to share your name?"

"No, not really. I almost didn't call."

Her voice was quiet, but not because she was trying to disguise it. It was almost as if she was trying not to be overheard.

"I saw Candace on Tuesday morning. *After* she was reported missing. But I didn't know she was missing then, so I really didn't think anything about it."

Regan asked, "How can you be sure that it was the Tuesday after she went missing?"

"I knew Candace, and she was supposed to meet with me and a couple others from our molecular biology class the night before. We were going to study because there was a huge test on Thursday and if you didn't pass it, well, you probably wouldn't pass the course, and we all needed it to graduate. We'd been meeting every Monday for the entire semester, and Candace really understood everything and could explain it in a way that helped. Anyway, she didn't show and she didn't answer her text messages, and I was kind of pissed. The next morning was Tuesday, and it was early. Cline Library had *just opened*, and I saw Candace walk out the side door, not the main door. She ignored me."

"You and Candace studied together, so she would recognize you."

"Yes. I mean, we didn't hang out or anything, but we had a lot of classes together over the years, so we were friendly."

"Go on," Regan encouraged.

"The library had literally *just opened*. I was on my way to a morning lab. I live off campus, but it's not far to walk. I always pass the library. It's sort of a shortcut across campus for me. Candace had an oversize bag, like a big, bulky purse. She walked right by me without looking, even though I said hello. I'd wanted to ask where she was the night before, but she looked mad, and she totally ignored me."

"Why did you think she was angry?"

"Her expression. Like she was furious about something, her mouth set, walking fast. She had on sunglasses, even though it was early, and she looked *determined*. She stomped down the path heading off campus. She was kind of a mess. Her hair sloppy, clothes all wrinkled. Every time I saw Candace she was always so put-together, you know?"

The more this student spoke, the more Regan believed her.

"What was she wearing?"

"I dunno. Just regular clothes."

"Jeans? A dress? A sweatshirt?"

"I—" The caller sighed dramatically. "Jeez. I really don't remember. Maybe a sweatshirt, but everyone wears sweatshirts, so I don't know. Not a dress or skirt. Just casual."

"And she came out of the library," Regan prompted. "It had just opened, which would be about seven thirty, correct? You had a lab at seven thirty?"

"My lab was at eight, but I usually went early so I could grab coffee and food at the student union on my way. And I just had this idea that she'd done an all-nighter, but I remember thinking she couldn't have done an all-nighter at the library. She never went to class looking like that. I had the feeling she'd spent the night at the library. Then I thought that was stupid, she was probably returning a book or something."

There were security cameras at the library, but they didn't cover the entire interior, and if someone didn't want to be seen, they might be able to hide from Security until after closing.

Would there still be copies of those tapes, three years later? Regan doubted it. She could ask, find out how long they kept recordings.

Maybe the caller was mistaken about Candace staying overnight in the library, but Regan believed that the anonymous caller *had* definitely seen her Tuesday morning.

Lucas asked, "Did you talk to campus police at the time? FPD?"

"No," the caller said. "I forgot about it. Really. And when I found out she was dead, I didn't know she'd been missing all week. We didn't have the same friend group, and we only had that one class together that year."

"Are you still a student?" Regan asked.

"No, but I work in town. I don't want to get into trouble, but my girlfriend says I won't. That I didn't know that what I saw might have been important. And when I listened tonight, and you talked about how we remember things, I was compelled to call. I don't know how it helps, but I want to do what I can."

"It helps," Lucas said, "because it adds one more point on the timeline. Thank you." He cut off the call and looked at the clock. "We're nearly at our allotted time for the studio, but I want to remind our listeners that you might not know what is important and what is not. We now have three sightings of Candace Swain after she left the Sigma Rho party. She was in Kingman, Arizona, two hours from campus, on Sunday afternoon. She drove into the Mountain View parking lot at ten that night. And she was spotted outside Cline Library around seven thirty Tuesday morning. Who else saw her? When and where? Call or email." He rattled off the number and email address.

Lizzy was frantically waving at them. "We have another

caller," Lucas said. He put the phone on speaker. "Hello, are you there?"

There was a long pause, and Regan thought maybe the caller had hung up.

Then a muffled, likely female voice said, "Maybe someone should find out what Taylor James and Candace were *really* fighting about at the party. Maybe not everyone who overheard the fight is telling the truth."

The caller hung up.

Lucas seemed stunned. "Well, that sounds ominous. But without more information, it's hard to know what to do with it. Right, Regan?"

"It's interesting, but I agree, without more details the caller sounds like she wants to stir the pot." Yet...Regan wasn't so sure about that.

It was definitely worth looking into.

Ten

Lizzy signaled to Lucas through the window that they only had five more minutes. Lucas needed more—there had to be more people with information. "Regan," he said, "you mentioned that the earlier caller was trying to 'stir the pot.' Is this common in investigations you've conducted? That people will make unfair or unsubstantiated accusations?"

"First, I didn't conduct investigations. I was involved first in courthouse security and witness protection, then fugitive apprehension. But it's true that in any criminal investigation, the police need to make assessments on the viability of statements, weighing the import of the information based on several factors, not just evidence—which, of course, is primary."

"But if you have two conflicting statements, how would that be resolved in the investigation?"

"The police would attempt to confirm each statement. If they conflicted, then one person would be lying, or possibly remembering an event differently. That's why witness testimony can be difficult. Take, for example, if I'm standing on one side of the street and you're standing on the other, and we both see a fight. Maybe I see a weapon and report that information. You don't see the weapon because you're at a different angle. You are emphatic that there was no weapon. The police would then search for evidence, as well as dig deeper into the interviews to determine exactly where we were standing, what might have been obscured, even ask if we are visually impaired."

Lizzy motioned that there was a caller. She sent him a text message, which he showed to Regan.

Male, no name, says he saw C Monday.

Lucas took the call. "Hello, sir, this is Lucas Vega and Regan Merritt. When did you see Candace?"

"I'm not one hundred percent positive," he began, "but after thinking about the last caller, who saw Candace on Tuesday morning coming out of the library, I'm ninety percent sure that I saw her *in* the library on Monday. It might have been Wednesday, but I think it was Monday. Before closing."

"How certain are you that it was during the week Candace was allegedly missing?"

"Well, I know it was a Monday or Wednesday, and it was in April—I was tutoring those two nights in one of the study rooms all month. Basically, from when I got back from spring break until finals in May, but she was already dead by then, right?"

"Yes. Her body was found April 19."

"So I don't hang out at the library, but it's convenient for tutoring. I was leaving, so it was between nine and ten. The library closes at ten, and my tutoring was from eight until whenever my student understood the lesson. I was walking out and I remember thinking she looked lost. I mean, she was hot, so I noticed her. I probably shouldn't say that."

"All memories are valid," Regan said. "Where exactly in the library did you see her?"

"The study rooms on the second floor. I was coming out, about to go down the stairs. She was coming up. She had this big, huge bag. Too big for a purse, but too small for a suitcase."

"Do you remember the color?" Regan asked.

Lucas wanted to ask why that was important, but remembered earlier when Regan said that asking about specific details could yield better information.

"Not really. Not black or anything dark, I don't think. Maybe gray or pink or blue or something. I really don't remember. Just a big bag, over her shoulder."

"Do you remember what she was wearing?"

"A Lumberjack sweatshirt, I'm almost positive. Just one of the standard gray sweatshirts, said Lumberjacks across the front. You see them everywhere on campus."

"So how can you be sure she was wearing one?"

"I don't know. Maybe I'm wrong. But she was cute, like I said, and I kinda knew her—she was a year older than me, but I was in a frat, and she and some of the sorority girls would come over when we had parties and stuff. So I did a double take, you know, because like I said, hot, and she was completely oblivious. Just walked by me, and I said something like, 'Good to see you, too, Candy.' She looked at me and gave me that *You're an asshole* look, and I laughed."

He remembered a lot. Was it a real memory? Or real... but the wrong time frame? Lucas wasn't certain. "Did you go to the police," he asked, "when you found out she had been killed?"

"No, but I remember telling my roommate that I'd thought I'd just seen her."

Regan asked, "You said that she was walking up the

stairs from the ground floor to the second floor, after nine on possibly Monday or Wednesday night. Do you remember where she went from there?"

"Yeah, she went up to the third floor."

"How can you be so sure three years later?" Lucas asked.

"I didn't really think about it until now, after listening to your caller, and then it just came back."

"And the police never asked you anything?" Lucas was having a hard time buying this story, that this guy saw Candace and then talked to her and never said anything to the police. "Did you ever talk to them?"

"I never even heard about what happened, I mean I heard she was dead, but no details, and it wasn't something that we really talked about. It happened off campus, and it was awful, but you know, finals were coming up and stuff." He paused. "That sounds callous."

Regan said, "I understand what you're saying. Did the police issue any kind of blanket statement? Asking for anyone to come forward?"

"Maybe? I don't know. I didn't hear about it."

Lucas said, "The university sent out a campus-wide email Monday after Candace's body was found, notifying the students that she had been found dead and the police were investigating. It said if you had any information about Candace's disappearance, to contact FPD. That was it."

"I didn't even see that," the caller said. "But I don't read most of the campus emails. There's a lot of junk in there."

Regan remembered that was true—she got dozens of emails a week from the university on her school email, and most of the time she ignored them.

The caller didn't have any other information, so Lucas wrapped up the call and, because Lizzy was frantically indicating to him that they had gone over their time, said, "We've learned a lot about Candace Swain tonight. Please dig into your memories and think about where you were the week she was killed. Did you see her on campus? In the library or her sorority or somewhere else, like our caller who saw her in Kingman? No matter how small a detail, if you saw Candace Swain, please call in. I'll be back Friday at seven."

Forty-five minutes later, Lucas and Lizzy were done with the technical end of editing and uploading the audio. Lizzy asked, "Wanna grab some food?"

"I would," Lucas said, "but I invited Regan over to show her what I have on the case. Maybe she'll see something I haven't."

"Good idea, because you stare at your walls too much." Lizzy said goodbye to both of them and left.

"Ready?" Regan asked.

"Do you mind driving? I took the bus here, but I don't live too far. Like, two miles, on the other side of downtown."

"No problem."

He locked up the studio, and they left the building. Regan was parked in visitor parking. Out of habit, she glanced around, assessing the people and cars in the area. Nothing suspicious jumped out at her, and she hit her key fob.

"Nice truck," Lucas said, climbing into the passenger side.

"Thanks. Address?"

He rattled it off, and she put it into her phone's GPS and hit Go to navigate. It wasn't far, six minutes. She backed out of the space and said, "You don't seem to be happy with what we learned."

"It's good information, but we're missing too many details, too many days. Lizzy showed me twenty-three emails that came in, basically telling me to go to hell."

Regan glanced into her rearview mirror. Someone had pulled in close behind her when she exited the university onto the main road, their lights bright. She adjusted the mirror.

"Do you think the guy who called in was Richie Traverton?" Lucas asked.

"The caller exhibited signs of betrayal. Have you spoken to Traverton?"

"I reached out via email, and he never got back to me. I go to his bar all the time, but I don't think he knows who I am, at least to look at me. I want to interview him, but if he doesn't call me back, what can I do?"

"Might be worth pursuing again," she said.

She didn't like the car following her so closely. It had been on the campus, though not in the visitors lot. No front license plate—Arizona didn't require it. Maybe they weren't following her. They could just be leaving at the same time and being jerks.

She turned left at the light, even though her navigation told her to go straight. She paused the navigation because the annoying voice told her to make a U-turn.

"What's going on?" Lucas asked.

She didn't respond. The car followed her.

Regan turned left at the next light, into a residential neighborhood.

The car slowed, followed.

"Okay, that's it."

She stopped her truck at the next stop sign. "Stay here,"

she told Lucas. She got out of her truck and approached the car.

The driver immediately put on the bright lights, which temporarily blinded her. They made a three-point turn and drove back the way they'd come, but because her eyes were still adjusting, she couldn't read the license plate.

"Dammit," she muttered as she climbed back into her truck.

"What happened? Who was it?"

"I don't know. A small SUV, possibly a Jeep. They followed us off campus, but I couldn't get the plates."

"Who would do that?"

She glanced at him, her vision clearing. "Someone who doesn't like the hornet's nest you've stirred up."

Eleven

Though Lucas was edgy, Regan seemed calm about the whole being-followed thing, though she didn't drive directly to his apartment. "Are they still following?" he asked her.

"No, just making sure."

"Are you sure they were following *us*?" he said as she parked on his narrow street.

"Yes," she said. "I don't know what it means—maybe someone wants to know where you or I live, maybe they want to know what we're doing now. Either way, it's a sign that your podcast is making someone nervous. You need to be extra careful."

They walked to his apartment. When he opened the unlocked door, she said, "Being extra careful means keeping your door locked, even when you're home."

"Okay," he said.

Lucas introduced Regan to Troy, who was watching basketball while doing homework on the couch. "What happened?" Troy asked.

"Someone was following us."

"No shit? Wow."

"Keep the door locked at all times," Regan said. She looked at it. "And use the dead bolt, okay?"

"Sure," Troy said.

"Everything's in my bedroom," Lucas said. He opened his door, cringing at how cluttered the space was. It wasn't a large room, and other than his twin bed—thank God he had made it this morning—he'd dedicated his room to *The Sorority Murder* podcast. Books, stacks of folders and papers, binders, notes, a corkboard with a timeline of Candace's missing days that he'd hung on the wall. The timeline was pretty bare. Regan was looking at it now.

Friday April 10: Sorority party in evening. Candace has argument with Taylor James and leaves @midnight.

Saturday April 11 12:20 a.m.: Candace's card key used to enter dorm building.

Sunday April 12: Abby from Las Vegas sees Candace in Kingman early afternoon.

April 12: @10 p.m. 'A Concerned Sister' sees Candace—Mountain View parking, driving.

April 12: 11:10 p.m.: Candace's card key used to enter dorm.

Monday April 13: 5:37 p.m. per NAUPD report—Annie Johnston, roommate, contacts campus police.

Tuesday April 14: 9:07 a.m. per NAUPD report—Campus police locate Candace's car in Mountain View parking structure (did anyone look on Monday?)

Wednesday April 15: NAUPD notified Flagstaff PD—FPD takes over missing person case.

Saturday April 18: Candace killed between 10 p.m. and 1 a.m. per ME; COD drowning (also manual strangulation, bruising on shoulders peri mortem; post-mortem injuries consistent with body dragged.)

Sunday April 19: Candace's body found @ 8 a.m. Hope Springs Lake, maintenance staff (Julio Dominguez, head of landscaping, Hope Centennial Golf)

April 19: Witness tells police they saw Joseph Abernathy jumping into freight car near Flagstaff station in the a.m. (Note: freight train slowed through town to <5 mph on April 19, no stop, at 9:10 a.m. per Union office.)

Lucas had other notes, including the name of the detective in charge of the case, the dates of key media reports. On April 20, the FPD had issued a statement that Abernathy was a person of interest.

Lucas also had Post-it notes on the days he'd talked to—or tried to talk to—Detective Young. There was a list of all the Sigma Rho girls living at the sorority at the time; another list was of all the sorority girls today. Twelve names were highlighted, and Regan asked why.

"They were all members of the sorority when Candace was killed, are still there. Ten are seniors, two are fourth-year students in a five-year program," Lucas explained.

"I think your Concerned Sister might be one of those girls," Regan said. "Though, it may be a member of a different sorority. They used to socialize together, at least when I was here."

"They still do. They all closed ranks."

He also had questions written on sticky notes.

Did Candace have a second phone?

How can someone go completely off-grid for seven days? (Sunday through Saturday.)

Was Candace hiding? Scared? A witness to a crime? Why didn't she go to the police?

What did Candace know?

What were Candace and Taylor really arguing about?

Check into stolen cars from week of Candace's disappearance.

Lucas's eyes drifted back to his note *What did Candace know?*

He needed more evidence before he revealed on his podcast the real reason he thought Candace had been killed. But so far that evidence hadn't come in.

Real reason? He actually didn't know *why.* He just didn't believe that a drunk drifter had killed her.

He wasn't ready to explain exactly why he had picked this cold case, either, why he was obsessed with Candace's murder. It hit way too close to home.

Lucas picked up the file that held a copy of Candace's autopsy and handed it to Regan. He'd compiled the file when he interned at the medical examiner's office over the summer. He shouldn't have made copies, but was relieved that Regan hadn't questioned him about it. She read the report, flipped through to his notes about the water found in Candace's lungs and his analysis that it couldn't have come from Hope Springs. Then she looked at the police report. A lot had been redacted, such as the names of witnesses who had been interviewed. He'd received the report through FOIA, but because it was an open case they wouldn't share everything.

Antsy, Lucas sat on his chair. "Um, do you want anything? Water? Coke?"

"No, thank you."

Regan read through the witness statements. Though the names were redacted, he'd written who he thought they were. Tyler Diaz, Candace's longtime boyfriend from campus, hadn't been at the party, and he hadn't seen her since the Wednesday before. Richie Traverton said she had come into McCarthy's the Sunday *before* the party when he was working and she had stayed until closing. They talked, and he drove her back to campus then went home. That was the last he'd seen her, he said. She'd called him on Friday night after the party at 12:27 a.m. and left a message that she wanted to talk, but he was working, and when he called her back at two, she didn't answer. The calls were confirmed by both her phone records and Richie's.

In fact, Lucas had a copy of Candace's phone records, thanks to her sister. Chrissy Swain had all her sister's passwords, which had also helped him confirm that Candace hadn't been on social media after the Friday-night party, nor did she use her phone after leaving a message for Richie. That's why Lucas thought she might have had a second phone—maybe a burner that was never found.

Knowing now from a caller that Candace might have been seen on that Sunday after the party, her whereabouts Saturday didn't seem to be as important, Lucas thought. She'd been angry, maybe decided to leave campus, get away for the weekend, and come back on Sunday night.

Then she left her car in the parking garage and disappeared. The only thing in the autopsy report that stood out to him, besides the water in her lungs, was that her stomach was empty and that she had probably eaten approximately eight hours before she was killed. Which would mean a late lunch or early dinner. Where did she eat? With whom?

Were people even telling the truth? Why would they lie?

He picked up a pen and added to the timeline the information they'd learned about Candace being seen at the library. He added question marks. He wanted to believe the two callers, but he couldn't shake the idea that maybe the guy who saw her Monday night was calling either to mess with him—like the plethora of nasty emails he'd been getting—or had seen her at an earlier date.

"Why are you nervous, Lucas?" Regan asked without looking at him.

"I'm not. I guess I'm trying to look at this through your eyes."

"You have good stuff here, quality research. I think you should have shared all of this on your podcast. It might have jump-started more of a conversation."

"I plan to. I have the podcasts sketched out while also leaving it open-ended so people will call in with clues."

"I get that. I'm looking at this as a whole. And there's an obvious answer."

"Which is?"

"Someone lied to the police. Your information is incomplete. You have documentation from newspapers, and the original report that indicates they spoke to her two boyfriends, her roommate Annie, Taylor James from the sorority, others from Sigma Rho, a senior who said he saw her talking to the homeless guy the evening of the party. But they must have also spoken to people on and off campus, especially after her body was found. A missing-person investigation is different than a homicide investigation. I'm really good with missing persons, it's what I did for years. I found people who didn't *want* to be found. And nine times out of ten someone lied to me about what they knew. Sometimes lies of omission, other times they lied to my face."

He was surprised he hadn't thought of that. But then again, he was a college student, and Regan Merritt was a thirty-five-year-old trained law-enforcement officer.

He asked, "So who's lying? And why?" and half expected her to already know.

"Those are the million-dollar questions. My guess? Someone in the sorority knew a lot more than they told the cops. Whether it directly led to Candace's murder, I don't know. But someone may have helped her disappear. No car, no phone, didn't use her credit cards—but records show she took out five hundred dollars on the day after the party, from an ATM in Flagstaff, the maximum allowed."

"How do you know that?"

"Detective Young wrote it in a sort of shorthand I recognized because I was looking for it. She withdrew that money after hours, early Saturday morning, after she left the party. If someone was being frugal, they could easily live on five hundred for a week, longer if they had a free place to stay. To find out where that place was, I need to learn everything I can about Candace Swain."

She tapped his list of questions. "By the way, it was smart of you to think about stolen vehicles. But more than stolen, I think someone may have loaned her a car. If we believe Abby that she saw Candace in Kingman, and the sister who saw her driving *to* campus on Sunday night, that suggests she left town after the party, returned, and then left again. But why not take her own car? Because of where she was going? Because her car was so recognizable? And if someone helped her that week, why didn't they tell the police after Candace was found dead?"

"Because they killed her? Or they were scared? Intimidated?"

Regan shrugged. "Any or all of the above. Or they thought they would get in trouble because they lied to the police about *not* seeing Candace during the missing-person investigation. We need to find that person, and then I think we'll break this case open."

"So you don't buy into the police theory that the homeless guy Abernathy killed her."

"I can't say. Would he have had the wherewithal to move her body, as you suggested? I don't know enough yet."

Lucas latched onto her comment.

Move the body.

So Regan believed him. That Candace was drowned elsewhere and dumped in the lake. Somehow, that gave Lucas confidence and hope—even if she didn't explicitly state it.

"Have you talked to Taylor James?" Regan asked.

"You're not taking that last caller seriously, are you?"

"Yes, I am. You're not?"

"The police took witness statements from dozens of people who had been at the party. Three people said they heard the argument, their names are redacted in the report, but one I figured was Taylor. Two other statements were from people not in the sorority who saw Candace talking to Abernathy. We know that he had been run off campus at least twice, and he would be going to jail if caught again. So it makes sense that they would have a disagreement about whether to call the police."

"I agree. But what if someone else at the party overheard the conversation? Maybe they didn't think much about it at the time, but now, when they heard your podcast where you state that they were arguing about Abernathy and whether to call the police? And they know that is not completely accurate. Maybe they are just learning that the murder investigation is still open. It might have motivated them to call."

"Then, why not give their name? Why hang up?"

"Because they don't want to get in trouble with the sorority," Regan suggested. "Any number of reasons. It's worth looking into. Did you reach out to Taylor?"

"I couldn't find her. She graduated, and I don't know where she went after that."

"I can find her," Regan said. "Finding people is something I'm really good at."

Twelve

Lucas Vega's stupid murder podcast had drained her.

Vicky Ryan poured herself a glass of white wine and drank half of it in one gulp. She didn't want to be drinking alone, but she was over twenty-one, and they were allowed to have alcohol on campus, and *damn*, she *was* alone and had a headache and didn't know what to do with this stupid podcast that was causing friction among her sorority sisters.

Half the girls thought the idea was smart and didn't like that the council had forbidden them from participating. The other half worried about the impact on the sorority and Candace's reputation. And people on both sides thought the police should handle it.

But her roommate, Nicole, had made a good point the other night.

"It's been three years and the police haven't solved Candace's murder. Maybe this could help."

Nicole might be right, but Vicky was worried about some of her sisters who were truly upset listening to the podcast. Vicky tried to be fair and impartial, but it was hard. She had to protect the sorority's reputation, and creating a safe space for the girls she was supposed to lead and protect was important to her. She couldn't stop Nicole and others from listening, but she could prevent playing it in common areas.

A knock on her door had her groaning. She didn't want to talk to anyone about the podcast. It had been the number one topic in the sorority for the last week, since Lucas Vega had aired the first episode last Tuesday night.

She opened the door and was surprised to find Rachel Wagner, their faculty advisor, standing there. She looked upset.

"Are you okay?" Vicky asked.

"Can I come in?"

"Of course." She opened the door wider, and Rachel walked in and stared out the window. It was dark, and Vicky could see her reflection in the glass. "Do you want some wine?"

"I'd love some, but no, thank you." Rachel turned around. She didn't look thirty-five. She was tall, model-pretty with silky blond hair and big brown eyes and could have passed for a student. She was one of Vicky's favorite teachers as well because she knew what she was talking about and she had more open office hours than most. She was up for a professor slot in the biology department, after being an associate professor for the past six years.

"You're upset about the podcast," Vicky said. It didn't take a rocket scientist to figure it out.

"I'm so frustrated and don't know how to handle this. I tried talking to Henry Clarkson last week, after the first episode, but he doesn't see this from our perspective. And then Henry hooked Vega up with a former US Marshal? Why?"

"Nicole has been talking to some of the girls, and they think this podcast is a good idea."

"I know. I had a long conversation with Nicole yesterday. I'm too close to it. I really liked Candace, and I told her she needed to do more to keep that man off campus, but she had such a soft spot for the troubled. I admired that about her, but at the same time she didn't have the street smarts to know who might really be dangerous."

"You think he really killed her."

"Yes! Who else?"

"Yeah, I know—you're probably right. But Nicole and some of the others are talking about other theories, and it's just exhausting."

"The police know what they're doing," Rachel said. "They've been up-front with us from the beginning. Abernathy is their primary suspect. He killed her and knew he did something wrong and left. It makes sense, and it fits all the evidence. I'm just surprised they never caught up with him."

"I wish I could get them to stop listening, because others are getting upset. I found Debra crying after the podcast. She's the sensitive type, said she now can't stop picturing Candace drowning, and it's interfering with her studies."

"I'll go talk to her if it'll help."

"I'm sure it would."

"Do you know who wrote that email?" Rachel asked. "The one Vega read on air, about seeing Candace driving onto campus Sunday night?"

Vicky shook her head. "I sent an email to everyone right after the podcast, promised confidentiality, but no one has gotten back to me. It makes us look bad. But I'll find out." Nothing could remain a secret for long here, and Vicky was good at getting information.

"I'm sure she thought she was doing the right thing, but if anyone knows *anything* they need to go to the police, not call into that sensationalist program." Rachel looked at her watch. "It's late, but maybe you can get everyone together for a quick meeting? I want to make sure that the girls know that they can come talk to me or the police about anything, but we don't want to contribute to an amateur podcast that is doing more harm than good."

"Yeah, I'll have everyone who can meet down in the Rose Room in fifteen minutes."

Vicky texted out the announcement to the Sigma Rho loop. "Done."

"I'm also going to reach out to Regan Merritt myself," Rachel said.

"Do you think that will help?"

"I don't know, but I want her to have the facts, not just Vega's twisted version. If the police believed that Candace was killed by someone other than Joseph Abernathy, they would be pursuing it. I have faith in the system, and more, I have faith in Steven—Detective Young—who has been straight and honest with us from the beginning."

"Maybe Regan Merritt should talk to him," Vicky said. "If she hasn't already."

"That's an excellent idea," Rachel agreed. "But I doubt he'd talk to her, not after she's aligned herself with Vega."

"Let me know what she says, because juggling all this with only two more months until graduation is stressful."

Rachel gave her a hug. "I know. It'll be over soon."

From the Missing Journal of Candace Swain

Yoda said, "Do, or do not. There is no try."

I'm not a *Star Wars* fan. I don't get it. I don't like science fiction or anything not set on this world, in this reality. But Chrissy has always loved *Star Wars*. I never understood how two girls who came from the same two parents and were raised in the same way could be so different.

I had promised to pick Chrissy up from a party. She didn't have her license yet, so my little sister became my responsibility. It didn't help that Mom and Dad were divorced and still fighting about everything. I thought that divorce meant silence, acceptance, an end to the constant bickering. But no. It just means fighting over the phone or using me and Chrissy to send messages back and forth.

I wish I could have escaped, but I couldn't leave Chrissy there, alone, to deal with the mess of our parents' lives.

Chrissy called me early, saying she wanted to be picked up now, that her friends were doing drugs, and she didn't want any part of that and they were calling her a party pooper and a baby. I said, "I'll try." I didn't want to cut my date short just because Chrissy couldn't wait.

My sister said, "Do, or do not, Candace."

She only called me Candace when she was really mad at me.

I did pick her up, asking my boyfriend to come with me. He was actually pretty cool about it. Chrissy was crying, and though she never told me what really happened at the party, it had to be worse than her friends getting high.

I've thought a lot about that quote, especially over the last three years. Three years of wanting to do the right thing...then doubting I even knew what the right thing was. I had to make a stand. I had to do, not just try.

Even if by doing meant I would be sacrificing everything I have worked for, everything I have achieved. Because as time passes, I wake up feeling less human, less real...just less.

Thirteen

Candace sat in her car in the middle of the parking lot, crying.

Pathetic, but she couldn't stop.

No one would help her.

She didn't blame Alexa. She had so much to deal with right now, Candace didn't blame her for not coming back and helping her convince Taylor to do the right thing. But she'd hoped. She'd really, really hoped they could present a united front and Taylor would change her mind.

The entire day she'd just driven around, trying to figure out what to do, and she came back to campus planning to forget everything. Just finish college and graduate and leave all these people. They weren't her friends, they weren't her sisters, not like she thought.

She was just one person, how could she do this all alone?

Maybe Taylor was right. That if they came forward with the truth, it wouldn't matter in the long run, and they would destroy their future for no real reason. Because what would change if they said anything?

She pounded the steering wheel. She didn't know what to do!

She pulled out her phone and considered calling Chrissy. Tell her everything, ask her advice. But Chrissy was preparing for a major swim competition at the end of the week. How could she put this burden on her?

No, this was Candace's burden to bear.

And she didn't want to disappoint her sister.

She wished she could talk to her dad. She used to be so close to him, up until her parents' divorce. It was like he was a completely different person. Dating a lot of women, buying an expensive car, working too much to make money to buy stuff he didn't need. He'd never yelled at her or hurt her, but sometimes she wished she had told him he'd become a jerk. It was like he had to prove to her mom that he wasn't the loser she thought he was. And her mom was no better. She remarried and raised a second family, her new husband's three kids, and it felt too much like she and Chrissy were being replaced. Candace knew that wasn't true, but nine times out of ten her mom opted to spend time with the younger kids over her and Chrissy. "They need me more," was her excuse.

No way was Candace going to share anything with her parents.

She looked at her phone. A prepaid phone she'd bought last week because she thought someone had been spying on her. It seemed ridiculous, but she couldn't shake the feeling, and after the party on Friday, she was pretty certain someone had been looking through her phone. Hard to prove, but she didn't bring it with her to Kingman. Couldn't risk getting Alexa in trouble if someone *was* tracking her.

It seemed unlikely when she thought about it, but so many odd things had happened she couldn't shake this uneasy feeling.

It was after eleven. She'd been sitting in her car for an hour feeling sorry for herself. She needed to sleep, she needed to think. Maybe in the morning she'd have answers.

She walked into the dorm. Since it was late, most everyone was in their room. She didn't see anyone as she went up to the third floor where she and Annie shared a room. She hoped Annie was there—she had the most level head of anyone she knew. Annie could talk sense into Taylor. Or tell Candace that she was wrong.

You're not wrong. Stop letting Taylor get into your head!

The room was dark; Candace flipped on the lights. Annie wasn't there. She hadn't come back yet. Her grandmother had early-stage Alzheimer's, and Annie went home almost every weekend to spend time with her. Candace understood that: if Chrissy had a serious medical issue, Candace would do everything she could to spend as much time with her sister as possible.

She hoped Annie got back soon.

Candace put her small overnight bag on the floor next to her bed and was about to change into her pajamas when something caught her eye.

Something out of place on her desk.

Her notebooks were in disarray, and the blue one that she *knew* she'd left on top was now on the bottom.

Candace was a neat person. She never left her desk a mess. She remembered where she put everything.

She looked in all three desk drawers; papers were disorganized. This wasn't how she left her space.

She reassessed her room. Annie's side was neat, as it

always was, her bed made, three oversize, fluffed pillows covering half the bed.

Candace looked at her own bookshelf. The books were jostled, as if someone had pulled every book out to look inside and put it back without care. Her small bird-of-paradise that she had growing by the window had been knocked over: soil had spilled on the floor, but someone had righted the plant again. One of the stems had broken.

Someone had rifled through her things. Why? Why would anyone want to look through her stuff? And how did they get in?

She sat on her bed and didn't know what to do. Suddenly, she was scared. She realized she couldn't trust anyone, not her friends, not her roommate, not her teachers—someone had been looking for something, but what could they possibly want? Money? No, that was silly.

She stared at her overnight bag and felt the blood drain from her face. She knew exactly what someone had been looking for.

And who.

She grabbed her bag and her car keys and left.

Fourteen

Wednesday

Regan woke up early Wednesday morning to find her father already eating breakfast in the nook. It was one of Regan's favorite rooms, and it reminded her of when life was less complicated, less sad.

"There's plenty left," John said when he heard Regan in the kitchen. She poured coffee, then dished up potatoes and eggs and sausage.

"And you said you couldn't cook," she said as she sat down.

Her father, who still preferred a physical paper to the internet, put his sports page down. He said, "Breakfast is easy. I can make you some toast."

"This is good."

She sipped her coffee. She hadn't talked to her dad, not more than a few words, since she'd walked out on Monday night. "I'm sorry about Monday."

"I know."

"It's hard for me to talk about it." By *it* she meant the

murder of her son. She didn't want to say it out loud. That probably wasn't healthy, but she didn't care.

"Regan," John said, "I miss him. It's not the same as your loss, but I miss Chase."

She cringed hearing his name spoken. "I know."

"When you're ready to find answers, I'll be here for you. You know that."

Answers. She'd left Virginia because her search for answers about the *why* of Chase's murder had left her angry and raw. She didn't like the person she had become, not in the months after she buried her son. Worse, the more she looked for answers, the more questions she had—questions that she couldn't answer. It tore her up, because her ex-husband believed it was her fault. Her job, her career, her life that had made their son a target.

It wasn't. She couldn't believe she was to blame in any way and still draw breath.

But she couldn't prove her career hadn't been the reason. When Chase's killer was stabbed to death in prison, everything shut down. Her private investigation, the Marshals investigation, the local investigation. She'd reached an impasse and decided to leave it all behind.

To save herself, she'd had to walk away. She still didn't know if it had been the right decision.

A moment later, when it was clear she wasn't going to talk more about Chase, her dad said, "I listened to the podcast last night."

Good. Change of subject. "Thoughts?" She shoveled eggs into her mouth.

"That dumb kid needs to turn everything over to the police."

"Lucas said they dismissed his theory. And he's not

dumb, Dad. He's young, not seasoned, obviously not a cop, but he's anything but stupid."

"So you think he gave them all the information he had?"

"I have no reason to doubt him, but I think..." She hesitated, unsure what she was going to say.

"You think...he knows more."

"I wouldn't say he's *withholding* information so much as I believe he hasn't told me everything about his interest in the case."

"Another reason for getting involved?"

"Perhaps. Maybe *he* has personal information about Candace that he hasn't revealed. Gossip? A deeper relationship? I can only speculate."

"Ask him. Direct questions yield more honest answers."

"I will. But before that I want to learn more on my own. I think he's a good kid."

"You always had the best instincts of anyone in the family."

She smiled, got up with her half-empty coffee mug, and kissed his cheek. "I get my instincts from you." She walked to the counter to top off her coffee. After sitting back down, she said, "I'm going to track down Taylor James, who argued with Candace that Friday."

"The argument about the homeless guy hanging around."

She nodded. "It makes sense. Candace was a do-gooder. She didn't want the poor guy to end up in jail. But from everything that I could glean from the police and media reports, Abernathy was over the edge. A serious alcoholic, but coherent enough to ride the rails. Maybe her sorority sisters were right to be intimidated or afraid of him. I wouldn't be too happy if I walked out of my dorm and saw a guy taking a leak against the fence."

"Can you honestly say Candace disappeared for more

than a week if she was seen by different people through to Tuesday? When she checked into her dorm, and someone saw her outside the library?"

She smiled. Her dad was already as invested in the case as she was.

"None of those sightings came up during the police investigation."

"Incompetence?"

"I don't know," she said. "I think they talked to everyone in the sorority, but did they expand to the rest of the twenty thousand students? How do you reach everyone if most of them don't even open their campus email? We know she didn't sleep in her dorm that night because her roommate came in late—after one o'clock, according to her statement—and Candace wasn't there. If she in fact entered late Sunday night, why did she leave again? She didn't attend classes, she didn't sleep in her dorm. My guess? She had another place to stay. She had two boyfriends, after all, although both were cleared by the police." She took a long gulp of coffee, considered what they knew, and said, "I think she *really* disappeared Tuesday morning, after the library sighting. She was preoccupied, possibly angry, ignored a classmate. Conflict in the dorm? Anger over the argument? Maybe she thought one of the girls had called the police on Abernathy. Maybe she was trying, on her own, to help him. There are many things she could have been doing, but why not tell someone?"

"All good questions. Maybe you should have been a detective instead of a marshal."

She smiled, shook her head. "Marshals have cooler toys."

He laughed. "You plan to reach out to the FPD detective? Young?"

"Not yet. I want to talk to Lucas again. This is his podcast, his schedule. I'd *like* to reach out to Young, see if there's anything he might tell me that he wouldn't tell Lucas. I might be a civilian now, but the Merritt name still holds a little weight."

"A little?" John said with mock insult.

"I reached out to the victim's former roommate, Annie Johnston, last night. She emailed me early this morning. She lives in Phoenix and agreed to talk to me on the condition she didn't have to talk to Lucas. I ran it by him, and he's cool with it. These sorority sisters seem to have blacklisted the podcast. Completely shut him out, so anything I can get from the outside might help." She paused, drained her second cup of coffee. "She works at Phoenix Children's Hospital, said I could call her before she goes to work."

John said, "Looks like you have a new cause."

"What does that mean?"

"A cause, a hobby, whatever you want to call it. You're helping this kid."

She shrugged. "Maybe. Last night went well, we learned more, and Lucas asked if I would return on Friday's episode. Why not? What else am I doing?"

"Now you sound like you're feeling sorry for yourself. Go ahead. Help the kid solve his friend's murder. It'll make you both feel better."

Sometimes, her dad just cut straight to the point.

"Anyway," she said, "Lucas had reached out to Annie earlier in the process, and she wouldn't talk to him. I'm going to have him listen in. It's his podcast. I don't want to just take it over."

He laughed.

"Really, Dad."

"Don't lie to yourself. You're a control freak, just like

I am. It runs in our veins. But he needs you. Maybe he's smarter than I gave him credit for, but he doesn't have experience. If he's right about any of this, he might draw the killer's attention." Her dad paused, then asked her, "Do you know if the police ever looked closely at Sunrise Center itself?"

"What do you mean?"

"Well, the victim volunteered there, and the suspect often stayed there. If I were planning a murder, having a guy with a habit of stalking sorority girls take the fall for me would be a big plus."

And that was one reason she loved her dad. He thought anyone was capable of a crime, under the right circumstances. She hadn't even considered the idea that someone at Sunrise might be involved, but it might explain why Abernathy had disappeared.

Still, it seemed far-fetched. Why would the director cooperate with Lucas for his podcast if she had something to do with Candace's murder? It seemed…odd.

Yet, people often behaved in ways that confused Regan. It was definitely something to think about.

Regan's dad had already left when Lucas arrived.

"I really like your place here," he said, looking out the picture windows at the trees and Humphreys Peak looming in the north. "You're, like, in the middle of nowhere, but only twenty minutes from downtown."

"Best of all worlds," she said. Peaceful. Beautiful. Now that she was back she didn't know if she would leave again.

"Only thing I don't like about this area is the snow," he said.

"It doesn't snow *that* much."

"More than enough."

"I hope you don't have to miss a class," she said. "I know the last semester can be demanding."

"I only have two classes this semester, Tuesdays and Thursdays, and they're both pretty easy, to be honest. My capstone is taking most of my time."

The capstone for a Criminology and Criminal Justice degree didn't involve any physical classes, but a lot of research, writing, and regular meetings with an advisor were required. If you didn't do it, or slacked off, it could mean the difference between graduating or not. But most advisors worked hard with their seniors to ensure they at least passed.

"I can't believe you convinced Annie to speak to us."

"To me," Regan corrected. "I appealed to her desire for justice, but she made it clear that she was irritated that you'd repeatedly called her. She mentioned *harassment.*"

"I called too many times, I know, but I really wanted to talk to her. She was Candace's roommate. I had Chrissy on board, and the Sunrise director, and even the campus police talked to me. I thought that having that support would convince her. Every time I got another interview, I called her. I shouldn't have."

"Live and learn," she said.

They went into her dad's office—a room he'd built on after she had moved to the East Coast. A wall of windows, built-in bookshelves, a potbellied stove in the corner, and her grandfather's antique desk that her dad had refinished. A couple of leather chairs and a small table completed the comfortable room. Lucas looked around and his eyes widened when he saw the stuffed black bear in the corner. "Is that real?"

"It is." In addition to the bear, there was the head of a pronghorn mounted on one wall, and the largest fish her dad had ever caught, a forty-two-pound rainbow trout, above his desk. Not world-record size, but close. A mountain lion head, a javelina head—they were nasty creatures. "Don't let them intimidate you. There's a story behind each one. My brother and dad go hunting every year, if they can get tags. I prefer pheasant to big game, but I was with my dad when he caught that fish. I don't know if I ever saw him more excited in my life."

She sat at the desk and motioned for Lucas to take one of the chairs. "I'll put her on speaker, but don't talk, okay?" she said. "If you have anything you want me to ask, write it down. I think we'll get more information this way."

Lucas agreed.

Regan called Annie at their prearranged time. She answered on the second ring. "Hello, Annie Johnston? This is Regan Merritt."

"Yes. I've been waiting—but you're right on time. I guess I'm nervous."

"There's nothing to be nervous about," Regan assured her. "As I told you in my message yesterday, I graduated from NAU, and as a favor to my college advisor, I'm helping Lucas Vega with his podcast, which seeks to solve the murder of Candace Swain."

"After you reached out yesterday, my boyfriend and I listened to all the episodes. I guess—well, I didn't believe Lucas when he told me he had Candace's sister helping. I thought he was lying to get me to talk to him. But I still don't want to call into the podcast. I have mixed feelings about the whole thing."

"That's okay. I appreciate you taking the time to talk to me now. You should know that I plan to share whatever you tell me with Lucas," Regan said, glancing over at him as he sat rigid in the chair across from her.

"I'm fine with that. Sigma Rho, my sorority, sent out an email six, seven weeks ago telling all alumnae that a student was doing a podcast about Candace and her murder and that they had voted not to participate. It made sense when I read it—the idea that the podcast would sensationalize her murder, that we didn't know whether Candace's name would be dragged through the mud, or the sorority itself, and the idea that this is better a matter for the police. But then, when I listened to the podcast, while a few things seemed a little over the top, I thought he did a good job being fair to both the sorority and Candace."

"How long were you Candace's roommate?"

"Three years. The way our sorority handles recruitment and housing is that we rush our first semester freshman year. Second semester we can move into the sorority dorms at Mountain View, or stay in our own dorm until our second year. Most of us move into the sorority because it's fun and exciting. I met Candace during rush, but she and Taylor were best friends and roommates in the dorms, so they stayed roommates at Sigma Rho. But something happened, I don't know what, and they had a falling-out. Second year Candace and I roomed together. She reached out to me, and it worked. We weren't best friends, but we were best roommates, if that makes sense. She was very considerate, respected my space, things like that. We were both very neat people. She was private. We were close, but we didn't do much together outside of the sorority."

"According to the police and media reports, you were away for the weekend and came back late Sunday, correct?"

"Really late. I didn't get back until after one in the morning. I went home most weekends, to Mesa, south of Phoenix. My grandmother was sick, and I wanted to spend all the time I could with her before she forgot me."

"I'm sorry."

"It was three years ago and she's still with us, but her Alzheimer's has progressed. I wouldn't have traded those weekends with her for anything. So I left Friday morning and didn't go to the party—which really wasn't my thing, anyway."

"Did you see Candace that morning?"

"Briefly. She was just waking up, maybe around eight? I was leaving and trying to be quiet. I told her to have fun for me at the party. She said she didn't even want to go but had to because she was on the sorority council."

"Was that like her? Not wanting to go to parties?"

"No. The police asked me a lot of these kind of questions— what was her demeanor, was she unusually stressed or depressed? This was when she was missing. I told them she had been preoccupied for a few weeks and hadn't talked to me about it. They asked me to speculate. I didn't know why then, and I still don't know. I don't even remember what I was thinking, and I'll admit I was caught up in my senior project and my grandmother and trying to juggle a bunch of stuff. I just had the sense that Candace had something heavy weighing on her, over and above graduation."

"Was that unusual? That she didn't talk to you?"

"No. Like I said, Candace was private. I think she knew that I had my own things and she didn't want to burden me. But she also never liked talking about her problems. Candace didn't want other people to know she even had problems."

"Who was Candace closest to in the sorority?"

"When she died? Just me, really. She had her boyfriends. She seemed to be spending less and less time at the sorority. She started to push people away. Probably I'd say when she came back from Christmas break, that's when I really noticed it."

That was good to know. What happened either before she left for the holiday or while she was gone that might have changed her? Regan made a brief note, then said, "Who had she been close to before her senior year?"

"Taylor James. Even after they had their falling-out, they were still somewhat friendly, were on the council together. She was pretty good friends with a girl named Alexa Castillo, and Alexa would sometimes volunteer with her at Sunrise Center."

"Do you know how to reach Alexa?"

"No, I'm sorry. She was one of the few non-science majors, and we didn't have any classes together or anything like that. She had her own group of friends, plus she graduated before I did." She paused. "Candace was mentoring Vicky Ryan, a first year who, I saw from the sorority newsletter, is now the president. I'm not surprised. Vicky had that personality, that she wanted to be in leadership, and she was very organized and together. Everyone liked Candace, but no one was her confidante."

Taylor James. Her name kept popping up. Regan wrote down the other two, Vicky and Alexa. But Taylor was definitely someone they needed to track down.

"When you returned on Sunday night, you noticed Candace wasn't there."

"I came in really late, she wasn't in bed, but at the time I didn't think anything of it, and I told that to the police. She was seeing two different guys at the time—I told her she should choose. She said that Tyler was a sweetheart and they had fun together, but Richie was someone who listened to her and had more life experience. I don't think she was serious about either of them, to be honest."

"Did the two guys know about each other?"

"Richie knew about Tyler; I don't think that Tyler knew about Richie. Richie dated other girls, but the funny thing is I think he really liked Candace. If she had split with Tyler and wanted to be exclusive, Richie would have jumped at it."

"You knew both of them?"

"I knew Tyler better because Candace had been seeing him on and off for two years. Very nice guy, the typical *too* nice, if you understand?"

Regan smiled. "I do know what you mean, Annie."

"No backbone," Annie said. "I mean, I wouldn't want to date a guy who just did everything I wanted and never had an original thought on his own. It's nice for a while, but it gets old fast."

"According to the police report, you didn't notice that Candace's phone was in the room until you woke up the next morning."

"I was exhausted when I got in. I unpacked and crashed. In the morning I saw her phone in the charger and thought she was around, but I didn't see her. Her bed was made, it didn't look like she'd slept there, but I didn't really think much about it until I came back that afternoon and everything was the same. I called around to see if anyone had seen her—then I started to worry. I looked at her phone—I didn't have her passcode—but I could see that she had a lot of missed calls and texts. That's when I contacted campus police."

"You were worried."

"Irritated more than worried, but by Monday night I was worried. Candace wasn't irresponsible. She didn't skip classes. It was the last six weeks of school. If she needed to get away, she would have told someone."

"Lucas has a statement from a sorority sister who said that she saw Candace speed into the sorority dorm lot around ten on Sunday night."

"I heard that on the podcast. Which surprised me, actually, because Candace was usually a good driver."

"Annie, based on what the police reports stated, and what we've learned from the callers, Candace left after the party and no one knows where she went that weekend. She returned Sunday night but didn't stay in her dorm, and the police cleared both Richie and Tyler. Do you know what she might have been doing or who she would have stayed with?"

Annie said, "I—I really don't know. If her car was gone, I could see her going to see family. She didn't get along with her parents, but I could see her hopping on a plane and flying to South Carolina to see her sister if something was wrong. She was pragmatic, like I said, but she was also bold. When she made a decision, she jumped on it. No looking back. When her parents came down to clean out her dorm room after her body was found, they were devastated. They told me the police were looking for Joseph Abernathy, the weird guy who'd been lurking around. I don't have any reason to think the police are wrong, but... I'll admit, the podcast has made me think."

Regan caught Lucas's eye: that was exactly what they wanted to do, have people start to think.

"Candace originally met Abernathy at Sunrise Center, correct?"

"Yes."

"Did she ever complain about him or anyone else from the shelter?"

"No. She wasn't a complainer. One time I remember, and I told this to the police because they'd asked about Abernathy, she was frustrated. I asked about it, and she said that Joseph—she always called him by his first name to show that she saw him as an individual—wouldn't stay in rehab. He didn't want it. He didn't want to be in recovery or do anything different, for whatever reason. He accepted shelter in bad weather, and he went there to eat a few times a week. She wanted to fix everything, and the fact that he wouldn't take the help bothered her. I think he was some-what fixated on Candace, which is why he kept showing up at the sorority."

If Annie had told the police that Joseph Abernathy was fixated on Candace, that would definitely put him high up on the suspect list. A troubled, homeless alcoholic who Candace was trying to help, turning on her. It would check all their boxes, especially since she'd confronted him the night she disappeared.

Except she hadn't been killed that weekend. And the police knew that.

"Other than you," Regan asked, "who else did the po-lice talk to in the sorority?"

"Taylor, because she and Candace had had the argu-ment about Abernathy. Probably other girls who were at the party, our advisor, but I didn't keep track of all that. Everyone was talking about it, but no one really had an idea about where Candace was. After her body was found at the lake, they talked to me again, but I didn't have any-thing new to add. They probably talked to Taylor again as well, but she was in shock—she almost left school. I don't know that she would have graduated at all if we hadn't all rallied and helped her with her finals."

"Did you see Candace with anyone you didn't know or recognize?"

"I really can't remember. She spent a lot of her free time

at the library because she liked the quiet. She spent more time there that last semester, but that could have been because of her finals."

Regan looked down at her notes and was about to ask about Taylor when Annie exclaimed.

"Oh! Her journal! She kept a journal and wrote it in often. Not every day, but a couple times a week."

A journal would be a valuable piece of evidence. Things that Candace had said or done, people she might have had conflicts with. If she was scared or intimidated, depressed or worried. "Do the police have the journal?"

"I don't know. I can't even remember if I mentioned it to the police. Chrissy asked about it, but that was a couple weeks after she died, and I said I didn't know where it was."

The police would have eventually given it to the family, unless the journal was considered evidence. Regan made a note and underlined it.

Where is Candace Swain's journal?

She glanced at Lucas. By his expression, he didn't know about a journal, either.

"One more thing," she said. "Are you still in contact with Taylor James?"

"Taylor pretty much disappeared at the end of the semester. She didn't even come to the graduation ceremony or the last Sigma Rho party. I heard she was still living in Flagstaff, but I have no idea where or what she's doing."

"Do you remember her major?"

"Chemistry, or maybe biology. Some sort of science. At least two-thirds of Sigma Rho were STEM."

Regan glanced at Lucas to see if he had any questions to add. He shook his head.

"If you think of anything else, please reach out to me," Regan said.

"Actually, I don't know if this is important, but when I was listening to the podcast and Lucas said that tests proved she didn't drown in the lake, I was stunned. I mean, that's what we all thought. That's where she was found, and the police didn't tell us anything different. Anyway, Candace was very close to her sister, as I said. Chrissy is a swimmer, a huge deal, got a scholarship and everything. Candace was extremely proud of her. Whenever she was homesick, she'd go sit at the aquatics center and watch them practice. She told me it helped her decompress."

That was valuable information. The aquatics center was a five-minute walk from the sorority. It wasn't the only pool in town—in addition to private pools, there was a recreation center downtown that had both an indoor and outdoor pool, and there was a pool at the high school, not far from the college. But knowing that Candace regularly went to the aquatics center on campus seemed important. By the look on Lucas's face, he thought it was significant, too.

Regan thanked Annie for her time and ended the call.

She said, "Well."

"The police don't have her journal," Lucas said. "I don't think her sister, Chrissy, has it, either, but I can ask her."

"How do you know the police don't have it? They might have kept it for evidence, not turned it over to the family."

"I have a list of everything they collected from her car and room."

She wasn't certain he was legally allowed to have that information, but she didn't comment.

"She drowned on campus," Lucas said.

"You can't know that."

"It's logical. It's the only thing that makes sense."

"Why would she disappear for a week, then go to the

aquatics center and not her dorm? Or if she was scared, why not go to the police?"

"Maybe she felt safe there, or was thinking things through, whatever was going on with her," Lucas said. "Haven't you ever gone someplace because it gave you peace? Or to work through a problem? A place where you could be alone?"

Regan was going to deny it, but Lucas was right. She often went on long walks or horseback riding when she was upset. It'd started when her mother was diagnosed with cancer: Regan needed the time to just *be* without worrying about her family. When she was married, it had irritated her ex-husband, Grant, that Regan could walk out of the house on foot and disappear for hours. But there was something about those walks that instilled calm, focus, so she could think through her problems. For her, it wasn't so much where she went as the activity—walking alone, especially in the woods or along a country road.

"Maybe she was meeting someone there," Lucas pondered.

It was possible.

"I'm going to incorporate this into my podcast. But," he said quickly, "I won't let on that you let me listen to Annie. I can get a lot of this information from Chrissy."

"I told Annie that I would be sharing with you, so you should be okay. She wants to help but feels like it's either a lost cause or she doesn't want to make waves with the sorority."

"Why the questions about Sunrise Center?"

Regan told him about her father's comment, that if Abernathy were innocent, someone at Sunrise might suggest that he be sent away for his own safety. Or, if they believed he were guilty, maybe send him somewhere to protect him—

though that seemed far-fetched and would be obstruction of justice. Regan couldn't imagine why anyone would want to help him, if he were in fact guilty.

"I found Taylor James," Regan said. "Through a combination of social media, white pages, and people-finder databases, I learned she's renting a small house just outside town."

Taylor had an old social-media page that she hadn't updated in months. Her profile picture showed a smiling young brunette with classy highlights; her background picture was her standing at the southern rim of the Grand Canyon, in a spot where millions of tourists had their photos taken. Her page wasn't public, only a few posts she'd made public were visible—mostly motivational memes. Those had few comments.

"I have a confession to make," Lucas said.

"Spill it."

"I should have told you right away," he said. "I tried to talk to Taylor, a couple months ago. She works at a bar in a sketchy area of town, kind of a biker bar, I guess. She wouldn't talk to me, and a bouncer type kicked me out."

"Why is this relevant now? Other than it would have saved me a couple hours looking for her."

"Because I don't think she'll want to see me. Maybe this is something you should do on your own."

"If you're cool with that, I will. I have her address. And you? What are your plans?" She'd been thinking about being followed yesterday, and she didn't want Lucas to go off on his own where he might be vulnerable.

"I'm going to look through my files for Alexa Castillo. I have a list of everyone in the sorority who overlapped with Candace. She's someone we should talk to, especially since she also volunteered at Sunrise."

Regan's phone rang. She motioned to Lucas to wait while she answered.

"Regan Merritt," she said.

"Hi, Regan. My name is Rachel Wagner. I'm the faculty advisor for Sigma Rho sorority."

She quickly put Rachel on speaker and motioned for Lucas to be silent. "Yes, Ms. Wagner. How can I help you?"

"Call me Rachel, please. I hope you don't mind that I tracked you down. Henry Clarkson kindly gave me your contact information."

"I don't mind."

"I was hoping we could meet?"

"About?"

"Lucas Vega's podcast, of course. I listened last night and was surprised that you agreed to talk to that student. I want to share with you how his project is affecting the girls here at Sigma Rho and my growing frustration with Lucas. I won't take much of your time."

"I'm happy to meet." She wanted to talk to Taylor first. "Later this afternoon?"

"I'm an associate professor in the Department of Biological Sciences and am done with class at four this afternoon. Can you do four thirty, my office? I'll text you the location. Or I can meet you somewhere else if you like."

"Your office is fine," she said. "I'll see you then."

That was fortuitous. She wanted to talk to the sorority advisor, and now she had an appointment. Rachel Wagner's assessment of these girls would be helpful. According to the notes that Regan had reviewed last night at Lucas's place, Rachel had taken over as faculty advisor the fall before Candace's murder.

Regan hoped she could convince Rachel to encourage the girls to call in to the podcast, especially those who had known Candace, but she would approach the subject carefully. She understood the need to protect the sorority, but she would not tolerate protecting it over bringing Candace's killer to justice.

Fifteen

Taylor James lived in a run-down neighborhood not far off Highway 17 south of Flagstaff, distinguished by winding streets and tall pines. Some of the small, mostly prefab homes were caged in by sagging chain-link fencing, but most were separated from their neighbors by trees rather than fences. Several of these dilapidated houses sat right on the road, others were far back, hidden behind overgrown brush and trees—a fire hazard waiting to happen. RVs and campers proliferated, unused and sagging alongside rusted cars in front yards as well as backyards. A few homeowners kept their houses up, bright spots in a depressed neighborhood.

Taylor's rented house was tiny with a sloping roof and peeling paint. Clearly, the landlord hadn't put any money into the place recently. Tall pines grew out front, almost obscuring the door. No sidewalk and no lawn, just packed earth littered with pine needles. An older sedan was parked behind the house in a detached carport. Taylor's closest neighbor had a truck up on jacks in the driveway, but based on the weeds growing underneath, it looked like it had been out of commission for a while.

Regan parked kitty-corner to Taylor's house and crossed the quiet street. While the neighborhood might be struggling, she inhaled fresh, crisp air, reminding Regan of everything she loved about northern Arizona.

As she approached the door, she heard a television, low, indistinct. Then came the sound of a baby crying from the house to the east. From the house behind Taylor's, a place she could barely see through the trees, a power tool squealed.

There was no doorbell. Regan rapped on the door frame. The two windows facing the street had closed blinds.

She heard footsteps. A woman swore, as if she'd kicked something. Regan was dressed comfortably: jeans, black T-shirt, her favorite boots. She'd left her wavy, shoulder-length hair down, figuring it would soften her look. She didn't want to look like a cop, but after her long career it was a hard image to break.

"Coming, coming!" a voice called from inside.

Taylor James opened the front door, looking nothing like the vibrant woman in her Sigma Rho picture. Through the screen, she appeared ghostly—hollow features, sunken eyes, underweight. Her hair had highlights that had mostly grown out. Stale cigarette smoke filled Regan's nose.

"You know, I work nights, so this is early for me."

"I'm sorry, Ms. James. My name is Regan Merritt, and I'm investigating the disappearance and murder of Candace Swain some years ago. It's my understanding that you were one of the last people to see her before she disappeared."

"Are you a cop?"

"No, ma'am. I'm just an investigator." She itched to say *private investigator*, and she could probably get away with it, but she wasn't licensed and didn't want to imply that she was. Her dad had brought up the subject a few months ago—that maybe she should consider private law-enforcement or investigative services. One of his buddies who'd retired early after being shot in the line of duty ran an agency in Scottsdale, mostly former law enforcement. But Regan didn't know what she wanted to do now that she was no longer a marshal.

Though having that PI license would be a real plus right now.

"The Flagstaff police talked to me back then. I told them everything I knew. I have nothing to add."

She was about to close the door, but Regan said, "Have you listened to the podcast about Candace's murder? Three episodes aired over the last week and a half."

Her face drained. "No," she said.

Regan wasn't sure that Taylor was being honest. She pushed, lightly. "But you've heard of the podcast."

"Sigma Rho sent out an email to alumnae. No one wants to be involved with this farce."

"I'm following up on a caller who said that you and Candace were not actually arguing about Abernathy, the homeless man who was seen at the sorority the night she first disappeared."

"First disappeared? What does that mean?"

"You might want to listen to the podcast. There have been several revelations. For instance, four people have come forward saying they each saw Candace after Friday night. Two sightings on Sunday, another on Monday night, and one Tuesday morning."

"Like I told the police when it happened, like everyone knows, I didn't see Candace after she left the party."

"You told the police that you were arguing at the party about whether to call campus police about the homeless man."

"Exactly. He was harassing people, and he scared everyone except Candace, but maybe she should have had a little more fear because then she would still be alive."

Through the screen door, Regan watched Taylor grab a pack of cigarettes from a small table in the entry. She pulled a lighter out from the package, shook out a Virginia Slim, and lit up. Relief crossed her face as she inhaled.

"Why do you people want to stir shit up?" Taylor said. "Candace is *dead*. She's gone. Nothing is going to bring her back. All you're going to do is create problems and get people hurt."

"How so?" Regan asked.

"I'm not going to talk about this."

"Are you scared of someone? I can help you. I used to be a US Marshal. I can get you protection."

"A marshal? What the fuck? What's going on? You said you weren't a cop."

"I'm not a cop anymore, but I am investigating Candace's murder. I *was* a marshal, and I can help you if you're scared."

Taylor took another long drag on her cigarette. Blew it out through the screen at Regan. She didn't react, not knowing if Taylor was trying to intimidate her or if she was just rude.

"I'm not scared," Taylor said, but her manner said otherwise.

"What was your argument with Candace really about, Taylor?"

"Look, the cops said some weird dude from where she volunteered killed her, the same freak that was hanging around for *months*. And yeah, I was pissed off at Candace for not taking care of the situation sooner by calling in the police." She took a long drag, then exhaled. "If you were a *real* investigator, you would know that. Candace and I used to be best friends, and then we weren't. Now she's dead, and sure, I feel like shit that we couldn't get through our problems, you know? So just *drop it*. That podcast is a fucking *stupid idea*, and if that asshole thinks he's going to find her killer or some such nonsense, he's got a screw loose. Go away and leave this all *alone*." She slammed the door, and that was that.

Regan's phone rang just as she got back in her truck. It was a call from Lucas.

"Can you come to my apartment? Like, as soon as possible?"

"What happened?"

"I got a letter. It's not signed. Someone left it at the studio. And it's—hell, I don't know what it is, but you have to read this."

"I'll be there in twenty minutes," she said, then drove off.

Taylor stamped out her cigarette, then lit up another one.

"Fuck, fuck, fuck!" Now was the time she wished she had a joint. But pot never satisfied her the same way heroin did. She'd had to quit all drugs because of the way they'd fucked her up, big-time. For her, pot *always* led her to crave heroin. But now she craved any kind of relief.

Stress accentuated her dangerous cravings. But Taylor didn't want to go back to rehab. She'd been clean for thirteen months. She had a job she liked. She was *not* going to fuck up her life again.

This just couldn't be happening.

In her dimly lit living room, she paced, smoked, paced, wished she had a beer. But she didn't buy it anymore because sometimes when she drank, she wanted *more*. Not more alcohol, but heroin. It was a disgusting, awful habit, and she knew from rehab that it had taken years off her life, and she wanted to live.

Why did you have to fuck everything up, Candace? Why did you have to be a fucking Goody Two-Shoes? Everything was fine. Everything! But you just wouldn't shut up.

She glanced at the clock. She had to be at work at four thirty. She wanted to call in sick, but if she did that, she wouldn't make rent next month. She was on a tight budget, and she had been doing well and was making it, with decent tips.

Now this.

She picked up her cell phone and dialed a number she hadn't called in a long, long time.

No answer.

She left a message.

"I need to talk to you. This podcast bullshit is getting out of hand. Today I had a woman come to my door, asking questions about what Candace and I were fighting about. I didn't tell her anything, but what if someone knows the truth? *Please.* We need to talk about this. I get off work at midnight."

She ended the call. *Damn, damn, damn.*

She stubbed out her cigarette and lit up a third. She needed a plan. If Regan Merritt came back, Taylor wouldn't answer the door. Who the *fuck* did she think she was, anyway? Not a cop but acting all tough, asking questions she had no business asking?

Maybe someone oughta teach that bitch a lesson.

From the Missing Journal of Candace Swain

I always thought loyalty was the most important thing among friends. Loyalty is why I joined a sorority. It's what most appealed to me: a sisterhood when I couldn't be with my real sister. I missed Chrissy. My high-school friends, too, but mostly Chrissy. With the sorority, I could have what felt like family. Friends who had my back. Friends who believed in me like I believed in them.

But what happens when loyalty turns dark? When your sisters demand allegiance even in the face of evil? Because what we did was evil. I didn't think so at the time… Fuck, who am I lying to? It's just me with pen and paper. I can't even write down what we did, I am so ashamed. I knew it was wrong, and I did it anyway. Evil… I never thought I was evil. I tell myself I would never do it again, that I am better than that.

But I'm not better if I ignore the past, pretend it wasn't wrong, pretend that I learned from my mistakes. I have told myself for nearly three years that if I told anyone what really happened, I'd sacrifice my future. For what? No one knew…no one would ever know. It's a secret we swore to keep. It wasn't like it was on purpose. It was an accident…

Yet, I made a conscious decision to erase a human being from the face of the earth. That was a choice I made.

The wrong choice.

I can so easily pass blame, and I did for a long time. I blamed everyone else, except me. We panicked. Every one of us.

But there's only one person to blame for my own silence, and that's me. If I had stood up then, would I be in so much pain now? I don't know. Maybe I will always suffer, remembering the choices we made. The choice I made.

Why am I the only one who is having a hard time living with the guilt?

Sixteen

Lucas:

I don't know where to start.

I've been listening to your podcast with both fear and trepidation.

I knew Candace Swain. I was a year ahead of her. We were friends, and I knew that she was wrestling with something very deep and dark. Maybe you'll expose the truth. I hope you do. But you have to be careful. I fear the truth killed Candace.

I was at Sigma Rho's spring party that night when Candace and Taylor James were arguing. Only a few people overheard them and would know for sure what they were arguing about. Their fight didn't last long—maybe five minutes? Ten tops. Then Candace left the party.

But they weren't the only two people in that heated discussion. Another sister, Kimberly Foster, an alum, was there, trying to mediate and keep them quiet. Kim would know exactly what Candace and Taylor were arguing about. I have no idea if the police *ever talked to Kim or what she might have said to them if they did.*

I am too scared to come forward because I can't prove anything.

I will not call in to your podcast because someone might recognize my voice. I've gone back and forth about even contacting you this way. Sometimes it's not as easy as it might seem to know what to do or even what's right or wrong.

Honestly, I'm scared. Because the person who killed Candace is still out there.

But mostly, I want justice for my friend. I want the truth to come out. I hope this helps.

The letter ended there. No marks on the folded note, which was typed and printed on a standard laser printer. No address, no stamp.

Regan sat at Lucas's desk and took a picture of the note with her phone and then studied it more closely. Lucas paced his small bedroom.

"What do you think?" Lucas asked. "We have to find Kimberly Foster, right?"

"Where did you find this?"

"At the studio. It was left under the door with my name on it."

The communications building wasn't locked during the day, but whoever left it was familiar with the campus. A student or alumni. Someone most likely local, since the note hadn't been sent through the mail.

Regan looked at the list of Sigma Rho sisters that Lucas had posted on his wall, ranked by graduation year. Kimberly Foster was two years older than Candace.

The anonymous letter writer didn't say she was in the

sorority, but if she were, she was in the class that graduated the year after Kim and before Taylor.

Regan read the letter again.

Maybe you'll expose the truth.

Expose? That implied the writer knew *what* hidden truth there was to be found.

Regan reread the letter again, trying to get inside the head of the author.

Female. Men would have been at the party but the letter sounded female.

Scared. She knew something—and hadn't told the police. Had the police questioned her? Regan didn't know. She had been an alum, and unless the police were given the guest list, the police might not have known to interview her.

Not only did this person know something crucial about this case, the writer felt that her knowledge endangered her. The tone suggested that she felt threatened. Murder was the ultimate threat.

Could Candace's murder *itself* be a threat to others to keep their mouths shut? About what?

Talk, and you'll end up like Candace.

"Regan?" Lucas said. "What are you thinking? It sounds like this letter writer knows more than what's on the page."

"She does," Regan said. "And so does Taylor." She told Lucas how her conversation had gone. "I want to go back and confront her, but I don't know if that's the best approach, at least not until we have more information. I'm hoping after our conversation that she'll listen to the podcast—if she hasn't already—and call in. Or be more honest when I talk to her again."

"You'll be there on Friday again, right?" Lucas said.

"Yes, I said I would." She'd become as invested in solving Candace's murder as Lucas.

"Because," Lucas continued, "if Taylor does call in, I have no idea how to get her to talk."

"If she calls in it's because she wants to talk," Regan said. "And that means we need to ask open-ended questions, get her to tell us more than she plans to. She knows something she didn't want to tell me. It could be innocuous—or it could be answers we need."

"I looked up the other sorority sisters Annie mentioned in your conversation," Lucas said. He flipped through a notebook on his desk. "Alexa Castillo is a year older than Annie, and I couldn't find anything on her. Castillo is a pretty common name, but I can't find an Alexa or Alexandra or Alexis who graduated from NAU in the last four years on social media, but I kept it narrowed to Arizona. Maybe I should expand it. The sororities all have online newsletters and webpages, but the newsletters are archived as PDFs so I have to click on each one before I can search for a name. But I think it's worth doing because they often post updates on graduates. I'll start in on it tonight and look for Alexa Castillo and Kimberly Foster."

"Good," Regan said.

"I called Chrissy to ask about Candace's journal, but she didn't answer. She's pretty good about calling me back. I'll text you if she has any information."

"On Friday, for your next podcast episode, I think you should push the report from the witness who saw Candace leaving the library on Tuesday morning. You can even replay a clip of that, right? To remind people? That might generate other viable calls. And whoever wrote this letter—they *say* they don't want to call, but there's no reason you can't read the letter on air. It could spur someone else to call."

"That's a great idea," Lucas said, making a note.

"I'll see what I can find out from Rachel Wagner, the advisor. Maybe convince her to be interviewed, since she knew Candace."

"That would be great."

"Don't hold your breath, but it's worth pursuing." She glanced at her watch.

"You have to go?"

"In a minute. But I wanted to talk to you about Detective Young."

He rolled his eyes.

"You said he wasn't forthcoming, but you talked to the public information officer, correct?"

"Yes, got the party line. I learned more in the media reports than I did from FPD."

"I want to talk to him. You have good information, and I want to see if he'll share why they are so hung up on Joseph Abernathy as the killer. You also had a clip from the director of Sunrise Center. Do you think she would call in?"

"Maybe. I can reach out to her. She said to call her if I needed anything."

"Good. You do that, I'll talk first to Young, then Rachel Wagner, and we'll touch base tonight. But be careful. You're asking questions that might upset someone, and that *someone* killed Candace. If not Abernathy, then the murderer could still be around and listening. Watch your back, Lucas."

Seventeen

The Flagstaff Police Department was housed on the opposite end of the same large government building as the Coconino County Sheriff's Office. Even though she hadn't been there since she'd left home after college nearly fourteen years ago, Regan knew the building well. It hadn't changed much. She expected there would be plenty of new faces, but the first one she saw was familiar and friendly.

"Regan Merritt, as I live and breathe," said the guard as she entered the building.

"Since when do you work for the PD?" she asked Raul Ramirez, who'd been a deputy who worked under her father when John was sheriff.

"Since my heart attack two years ago," he said. "Lateral move. Flagstaff needed a desk sergeant, I qualified, no patrol. The chief and the new sheriff worked it out, and I appreciate it. I still have eighteen months before I can retire with full benefits."

"I'm happy for you."

"Growing old isn't fun," he said. "Though, I'll admit I do like the regular hours and more time to play with my grandkids. Amber had six kids, can you believe that?" Raul had one daughter, she remembered. She was a few years older than Regan.

"Six? Wow! Good for you."

He laughed. "She barely remembers what day it is, but Josh has a good job so she's able to stay home until the youngest starts school. Makes it tight on them financially, but we gave them the house a few years back, and my bride and I moved into a town house on the golf course. No maintenance, no stress, and a much smaller place to keep clean."

Raul had been married for at least forty years and always called his wife his *bride*. It was endearing.

"How can I help you this afternoon?"

"I'm here to see Detective Steven Young. Is he in?"

"I believe so. He'll want to know what it's regarding."

"The Candace Swain homicide."

"Give me a minute."

She nodded, walked around the lobby looking at the photos—two officers lost in the line of duty since FPD had been founded more than a hundred years ago. She knew one of them: they'd gone to the same high school, and he was a year behind her. He'd only been twenty-eight when he was killed. Risk was part of the job they signed up for, but his murder was completely senseless. She had adjusted to her dad leaving every morning with the idea that he might not come home. He'd once told her that no matter what, when you leave your family, tell them you love them.

"It doesn't matter if you had a disagreement, a fight, if you're still angry even after a good night's sleep. Tell them you love them and you'll work it out, no matter what. Because tomorrow is never guaranteed."

She understood more than she wanted to. She had accepted that she might lose her dad in the line of duty. She'd accepted that she might lose her own life in the line of duty. She had never conceived of losing her son.

She still didn't know *how* to accept it. She could face the truth: Chase was dead. But accepting the facts was a world different than accepting that she would never hold her son again, watch him play ball, hear his laugh.

Raul called over to her. "Young is coming out."

She breathed deeply, controlled her emotions, turned to face her friend. "Thank you."

Five minutes later, a man she suspected was Steven Young turned down the hall and walked toward the lobby. He was tall with dark eyes. Late thirties, early forties. Well-dressed. He wore black-framed eyeglasses and a gun in his shoulder holster.

"Merritt?" he said.

"Detective." She extended her hand. He hesitated, then shook it.

"Follow me."

He knew why she was here. His poker face was good, but the tension in his grip revealed him.

She followed him down the hall to a small conference room, the first on the right, and he motioned for her to sit, which she did. He closed the door and sat across from her.

"You know why I'm here," she said.

"I listened to Vega's podcast," he said.

That didn't surprise her. If she were in the same position, she would have listened as well.

When she didn't say anything, he added, "I was surprised that a former US Marshal would participate in something like that."

"Like what?"

He frowned, leaned back. Assessed her. "A sensational program like that podcast."

"My former advisor from NAU asked me to talk to Lucas. I was intrigued by his program so agreed to be interviewed."

"I wish you had talked to me first."

"I'm no longer in law enforcement," she said, which should explain why she felt no need to go to local cops for permission to talk about a cold case. "I know Lucas talked to you at one point."

"Lucas Vega is a smart, stubborn, angry young man. Emphasis on *young*. I don't know what he told you about his conversation with me, but he essentially accused me of being lazy and not caring about the victim. He threw information I already knew at me and demanded I answer his questions. I showed him the door. Why are you helping him?"

Carefully, she said, "I've become invested in this case, primarily because it's attached to my alma mater. Lucas's quest to retrace Candace Swain's steps from when she left Sigma Rho until she was found dead is a viable approach."

"Most of the people who knew Candace are no longer around campus. Maybe a dozen or so are still in the sorority."

She nodded. "If you listened to the podcast, you know several people have come forward with sightings of the victim during the week she was supposedly missing."

Young said, "I can't take as statements people remembering—*possibly* remembering—something that happened three years ago, through a podcast. There is no way I can verify that they are remembering the correct day. And why would the person who claimed to have seen her at the library not have come forward? All security footage is erased after thirty days, unless campus police flag it. There's no way to verify that information. She could be making it up."

"She may not have thought about it at the time, or not have known Candace was missing. She wasn't in a sorority, and most people on campus were in the dark until after Candace was killed. Also, in my experience, people rarely come forward. They have to be asked."

"Do you think I didn't do my job?"

He was antagonistic, for no reason. "I didn't say that."

"You implied it."

"No, I didn't."

He scowled. "I'll tell you this, Ms. Merritt. If my department had had the case from the beginning, it would have been handled differently. The campus police were out of their element and should have called us in right away, but they didn't know what they were dealing with. I don't blame them—as soon as she was missing for more than forty-eight hours, they called us in, plus the sheriff's department and the troopers. Every agency was looking for her by that Wednesday afternoon. Once it became a homicide investigation, I got involved. Though campus police did basic work—talked to Sigma Rho, Candace's family, her professors—it wasn't treated as a serious investigation until she was found dead. Then my team talked to everyone again. I don't have to tell you that memories fade over a week. Can you imagine what three years does to them?"

She saw his point. "I read the public reports and the autopsy report, which included an analysis of the water found in Candace's lungs."

"Yes, I'm aware."

"And?"

"And what?"

"Lucas believed that you dismissed his theory that she drowned in a chlorinated body of water."

"I dismissed *Lucas*. He's into television forensics—he thinks everything is instantaneous. We didn't know for *weeks* that the water samples didn't match Hope Springs Lake. Not because of any incompetence but because of a backlog in the state lab." He paused. "I made an assumption that she drowned in the lake because the autopsy said she drowned and she was found in the lake. By the time we learned that she drowned in a chlorinated body of water, it was too late to collect evidence from any other potential crime scene. Security tapes were already gone from the campus—as I said, they automatically get erased after thirty days unless specifically flagged. We had flagged all the tapes from the dorm, but there was nothing of value on them. No one came forward stating that they'd seen her after the party on Friday night. We knew her card key had been used late Sunday night, but no one in the sorority saw her, and there's no camera on the side door, only the main entrance. We had evidence that Joseph Abernathy harassed the women at the sorority house, and Candace knew him through her volunteer work. We had witnesses stating he was yelling at her at the party when she asked him to leave. When he was seen hopping a train the morning her body was found, it was pretty damning."

"But he hasn't returned. Was he found jumping off? Caught on security at another station?"

"Again, you're questioning my diligence."

He was angry, and she didn't see why. She was asking basic questions, calm.

"Detective, you can see why Lucas is skeptical. Why I'm skeptical that Abernathy killed Candace and moved her body."

He stared at her. "We notified the railroad, but we weren't informed that he was seen until the day after we found her body. He had more than twenty-four hours to disappear."

"Do you have any other evidence—"

"We have *no* other evidence. I've wanted to talk to Abernathy. He's fallen off the face of the earth, but every law-enforcement agency in the country has his stats, and we sent out a BOLO to every shelter in the database more than once. I know how to do my job. Look, I don't want to be a hardnose, but Lucas Vega has no personal or firsthand knowledge of Candace Swain's disappearance or death. I asked him. He saw her before the party the night she disappeared. I checked his alibi, just for kicks. He's acting like a reporter, but without training, experience, or employer."

"Look, Detective, I get it. You have experience, you know what you're doing. You want to solve this case. But Lucas has something good here. He's getting information. You know that because you admitted to listening to the podcast."

Young didn't comment.

"Do you really believe that Abernathy killed her?"

"Usually, the most obvious answer is the correct answer. Occam's razor." He hesitated, then added, "Abernathy is a person of interest. We've wanted to talk to him. It's that simple. The truth? I have nothing. There is no physical evidence. Water is a great way to destroy evidence, especially chlorinated water combined with the high-algae content of the lake. I won't say that Abernathy is straight-out guilty, but he is the most likely suspect. And if he's not guilty? He knows something. His disappearance tells me that. If I think that Lucas Vega finds anything useful, bet your house I'll follow up. But right now all he has are conjecture and rumors."

"Fair enough."

She wanted more information but wasn't certain how she could get anything more out of him. Young would know if she was fishing. She decided to share part of what she'd learned in the hopes that he would share other information.

"Did you know that Candace often spent time in the aquatic center? It's not far from the sorority."

He nodded. "Yes."

"And?"

"And what? By the time I learned that she didn't drown in the lake, all security tapes were erased. At the aquatic center the only cameras are on the doors. It's easy to get in and out. A lot of people have access. They are not monitored 24/7. When we looked, we found no evidence of foul play, but weeks had passed—I didn't expect to find anything, even if she had been killed there. No one reported anything out of the ordinary. I spoke to members of the swim team, janitorial staff, the coach. While it might be the most logical crime scene, it's impossible to prove. There are plenty of other pools in town that she could have drowned in. It still doesn't explain where she went, why she didn't use her phone after the party, or why she left campus, returned Sunday night, then left without sleeping in her bed."

"And that's where Lucas can help."

"Maybe." Young took off his glasses and rubbed his eyes. "You know, I hope he gets something, but I'm not holding my breath."

"Did you know that Candace kept a journal?"

"We had her computer. Nothing of interest was found on it."

"No, a physical journal. Like a diary."

"That she wrote in?"

"Yes. Her roommate told me she wrote in it regularly, and that she didn't think about it until the family came to clear out her dorm room and her sister asked about it."

"I interviewed her roommate. She never mentioned it to me."

"Maybe you didn't ask the right questions."

She wished she could take back the comment. Young clammed up, his jaw set in anger.

"I take it you're not done with the podcast," he said, his dark eyes meeting hers. Yes, he was very angry.

"Correct."

"I have no doubt that Lucas Vega is going to cross a line, if he hasn't already."

She had more questions, but Young kept looking at his watch, and she doubted he'd share anything more about his investigation after she'd slighted him. Sometimes, her tongue spoke before her brain thought things through.

She hoped in a day or two he might be inclined to share more. Especially if she and Lucas uncovered a witness that might help him solve the case.

He looked at his watch again, then said, "I have to get back to work, but I hope you'll keep me informed of anything relevant you learn."

She wouldn't withhold important information from the police, but she wasn't one hundred percent sold that Detective Young was as invested in this case as she was. "Thank you for your time," she said, extending her hand again; he shook it.

"I can walk you out."

She was going to decline, but the offer sounded like an

olive branch, so she took it. As they exited, she said, "I have another question. Do you think Candace's disappearance is directly related to her murder?"

"It would seem so. It's logical, yes, but I have no proof either way."

He held the main door open for her, and they stepped out into the sun. "If you want to know what my gut says, I'll disappoint you," he said. "While I understand and appreciate a cop's intuition—which is basically experience—I still rely on facts. Right now there is no evidence of any connection between Candace disappearing for over a week and then being murdered the night before her body was found, yet that is the most logical assumption. I feel someone has lied to me, but I don't know who. I interviewed many people more than once, including the sorority girls, the staff at the shelter where she volunteered, and Candace's boyfriends. If someone is lying, who is it? And why? And why would they want Candace dead? By everyone's testimony, she was well-liked, popular, kind, smart. It could be random. It could be a psychopath who held her for eight days before he killed her. I'm stumped. I have dozens of other cases in major crimes to investigate. So if you get something solid, I'd appreciate if you tell me. But I can't spend time and resources investigating a case that's three years old without new evidence."

That she understood. His frustration came through loud and clear.

Yes, someone had lied. But alibis weren't the only thing people lied about.

Young looked at his phone, sent a quick text.

"Go ahead," she said, nodding to the phone. "I'm good."

He finished his text, then said, "I'm sorry I came down

hard on you at the beginning, but I mean it—you find something, I need to know."

"Understood."

Eighteen

Regan hated being late. She briskly walked from the public lot to the Biological Sciences building and made it to Rachel Wagner's office with one minute to spare.

The door was open, and Rachel sat at her desk, her phone to her ear. She waved for Regan to enter, putting up a finger that she would just be a minute.

Regan remained standing while surveying the small, tidy, bright office. Like most professors, there were multiple bookshelves packed with tomes—in Rachel's case, mostly science-related. There was one shelf of fiction, a variety of popular books. Also many knickknacks, trophies, and plaques. On the walls, lots of pictures—of the Sigma Rho sorority, of a younger Rachel in a cheerleading uniform. Regan moved closer and realized that Rachel had cheered for the University of Arizona in college. There was also a photo of Rachel and a large group of women, framed with a plaque underneath that read *Sigma Rho, University of Arizona, Class of 2008*.

Same year Regan graduated from NAU. Had she gone to U of A she might have known Rachel. Small world.

Rachel was an attractive woman, with a tall, athletic build that suggested an active life.

"Thanks, honey, I'll see you tonight," Rachel disconnected and looked up at Regan. "Sorry about that. Finalizing date night with my boyfriend."

"No problem." She nodded toward the photo. "You and I graduated college the same year."

"How neat! Please sit. Can I get you coffee? Water?"

"I'm good, thanks." She was starving, because she'd only had an energy bar for lunch, but she didn't think this would take too long. She sat in a comfortable guest chair in front of Rachel's desk. Her desk was uncluttered with only her laptop computer in the corner. Regan wouldn't call herself a slob, but she wasn't that neat. Her style was more like Henry Clarkson's organized chaos.

But the atmosphere fit Rachel's sunny disposition.

"First, thank you for meeting with me," Rachel said. "I'm sure you're busy, and I appreciate it."

"I'm glad you reached out. I had planned to talk to the president of Sigma Rho to see if she wanted to talk about the podcast. It's my understanding that the sorority is unhappy with it."

Rachel frowned. "They are, especially the girls who knew Candace. I wouldn't say *unhappy*. They're more upset than anything. I'm sure you can understand."

"Yes," Regan said, though she didn't, not completely. Wouldn't they want closure? "They went through a traumatic experience having one of their own murdered."

"Exactly. But not just that, though that was the worst, but they were questioned by police, they were put into the awful position of hearing negative things about their sorority sister, who wasn't here to defend herself. They feel—and

I concur—that the podcast is only serving to victim-shame and to tear down the sorority."

"I think Lucas has been very respectful of Candace Swain and her life."

"Talking about Candace having two boyfriends, both of whom, I've been told, were cleared by the police, it makes her seem unappealing."

"Lucas hasn't implied that Candace was in any way to blame for what happened to her, and there's no victim-shaming going on. I listened to each episode twice, and heard nothing to suggest it. If anything, he was more than a little respectful. As you probably know, too often when a woman ends up dead, it's a boyfriend or ex-boyfriend that's involved. The fact that Candace had two boyfriends, whether or not they knew of the other, is logical for the police to pursue."

"See? It doesn't do her reputation any good, and she's not here to stand up for herself."

"That's not what I said, or what I meant."

"And if she had two boyfriends, who cares?" Rachel continued as if Regan hadn't spoken. "No one should pass moral judgment on her, but people do, even when they didn't know her or know how wonderful she was. And the talk about the disagreement at the sorority's spring party— it makes it sound so much worse than it actually was."

"Were you there?"

"For a while."

"You were the sorority advisor when Candace disappeared?"

"Yes, but I don't live at the sorority. I was a Sigma Rho alumna, so I was thrilled to take on the role. The value of a sorority—the relationships, the support, the future connections—cannot be taken lightly. To help guide these amazing young women through college and on to the next stage of their lives, I feel both blessed and lucky."

She sounded like she was selling the sorority to Regan, but that was probably par for the course. A lot of clubs had that rah-rah attitude. But there was a lot of truth to what she was saying: any organization that had a common, uniting element—like Greek Life—often helped graduates find jobs down the road, making connections that benefited their members.

"How well did you know Candace?"

"I—well, can I be honest with you?"

Odd question. "Of course."

"I invited you to talk about the podcast, but I don't want anything I say to be used on the podcast, out of respect for the young women I advise. What I really want is for you to understand how the podcast is distressing them."

"So you said. They are upset and feel that Candace and their sorority have been treated unfairly."

"Not so much unfairly, but bringing up negative stuff hurts the reputation of the sorority, as well as the girls emotionally. Some of them were friends with Candace, and even those who weren't want to remember Candace in the best possible light. And there was so much good that she did in her life. You know that she regularly volunteered at a homeless shelter downtown. Yet it was that good heart that may have gotten her killed."

"I'm aware of the situation with Mr. Abernathy."

"I trust the police to handle the investigation. Candace had so much love and compassion. That's what I want her to be known for, not that she was murdered and her killer was never found."

"I understand."

Rachel smiled. "I knew you would. You sounded both

intelligent and experienced on the podcast last night. Now, I know you probably can't convince Lucas Vega to put an end to this, and I understand that it's his capstone project. But perhaps you can help steer the show into something less inflammatory, considering the psychological damage that it's doing to my girls."

"I was interviewed last night to share my perspective in how law enforcement conducts investigations into missing persons. It's not my podcast."

"Of course, but you still have influence over the student."

Regan didn't respond to the comment. She said, "Vicky Ryan, the current Sigma Rho president, had been mentored by Candace when she was a freshman. I was hoping to be able to talk to her."

"Vicky wants nothing to do with the podcast. She already told Lucas that. She was very upset last night. I sat up half the night with her."

"I'm trying to piece together a few disparate facts, and I thought she might have some information."

Rachel frowned, leaned back in her chair. "Well, I'll ask her, but we are both of the opinion that the police are far better equipped to handle a murder investigation than a college student."

"I generally agree. But three years is a long time. They're called *cold cases* for a reason."

"I'll talk to Vicky, and if she agrees, I need to be here for her. I'm the one who dries their tears, who tells them it's going to get better—even when I have my doubts."

"You have my number. Let me know."

Regan rose from her chair, then said, almost as if she just remembered to ask—when, in fact, she had been thinking about how to ask it for the entire time she'd been sitting in

Rachel's office—"Do you know what Taylor and Candace were actually arguing about at the party?"

"That was fully investigated by the police."

"Still—"

"You actually believed that anonymous caller? People who don't want to give their names are probably lying," Rachel said.

Regan didn't agree, nor did she comment.

Rachel continued to fill the silence. "Taylor told the police exactly what the argument was about. That homeless man. Taylor and several of the other girls wanted to call the police, and Candace put her foot down. When Taylor heard that Candace had confronted him alone, she was worried, and then the conversation deteriorated into an argument. Taylor is heartbroken that her last conversation with Candace was one of anger. She said hurtful things that she regrets to this day."

"Maybe," Regan said carefully, "but someone who was there claims that their argument wasn't solely about Abernathy."

"I can't imagine what. Taylor spoke to the police. She told them everything she knew."

"I tracked down Taylor, asked her about that night, but she wasn't very helpful."

Rachel looked surprised. "You talked to Taylor?"

"I just want to get the facts straight."

"Taylor has a serious drug problem. I don't know that she'd remember what happened yesterday, let alone three years ago. Her problem started at the end of her senior year—related to the fact that one of her closest friends had been killed. I was the one who took her to rehab the first time, got her cleaned up. But a second time? I can't do it. It hurts too much to help, only to have her go back to her old ways."

"She seemed to be doing okay. Thank you for your time, Rachel. Let me know what Vicky says about talking to me."

Regan left, thinking about the conversation. Rachel was protective of the sorority, but Regan still didn't understand why she didn't want the truth. Yes, the police were generally best at solving capital crimes, but they were stuck. Young had said as much. So having Lucas shake things up was a good thing. Rachel's concerns seemed minor and almost petty, as if she had a personal problem with Lucas.

Still, maybe Vicky Ryan would talk to her. If not, Regan might just have to seek out other sorority sisters.

Regan had said to Lucas that someone had lied to the police; Young had confirmed the same gut feeling. Who? And why?

Someone in the sorority knew more than they had told the police, and whoever it was may be too scared to come forward. Both the letter to Lucas and the call they got about Candace driving on campus Sunday night had been anonymous. Even Annie's reticence to call in to the podcast was odd. Was something more going on with the sorority? Too many people were acting odd, almost scared.

Regan slipped on her sunglasses, breathing in the fresh spring air as she crossed campus to the public lot. It was a beautiful afternoon, and the sun revitalized her. Even being on campus wasn't as weird as she'd thought it might be. There was a warm, familiar nostalgia as she recalled friends and events during her four years here. Playing spontaneous games of beach volleyball in the sandpit in the middle of campus; hiking to the bottom of the Grand Canyon with her geology class; going to the football games with Jessie and their small group of friends. Regan never had a large friend group, but the friends she had were good ones, men and women she still kept in touch with.

Not so much in the last year, she realized. But grief did that to you. She hadn't wanted to talk to anyone after Chase died.

She shook the thoughts of the past from her head and focused on the present. Rachel was protective of Sigma Rho, and she had been around when Candace disappeared. She very well might know more about what had happened than she let on. Perhaps she was protecting one of her sorority sisters. Taylor? Would Rachel protect a killer? What would Taylor's motive be…and why on earth would a professor protect her?

Maybe Regan was jumping the gun on this, but she couldn't shake the thought that both Rachel and Taylor knew more than they'd told her or than they'd told the police. Whether that information was directly related to Candace's murder was anyone's guess.

But Regan was determined to find out.

Nineteen

It was after five thirty by the time Regan arrived back at her dad's house. She tried to recall what was in the refrigerator for her to eat. She was famished.

There were packages at the front door, so her dad wasn't home yet, which surprised her. She walked up the stairs and picked up two small boxes, both addressed to John Merritt. There was also a large manila envelope that had been sent two-day mail. For Regan.

The return address: Dyson, Brooks, & Shapiro, Attorneys-at-Law.

Regan's lawyer was Beth Shapiro.

All thought of food left her head. She unlocked the front door, dropped the boxes on the counter, and took the envelope to her dad's office. She sat at his desk and stared.

She knew what this was.

As soon as she signed on the dotted line, her divorce would be final.

She could wait, but why? Regan couldn't imagine that there were any outstanding issues. Beth would have called her.

Regan opened the package, and it was as she'd expected,

though she was somewhat surprised Beth hadn't called to tell her the papers were on their way. She read the brief letter attached to the documents.

Blah blah blah.

Sign all three copies and keep one for yourself, return the other two in the postage-paid envelope to their office. Colorful arrows pointed to where she was supposed to sign. As if there was anything cheery about divorce.

Grant had already signed. Of course he had. He wanted the divorce as much as she did—maybe more—and he was local. Easy to go into the lawyer's office to sign away the twelve years they'd shared.

Regan flipped to each arrow and scrawled her name. Took one copy and put it facedown next to her—she didn't want to look at it—and put the other two in the designated envelope, sealed it, and walked down to the mailbox at the end of the long driveway. Their road was private, remote. Twenty minutes to campus, but it felt like they were in the middle of nowhere. Only a few other people lived in this idyllic area, and she didn't see anyone, only a few houses set far up their own driveways, partly hidden by tall pine and juniper.

Regan retrieved that day's mail and stuffed the envelope in the box, then walked back up the driveway.

There was nothing left between her and Grant. When Chase was gone, they both realized that their son was all that had bound them together for the last few years. Why couldn't she have seen it before? Would it have even made a difference?

Dammit! She would have stayed married to Grant forever if it could bring Chase back to life. He shouldn't be dead!

She walked into the house and screamed as loud as she could. All the pain, all the frustration and anger, and deep, unyielding sorrow at her life over the last eight months streaming out on a wave of sound so loud that she almost scared herself. When she was done, the silence surprised her. Her throat was raw, and she wiped away tears.

Well, damn. She wasn't a crier. She had cried just twice after Chase was killed. The night he was killed, though those tears were constrained: she'd forced herself to cut them off even though it physically pained her.

Then, after the funeral.

Regan had just buried her baby boy. Ten years old. In his baseball uniform because he loved baseball more than anything. With his mitt and the ball he caught at a Nationals game signed by Bryce Harper. A collector's item now because the player was no longer with the team.

She'd had dry eyes all day. Her dad, brothers, and sister wanted to come home with her, but she said no.

She regretted that.

She'd found them a weeklong rental. She should have gone with them. She knew that Grant was no longer her husband, except in name. She knew it was over, but they had just buried their boy. He had held her hand. And for a while, she thought that maybe...maybe...they would find a way to get through this.

He slammed the door. His tears were real, pain and anger rolled together. For all of Grant's faults, he'd loved their son.

He'd once loved her.

She reached for him. Tried to push aside what he said one week ago, when Chase was shot and killed by a man who she had once apprehended.

Grant stared at her. "I told you your job was too dangerous. I thought you would be killed, and it tore me up, but I learned to live with the risk. But it was our son. Our baby boy. Chase is dead because of you."

"That's not true." She didn't know if she spoke or not.

"I can't even look at you. I can't—just go to your family. Leave me alone."

"Grant, you don't mean it." She knew he did. She wanted to be strong; she wanted to fight, to scream, but she had nothing left inside.

"My boy. Gone."

Grant was in pain, just like she was.

"He was my boy, too, Grant. I—I'm sorry."

She was sorry. It wasn't her fault, no matter what Grant said...was it? Had she missed something? Nothing made sense about the last week. Nothing made sense about Chase's murder.

Grant stared at her, his face radiating the pain she felt inside. "I wish it had been you."

Her shredded heart bled more. She had nothing to say as Grant twisted the final knife.

"So do I," she said and meant it. In that moment, she wished the bullets that had ripped into her son's body had torn her apart instead.

She stood in the entry, feeling helpless and grieving more than she could bear.

"Get out," Grant said. "I can't look at you."

She turned and walked out. Their marriage was over.

Regan showered, then sat down at her dad's computer. It was now after six thirty, and she texted her dad, concerned about his whereabouts. She shouldn't be. Even though he was retired, he was a big boy with a lot of friends and things to do.

He responded almost immediately.

Home by seven. La Fonda tonight?

She sent him a thumbs-up emoji: it was her favorite Mexican food restaurant, and she could use a margarita. Or three. She'd make her dad drive so she could down a few drinks.

She sent an email to Beth that the divorce papers were signed and out in tomorrow's mail. She checked her emails, ignoring most.

Her old boss, Tommy Granger, had emailed her twice, on Monday and again this morning. She'd been avoiding his messages. She really didn't want to talk to anyone from her previous life.

Especially Tommy.

He was angry with her because she let her sabbatical lapse without applying for an extension. The sabbatical was part of her benefits: she received three paid months off for every five years of service. She'd never taken her first sabbatical, and they could be rolled over once. She didn't argue with him when he put her in for a six-month sabbatical, even though she'd told him she wasn't coming back.

He kept pushing, and while she respected her boss, she wished he would drop it.

His email this morning was clear.

Regan:
You won't answer your phone. You don't respond to your emails. I haven't seen you since you left Virginia. I feel your pain. I wish I could take it away from you, that I could go back in time and protect Chase. I loved that kid, but that is nothing compared to you. Losing a child is the worst thing a parent can suffer. I never expected you to bounce back. That's why I insisted on the sabbatical.

You are one of the best marshals our service has to offer. You are dedicated, well-trained, experienced, and your instincts are better than anyone I have ever worked with. I want you back. I want you here, in Virginia, but I get that you can't be here. For a lot of reasons. I respect that. Hell, I respect you. And more. You know it.

But don't leave the service. I just got the message that you didn't fill out your returning paperwork. I got you an extension, but they have to receive it by the close of business Friday. Then a week at FLET-C to requalify with your weapons and take your psych test. I know neither will be difficult for you.

I can get you into any office you want. Any division. If you want to stay in Arizona, there's a place for you there. I know the director: he would be over the moon to have you. Or Texas. Florida. California. If you want the wide-open plains of middle America, I can make that happen. Anywhere.

You're too good to walk away.

Please call me. I miss you.

Tommy

Dammit. She didn't want to call him. For lots of reasons, but mostly because he was the only person on earth who might be able to talk her into going back to the Marshals.

She couldn't go back.

It was both complex and simple. She grieved for her son. Her focus wasn't one hundred percent on the job after Chase was killed, and she didn't know that it could be. A marshal needed to be completely clearheaded. They couldn't risk a mistake when other people's lives were on the line. She felt as if she'd been split in two, and without her sharpness, without being whole, she wouldn't survive.

She didn't want to die on the job. Marshals took daily risks. That's what they signed up for. But Regan knew herself too well—without her family, without a foundation, with her grief clawing at her soul, she would make mistakes, possibly putting other people's lives at risk.

She wasn't going to do it.

But mostly, her heart wasn't in it. She'd once loved her job more than anything except her son. Yes, she loved her job more than her husband. She and Grant had had many rough patches. They'd even separated for six months. Saw a counselor. Got back together to give Chase a foundation because their love for him was the single thing that united them. And for a while, things were even better than before. They took the time to be together, both with Chase and alone. They went away, just the two of them, and talked about having another child. That was when Chase was five. But it was talk, and they both loved Chase and loved their jobs, and time slipped away.

But the last year of their marriage, before Chase died, things weren't as they had been. Regan didn't notice because she was busy, between her job and her son. It was like time sped up and suddenly Grant was distant, argumentative, working longer-than-usual hours. She thought he was having an affair, confronted him. She remembered exactly what she said and how she said it. Unemotional. Cold.

"If you want out of this marriage, just tell me."

He stared at her. "I'm not fucking around, Regan. Work is just overwhelming right now, and you're never around to talk about anything. Not everyone is a cool cucumber like you."

It was the way he said it, as if he resented her ability to be calm in the face of chaos. And he'd hit on the reason they had gone to counseling in the first place, five years before: because they were both so busy they didn't talk.

She believed he was faithful, but they still didn't talk, and when she pushed he pushed back. And she buried it. She compartmentalized her marriage so she could do her job.

Maybe that had been the wrong approach. Hell, she didn't know anymore. And what did it matter? Chase was dead, Grant hated her, and she was officially divorced and without a home or a career.

She stared at Tommy's email, opened up a window to respond…then she called him.

She wanted to ignore him—her boss, her friend—but she couldn't.

He answered on the first ring.

"Regan? Is that really you?"

"Yes."

"Thank God. You haven't returned any of my messages."

"I'm sorry."

"Don't lie. I know you didn't want to talk. But we have to get your paperwork in by Friday."

"I'm not coming back."

"You don't mean that."

"Did you think I didn't mean it when I left Virginia? That I didn't mean it when we talked over Christmas? I'm not coming back. I really appreciate how you've tried, that you were willing to do so much to put me in any office, but my heart is not in the job. When you lose the spark, it's over. You told me that, time and time again. I have no spark."

He was silent for a long time.

"Tommy?"

"Dammit, you're too good to walk away. But I get it."

He took a deep breath. "I miss you here." He cleared his throat. "The team misses you."

I miss you, too. But she didn't say it. He'd been there for her after Chase, after her marriage fell apart, and they might have been able to have something if she wasn't so damn broken and grieving. Now...whatever might have been was gone.

But he was a friend. A good friend.

"You staying there? In Flagstaff?"

"I'm not making any long-term decisions right now."

"But you are."

"Yes."

"What are you going to do?"

"My dad thinks I should get my PI license. One of his former deputies runs a security company, and they hire mostly former law enforcement. I'm thinking about it." She really hadn't, not more than once or twice, but it was the only option she thought was viable.

"It's a good idea. And you're staying with him?"

"For now. I'll probably get my own place, but I don't think either of us are in a rush. And until I have a steady income, I should probably be frugal with my living expenses."

"I saw that you sold the house."

"I have money from it. Good money. Might be enough to buy a condo."

He laughed, and that somehow made her feel better. "A condo? Regan Merritt in a condo? Never happen."

Now she laughed. "You're right. Maybe I'll buy a tent and live in the mountains."

"Don't go that far. Where will I sleep when I visit?"

Her heart skipped a beat. They had never talked directly about their mutual attraction. She knew he had feelings for her. She was pretty certain he knew how she felt. But they didn't talk about it. Ever.

"Okay, I'll get a real house."

- "Good."

"I…" How did she tell him goodbye? For good? "Be safe out there, Tommy."

"You, too, Regan."

She ended the call before either of them said the one thing they had avoided all these years. She harbored no illusions that she and Tommy would ever be together. The time had passed, and it had never really been an option. A relationship born out of pain and grief couldn't last.

But, she realized, it was okay. She felt a burden lift off her chest that avoiding Tommy was over. That she could call him, and maybe they could reclaim the friendship they'd had before they'd started dancing around their feelings.

It gave her hope.

Twenty

Professor Clarkson had office hours from three to six today, but it was nearly seven o'clock when Lucas arrived. Clarkson was at his desk, reading term papers. He was old-fashioned; while the school required that all homework be submitted online, the professor printed out his students' essays and wrote in their margins, returning the hard copy. People called him a dinosaur, but Lucas found him to be one of the most interesting of all his teachers. He'd been a criminal-defense lawyer, worked on several high-profile cases, and wrote a book about how the system failed both the guilty and the innocent. In the end, it was the best system of justice yet devised, and they only needed to work harder to make it work for everyone. Lucas had read the book twice.

He wanted that. He wanted to be that pillar of truth that Clarkson often talked about.

He knocked on the open door. "Sorry I'm stopping by after office hours," he said.

Clarkson looked up. "Nonsense. Come in, Lucas. It's not like I have anywhere else to be. Sit down, please."

Lucas was pretty sure that wasn't true. While the prof

wasn't married—Lucas heard through the grapevine that his wife had died in an accident a long time ago, and his only daughter was a corporate lawyer in California—Clarkson had many friends. And even though students called him old-fashioned, he was one of the most popular professors in the criminal justice department.

Lucas didn't know what to say. He knew what he *wanted* to say, but he didn't know how to talk about it. His friends either thought he was crazy for doing the podcast or thought it was a cool idea and had a hundred ways to help him—most of which were over the top. Lizzy had been a rock, but he'd complained to her far too much, and she had to be getting tired of it. Troy, his roommate, was a good person to talk to, but since he'd met Denise, Lucas thought he now only half listened to him.

So that left Professor Clarkson. Lucas hoped he didn't mind, but he trusted Clarkson more than anyone.

"Lucas? What's on your mind?"

"I don't know."

Clarkson leaned back in his leather chair. "You don't know why you came to talk to me?"

"Last night's podcast with Regan was excellent. I got a great response. Four times more calls than in the previous two episodes. Afterward, Regan seemed to be invested, and we talked about next steps… She got Candace's roommate to talk. Not to me, but Regan had me sitting in the room while they were on speaker. Now she's talking to Detective Young."

"And that's a problem?"

"No. Maybe. I don't know. What if he convinces her not to help me? I mean, I thought I could do this on my own, but I realized after last night that I need Regan's help."

Clarkson leaned back and steepled his fingers. "I'm not sure I understand why that would be the case."

Lucas squirmed in his seat, unsure what to say, why he'd even come here in the first place.

Finally, the professor said, "What do you think Regan can do that you can't?"

"I don't understand."

"Your proposal was to create a podcast to crowdsource information on where Candace Swain was for the week before her murder and ultimately find out who committed the crime. So far, you have made considerable progress."

"Yeah, we have. It's okay that I keep her on, right? She already agreed to come back on Friday."

"Of course. It was my idea, remember?" Clarkson smiled. "You're a smart young man, Lucas. I have enjoyed our time together, our conversations, your ability to see possibilities. You're going to go far in this world, in whatever your chosen career. Anyone who succeeds does so in part because they recognize when they need help, and take it when offered."

"I want to find the truth so bad. I want to know what happened to Candace."

"Everyone does, but some more than others," Clarkson said. "Do I need to be worried about you?"

"No. Why?"

"No particular reason." He said it in a way that suggested he in fact had a reason but decided not to share with Lucas.

"You think I'm obsessed."

"Are you?"

"Now you sound like a shrink or something."

Clarkson smiled. "Maybe I do." Then, more serious, he said, "It comes from years working as a criminal-defense lawyer. People have secrets. Most of the secrets they keep aren't criminal, just private. Yet, some secrets are worth dying for—or killing for. I have a confession to make. I suggested you bring Regan on board not just because I thought she might be able to help but because I am worried."

"About what?"

"You're airing a podcast where you are trying to find a killer. If you are right—and based on what I've heard, I think you are—Joseph Abernathy didn't kill Candace. If you get too close to the truth, you could get hurt. I don't want to see that happen."

"Regan said pretty much the same thing."

"Good. Then, she knows you're onto something."

Lucas actually did feel better talking it all out. "I appreciate your time."

"Stop by anytime."

Lucas left and walked across campus to the recording studio. Hoping to see if he might spot or identify the person who'd dropped off the anonymous letter, he'd already asked campus police if he could look at the building's security cameras; they'd said no. If there was a crime committed, they would review the footage. There was only one CCTV camera at the main door.

Entering the studio, Lucas saw a group was working in the main conference room, some sort of planning session. Pizza and sodas littered the table in front of them. He waved and continued on. The studio had the recording light on, so he passed it by. At the end of the hall, he turned right and unlocked his office door.

He grabbed a granola bar from his top drawer and munched as he checked his email. Nothing in any of the messages that might help him with his timeline of Candace's disappearance.

He kept thinking about the anonymous letter. Its writer knew more than what was on the paper. Lucas needed to talk to her, to convince her to share the details with him.

Spontaneously, he opened his web page editor and posted a message at the top of the main page, where all visitors would see it.

To the person who contacted me after Tuesday's episode: we need to talk. Pick the time and place, and let me know. * Lucas

Before he could change his mind, he hit Upload.

A knock on his door made him jump.

He opened the door.

"Lizzy."

"Scare ya?" she said with a laugh and handed him a bag from Crumbl Cookies.

He took the bag, at first confused. "You got me cookies?"

"I was out with my roomie, and we walked by. I was just lucky you were still here, otherwise I'd be eating it."

Inside was a giant chocolate chip cookie, his favorite. "Want to split it?"

"I already ate two."

She sat down and said, "How'd your convo with Clarkson go?"

"Good. I don't know why I was so nervous, but he gave me a pep talk."

He turned his computer screen around so she could see what he'd done.

"Think whoever wrote the note will reach out?" she asked.

"I hope."

They chatted while he ate his cookie. It was nice spending time with Lizzy. She told him about all the drama in her apartment—she lived in campus upper division housing with three other girls on the far southern tip of campus. Ten minutes later, he was laughing as much as she was.

"I'll walk you home," he said.

"My place is in totally the opposite direction from your place."

"But I can catch the bus down there, it's not a problem."

"Then great!" Lizzy said.

He locked up and they walked out. Lizzy was the first person—okay, the first girl—that had him not thinking constantly about his ex-girlfriend, Amanda. He'd tried dating for a while but realized that he compared everyone to his longtime high-school sweetheart. That wasn't fair to them, and he recognized that he wasn't over Amanda. But Lizzy…he didn't compare her. That had to be a good thing.

Except he had no idea what Lizzy actually thought about him, other than they were friends and they spent a lot of time together.

"Quiet all of a sudden," she said.

"It's cold." They headed down the path that led to the southern edge of campus.

"Snow's gone."

"Still cold."

"Can't argue with that. It just doesn't bother me."

He wanted to ask Lizzy out, but not now—not when he was in the middle of the project. Would she go out with him, knowing that he was going back to Phoenix as soon as he graduated?

"When I'm done with this podcast, maybe I can take you out or something."

"Depends."

He didn't expect that answer.

"Depends on what?"

"Do you want to take me out as a thank-you?" she said as she glanced at him. "Or on a date?"

He didn't know what to say to that. If he said as a thank-you, she'd never know how he was beginning to feel about her. If he said on a date and she wasn't interested, it would put their friendship in a weird place.

He really hated being this indecisive.

"Earth to Lucas Vega. What is it?"

"Date?" He squeaked out the word.

"Is that a question, or do you really want to go out with me?"

"I really want to go out with you." He cleared his throat. "But if you don't, I don't want you to think that I'm going to get all weirded out on you or anything. I mean, I can handle rejection and stuff."

"For a smart guy, you're really clueless."

They'd reached the quad that housed her apartment and she stopped, turned to face him.

Then she stood on her tippy-toes and kissed him. It wasn't a long kiss, but it was on the lips, and he stared at her in surprise.

She laughed. "Lucas, you're so damn cute, and you don't even know it. I'll see you tomorrow." She waved and walked upstairs to her apartment.

Half dazed, half confused, and fully happy, Lucas waited for the bus, barely even noticing the cold anymore. He really hadn't seen that coming.

* * *

Lucas was still thinking about Lizzy when he exited the bus and walked six blocks uphill to his apartment.

He didn't know when it happened, when he'd really got over Amanda and let himself be open to falling for someone else. Maybe it was a long time ago, but he'd been so obsessed with Candace Swain's murder that he couldn't see it. All he knew was that for the first time, he was optimistic—that even though it took him nearly four years to find a girl, he'd found someone he really liked, who was smart and funny and cute. Maybe it wouldn't work out. Maybe it would. But it was okay…because he felt like an unacknowledged weight had suddenly been lifted off his shoulders.

He was really looking forward to finishing this podcast, solving Candace's murder, and putting the past completely behind him.

When he reached his apartment door, he noticed the lights were all off: Troy must be out with Denise. He unlocked the door and as he opened it, he noticed a paper sticking out from under his mat. He picked it up and flipped on the lights.

Lucas dropped his backpack on the couch. The envelope was standard, plain and white. On the front, his name was written in a red Sharpie in thick, perfect block letters.

His stomach tightened. Something felt creepy, like he was being watched. But that was stupid—he was inside his apartment.

He looked out the front window. The street was quiet, dark, except for a streetlight on the corner. Cars were parked up and down both sides, which was common for this area. He didn't see anything out of the ordinary.

"Don't be so paranoid," he said out loud.

He opened the envelope. Written in the same red marker, in the same perfect block letters, was a short message.
LEAVE IT ALONE.

Twenty-One

After having one too many margaritas, Regan tossed her dad her car keys. She'd told him about Lucas's call and the threatening letter. "I know it's serious, not only because he called instead of texting me but because he sounded scared."

"He should call the police."

"I'll check on him first, see what's going on. You're probably right. It's not far from here." She wasn't drunk but figured her BAC was over the legal limit. She asked the waitress for coffee to go to help clear her head, then over her objection her dad took care of the bill.

Over dinner, she'd told her father about her divorce being final, as well as her decision not to return to the Marshals Service. Neither was unexpected, but both brought about a sense of closure that made her feel simultaneously lighter and sad. And her dad didn't judge her or question her, just accepted her decision.

She directed her dad to Lucas's apartment. "You can wait here, if you'd like," she said.

"I'd like to meet this young man," her father said.

Before she knocked on the door, Lucas opened it. "I'm probably overreacting, but...it's just weird."

"I'm glad you called," she said. "This is my dad, John Merritt," she said as they stepped inside. "Is your roommate home?"

"Troy's at his girlfriend's. I called him after I talked to you. He said the note wasn't there when he left at seven."

"I assume there are no security cameras?"

"No," he said. "I don't have a Ring or anything. This is a pretty safe neighborhood, you know—nothing much happens in Flagstaff."

Of course, having grown up here Regan knew that wasn't true. There were plenty of car thefts, burglaries, assaults, and rapes. Maybe to Lucas it just seemed that way because it was safer here than where he'd grown up in Phoenix.

"Where's the letter?" she asked. "I assume you touched it."

"I didn't know what it was. It could have been from my landlord."

Regan slipped on gloves that she'd had in her truck. Not that it would matter: Lucas's prints were all over it, and if someone didn't want to be identified, they would also have worn gloves. But it was a good habit to maintain, not touching potential evidence.

The standard white envelope was generic. The Sharpie and painstakingly formed letters helped disguise any distinctive characteristcs. It was difficult to tell if the writing was male or female.

The message brief and to the point.

LEAVE IT ALONE.

The author had put a period after *alone*, bold and larger than a dot, as if they held the marker down for a length of time. To punctuate the point? Or because they were angry? Thinking about writing more? Considering?

The red ink was ominous. Danger, a threat, blood. The method of delivery—at home, under the mat—sent another message: *I know where you live.*

The threat was subtle, but Regan was certain it was meant to coerce Lucas to end the podcast.

Regan asked Lucas for a plastic baggie, then slipped the letter and envelope inside so it could still be read. She handed it to her dad. "What do you think?"

"The police won't do anything. It's not a clear threat, but you should contact Detective Young and let him know about it."

Lucas glanced at Regan. "How'd your conversation go?"

She should have called him after, but that's when she'd received the divorce papers and she wasn't in the mood to discuss the podcast. "Can we talk about it tomorrow? I'll take you to breakfast."

"Okay," he said.

She took the baggie back from her dad. "May I keep this?" she asked Lucas.

"Sure." He glanced at John, then said to Regan, "I updated my website tonight. When I was at the studio, about an hour before I got home."

"Do you think that's relevant to this message?" she asked.

Lucas pulled out his phone and showed her what he posted.

To the person who contacted me after Tuesday's episode: we need to talk. Pick the time and place, and let me know.
* Lucas

"It's a good idea, but I wish you'd have talked to me about it first." A dozen thoughts were running through her head simultaneously. Who saw the update? Is the killer tracking the podcast or website? Were they concerned about this letter and what it might contain? Would they pretend to be the letter writer in an effort to get close to Lucas, find out what else he knew?

"Why?"

"I'm concerned about your safety."

"Because of this? Or because someone followed us last night?"

"You were followed?" John asked.

"I couldn't get the plates, but yes, someone followed us off campus. I lost them, but they could have followed Lucas earlier, know where he lives." She said to Lucas, "I don't know if this threat is just to scare you or if it's serious. But clearly, whatever you're doing has someone concerned. Maybe it's innocuous—someone at the sorority who is mad about the podcast. Maybe it's dangerous, someone who knows more about the murder—or the killer himself."

"Do you think whoever wrote the letter sent this threat? After knowing I want to talk to them?"

"No, I don't think so."

"I'm in the dark," John said. "What are you talking about? What letter?"

"Do you have it here?" she asked Lucas.

He went to his bedroom, and she said to her dad, "Someone left an anonymous letter at the studio for Lucas."

Lucas handed the letter to John. A moment later he said, "She knows something. You're right, it doesn't seem to be the same person who sent this latest message."

"Lucas, how do you normally get to and from the campus?" asked Regan.

"The bus."

"Do you have a car?"

"Yes, a pickup truck, but—"

"For the next couple of days, don't take the bus. Change your routine. Drive to campus. Take Uber. Go with Troy. Don't walk the same path to classes. Don't eat in the same place, don't go to the same coffee shop. Change your habits—at least until I can find out more information. You can't be too careful. Agreed?"

"I guess. But why? Do you think this is serious?"

"Part of my job was threat assessment. On the surface, this doesn't seem to rise to that level, but I want to be cautious. You might consider informing Detective Young, even though the note is vague. Get it on record in case it escalates. He might be able to ask patrol to drive by your place a couple times a day, make sure everything is okay. Tell Troy about it, too, just so he can keep his eyes open."

"If you think it's necessary."

"Personal security is always important. Just be careful. You're beginning to grow on me." She smiled, trying to make the conversation lighter so Lucas didn't get too freaked out. She recognized that her time as a marshal made her see the world through different lenses. Personal security had become part of her life, a part that had become so routine she barely noticed.

But even being smart, safe, and cautious couldn't protect everyone every minute of the day. She was a testament to that.

"Do you think Taylor James did this?" Lucas asked. "I mean, you talked to her this morning about the podcast. Maybe she knows where I live."

Possible, she thought. She opened the baggie with the note again and smelled deeply.

"What are you doing?" Lucas asked, his nose wrinkling.

"Taylor is a chain-smoker. Anything she touches would likely smell of nicotine. She seemed jumpy, agitated, angry to me. Defeated. Clearly she's not living the life she expected after graduating. I don't smell anything." She paused, considered. "But still I'll talk to her again. Do you mind if I check your windows and locks?"

"Go ahead."

She walked Lucas through basic home security measures. She wasn't sold that the note was a threat, but it was odd, and clearly geared to discourage Lucas from continuing the podcast.

Lucas agreed to meet her at Marcy's Grill at seven, then Regan and her dad left.

Back in her truck, John said, "You might want to hand this all over to Detective Young."

"You and I both know that the police won't do anything. They can't. There's no connection between a vague threat to Lucas and me talking to Taylor James, or even directly to his podcast. The police have sat on this case for three years. And after my conversation with Young today, barring any physical evidence linking another suspect to Swain's murder, his hands are tied. Other cases, other priorities."

Her father conceded that three years put the case at the bottom of the inactive pile. "But," he said, "while I trust your instincts, something Lucas said on the podcast—or you, last night—may have rattled Candace Swain's killer, if he's still in the area. You're on the right track…but are you going to find the answers before the killer panics?"

She didn't know. "Friday night's podcast will be very interesting. I'm going to have Lucas lay all his cards on the table and see what happens."

And if they did that, she would have to stick close to

him, in case they did ruffle the wrong feathers. Which meant she'd have to cancel her hike with Jessie in Sedona. Her best friend was not going to be happy.

From the Missing Journal of Candace Swain

Erica Jong said, "I have not ceased being fearful, but I have ceased letting the fear control me."

I am so scared. Not about doing the right thing, not anymore. I am in control of my decisions for the first time in years. I will no longer be manipulated, lied to, plied with guilt about how doing the right thing is wrong. Told that up is down, right is wrong, wrong is right. I'm so tired.

I am scared that they will stop me. But the only way they can stop me is to kill me.

Twenty-Two

Lucas couldn't sleep.

Finally, after midnight, he climbed into his old pickup truck and drove over to Taylor James's house. Regan was confident that Taylor hadn't sent the threat to him, so he didn't feel particularly scared to confront her, especially at this hour.

He never told his advisor his real motivation behind the podcast but justified that omission by knowing it was for the right reason. To find the truth.

He should have manned up, as his brother used to tell him when he was indecisive, and confronted Taylor months ago. But being run out of her bar had intimidated him, and the podcast idea seemed much safer—and smarter.

Most bars closed by midnight during the week, and he hoped to catch her when she was coming home. He'd thought about coming in the morning, before his breakfast with Regan, but if she had been working until late he didn't want to wake her up as it would probably make her less likely to talk.

He turned into her neighborhood, narrowly missing a Jeep driving with only the fog lights on. He flashed at the driver—they were going to get someone killed. Glancing in his rearview mirror, he saw that the driver flicked on his lights.

Lucas drove slowly past Taylor's house. One light was on in the back of the house, but that didn't mean she was home. Lucas's mom didn't like coming home to a dark house and always left the stove light on. He turned around in a gravel driveway down the street and looked for a place to park where Taylor might not be able to see him when she came home. Then he saw a car in her carport, behind the house. Dammit, she was home; would she even answer the door this late?

He had to try.

Lucas parked in front of her house and got out. He'd been thinking about how to approach her on the drive over, and thought he should tell her who he was and then tell her everything he knew about Candace and why he thought she'd been killed.

What are you hiding, Taylor?

Maybe if he came clean with her, she'd be honest with him. He'd show her the letter. Ask what they were arguing about. What was *really* going on between her and Candace the night she disappeared. Maybe even tell her his theory, the one he hadn't yet shared with anyone. If she slammed the door in his face, then he was back to where he was now, so it was worth trying.

Having a plan helped bolster his confidence.

There were few streetlights out here, it was dark, and the only sound was a television turned too loud in a house across the street.

He stopped pacing in front of his truck and walked to Taylor's front door and knocked before he could chicken out, then rang the bell for good measure. It wasn't as cold as last night, but it wasn't warm, and he immediately put his hands back in his pockets.

No answer.

Dammit. Maybe that car wasn't hers. Maybe she *was* asleep.

He went back to his truck and rummaged around for his notebook. He wrote out a note.

Taylor: We need to talk. You can remain anonymous— I promise. But I have information...and I know you do, too. Lucas Vega.

He didn't want to say anything too specific in case someone else read it, but he wanted Taylor to know that *he* knew a lot more about why Candace was killed so that she might agree to talk to him. If she'd come clean and tell him the truth, he would help her stay anonymous. There were ways to disguise voices on the radio: he could help her hide her identity.

Once he could get a confirmation of his theory, then he would share his story.

The *entire* story.

Without outside confirmation, he couldn't say a word.

Before he changed his mind, Lucas folded his note and was about to walk back to her door but then decided it was more likely that she would see the note if he left it under her car's windshield wipers.

He walked down the packed gravel-and-dirt driveway. When he saw Taylor's back-porch light on, he hesitated. Maybe he should knock on the back door.

Then he froze.

A covered patio, large enough for two lounge chairs and a small table, was illuminated by a sickly yellow light. Someone was lying on one of the chairs.

This was it. Now or never.

Lucas stuffed the note into his pocket and stepped out of the dark.

"Taylor? Hey, Taylor, it's Lucas Vega."

The woman didn't move. Was she sleeping? Passed out? *Dammit, Lucas, just leave the note and go!*

Even though she was thirty feet from him, she didn't look right. Maybe because the porch light was yellow, but her coloring was strange and her arm was hanging over the lounge. Even though it was chilly, she wasn't wearing a jacket; she didn't have a blanket or sleeping bag. Her head slouched at a strange angle, as if she were in a deep sleep, her mouth partly open.

Lucas stared at her arm. Then he saw the needle on the ground.

"Taylor?" Still cautious, he approached her slowly. "Taylor, are you okay? Do you want me to call someone?"

No answer. He reached her body and stared. Her eyes were half-open. He didn't want to touch her, but he had to wake her up because something was wrong.

He shook her gently. "Wake up. Taylor? You need to wake up."

Her body rocked under his hand, but she didn't move.

He jumped back. She was unconscious. "Oh shit, oh shit, oh shit."

Was she dead? He leaned over, tried to find her pulse. Was it there, on her wrist? Or was that wishful thinking?

"Taylor? Can you hear me?" He gently shook her body to see if he could wake her, but she was limp.

"Don't die. Please don't die," he said. "Dammit! you're the only one who knows what happened to Adele!"

He pulled out his phone and called 9-1-1.

Regan arrived twenty minutes after the paramedics. Taylor had been declared dead on scene, and she heard

rumblings about an overdose because they found drug para-
phernalia but knew there would be an autopsy to confirm.

Lucas stood next to a sheriff's patrol car because they
were outside the city limits. A plus.

Regan walked up, put her hand on Lucas's arm for support, and said to the deputy, "I'm Regan Merritt, a friend
of Lucas."

"Merritt—John's kid?"

"One of them." She looked at the badge of the young
deputy. "Deputy Prince? I don't think we've met."

"I started two years ago. But everyone knows the old
sheriff. I'm just getting Mr. Vega's statement."

"Lucas called me after he called 9-1-1. I saw the paramedics packing up without a body."

"The victim's dead. We've called for the coroner, their
ETA is sixty minutes." Prince looked at his notes. "I think
I have everything, Mr. Vega. And this is your correct ad-
dress?" He handed Lucas back his driver's license.

"Yes."

"A detective will be contacting you in the next day or
two to confirm your statement and may have more questions."

"Thank you, Officer," Lucas said politely. He looked upset.

"You okay?" Regan asked.

Lucas nodded, but he still didn't look comfortable.

Deputy Prince said, "Lucas was on the phone with the
9-1-1 dispatch trying to save her life. The paramedics said
you did everything you could. I know this is difficult, but
you tried, which is more than I can say for some people."

Prince asked her, "Ms. Merritt, did you know Ms. James?"

"I met her once. I wouldn't say I knew her."

"Can I get your contact information in case the detective has questions?"

She gave the deputy her info, and then Lucas asked Prince, "Can I go home?"

"Yes, you're free to leave."

Lucas walked over to his truck; Regan followed. "Lucas, why'd you come out here? Wasn't I just telling you not three hours ago that you needed to be cautious?"

"I know. I'm sorry."

She tried to look at the situation from his point of view. "So explain?"

"I thought I could just talk to her. Convince her to come on the podcast."

He handed her a crumbled note. She read it. "You were going to leave her this?"

"I didn't know if she was home. She didn't answer the front door when I rang the bell, but I saw her car in the carport. I thought I'd leave the note on the windshield."

"What information were you going to share?"

"Everything. All the research I've done, the facts of the case, the anonymous letter. I wanted to push her about what they were arguing about. I thought—maybe if I told her why I was so invested in Candace's murder, that she might be willing to help."

Regan hesitated. There was something odd about Lucas's tone, but she couldn't quite put her finger on it. She was about to ask *why* he was invested in Candace's murder, because it sounded like there was more to it than what he'd originally told her.

"It's my fault," he said.

"No, Lucas. This isn't on you."

"But it looks like she overdosed. There was a needle on the ground. What if she listened to the podcast? What if she did know more like we thought and killed herself on purpose out of guilt? Or…or she was upset and wanted to just get high but took too much? I don't know, but this is wrong. It's not fair."

"Taylor's choices are her choices, Lucas. Not yours. You can't be responsible for what other people do. Go home. We'll talk about this in the morning, at breakfast."

"I'm sorry. I should have called you before I came here."

"Yes, but I understand. It's going to be okay."

Lucas retreated to his truck and drove off.

Regan walked back to Prince as he was writing his report. "Deputy."

"Are you the US Marshal or the deputy from Maricopa?" he asked. "For my report."

"Good memory. Former marshal."

"I didn't work under Sheriff Merritt, but everyone liked him. I voted for him."

"So did I, once, when I was still living here. I'm biased." She smiled, putting the cop at ease. "Did Lucas tell you about his podcast?" She wanted to know exactly what Lucas had said to the cop. She had this nagging feeling he wasn't telling her everything.

Prince nodded. "I asked him why he was here so late, and did he know the woman? He said he wanted to talk to her about a podcast he was doing about her best friend's murder, and because she had been avoiding his calls and she works late, he'd hoped to catch her when she got off work. He was shaken, but that's to be expected. He was clear when he answered my questions. Do you think something else is going on?"

"I couldn't say. I've been helping Lucas and I talked to Taylor yesterday."

"Oh?"

"You can have the detective call me if he needs to, but I don't know what more I can say. All I know is that she was a recovering drug addict but apparently had been clean for a while. Went through rehab a while back."

"I've responded to far too many overdoses in my time, and often people who have been clean have the worst reaction. They don't realize they can't go back to the previous levels of self-medication."

"I hear you there." It was a logical conclusion.

"But I'll make sure the detective has your contact info. The paramedics said it was a likely overdose, but we'll make sure there's nothing else going on."

She thanked the deputy and walked back to her truck.

Did Taylor James overdose by accident?

Or did she OD on purpose?

Either way, Lucas was going to be troubled.

It didn't sit well with Regan, either. Something was off... It wasn't the first time she'd thought that, but the feeling was getting stronger. Now she had to figure out why.

Twenty-Three

Three Years Ago
Saturday, April 18

Candace had failed.

She sat on a rock, high up in the mountains as the sun set, and considered her options.

Go back to campus and pretend nothing had happened. She'd probably have to explain where she'd been and what she was doing; she would lie, of course. Because without evidence, she couldn't tell anyone the truth.

Go home. Find a way to take her finals online. Go do something with her life, anything, and get away from the toxic people at Sigma Rho. Try not to let the guilt destroy her.

Right. Because that's worked so *well for you...*

Go to the police. Tell them everything and...then what? Ruin her life, ruin others' lives, through innuendo because she had no proof of anything? No evidence, just her clouded memory. And if Taylor denied telling her the truth back then—what Candace knew to be the truth—why would anyone believe her now? And if they did believe her, what could they do about it?

Her head ached. She'd been living in a tent for the last four nights searching for answers in the middle of nowhere. She was tired and sore, and she hadn't showered, though she'd jumped in a small freezing-cold lake yesterday because she stank.

Four full days of searching for the body…and nothing.

Maybe Taylor had lied to her. Maybe she didn't remember correctly. Maybe Candace's research was flawed.

But she knew what the problem was. She had some tools—a shovel, rope, lights—but she couldn't go deep into any of the mines. It was too dangerous. She'd spent far too long trying to figure out *how* when she really should have spent the time figuring out what to tell the police.

Candace still didn't know what she was going to do, but she needed to at least go back to NAU and return the truck she'd borrowed—borrowed without permission—and pack up her dorm. She couldn't stay in the sorority, not anymore. She should have moved out long ago, but she hadn't had the backbone until now.

Richie would let her stay with him, she was pretty certain. If she hadn't burned that bridge along with all the other bridges she'd crossed.

When she packed up her tent and her supplies, she took one long look at the mountain she had scoured for four days. The proof was here. She just couldn't find it.

She climbed into the truck, and as soon as she had cellphone coverage, she took the prepaid phone she'd bought before she left Flagstaff and called Taylor. Taylor answered immediately.

"Hello?"

"Tay, it's me. Candace."

"Oh my God, where have you been?"

"I told you."

Silence.

"Don't do this," Taylor finally said. "Please don't."

"I didn't find anything. You win."

"It's not about winning, Candace, it's about survival."

"It's about doing the right thing."

"The police are looking for you. Everyone is. Annie reported you missing. What are you going to tell them?"

Maybe this was her chance. Her opening. And maybe, just maybe, they would listen to her, even if Taylor refused to back her up.

"Candace, tell me what you're going to do."

"I don't know."

"That's not an answer."

"Please, Taylor. Please understand that this is the *only* thing we can do."

"This is about that little punk, Lucas Vega, isn't it?"

"No." *Yes.* "Sort of."

"Don't do this to me."

"I'm not going to *do* anything to you, Taylor. But if you join me, we can give Lucas, we can give everyone, closure. It's the right thing to do."

"I don't know." Taylor sounded like she was on the verge of tears.

This was the opening she needed to convince Taylor to join her.

"I'll be back in less than three hours," Candace said. "Let's talk, just you and me." If she could get Taylor alone, convince her, they'd go directly to the police. Before anyone else talked to Taylor and changed her mind.

"Okay. Come to my dorm."

"No. I'm never going back there. The aquatic center, okay? It's private, it's quiet, just you and me, and we'll hash this out, and together we'll figure out what to do. I promise, Taylor, I won't do anything without you."

"You mean that?"

"Yes." *No.* She didn't know if she could trust Taylor, but she wanted to. Deep down, Taylor was a good person, she just needed to be reminded of that.

"Okay. Three hours. I'll be there."

Twenty-Four

Thursday

After only a handful of hours of sleep, Regan needed both food and coffee. She arrived at the diner at quarter to seven so she could caffeinate her system before Lucas showed up.

She saw Jessie sitting in her favorite corner booth and slid in across from her. "We didn't have a date, did we?" Jessie asked.

"Nope."

Susan brought over coffee. "What can I get you this morning?"

"Nothing yet. I'm meeting someone."

"No problem, let me know when you're ready." Susan walked away.

"Tripp?" Jessie asked.

"Why would you say that?"

"He's back in town. I see him in here all the time. I thought you knew."

"I ran into him the other day."

"He's always had a crush on you."

"Bullshit," she said.

Jessie laughed. "You're cute when you're angry. But you know I'm right."

"He's JT's best friend. I'm not even going there." She paused. "Jess, I have a conflict this weekend."

"You're fucking canceling on me?" Jessie said. "I won't let you. We haven't gone out *once* since you've been back."

"Lucas Vega was threatened, I need to keep him close," Regan said. "And he found one of Candace's friends dead last night. He took it hard, feeling guilty that his podcast may have led her down a dark road—it's a probable OD. He tried to save her."

"Poor kid, I get it, but dammit, Regan, the weather is finally perfect, and you're playing psychotherapist." She drained her orange juice. "Bring him with us."

"I doubt he could keep up. He's a beanpole and doesn't look too robust."

"I'm not happy."

"As soon as this is over, we'll go."

Jessie snorted, finished her waffles. "You're buying my breakfast."

"Fine."

Jessie nodded toward the door. "That's him, isn't it?"

"Yep." Lucas didn't look like he'd had much more sleep than she had.

"You're right. Scrawny. A hike would do him good."

Jessie got up, introduced herself to Lucas as he approached. "I'm Jessie Nez, Regan's best friend, and she bailed on me for you, so I hope you appreciate it."

"You're impossible," Regan said and shook her head.

"I gotta bolt. Dead deer off Route 66 in Bellemont. Doesn't seem to be a vehicle involved, but I need to check things out. Be careful, Regan."

"You, too, Jess."

Lucas sat down across from her and Susan came over with menus and more coffee for Regan. "Coffee for you?" she asked Lucas as she put a mug down before grabbing Jessie's empty plate.

He grimaced. "Yeah, I need it." He liberally poured sugar in his cup.

They ordered, and then Regan said, "How you holding up?"

"I didn't sleep. I feel awful about the whole thing."

"Like I said last night, Taylor's OD is not on you. How are we going to handle this on your podcast?"

"My plan was to recap what we know, read the anonymous letter, and then I guess now talk about Taylor's death. But I feel bad about that. I don't want to say she ODed without knowing it's true or not. Will they have the autopsy done by then? It's usually twenty-four to forty-eight hours, but I don't know if I'll be able to get it before it's official."

"You don't have to give cause of death. The media would say an *apparent* drug overdose, pending investigation."

"Right. So talk about that, and how people need to dig deep because what one person remembers another might remember more, and so on."

"We already have solid sightings. I'm particularly interested in the library sightings. And," Regan continued, "I think you need to share all the details about Candace's death. Beginning to end."

"I planned to. I just wanted to do this chronologically."

"That makes sense on paper, but consider this. You received a possible threat. We were followed. Taylor died, either on purpose or by accident, we don't know. And you have more information about Candace's death. You mentioned that she didn't die in the lake, but you need to reveal *all* the details. It will interest some people, horrify others, and they'll talk—and talking is where people will remember. Okay?"

He nodded. "I can do that."

Susan brought over their breakfast and poured more coffee. When she left, Regan said, "I want to talk to Richie Traverton, just to get his take on Candace and the investigation. You should be there."

"I don't know. You got more out of her roommate because she didn't know I was there."

"Think about it, okay? And I'd like you to research more about the sorority, Candace's peers, and the current president."

"Okay, but why?"

"Because if we find anything good, you need to expose it on the podcast."

"Expose? That sounds ominous."

"They're not talking, but I find it hard to believe that everyone there agrees on this. Isn't at least one person curious? And after Wagner gave me a hard sell about the mental health of the girls. I'm sure there are some who are seriously troubled by what happened, but so troubled that they want to shut down all conversation? It rubbed me wrong. Candace wasn't last seen at the sorority party, we know that now, but the reason she left in the first place may be directly connected to something that happened at the party. It's the only thing that makes sense. If we can stir the pot a bit, it might encourage one or more of them to break ranks."

"I like that idea. But I don't want anyone else hurt. Seeing Taylor last night… I just…" He looked pained, and Regan felt for the kid.

"She may not have intended to kill herself, Lucas. It could have been—probably was—an accidental overdose."

"Yeah—but on purpose or not, I didn't start this podcast to hurt anyone. I did it to find the truth."

"That's a good thing, Lucas. You can't blame yourself for the decisions other people make. The truth is always important."

He stared at his half-eaten meal, then said, "How about if you talk to Traverton, and I'll continue my research on the sorority as soon as I'm done with my morning class."

"Then, after that, we should go to Sunrise Center. You have a relationship already with the director, but it might be time to follow up."

"Okay. I have an afternoon class at two, so I can meet you there by four."

She agreed. "Remember what I said last night." Regan drained her coffee.

"Be careful, watch my surroundings, do things different than normal."

"You're a quick study."

Twenty-Five

After Regan learned from McCarthy's that Richie Traverton would come on shift at eleven, she spent the morning doing basic research. Having the Merritt name helped tremendously: anyone who'd lived in Flagstaff for more than ten years knew who her father was, and many of the old-timers still remembered her grandfather. Her generation remembered that her brother had broken the RBI record in high school—43. It didn't break the state record, but no one had matched it at their high school since.

People in the know informed her that Detective Young had a decent record. He'd made a lateral move from Phoenix PD four years ago after his divorce, bringing along his daughter, now nine. He had full custody, so there might be something to the rumors she'd heard about his "crazy" ex-wife. Not relevant, but it was always good to know as much as possible about the background and motivations of the people around you. The big plus was that he was considered a good cop; the big negative was that he rarely worked overtime and didn't pick up the slack, causing some friction among his colleagues. That could be because he was a single dad, or it could be because he was lazy, or a combination of both. The Candace Swain homicide was the first homicide in Flagstaff that he'd worked, but he hadn't been in homicide in Phoenix, which suggested that it may have been the first homicide he had *ever* worked.

After chatting with local cops who still knew and loved her dad, Regan headed over to the campus. She confirmed with NAUPD that security tapes were deleted after thirty days; nothing had been saved from the week Candace had disappeared, except for the dorm recordings from that weekend when she first went missing through the Sunday her body was found.

Young most likely had possession of that tape. She wondered why he hadn't requested more. But with a property that size, she supposed if he asked for the whole week for the entire campus it would be a substantial amount of data. By the time he'd learned that the victim hadn't drowned in the lake, the aquatic center recordings had been erased.

She also learned more about security at the library. Doors and windows that opened were wired. No motion sensors inside that might have tripped an alarm. Security cameras in the lobby, the information desk, the entrances, elevator interiors, technology wing, and rare-books room. That left more than half the square footage not covered by cameras, including none of the bathrooms or study rooms.

Regan decided to take a walk around the library herself to identify all the cameras. The library had changed quite a bit since she'd been there. The lobby had been remodeled and felt more open; the study rooms on the first and second floors now had glass walls, and they didn't feel as claustrophobic; and the technology center had moved over. The tech center had its own wing and a secondary door, which could be locked separately from the main library.

Where would someone hide at closing time? She was surprised by how much space was not covered by cameras—such as the entire third floor, outside of the elevator bank, and the staircases.

She had no idea what the exact process was for the librarians or security guards when they closed the building for the night. Did they do a walk-through to make sure no one was inside? Check each of the bathrooms? Each study room? If someone wanted to hide, Regan figured they could, if they were familiar with the library. After an hour of exploration, she determined that the best way to intentionally get locked in would be to stay on the third floor in one of the study rooms along the north wall. Candace could have easily hidden in the book stacks, then slipped into one of the rooms until the library officially closed. She could have slept there, and the bathroom on the third floor didn't have a lock, and there were no cameras between it and the study rooms.

But why? It made no sense to Regan why she would do that when she had a dorm room on campus, at least one boyfriend off campus, and her parents only a day's drive away.

If the callers from the last podcast episode were accurate, Candace was seen briefly in the library Monday night…and exited Tuesday morning. That suggested she stayed the night.

Without more information, Regan couldn't figure out the *why*.

Regan waited until after the lunch rush before she headed to McCarthy's to talk to Richie Traverton. She arrived at two and ordered a cheeseburger and sweet potato fries while sitting at the bar, the best place to engage in a conversation. The burger was good, and the fries were better than expected.

Regan's phone vibrated, and she had a text message from Rachel Wagner.

Vicky agreed to talk to you on the condition that I'm there with her. I don't think this is a good idea, but I agreed. Can we meet tomorrow?

She didn't immediately respond because Richie approached her at the same time and took her empty plates. "Can I get you anything else?"

She glanced around the sparsely populated bar in the middle of the afternoon. Happy hour started at four, so she was glad she had come now, before they got busy.

"Five minutes of your time. My name is Regan Merritt. I was hoping to have a word with you about your former girlfriend Candace Swain."

Richie was twenty-seven now, had dropped out of college after two years, and had been working here ever since. He was attractive though not her type: his hair was a little too long, his smile a little too cocky, his clothing a little too grunge, and he had a few too many tattoos. But she'd done her research and knew he was a responsible employee, respected by his coworkers, and had no criminal record. A year ago, he'd bought a small house up the hill from the pub, not too far from Lucas's apartment. Nothing expensive, but she'd driven by it on her way here and it was clean and well maintained.

He frowned at the mention of his former girlfriend. "Who are you again? The name sounds familiar."

"I'm doing research for the host of a podcast about Candace's disappearance and murder. You might have listened to it."

"That's it. Yes, I heard you the other night. You're the marshal."

"Former," she corrected.

"I've been ignoring Vega. I don't want to get in the middle of this."

"But you listened to the podcast."

"Wouldn't you?"

She nodded. "You might be able to help solve her murder."

"I talked to the police before and after Candace was killed. I know they were first looking at me because I was her boyfriend, but they know I didn't kill her."

"I believe you."

"So why do you want to talk to me?"

He didn't seem defensive, only curious. She liked his straightforward personality.

"Since you've listened to the podcast, you know what Lucas is trying to do."

"Figure out where she was before she died. Right. And I told the police I didn't know. And I don't. Candace was her own person. I cared about her, a lot, but I knew it wasn't going to last. She was planning to leave Flagstaff, and I'm not. I love it here, my mom is here, my grandmother, my little brother. I can ski in the winter, and there's nothing better than loving where you live."

"I agree. Born and raised here."

"So you get it. And Candace would never be happy living here for the rest of her life. And I guess, well, I loved her too much to push her to stay and didn't love her enough to follow wherever she went."

Pretty astute observation from a twentysomething.

"All I know," Regan said, "is what the media reported, what her roommate said, what her sister said. But you really knew her."

"No one really knew Candace. I might have known her better than most, but even I suspected she was different around me than she was around others, if that makes any sense."

"A woman of a thousand faces."

"In a way. Excuse me." He stepped aside to refill a pint for an older guy at the end of the bar and to ring up a tab for another customer. He returned a few minutes later. "So what do you want to know?"

"Why didn't you respond to Lucas Vega when he reached out to you?"

Richie shrugged. "I didn't know what he planned to do, and I'm actually pretty busy. I work here full-time and work on ski patrol in the winter. And I didn't want him to use me to create some sort of, I don't know, tell-all about my dead girlfriend. She deserves more respect than that."

"So you're saying he didn't make it clear what the podcast was about."

"Right. All he said was that he was doing a project for his capstone about Candace's murder and wanted to interview me."

"Now that you've listened, do you have a different perspective?"

He shrugged. "Maybe."

"Where do you think Candace was that week?"

"I don't know. I've thought about it a lot, but other than her sister, she wasn't all that close to anyone. She had a lot of friends, but no close friends."

"Did she have a friend that she might have visited? Maybe just a casual friend? In or around Kingman?"

"Yeah. I thought about it after I listened to the caller who saw her there. One of the Sigma Rho girls who had already graduated lived there, and I wondered if she was who Candace had visited. Now that I think about it, they were pretty tight—it wasn't the first time she'd driven out there. But not so close that Candace talked about her a lot."

"Do you know her name?"

"Sorry, I never met her. Candace might have mentioned it once or twice, but I don't remember."

It should be pretty easy to find a sorority sister from Kingman.

"So that caller didn't surprise you."

"No."

"What about the library? I walked through there this morning, and there are several places she may have hidden."

"Hidden? Like, you're thinking she spent the night?"

"Yes."

"I guess it's possible, but why?"

Million-dollar question, she thought.

"I'm trying to think like her, figure out what her plan was, if she even had a plan. Or if she might have been scared or intimidated or worried. You were close to her."

"I really wasn't," he said quietly. "I wanted to be. But Candace didn't let anyone inside. I guess three years ago I didn't care all that much. She liked me, we had fun, sex was great, she was smart, and I always had the feeling she came over to my place because she wanted to get away from her sorority."

"Do you know if she was having problems with any of the girls there?"

He shrugged. "I couldn't tell you."

"Taylor James?"

He frowned.

"You know her."

"Not well."

"But?" she prompted.

"They used to be best friends, but something happened, and Candace said Taylor wasn't the person she'd thought she was."

"What about Kimberly Foster?"

"Don't know her."

"Annie Johnston?"

"Candace's roommate? Real sweet. Kinda on the wholesome side. Annie was the only one who Candace brought here, like when she'd stop in here to see me. She'd come alone or with Annie."

"Do you know if Candace had a second phone? Or access to a vehicle that wasn't hers?"

"Now that you mention it, I saw a flip phone in her purse the last time I saw her. She was here, had her purse on the bar, and I commented on it. What happened to your phone? I think I said. She said it had a cracked screen so she got a prepaid one until she got it fixed. Something like that. It was in passing."

Interesting...and odd. There was no mention of a prepaid phone *or* a nonworking smartphone. In fact, Annie had mentioned the many calls Candace was getting, and the notifications on her screen. It could have been cracked, but it was functional.

"Is that important?" he asked her, interested.

"Possibly. According to the police report, she made no outgoing calls, nor did she answer her phone or respond to messages, after Friday night. You were the last person she called. And you know now that she wasn't killed in the lake."

"Right. Vega said she drowned in chlorinated water, like a pool."

"Do you know who she might have been with who had a pool?"

"No, I mean, a lot of people have pools. She loved the aquatic center because it reminded her of her little sister. She talked about Chrissy all the time. In fact, I went to her funeral and met Chrissy for the first time. She's a sweet kid, heartbroken. I reached out a few times, sent her some pictures I thought she might like, of Candace and me. She seemed to appreciate it."

That was a thoughtful gesture, she thought.

"Did Candace ever mention Joseph Abernathy to you?"

"No. I mean, I had heard about him from the police and everything, but she never mentioned him. Like I said, she didn't talk much about herself or her life. She was very private."

"Can you think of any place she might have gone where she felt safe, or disappear to while she was maybe studying or collecting her thoughts? A person or place?"

"Other than her sister, no. When Chrissy said she hadn't talked to Candace, when Candace was still missing, I figured she was dead. Because there wasn't a week that went by that she didn't talk to her sister. So when I found out that she was alive that whole week? It surprised me."

"Was Candace having problems with anyone on campus?"

"If she was, she didn't tell me. There was one odd thing, though. Candace was in an off mood one day after tutoring, and then she quit the writing lab suddenly. She liked tutoring there because it gave her a break from the hard sciences she was studying. She was very creative and a really good writer. I asked her why. She got paid for it, and I know she was saving up so she could go on a trip with Chrissy over the summer, after her graduation. She said she needed to focus on school for the last semester."

"Makes sense."

"Not for Candace. She had outstanding grades. She didn't struggle academically. And—well, I thought she was lying. I don't know why, but it sounded like an excuse to me. Not what she said, but how she said it."

"I really appreciate you talking about this, Richie," she said. "If you can think of anything else—especially where Candace might have gone that week—I'd encourage you to call in to the podcast."

"I really don't know where she went. I've thought about it all week since I listened to it, and her disappearance just doesn't make any sense. Are you sure that this Abernathy guy didn't kidnap her? Hold her captive somewhere? I mean, I know that she wasn't assaulted, you know, like that, but maybe it was something else."

"I suppose anything is possible, but I think Abernathy is way down on the list. He was a barely functioning alcoholic." She paid her bill and said, "Oh, one more thing. Do you know about Candace's journal?"

"I know she had one, but I never saw it. She told me she'd been keeping it since she was thirteen, when her parents were going through their divorce. Candace said journaling helped her more than talking to the psychologist they sent her to. That I understood. I've always preferred writing out my problems than talking about them. Why do you ask?"

Regan had been hoping Richie had the journal or knew where it was.

"The police never found it in her room or car."

"That's weird," he said. "That journal was important to

her. I had a feeling that she wrote down things she wouldn't say out loud."

He was right. Weird. And suspicious.

Because now Regan thought her killer took it. And maybe the reason Candace was killed in the first place was because of something in her journal.

Twenty-Six

After his morning class, Lucas grabbed a sandwich and went to his office in the communications building. He propped the door open with his garbage can because the small window didn't open and the room was stuffy.

He had a list of everything he needed to investigate about Sigma Rho and the girls who went there, both with Candace and before her time. He'd done basic research before launching his podcast—he knew the names and graduation status of every girl who was at Sigma Rho during the time Candace was there. But finding most people after graduation hadn't been his focus.

He started reading the Sigma Rho newsletters from her first year. The rush class, pictures of the girls, events, names. Candace was all over it: she had been popular then as well as when she died.

"Hello!"

He jumped.

Lizzy stood in his door and laughed. "Scared ya." She pushed aside the garbage can so she could walk in. "Whatcha doing?"

"Researching the sorority."

"Fun. Need help?"

"It's not fun."

She sat on the chair across from him. "Maybe I just want to spend time with you."

He warmed at the thought. Lizzy was flirty—she always had been, he now realized—but he'd never thought she was interested, until last night.

"You can start digging into Vicky Ryan while I finish reading these newsletters." He pushed over his notebook where he had a list of questions about Vicky Ryan.

"It *is* fun. I'm looking for dirt."

He quickly wrote out the other names he was looking at—every name that had come up over the course of his research—and slid that to her. "If Vicky has a connection with any of these girls, make a note."

"You think she's the one who killed Candace?"

"No."

"Then, why do this?"

"Candace mentored her, she was at the party, and she doesn't want anyone in the sorority to help us solve Candace's murder. And Regan put her on the list."

"I like her."

"Vicky?"

"Regan. She's a sharp tack. All calm, cool, and collected. I can totally see her as a badass marshal. Do you know why she left?"

"Not really. I know her son died, but Professor Clarkson didn't say anything more."

"That's so sad."

They worked in silence for several minutes.

Lucas went through each person on his list, starting with Kimberly Foster, the alumna who had allegedly been a witness to the argument between Candace and Taylor.

Kimberly Foster—middle name Anne—was from Payson, Arizona, a small mountain town famous for hunting and gold mining, though that industry had mostly dried up decades ago, going from over eight thousand mines to fewer than three hundred. Still, it was a nice area to camp, fish, hike, and hunt. Lucas and his brother used to go up there to fish with his grandpa, before he died when Lucas was in high school. They were some of his favorite memories.

Kimberly had graduated cum laude from the Health and Human Services College. He wished he could do a wide search on the Sigma Rho website, but all the newsletters were PDF documents, and he had to search each one separately, which was time-consuming. He almost wished he had asked Lizzy to split the newsletters with him.

He found Kimberly's rush statement, which clearly showed she was an overachiever.

Extracurricular activities in high school: Varsity Cheerleading, 4 years. Captain, senior year. Student Council, 4 years. Senior Class Vice President. Varsity Cross-Country, 4 years. Peer tutoring, 4 years. Debate Club, 2 years. Class Valedictorian.

Rush Statement: Sigma Rho is the only sorority I wanted to join. The smart women here are focused on the future, with the overwhelming majority majoring in science and math. I am an only child and have always wanted sisters— joining Sigma Rho would complete me in ways that only another only child would understand. My strengths are organization, coalition building, and loyalty. I will always support my sisters in whatever they choose to do, and I look forward to lifetime friendships.

Lucas cringed. Were all of these things so sappy? Maybe he was being negative because the sorority had closed ranks and wouldn't talk to him.

He saved each page to his desktop so that he could review them later. He already had all of Candace's information; it had been one of the first things he'd done. He found Taylor James, Annie Johnston, Alexa Castillo, who Annie had mentioned as having volunteered with Candace, and Vicky Ryan.

He then started running a variety of Google searches on Kimberly Foster, and after several tries, he found her.

Kim was now the public information officer for the largest biotech company in the southwest. She made six figures and lived in Old Town Scottsdale in a condo now worth more than $600,000. She was single but had dated a professional baseball player, as well as the CEO of a software company. Kim had been profiled as one of the Top 30 Women under 30 in a statewide business magazine last year.

She had done very well for herself. He wondered if she would talk to him, or Regan, about Candace. He saved her social-media pages and her work email and phone number and made a note to talk to Regan about how to approach her.

Kimberly Foster had been privy to the fight between Taylor and Candace, and now two of those three were dead.

He looked again at Candace's profile. She'd been so optimistic in her rush statement, but then seemed quite different as a senior.

Rush Statement: When I came to NAU, I was homesick. I have a little sister I love and miss so much that I thought about dropping out and going back home. Instead, I found Sigma Rho and knew as soon as I stepped in the front door that this was my place. The support and love from girls I just met sustains me and helps me overcome missing my own family. Now I have a house full of sisters, and I could not be happier. I hope to help create an atmosphere of volunteerism and community service, for the campus and our community at large. The future has never looked so bright and shiny, and I look forward to what it holds for both me and all my sorority sisters.

She sounded so happy, Lucas thought. But then as a senior…she sounded just like he felt, pessimistic. Aren't you supposed to be happy, the world-is-your-oyster type of happy, when you're on the verge of graduating from college with a degree in the field you love?

NAU Accomplishments: Volunteering and community involvement, including building homes for homeless veterans; working at Sunrise Center homeless shelter; reading to pediatric cancer patients; creating and maintaining the Greek Life Food Drive that last Thanksgiving bought four hundred and twenty turkeys for struggling families.

What do you plan to do when you leave NAU? Since I was little, I have wanted to be a nurse and take care of people. I have always wanted to give back, to help people, to do something more for my community, so I volunteered each academic break and summer to aid those who needed a helping hand. I want to continue a life of service.

What advice can you offer the incoming rush women? Trust yourself and don't let anyone make you feel less.

*Senior Quote: "The future influences the present just as much as the past." * Friedrich Nietzsche*

Odd quote, he thought.

Odd, and he feared he might have had something to do with Candace's negativity. He hoped not, but he couldn't help but think about his last conversation with her, and his suspicion about why she no longer wanted to tutor him.

He put Candace aside and turned to Taylor James. He looked at the photo of Taylor from first year and mentally juxtaposed that image with how he had found her, dead of a drug overdose. A pang of guilt overwhelmed him. He couldn't help but think that he'd had something to do with her death. That because he was pushing the investigation into Candace's murder, Taylor had gone back to using drugs.

Stop it, he told himself. Regan had reminded him that it was Taylor's choice, which he understood intellectually, and he couldn't figure out what he could have done different. But his heart hurt.

He believed that she knew more about Candace's disappearance than she'd told anyone.

Could she have killed her?

"What?" Lizzy said.

"What what?" he asked.

"You just said something. Were you talking to me?"

"Guess maybe thinking out loud. What if Taylor James killed herself out of guilt? What if she killed Candace?"

"Whoa, slow down, Lucas. You've really jumped the shark."

"Have I? Consider that Taylor and Candace fought about something. Everyone claimed it was about Joseph Abernathy, but then we get that letter that it was about something completely different, and the odd call. Maybe Taylor kills her accidentally, panics, moves the body, covers up the crime. But she feels guilty and starts doing drugs."

"I can see it, but do you have any evidence?"

Of course he didn't, and she knew it.

"Now she's dead," he said. "And if she *did* kill Candace, I'll never prove it."

"Stop with the fatalism. Breathe. Now, you wanted info on Vicky Ryan?"

"Find anything?"

"Nothing particularly interesting. She's a nursing major, an overachiever. Loves planning parties, loves socializing, has her photo all over everything. Outgoing. Pretty. From a teeny-tiny town west of Phoenix, called Buckeye. No boyfriend now, though had one until the fall. Her best friend is Nicole Bergamo, a math major. I actually know Nicole. We're not besties or anything, but I was in a couple classes with her. She's super smart, totally like—who's that guy?—the *Beautiful Mind* guy, she just gets math on a level most people don't. I think she wants to teach, but I could remember it wrong. Anyway, they're roommates, have been for all four years, so they must be tight. Oh, shit. I need to run. I can't be late for my class."

"I'm already late," he groaned. "Go, I'll wrap up here." Maybe even skip his class. He had an A: he could get the notes from someone.

She leaned over and gave him a quick kiss. "See you later."

Lucas watched Lizzy leave, thinking about her, them, what might be, then he shook his head to clear it. Thinking about the future wasn't going to get the work done.

He finished going through all the sorority girls on his list. As he pulled down Alexa Castillo's profile, something jumped out at him.

Hometown: Kingman, Arizona.

Was that a coincidence? That a sorority sister who graduated the year before Candace was from Kingman? Had she returned after graduation? Were they close?

Could Candace have been visiting her that weekend?

If so, why didn't she come forward?

He did another quick search but couldn't find Alexa Castillo anywhere on social media. It was a common name, but no one fit on Facebook or Twitter or Instagram. He searched for alumnae news in the Sigma Rho newsletters: nothing. The only thing he could find was her senior statement, where she said she planned on teaching elementary school. Nothing about where she would be teaching, no follow-ups.

He looked at his phone and realized he was going to be late meeting Regan at Sunrise Center.

He quickly packed up his backpack and left.

Twenty-Seven

Regan arrived before Lucas at Sunrise Center, though he'd texted her and said he was running late. She introduced herself to Willa March, who was happy to give her a tour of the facility while they waited. Willa was sixty, tall and slender, with blue eyes and gray hair.

The homeless shelter was on the edge of downtown, more than a mile east from the northern boundary of the NAU campus. It was in a semi-industrial area, away from homes, near public transportation, an urgent-care facility, and two churches. Willa had done an excellent job making the facility look inviting. It had once been a church and small school. The church was now the dining and recreation hall, the garden that separated it from the school was clean and well-maintained, with several tall trees in the center, and the school had been converted to both offices and dorm-style rooms for men. A building in the back—Willa said it had once been a strip mall—had been refashioned into small two-room apartments for families, mostly women with children.

"We have four full-time staff members, including myself, and dozens of volunteers. A drug counselor is here through a county program two days a week," Willa said. "We can have a maximum of forty men in the dormitory, and six families in the apartments. I have a temporary permit for two four-bed dorm-style rooms for women downstairs, but usually the women here come in with their children. One person is on duty at night, and we have a staff suite."

"The facility is impressive. Clean and functional."

"We've accomplished so much from our humble beginnings. The city and the county provide some of our funding, churches provide most of the volunteers and help with the food program, and we have generous donors. Our clients work to keep the facility clean."

Lucas approached them as they were talking in the garden. "Sorry I'm late. Hi, Ms. March."

He glanced at Regan, and she knew that he'd found something, but he didn't say anything.

"Willa. I told you," the director said.

Because it was a pleasant afternoon, in spite of a steady wind, they sat outside at a picnic table. Regan noted that four men were gardening on the opposite side of the yard, and two young mothers were watching five children play on a jungle gym. Regan stared a moment too long, memories of her watching Chase laughing as he swooshed down the tall slide at their old neighborhood park. The feelings of grief and sorrow were momentarily overwhelming. She almost got up to leave, but she buried it. Pushing it aside gave her a headache.

She also felt something unfamiliar, a bittersweet sensation that swept over her. Chase was gone, she'd never hug him or watch him play or see his eyes light up when they went to baseball games. But she could remember. For the first time, her memories weren't solely clouded by pain.

She averted her eyes, redirected her attention fully to the matter at hand. If anyone noticed her emotions, they didn't say anything.

Lucas said, "Did you listen to the podcast this week?"

"Yes," Willa said. "You want to talk to me about the gentleman who called in."

"Yes. Do you know who he was?"

"I believe I do. I haven't seen him here in a while, but I know he has a steady job. Travels for work."

"Who is he?"

"I don't feel comfortable saying, considering he didn't share his name with you."

Regan said, "But you do remember him coming to you about Abernathy sleeping near the tracks."

She nodded. "He—I'll call him Doe, for clarity—had lost so much in such a short time. He needed us, to help him get back on his feet. He could have gone the way of Joseph, all too easily. Loss, pain, suffering—it can destroy a soul. Some people never find their way out of the abyss."

"Like Joseph Abernathy," Regan said.

"Yes. I don't know his story. He never shared it." She reached up and played with a crucifix hanging from a simple gold chain around her neck. "But I saw it on occasion, because I have worked with men like Joseph for more than thirty years. My father had been in Vietnam. He came home a different man, turned to alcohol, left. I don't say he left *us*, though he did and my mother resented him and her plight, but he didn't really leave us. He left because he felt he had no hope, no future, and drinking numbed the pain. He died. I didn't know until years later. I say he died of hopelessness. But he drank himself to death. Joseph was doing the same thing, but I felt that, with patience and firm boundaries, he might see a path out. We don't allow alcohol or drugs here but take in those suffering from addiction. They come here, try to get clean, we give them help—counseling, medical attention, food, fellowship—but men like Joseph can only take it for a short time before they leave to drink. It was a cycle. But I would—we would—never turn him away for a meal. So I saw him regularly back then."

"But he often left, correct?" Lucas asked. "He didn't live here year-round."

"No, he would jump on a freight train and disappear for months at a time, usually in the winter months," Willa said. "But three years…that's too long. I agree with Doe. Something must have happened to him."

Regan steered the conversation back to Candace. "Candace volunteered here for several years."

"Yes. I adored her. She was kind and compassionate and would have made a wonderful nurse. Maybe she was too compassionate. I know, that sounds odd coming from someone like me, because I try to always see the good in people, but I also recognize that some people are beyond help. You can only hold out your hand so many times for people to grab onto before you get bit one time too many. I told Candace to call the police if Joseph showed up on campus again. Not because I thought he would hurt anyone but because, if confronted, he could become belligerent. Someone *could* get hurt—or someone could hurt him."

"Do you think he killed her?"

"Before meeting Lucas earlier this year, I would have said yes, I think it was possible but unlikely. Not because he had a problem with her, but when he was drinking he sometimes lashed out. Hit someone, pushed them. Could he have pushed Candace and accidentally killed her? Yes, I could see that. But now that I know exactly how she died, I don't think Joseph had the mental capacity to move her body, cover up evidence, disappear. Not with what I knew of him."

"What about someone else?" Regan said. "Someone here who might have become fixated with her. Someone she tried to help, or maybe someone who she couldn't help."

"The police asked me similar questions three years ago. I can't think of anyone. People with mental illness and serious drug addiction can become unpredictable, but to the point of murder? No one then had any issues with Candace, not anger or a fixation or anything that would put her in danger."

Lucas said, "Did you follow up on Doe's sighting of Joseph near the tracks?"

"Yes, but this was before I knew Candace was dead. I went down there with one of my employees on Thursday or Friday, I don't remember exactly. It was after she was missing. He wasn't there. No one had seen him that day."

"Candace was a regular here," Lucas said, "but I learned that she sometimes brought others to volunteer."

"Yes, especially during the holidays. She had many girls in the sorority helping with food drives."

"Did a student named Alexa Castillo work with her?"

"Alexa? Yes! I haven't seen her in years. She came with Candace several times. Kind, very quiet."

"So would you say she was a regular?"

"Semiregular. She probably volunteered ten, twelve times? I keep track of my volunteers, but it was quite some time ago, so I would have to look up the records."

"That's okay. That's all we need now."

They thanked Willa for her time, and Regan walked Lucas to his truck, which was parked down the street from hers.

"What do you think?" he asked her.

"I think it would be difficult for that woman to cover up a murder to protect the killer. She doesn't seem to have motive to lie. Now, you asked about Alexa. Why?"

"I might have found something," Lucas said. "Candace was in Kingman. Alexa Castillo is from Kingman. She graduated the year before Candace. I tried to find her, but she doesn't appear to have any social-media profiles, and the name is too common to do a broader internet search. A basic search came up with more than a dozen in Arizona alone. There's nothing about her in any of the alumnae news, but she majored in elementary education."

"That confirms what Richie Traverton told me." Regan gave Lucas the basic rundown on her conversation with Richie, including that he'd seen Candace with a prepaid flip phone the week before she disappeared. "Richie said she was close to a sorority sister in Kingman. It's not a large city."

"Only three Sigma Rho members are from Kingman who overlapped with Candace."

"You *have* been busy," Regan said. "What do you want to do about it?"

"Like you said, lay everything out for my listeners. Tomorrow's podcast is going to be explosive."

"I'll see what I can do to track down Alexa Castillo."

"I'll send you everything I have on her," he said. "But I found something else." He reached into his back pocket and handed her an envelope. The same type of red letters spelled *LUCAS* on the front as the note from yesterday. It wasn't sealed, the folded paper simply tucked in.

She unfolded it.

END IT NOW.

Like the first note, there was no explicit threat. But the message was clear: *I know who you are, I know where you live, I know the car you drive. I can find you if you don't do what I want you to do.*

It was an intimidation tactic, pure and simple.

Twenty-Eight

"We need to talk to Detective Young," Regan said. "He should be aware that your podcast is riling up someone on campus or nearby. Someone who may personally know you. It's for your protection."

"No one I know would do this," he said.

"Someone followed us. They know where you live, they know the car you drive. They could have been following you for a while, or may have access to college records."

"I don't have a parking pass."

She pointed to a sticker on his rear window.

"That's just so I can park in the student lots cheaper, as a commuter student."

"The university keeps records. Trust me, for someone who has accessed the university system, it's not difficult to find info—especially for a staff member or student who works in one of the administrative offices."

She pulled out her cell phone and dialed Young's number. It took him a few rings to answer.

"Young."

"It's Regan Merritt."

"Is something wrong?"

"Possibly. Can I meet you at the station?"

"I'm off duty. It's dinnertime. What's this about?"

"Lucas Vega has received two vague warnings connected to his podcast, which the note writer wants him to stop. They are not overtly threatening, but I think you should be made aware of the situation."

"Duly noted. Drop the notes at the station to my attention, and I'll see if there's anything similar in the system, do an analysis of the notes. I don't know how fast I can get it done—are they direct threats to harm him?"

"No threat of violence, but it's implied."

"I'll do what I can."

"Thanks, Steven," she said and ended the call. She needed to keep on his good side because she had a feeling they might need him sooner rather than later.

Regan added the note to the same large plastic envelope as the first, which was still in her truck. "I'm going to follow you to your apartment, Lucas," she said. "Make sure everything is kosher inside, then go home. Tomorrow what time do you need to be on campus?"

"I don't have any classes on Fridays. I'm going to the studio about an hour before the show. We air at seven on Friday."

"I'll pick you up at your apartment at five thirty. Can you stay inside for the day?"

"Why? I mean, these notes don't mean anything. They just want to scare me."

"We don't know what they will or will not do, but you need to be cautious. Promise?"

After Regan made sure that Lucas's apartment was secure, she dropped the notes off at the police station in a large envelope labeled with Young's name, then left town for her dad's house. It was nearly eight. He was listening to sports news on the television while reading a book on World War II.

"I ordered out for pizza," he said. "Enough for both of us. Should be here in twenty, thirty minutes."

"Late for dinner."

"I suspect you didn't eat." He put his book down and smiled.

"All in a day's work. Do you mind if I use your office for a bit?"

"You don't have to ask."

She felt she did. This had been her home growing up, and she still thought of it as her home, but it was mostly her dad's place now. He had done so many things to make it his space.

She was going to have to think about finding her own place. She just didn't know where and wasn't even sure what she wanted: staying here, heading down to Phoenix closer to her brother JT and sister, Bri, or someplace completely different. If she didn't know what she wanted to do with the rest of her life, and if she didn't have a plan, how could she put down roots?

She pushed all that aside and sat at her dad's desk. She had a laptop, but she preferred her dad's larger screen and faster computer. Plus he had a dedicated phone line for the internet, since the Wi-Fi connection wasn't strong.

She pulled up her email. Lucas had in fact sent her not only everything he'd found on Alexa Castillo—which wasn't much—he also had information about Kimberly Foster, Vicky Ryan, and others.

He was right in that Alexa Castillo didn't have any social-media profiles, but if she was a teacher, Regan knew how to dig around and find her. It took a while—her dad brought her two slices of pizza and a beer—but through a series of education links and news articles, she learned that Alexa taught second grade at one of the three elementary schools in Flagstaff. Prior, she'd done a year of student teaching in her hometown of Kingman. Which meant she would have been in Kingman when Candace was seen there three years ago.

Is that who Candace had met with?

Likely, Regan thought. Very likely.

She couldn't find a phone number for Alexa, but she had the school name, and tomorrow was Friday. Regan would track her down at work. If Alexa could confirm their suspicions, she might also know exactly what had been going on with Candace that week.

Regan had created her own timeline of events based on what Lucas had started. She wondered why someone would leave a second note less than twenty-four hours after the first one. To make sure he got the message? To underscore the threat?

Her phone rang. She glanced at the screen: Rachel Wagner.

"Merritt."

"Hi, Regan, it's Rachel Wagner. I sent you a message earlier. I wanted to make sure you got it."

"I'm sorry I didn't respond. What time is good for you and Vicky?"

"Anytime tomorrow. I only have a class in the late morning, and I have office hours after lunch. So either before my class starts at eleven or after two."

Regan wanted to talk to Alexa right when school got out, so she said, "Morning would be better."

"Ten? Is that good? My office. I'll ask Vicky to meet us there."

"Ten. Thanks."

She ended the call, put her work aside, and went out to the kitchen to finish her pizza with her dad. They ate in silence for a few minutes. They'd eaten a lot of pizza in their lives, but Regan never grew tired of it.

"Lucas got another note today, almost identical to the first," she said as she grabbed her third slice. Her dad was like her: they both loved their pizza loaded. All the meat, all the veggies, the more toppings the better. Made it messy, but there was nothing better.

"Did you talk to Young?"

"Yes. I dropped off the threatening notes at the station on my way home."

"If the notes are from the killer, it means he is within listening distance of the station."

"Not necessarily," she said. "He could be streaming or listening to the podcasts after the fact."

"Except that someone personally delivered the notes."

True, she thought.

"I wonder if he's tipping his hand," her dad continued. "Since he's remained at large all this time, silence would be the smarter move."

"Criminals are not always smart. And the notes may not be from the killer."

"Then, why would they want to shut Lucas up? Whoever is trying to intimidate him doesn't want the truth to come out."

"That, or someone in the sorority doesn't like the podcast because she thinks it makes them look bad, or someone's messing with him."

"Do you believe that? It's a joke?"

"No. I think—well, I don't know, to be honest. I was leaning toward someone at Sigma Rho. The current sorority as a whole doesn't want the podcast aired. They closed ranks and won't talk to him. I had that confirmed by an alumna who got a message from the sorority suggesting that no one speak to him, and from a current sister who wanted to give us information but not use her name. But I'm meeting with the president tomorrow, and I'm hoping to get more answers. The veiled threat feels more like someone who isn't going to act on it, but I can't be certain."

"Any idea who wrote the anonymous letter?"

"No. I have an idea, but I need to confirm it. It was someone who attended the party, an alumna. They want the truth exposed, but don't want to be the one who talks."

"Loyalty in Greek Life is both good and bad, same with us in law enforcement."

She drained her beer and got up to retrieve a water bottle. The sausage on the pizza was spicy, just the way she liked it.

"I'll listen to the podcast tomorrow, see what you come up with."

"Do that. And if you think I need to go in a different direction, text me."

"I've been thinking," her dad said.

She started to clean up. She didn't want to know what her dad was thinking, not with the tone he had.

"Listen," he said.

"Dad—"

"No, listen, Regan Marie. You're a grown woman, and you can make your own decisions. I understand not wanting to go back to the Marshals Service. And I like having you around. We're both adults, and I know you don't want to live under my roof forever. I want you to consider Granddad's apartment, above the barn. It's structurally sound and wouldn't take too much money to remodel the space, put in new appliances, paint it, do whatever you want. If you live there for a few months or for years, I don't care, but you'd have your own space. For you—not so much for me. Like I said, I like having you here."

That was the last thing she'd expected from him. She thought he was going to push the security job with his friend, or encourage her to apply for the sheriff's department or something…but the apartment?

"I like being here," she admitted. "Can I think about it?"

"Of course. No rush. Just wanted you to know that it's there if you want it."

She finished cleaning up and put the last two pieces of pizza in a baggie for breakfast.

Then she sat back down and said, "I think Lucas has a personal reason for pursuing this podcast. I just can't figure out what it is. It was just an odd comment he made the other day that I've been twisting around in my mind."

"Have you looked at his background? Didn't you say his brother was in the police academy?"

"Phoenix. I know a bit about his family. He hasn't lost anyone to violence. Two sisters in high school, older brother, single mom. I had the sense that the father just left or they divorced and he doesn't see his dad. Mom is a nurse, which might be a psychological reason for Lucas's obsession with the Candace Swain murder." She paused, considered maybe a friend…extended family…neighbors. She asked her dad, "Do you remember any other murders on campus?"

"NAU is pretty safe," said the retired sheriff. "There was a tragic shooting—alcohol-related—that ended up with a plea deal and manslaughter charge. It started off campus. Rape is the number-one violent crime, and my guess is that the majority of those cases involve alcohol."

"That doesn't make it justified."

"No," he said, "but it makes it a lot harder to get a clean prosecution."

"Missing persons?" she asked her dad. "An off-campus, unsolved homicide?"

"I'm sure there must be some," he answered. "I don't know off the top of my head. I'll look them up for you tomorrow, give me something to do."

"Thanks, Dad."

"I may be retired, but I still have a sharp mind."

"Then answer me this," she said. "Taylor James is dead. She died of a drug overdose. I think she knew a lot more about Candace's death than she said, but I didn't get the vibe when I talked to her yesterday that she was going to fall off the wagon."

"Do you want me to find out more?"

She nodded. "I'd really like to know if there is any chance that the overdose was intentional."

"Suicide."

"Or homicide."

Twenty-Nine

Friday

On her way to town Friday morning, Regan stopped by Lucas's apartment to check on him. She wasn't positive that the notes he received were a prelude to a physical attack, but she was cautious by nature.

She also wanted to give him an opportunity to talk more about his motives. She didn't think he was being deceptive, but she kept going through all their conversations, and there was just a little niggle of a doubt that he hadn't been completely up-front with her about his motivation.

"I'm meeting with the sorority advisor and president in an hour," she said.

"Ask if Vicky will let me interview her for the podcast," he said. "Maybe come on live. She can say anything she wants—talk about how Candace mentored her, how her death impacted her. And I can ask about the last time she saw her."

"I'll do my best," she said.

"They won't even talk to me, so you're my best hope."

"I was going through all my notes last night and listened

to the podcasts again, trying to wrap my head around a few things."

"I went through my notes, too. Great minds," he said with a laugh.

"Yeah, well, one thing you said about the last time you saw Candace. You were at the sorority to go to the party—"

"No, I went to talk to Candace. She'd quit tutoring, and I really needed her help for my English class."

"When I was talking to Richie, he said that she quit tutoring before spring semester."

"Yeah, so?"

"The party was in April."

"I used her in the fall, and I wanted to use her again. She helped. She said she was too busy. Why does it matter?"

"I'm trying to determine what was going on in her life, what might have led up to the argument with Taylor. Richie implied that she was irritated with someone she was tutoring. I thought you might have known something about it."

"No. We weren't friends, just friendly."

It wasn't what Lucas was saying, it was his tone and the way he averted his eyes.

Did she press now? Or wait? Would he come around on his own? He was a smart kid, and she had grown to like him quite a bit. He pushed when warranted, listened when he didn't know something, and assessed information critically. She liked that.

She wanted him to tell her everything, even if it wasn't important to Candace's murder. Because if his motivation was personal, it might cloud his judgment if there was an actual threat to him. She didn't want anything bad to happen to him.

She decided to wait. Maybe it was nothing.

"I also found out Alexa Castillo teaches in Flagstaff. Let's go pay her a visit this afternoon, okay?"

"How'd you do that?"

"Lots of patience and false leads, but she's a teacher, and there are public records. So I went down a rabbit hole and got lucky."

"What time?"

"I'll pick you up around two thirty? We'll head over there, catch her right after classes end."

"This might be it."

"Don't get your hopes up," she told him, "but it's a good lead."

When Regan drove to the campus, she kept looking up at the gray sky. Yep, it was going to rain. Not a little drizzle like earlier in the week but a hard, pounding rain that might last most of the weekend. By the time she arrived at campus ten minutes later, the first raindrop fell.

She pulled on the hood of her Gore-Tex jacket. She loved the rain and didn't mind getting wet, but she didn't relish the idea of sitting around damp for the rest of the day.

She headed directly to Rachel's office. The door was open. She rapped on it, and Rachel looked up with a smile. Like yesterday, she was dressed both impeccably and trendy. "Thank you for coming to campus," she said.

"It's not out of my way."

"Vicky will be here in a few minutes. Come in, sit. Would you like some coffee?"

"I'm good."

Regan took off her jacket and hung it on a hook by the door, where Rachel had her own coat hanging. It was quiet, but it was Friday. Fewer classes in session, many students leaving campus for the weekend.

Rachel took a bottle of water from a minifridge under the table behind her desk, and offered one to Regan, which she declined.

"I was hoping the rain would hold off until tonight," Rachel said. "But I did come prepared." She laughed lightly and gestured to the umbrella next to her coatrack.

"I don't trust the weather, especially in the mountains," Regan said.

"I've learned that the hard way," Rachel said. "I still hold out hope!"

"Anything I should know about Vicky Ryan?"

"Vicky is a wonderful young woman. She's been accepted to a specialty program to get her nursing certification in geriatrics. After her great-grandmother died in a nursing home, she decided she wanted to change the way nursing homes are certified and run. Very strong ethics, solid foundation. She'll go far."

Regan nodded. Not exactly what she had been searching for, but everything she could learn about the student would help her assess the situation.

Vicky stepped inside the office. "Are you ready for me?"

"Come in," Rachel said. "Vicky, this is former US Marshal Regan Merritt."

"Right. You went on that ridiculous podcast."

Vicky sat down next to Rachel, her lips a firm line, arms across her chest.

"Thank you for agreeing to talk to me."

"I didn't want to, to be honest. I am so angry about that podcast I could scream. I tried to get the department to shut it down, but because it's a capstone project and already had approval from Lucas's advisor and the CCJ department, I was stymied."

"Why did you want to shut it down?"

"Why?" She said it in such a way as to make it seem that Regan was stupid for not knowing. "It's triggering to most of us who knew Candace. Lucas is bringing up all these feelings of fear, uncertainty, anger. You name it. We all liked and admired Candace. She volunteered more hours than any other NAU Sigma Rho sister *ever*. No one will break her record, and then she was killed—it was awful."

"You were a first-year student."

"Yes. Why would that be relevant?"

"I'm just keeping my facts straight."

"She was my mentor," Vicky said. "I loved her like a blood sister, over and above being in the sorority together. I saw her that night. We organized the party together, and she taught me everything I know about event planning." Her voice cracked and she glanced at Rachel for moral support.

"I know this is hard," Regan acknowledged.

"I just wish that Lucas would let the police handle this, you know?"

"Generally, the police are more capable than anyone else at solving a crime, but when it comes to a cold case, the police are often at an impasse. They can't put aside their current caseload to focus on an older case with little to no evidence."

Rachel sighed, glanced at Vicky. "Do you have anything else to share, Vicky?"

"Only that I just heard this morning that Taylor James died of a drug overdose the other night. I can't help but think that the podcast had something to do with that."

"Why would you think that?" Regan asked.

"Because while I think Candace was treated fairly, I felt that Lucas was snide and accusatory toward Taylor, as if she'd lied to the police. He didn't flat out say that, but he kept bringing her up. Their stupid argument and all that.

Taylor cared about Candace, and we were all concerned about that weirdo who was hanging around. I mean, I felt bad for him, but he creeped us out. Taylor tried to get Candace to understand that he could be dangerous."

"Did you overhear their argument?"

"Just a small part of it," she said. "They weren't shouting or anything, just talking emphatically. Rachel was there."

That was the first Regan heard that Rachel had been part of the conversation.

Rachel said, "I came over to mediate. No one could get Candace to see the truth, and that's why she walked off. I guess I never thought that man would actually hurt her. If I had, I would have done something right then, called the police myself. But he was gone, and I didn't think he would come back."

"Was there evidence that he returned?" Regan asked.

"I figured either he returned, or Candace went to Sunrise Center and something happened there," Rachel said. "When the police told me she'd been alive during the time she was missing, I was surprised, and I understand why Lucas thinks that seems suspicious, but I'm sure there's a logical explanation for it."

There was, but they didn't know it, and that these women weren't more curious surprised her.

Not everyone is compelled to find justice.

"Taylor's overdose is tragic," Rachel continued. "We're having a memorial for her Monday evening. You're welcome to come," she added, "but not Lucas. That would stir up too much anger and emotion. Many of the girls feel the podcast sent Taylor over the edge. She was a sensitive young woman, and Candace's death nearly destroyed her."

"I hope you understand how we feel about this," Vicky said.

"I do. But I would want to know the truth."

"Of *course*," she said, emphatic. "But I doubt he'll accomplish anything, and it's at the expense of our mental health. This is a college podcast. People talk, and some are not very nice."

Vicky didn't come off as being the type to struggle in any capacity. She was confident and articulate, but Regan could imagine how others might not be—like Taylor.

"I appreciate your time," Regan said. "I'll talk to Lucas about your concerns, but he still plans to finish the scheduled episodes."

"I appreciate whatever you can do. I have to run to a study session, but it was nice to meet you, Regan."

Vicky left, and Regan rose from her seat. "I hope," Rachel said, "that you'll convince Lucas to treat Taylor James with respect on his podcast in light of the circumstances of her death."

"I have no reason to think that he wouldn't."

Rachel rubbed her eyes. "I'm sorry. I was trying to put on a brave face for Vicky, but Taylor's death hit me hard."

Regan sat back down. "Can I get you anything?"

"No, I'm sorry, really. There is some truth to what Lucas Vega is doing. I might not like his approach, but... he touched upon some animosity between Taylor and Candace that went far beyond Taylor's concern about the homeless man."

"Do you know what it was about?"

She shook her head. "I had just started as the faculty advisor, and the girls were only beginning to know me. Now I like to think that any of them would come to me if they were having difficulties."

"What do you think was going on between them?"

"I don't know the details. Just rumors and innuendo, and I don't feel comfortable sharing any of that." She paused, then said carefully, "It would not surprise me if I learned Taylor had...*hurt*...Candace. She fell apart after Candace's murder, and I just had this odd feeling... Anyway, guilt is a powerful emotion. For three years Taylor struggled with addiction, and I fear the podcast sent her over the edge."

"Do you have anything concrete that makes you think that Taylor was involved in Candace's murder?"

"Of course not! Just...a feeling. She spiraled after Candace's death, more than anyone. But it was such an awful time for the sorority. Sigma Rho almost didn't get through it. But we did, and we're stronger for it."

Lizzy Choi loved being a TA for what she affectionately called Math for Dummies. Probably not politically correct, but teaching artsy types how to do basic math that they should have learned in elementary school was actually fun. Her mom always thought she should be a teacher herself, but the idea of being trapped in a classroom doing the same thing every day, every year, just with different kids? No thanks.

She didn't care that the professor rarely showed up. She was on full scholarship *and* got paid for being a TA. She was putting virtually every dime in the bank because who knew what was going to happen when she graduated? What if she couldn't find a job right away?

Right. Someone with your brains majoring in engineering? You'll land somewhere fast.

Still her parents were old-school. Save your money, don't go into debt, get a good job, buy a house, get married, have a family. She wasn't quite sure about the last two on the checklist, but she was only twenty-one: she had time.

Well, time was relative. She had a heavy class schedule, she was the TA for this class, and she was working on Lucas's podcast. Free time was at a premium, and she wanted to spend it with Lucas. Which was *so* unlike her.

She was about to call him and see if he wanted to meet for lunch when Nicole Bergamo approached her. She did a double take. She had *just been* talking about Nicole with Lucas last night, and now she clearly wanted to talk to her, even though they hadn't had a class together this year.

Nicole was another super smart math person, but not a geek like Lizzy. Nicole was definitely the type to become a math teacher.

"Hi, Lizzy. I'm so glad I caught you here."

"Almost missed me! I let the children out early today because I was hungry. Do you want to get lunch?"

"I can't. Can we go back into the classroom where we have some privacy?"

"Sure." Weird. Lizzy led the way to the class, opened the door. Yes, her math-challenged kids had fled quickly, and the room was empty.

Nicole relaxed and sat down on one of the desks. "Thanks," she said. "You're probably thinking, *What does Nicole want? I haven't talked to her in a year.*"

"I know what you want."

Nicole stared at her. "You do?"

"Yeah. We haven't talked in over a year, and now I'm helping Lucas solve Candace Swain's murder and you're coming to me because we know each other."

"Oh. Yeah. Okay."

Nicole was math-smart, but there wasn't a lot of common sense there, Lizzy realized.

"So? What's up? You're not going to convince me to work on Lucas to dump the podcast."

"No, why would I?"

"Because…your sorority is all *hush-hush, shut it down.*"

"No. I mean, yes—officially—but there's a group of us who really like what he's doing, and we want to help, but we can't."

"Define *can't*."

"I don't want to get kicked out of the sorority."

"Can they do that?"

"Yeah. They can, if Vicky has enough votes."

"She's your best friend."

"And I really thought I could convince her to at least let those of us who want to call in do so. That girl? Who said she saw Candace on Sunday night, in her car? That caused *huge* problems. Vicky and the council figured out who she was, brought her in to talk. Said if she knew anything about Candace to go to the police and not talk to anyone else or she would be out of here, period. She'll be on probation through graduation, and she could lose her pin and all alumnae perks if she breaks the agreement. She's heartbroken."

"So you're taking a risk talking to me?"

"I don't want to lose this sisterhood. I mean, you're not in a sorority. I don't think you understand how much having this group of women helps. Not just now, in college, always having people you can go out with and talk to, but in the future, the connections and job opportunities that can come your way."

Lizzy shrugged. "I've heard. Not my thing, but I'm not judging you because it's yours. But I don't understand why you're coming to me."

"I've been roommates with Vicky for four years. If I call in, she'll know it's me. And I've been pushing her to cooperate."

"Okay, explain me this," Lizzy said. "Why *wouldn't* she cooperate?"

"Because Lucas is a student, not the police. Vicky is very law-and-order, which is great, but I think she has too much faith in them. It's been *three years*, and they haven't figured out what happened to Candace. And they don't care. I mean, I'm sure they *care*, but it's not the same. Vicky is positive that the homeless guy killed her. I mean, she believes it like she believes the sky is blue."

"You don't?"

"No. I mean, I suppose anything's possible, but Candace was acting really, really weird before she disappeared."

"How so?"

"Mostly, she kind of removed herself from the sorority her last semester. I mean, she lived there and everything, but she didn't do anything with us, didn't come to movie nights, missed several council meetings. Vicky was on the council as the first-year representative, and she complained about Candace all the time. Candace was Vicky's mentor, and she felt she was getting the short end because Candace kept canceling on her and not telling her why. But at the same time, Vicky worshipped her. Candace was smart and beautiful and everyone liked her. Vicky wanted to be just like her."

"So if you don't think that Joseph Abernathy killed Candace, what do you think happened to her?"

"I don't know. That's why I think this podcast is a good idea." She leaned forward and whispered, "What if it was someone in the sorority? We were talking last night, the group of us who are fascinated by this case, and were wondering if maybe Taylor James killed her, and that's why she overdosed. They were arguing a lot, not just at the party."

"About what?"

"I have no idea, because anytime someone would walk into a room, they'd stop talking. The night of the party, I heard Taylor call Candace a *selfish bitch*. I don't know the context or anything, but it was harsh."

"How long was this going on?" Lizzy felt like a detective, asking questions of a witness. It was kind of thrilling.

"I don't know. They never really liked each other as long as I knew them, but they did things together."

Lizzy considered her options. "What if you call in tonight and share what you know, except for the really personal stuff that someone might know you'd be the only one to know."

"I told you, I can't. They'll recognize my voice, just like Nia." Nicole put a hand to her mouth. "Dammit."

"I won't say anything. But I can disguise your voice. I can run it through a program so it'll be totally distorted."

"I don't know."

"You can pass my offer along to anyone else who wants to talk. I answer the calls during the podcast. All you have to do is tell anyone at the sorority that when they call, they can tell me they want their voice disguised. I'll have it all set up. I promise."

Nicole was thinking, but she didn't commit.

Lizzy needed to push her. "Regan Merritt is coming back tonight. Lucas is going to detail everything about Candace's death and everything he's learned since Tuesday night. There's a lot. And I think you might have information that you don't know is important to put this all together. Regan said the police are listening to the podcast, and if we find something, they'll investigate. Someone needs to answer for Candace's murder, don't you think? Don't you think her sister would rest easier knowing what really happened?"

"Okay," Nicole said. "My group and I will listen, and if we're all in agreement, I'll call. If you promise you'll keep my name out of it. Because I don't know if I can really help. I just came here to tell you that there are many of us who think the podcast is a good idea because we want to know what happened to Candace."

Nicole walked out first, alone. Lizzy called Lucas. "Where are you? We need to talk, right now."

Thirty

Lucas sat in his truck across from Taylor James's house. Lizzy wanted to talk to him in person, said it was important, so he agreed to meet her at his apartment in an hour. He should have asked why—she sounded super excited about something—but he was preoccupied with what he planned to do.

When he ended the call, his roommate, Troy, said, "Lizzy? Wow, she can talk a mile a minute, can't she?"

"Yeah," he said, noncommittal.

He'd brought Troy along with him because he wasn't an idiot: he knew there was safety in numbers. And Troy was built like a football lineman, which could be intimidating if you didn't know him.

The neighborhood might have been nice if more houses had been fixed up. But most were falling apart, separated from their neighbors by tall trees and overgrown shrubs. A fire hazard, he thought.

He shouldn't be here. He had wanted to tell Regan his full theory. He almost did earlier today because he had a feeling she was fishing around for something, but he didn't know how she would take it. He hadn't shared it with anyone, not even Lizzy—though Lizzy knew about his ex-girlfriend, Amanda, and she knew about Amanda's missing sister, Adele.

Regan wouldn't be happy if she found out he was here, even with Troy. But he couldn't help himself and he'd been careful—no one had followed him. It was the middle of the day, overcast, drizzly, no one was around. He could do this.

He'd spent most of the morning going over all the files he'd downloaded about Greek Life. He hadn't made any further connections between any of the sisters to Candace, and most of the newsletters were filled with fluff.

"Hey, buddy, are you sure you should be doing this?" Troy asked.

"I'm just going to walk around. I can't really sleep, after finding her. I'm hoping, I don't know, that I can just let it go." He wasn't being completely honest with Troy, and he felt bad about that, but it was true that he couldn't get dead Taylor out of his head. When he did sleep, his mind replayed trying to save her life, hearing the voice of the 9-1-1 operator telling him what to do, but she still died. Over and over and over.

"Do you want me to go with you?"

"No, that's okay. I'm just going to walk around the house, ten, fifteen minutes? Just let me know if anyone comes. I don't want people to think I'm doing anything wrong."

Even though he was.

"No problem." Troy leaned back in the passenger's seat.

Lucas had to do this because he couldn't shake the idea that something he'd said had pushed Taylor to kill herself. In the back of his mind, he'd thought Taylor was involved in Candace's murder. They were first friends, then enemies. His research, everyone he talked to, all the anonymous notes supported the idea that they had a major falling-out.

But just because you didn't like someone didn't mean you wanted to kill them.

Trying not to look suspicious, Lucas walked purposefully to the front door, knocked. No answer—he didn't expect one. Taylor had lived alone.

He jiggled the knob. Locked.

The blinds were closed in the front. The carport was in the back of the house. No fences to stop him from walking around to the rear door.

Aggressive weeds pushing through the cracked concrete on the back patio. A weathered picnic table, splintered to the point that no one would want to touch it, sat on one side; a couple chairs and a sagging plastic lounge were on the other side. Multiple coffee cans were half-filled with dirt and sand, in which hundreds of cigarette butts were stuffed. It looked even worse in daytime than it had the other night.

He saw the trash left by the paramedics: a couple gauze wrappers, latex gloves, all tossed in a garbage can that was outside the back door.

Taylor had died here. Right here, outside, alone, and Lucas hadn't been able to save her.

He stared at the lounge chair where he'd found her, almost saw her again, her bare arm hanging over the edge, her eyes half-open.

Maybe she didn't die alone.

Where had that thought come from?

Suicide made sense. Sure, the timing was suspicious, but it would be confirmed at the autopsy. Unless it was inconclusive. Or they suspected accidental drug overdose so that's what they would see. None of this sat right with him. He hadn't wanted her to die. He'd only wanted answers.

Answers he'd known Taylor had.

He tried the back door.

It was unlocked.

He didn't hesitate. He went inside, hoping no one saw him.

The house was dark because of the closed blinds. It reeked of cigarette smoke.

He pulled on the latex gloves that Regan had left at his house after she handled the letter he received. He meant to throw them out, but when he saw them this morning he reconsidered, thinking they very well might come in handy.

He went back to the rear door and wiped the knob. Just in case. He wasn't planning on taking anything—he just wanted to see if there was any connection he could find to Candace's murder.

Even though Taylor had died outside, he assumed the police had gone through the house when her body was found. To make sure nothing was turned on, like the stove, no potential dangers, no visible drugs, no other victims.

Why was she outside in the middle of the night when it was so cold?

The police would follow up at her work, with her neighbors, just for the report, even if they thought she overdosed. Verify she had been at work, see if they could trace where she'd gotten the drugs, find out if anyone had been with her. Try to figure out her state of mind to help determine if this was an accident or suicide. And if someone had been with her, left her to die? That might be considered manslaughter.

Regan could find those answers faster, and Lucas would ask if she'd followed up with the detective. Lucas hadn't been called, which surprised him. Did they not care? Or was a drug death not a priority? Right now he was wondering why—when it had been forty degrees that night—she hadn't been inside her house when shooting up.

He'd never done drugs, so he didn't understand Taylor's

thinking. They screwed you up. One of his best friends growing up had gotten into drugs in high school, ended up dropping out and getting arrested when he was seventeen, and again when he was eighteen. The third time landed him in prison for five years. Lucas believed in second chances, but he always wondered if maybe Greg had gotten help the first time he was arrested, he might not have found himself in the same cycle of stealing to feed a worsening drug habit.

The cigarette smell was overwhelming. He'd need a shower when he got home.

Lucas scanned Taylor's house. He could see the front door from the back door. A tiny kitchen, a counter with two bar stools. Though the house wasn't clean, it wasn't a total disaster. No dirty dishes in the sink. No dishwasher, but clean dishes were stacked in a rubber rack next to the sink. The counters were cluttered with spices and old mail but had been wiped down. A table by the window facing the back had stacks of paper and books—mostly paperback romances. An ashtray that had a few butts in it sat next to an empty beer bottle.

The living room had a sectional sofa, old but clean. A television was mounted on the wall. More half-filled ashtrays, all the same brand of cigarette, lots of magazines. Lucas's stomach flipped when he realized she read nursing and other science magazines. Did she read the articles and regret her life choices? Taylor had once had a promising future—what had happened? She was only twenty-five. She could have turned her life around, but it was as if she'd given up.

There was one bedroom off a short hall near the front door. He didn't want to search her room, but now he was compelled. He'd already entered her house. What was five more minutes?

Her bedroom was cluttered but clean. No ashtrays in here, but the smell was nearly as strong. She'd made an attempt to make her bed—pulled up the comforter over her sheets. A stuffed dog sat on top.

It was unbelievably sad.

The bedroom was a good size, and she had a desk in the corner piled with books and papers. He glanced through them and found a lot of newsletters from NAU stuffed in every nook. On the shelf above the desk were college yearbooks. He had never ordered one but planned to for his senior year.

He flipped through the yearbooks, hoping that something would jump out at him. Like if she'd scratched the eyes out of Candace's photos. Or written a confession in the margins. Nothing. The books were pristine.

What was he thinking? That she would keep damning evidence here at her house? If there was a suicide note, Regan would have found out, right?

He stared at the desk. It was small, uncluttered—but there were cords going to the wall. Computer cords?

Had the police taken her computer? Why? Because there was evidence on it—or a suicide note—or something else?

Or was it missing? Stolen? Had she hidden it?

On the top of her dresser was a lot of makeup, perfume, photos, scraps of paper. Mostly sticky notes to herself about work, doctors' appointments, phone numbers with only first names.

In the dim light, Lucas caught his reflection in the mirror attached to the dresser. What the fuck was he doing going through a dead woman's house? He could lose everything. He could be expelled. He might not be able to get a job in law enforcement.

Then he saw the picture, partly hidden behind a bunch

of other photos that were mostly of Taylor in college. He stared at it for a long minute, almost thinking that he had conjured the photo in his imagination.

He reached out and gingerly touched it.

It was real.

He pulled it out. A couple other photos tumbled to the dresser top, but he ignored them. He stared at the familiar faces.

Candace. Taylor.

Adele.

He had been right from the beginning.

He *knew* that Candace and Taylor had known Adele, even though they'd both denied it to him. There was no denying it now. Here was a photo of the three girls from their first year in college, arms around each other. Proof. Proof that they'd lied to him.

But what could he do with it? Was it proof when both Candace and Taylor were dead? Proof of what?

All three of them were now dead.

His phone vibrated, and he jumped.

He looked at the message. It was Troy.

It's been 20 minutes—you good?

He pocketed his phone—and the photo—and left the house.

Thirty-One

Regan grabbed a quick lunch, then drove to Lucas's apartment. Lizzy was on the couch when Lucas let Regan in. Remnants of deli sandwiches sat on the coffee table in front of them. Lucas quickly picked everything up as he said, "Nicole Bergamo reached out to Lizzy. This could be big."

Regan listened as Lizzy recounted her conversation with Nicole and her offer to disguise her voice.

Based on what Nicole told Lizzy, she didn't know anything about Candace's disappearance though had some interesting insight as to the division in the sorority. What *was* interesting was Vicky Ryan's anger toward her mentor.

Thirdhand information was harder to work with, but if Nicole called in, Regan had more questions to ask. The fact that she seemed adamant that Abernathy had played no role in Candace's death made Regan think she knew something else—even if she didn't fully understand what she might remember. Which was, unfortunately, the biggest problem with accessing three-year-old memories and observations. Time often slanted perception.

"What do you think?" Lucas asked Regan. "Do you think this is important?"

"What's curious to me is that the sorority is divided. It makes me wonder if there's something else going on there, maybe someone who knows more than they're saying."

"Why?" Lizzy asked. "I mean, you don't actually buy into Nicole implying that Taylor might have killed her, do you? And like what? They're covering it up?"

"Actually, it's a viable theory," she said. Rachel had also implied the same thing. But it was just conjecture and rumors, something Regan didn't put much stock in, until she could find evidence.

"I'd been thinking the same thing," Lucas said. "That maybe Taylor is responsible. But it'll be impossible to prove."

"Not necessarily," Regan said. "If you came to that conclusion, others may, too. We'll see what happens tonight on the podcast and go from there." She glanced at her watch. "We should go. Alexa Castillo's school day ends shortly. She has little digital footprint, so I don't know how else to find her through public channels."

Lizzy popped up. "I'll see you at the studio tonight."

"Lizzy," Regan said, "I told Lucas to watch himself, because he's stirred up a lot of anger over at the sorority. I'm telling you the same thing."

"He told me about the notes. I'll be super cautious."

They walked out together. Lizzy planned to take the bus back to campus, but Regan gave her a ride as it wasn't too far out of the way. She didn't think that Lizzy would be in danger—Lucas was the face of the podcast—but as Lizzy said, it was best to be *super cautious*.

Regan couldn't find parking anywhere close to the elementary school because dozens of cars were lined up to pick up kids. She parked around the corner and waited.

She'd wait until most of the kids and parents were gone, then head in.

While they waited, she said to Lucas, "Vicky Ryan seems to be at the center of this. She wants to end the podcast. She knew Candace, had seen her that night, witnessed part of the argument. She claimed she didn't hear what it was about but mentioned that Rachel was there as well. Did you know about that?"

"No, it has never come up, and it wasn't in the police report."

"So Rachel was there during the argument, along with Kimberly Foster and possibly others. Why would anyone lie about what the fight was about?"

"Maybe," Lucas considered, "the fight was about *more* than Abernathy. Maybe it started out that way but devolved into something else."

Possible, but without someone who was there to confirm, they could only speculate.

"Rachel simply confirmed what we have already been told, then went on to say she should have called the police on Abernathy, and Candace may still be alive. Rachel and Vicky believe he's guilty. They don't even question it. Though Rachel said something interesting, that she wouldn't be surprised if she learned that Taylor had *hurt* Candace."

"Hurt? Like, her feelings?"

"Her tone said *killed*. She just didn't use the word."

"Wow."

"I don't know what to think, but someone in that sorority knows exactly what happened to Candace Swain, and I'm at the point where I'm more than a little irritated. At the people keeping secrets and at the cops for not digging deeper. Abernathy looks good on the surface, but it doesn't make sense when you look at everything else."

Cars started easing up from the front of the school as parents and caregivers picked up the children. When the second of three buses pulled away, Regan and Lucas walked to the school.

If Taylor had lied to the police—or intentionally misled them about the argument—she could have lied about anything. She might have seen Candace during the time she was missing. She might have loaned her a car or money or even driven her somewhere. But why? And when she turned up dead, why wouldn't Taylor have spoken up? Would someone at the sorority cover up a murder? An accidental death? What would be the motive for remaining silent?

Based on what they knew, Candace's disappearance was voluntary. She had a prepaid phone and didn't use her regular cell, which didn't make sense. Maybe Candace didn't want anyone to find her.

According to the police report, the phone left in the dorm had contained no information about Candace's plans.

Regan pushed her questions aside as she and Lucas approached the main entrance. While schools had pretty tight security these days, and visitors had to go through the office to access any of the classrooms, once school was out for the day, the gates were often left open. That was the case here.

It was pretty easy to find Ms. Castillo's classroom: the rooms were grouped by grade with teacher names on the door. Helpful arrows pointed her to the wing that housed grades one through three. Alexa Castillo's room was in the far corner.

Through the windows, Regan saw Alexa working at

her desk in the empty room. The door was locked so she knocked.

Alexa opened the door but stayed a step back, clearly telling Regan not to invade her space. She was an attractive young woman. Twenty-six, but she looked older, her hair up in a bun, wearing sensible pants and a blouse that was a generation too old for her. Little makeup, with blemish-free light brown skin and long lashes.

"May I help you?" she asked, smiling at first Regan, then at Lucas.

"I'm Regan Merritt. This is Lucas Vega. We're looking into the death of Candace Swain for a podcast."

Her face paled. Alexa would never be able to play poker. As soon as she said her name, Alexa knew who Regan was. She'd clearly listened to the podcast.

Alexa stepped back, cleared her throat. "I—um—yes? I don't know how I can help you."

"We'd like to talk to you about Candace Swain from NAU. You knew her."

"Yes."

Lucas said, "Were you at the party when Candace disappeared?"

"I don't understand what you want from me." Alexa was nervous, her eyes darting, as if looking for an escape. Guilt? Fear? Both?

"May we come in?" Lucas asked. "You'd probably like to sit down."

"No, I'm sorry, this is my classroom. I can't have personal business here," she said firmly.

"Ms. Castillo," Lucas said, "Regan has been helping me retrace Candace's steps from after the party until she was found dead. We know she was in Kingman that weekend— her boyfriend said that she often visited a sorority sister

who had already graduated. I narrowed down the possibilities, and you're the most likely from that list. Did you
see Candace that weekend?"

"Why?"

"Because I think you know why she disappeared and
what she was doing. That will help us figure out what happened to her."

"I can't talk to you."

Regan was watching Alexa carefully as Lucas questioned her. His words were straightforward, and his tone
matter-of-fact, not confrontational. But the more questions
he asked, the more agitated she became.

"You mean, you won't talk to us," Lucas said.

"I don't know what you want, I don't know why you're
here, I want you to leave. I'll call security."

She hadn't denied seeing Candace.

Regan said, "Do you know that Taylor James died of an
overdose Wednesday night?"

Her eyes widened. She hadn't known, and she looked
terrified.

"Go away. Please. I have nothing to say to you. Nothing.
Do not come here again. This is where I *work*."

A teacher walking through the courtyard had slowed
and was watching them, perhaps picking up on the panic
in Alexa's voice.

Lucas said quietly, "You really need to talk to us, Alexa.
I know you've listened to the podcast, and my guess is that
you're the one who sent me the anonymous letter about the
argument between Taylor and Candace. You gave us Kimberly Foster's name. We also know that you volunteered
with Candace at Sunrise Center. Anyone else we need to
talk to? Do you know who killed Candace or just suspect
someone other than Abernathy?"

At that moment, an older woman approached holding the hand of a little girl, two and a half or maybe close to three, with curly brown pigtails. "Mommy, Mommy, Mommy!" The girl ran full-speed toward Alexa with a huge grin on her face holding a paper with bright colors in what Regan suspected was a rainbow.

Alexa stared at Regan, then she grimly shook her head before turning to the girl and plastering a smile on her face. "Bella! How is my angel?"

"See my pit-cher? *All* the colors!"

"It's so pretty, it is *definitely* going on the refrigerator when we get home."

Alexa barely looked at Lucas and Regan when she said, "I need to go. Thank you for your time." She ushered Bella and the older woman into her classroom and closed the door.

Everything Alexa said—and didn't say—confirmed what Regan and Lucas suspected.

She was the anonymous letter writer.

She was terrified of someone.

And now Regan understood why Alexa hadn't wanted to come forward. She had a little girl, and she was scared. Fear was powerful, especially when you had more than yourself to protect.

But if she feared Taylor, why would Alexa still be scared after learning she was dead?

Thirty-Two

Regan let Lucas talk about his impressions of Alexa Castillo, which were very similar to hers: yes, she wrote the letter; yes, she knew more than she said; yes, it was most likely her that Candace visited in Kingman. He was excited about their discovery and wanted to brainstorm ways to convince her to talk.

"She's scared," Regan said simply when Lucas took a breath.

"I know, but—"

"There are no buts. She's scared because she has a young child to protect. That little girl was between two and three. Want to bet Alexa was pregnant three years ago when Candace visited her?"

"So?"

Lucas didn't understand what she was trying to say, maybe because he wasn't a parent himself.

"She said in the letter that she'd been at the party, and based on that little girl, she was very likely pregnant—maybe very pregnant. She never came forward after Candace's disappearance or her murder. She wasn't living in Flagstaff, maybe she didn't hear immediately, but she would have sooner rather than later."

"Why didn't she? Was she involved?"

Good questions, but Regan didn't think so. Alexa had become more fearful after she'd heard that Taylor James was dead. Concerned, maybe worried, when Lucas was talking about Candace—but absolutely terrified that Taylor was dead.

Maybe she hadn't been at the party. Maybe she'd known about it, *said* she was there because Candace told her about the argument and what her plans were. Maybe Alexa knew exactly where Candace had disappeared to. Had Alexa gone with her? Now, Alexa was trying to help them on the podcast without letting on that she was the one who'd helped Candace. Because she didn't want to put herself or her daughter in harm's way.

"She knows something, possibly even suspects who killed Candace," Regan said. "But without evidence, she's smart enough to know talking might put her in danger. We need to proceed carefully."

"So what do we do?"

"Maybe we can convince Detective Young to come on the podcast tonight."

"He won't. He hates me."

"*Hate* is a strong word. *Irritated* is probably better."

"Why?"

"Two reasons. First, we can share this information with him about Alexa. I suspect that if Alexa is questioned by authorities, she'll come clean. She has that civic-minded vibe to her."

"Second," she continued, "Nicole told Lizzy that some of the sorority girls wanted to help. That tells me that some of them know more information about Candace but have been bullied into being quiet by Vicky and the council primarily because they believe only the police should be investigating. If we have Detective Young on the podcast, that just might open them up. They may call and tell all. I still think the police know more than they've said, publicly or privately. But they are still stuck on Joseph Abernathy. This might get them unstuck."

Lucas didn't say anything.

"Okay, what's wrong?" Regan asked a couple minutes later.

"Can he shut me down? I have four more episodes after tonight. What if he says end it?"

"He can't. You have the first amendment on your side."

"I want to solve this."

"I do, too. I think we will—if we can get those girls to open up. Having the support of the police might make the difference."

"All right," he reluctantly agreed.

"If you don't want to, we won't, and we can try Alexa again on Monday."

"No, let's do it, but I also want to try Alexa again," he said.

Regan turned south and headed toward the police station. When she pulled into the parking lot, she saw a familiar person exiting the building: Rachel Wagner.

Instead of pulling into the first available parking place, she drove past it, and stopped, looked in her side-view mirror.

Detective Young was right behind Rachel. They crossed the lot together, talking.

Lucas turned in his seat, and Regan hit him. "Don't draw attention to us."

"Is that Rachel Wagner?" he asked as he faced forward again.

"Yep."

As Regan watched, Young kissed Rachel. Then she got into a Jeep and drove off, fortunately in the opposite direction from Regan.

Instead of going back into the building, Young walked around the side to where employees parked. A minute later, he left the lot, heading in the same direction as Rachel.

Well, *that* was interesting.

Rachel was dating the lead investigator in Candace Swain's murder. Was that a conflict?

Maybe. Maybe not. Yet, it rubbed Regan the wrong way. It wasn't that Young should have said he was dating the sorority's advisor… It just *felt* like a conflict.

"What does this mean?" Lucas said.

"I don't know. But I need to think about how we approach Young. Maybe not tonight."

"I trust you, Regan. Whatever you think is best."

She wished she knew, because something wasn't adding up.

"Let's talk to Kimberly Foster."

Lucas glanced at her sheepishly.

"What?" she pushed.

"I left a message for her. She hasn't called me back."

"Okay. Let's try again. This time, tell her we have a witness to the argument between Taylor and Candace, we know that she was there, and the argument wasn't solely about Joseph Abernathy. Call us back, or we're going to bring the witness on the podcast."

"Are we?"

"No—unless Alexa calls in, which I doubt. She'll be listening, especially after we confronted her today. She has my card. I'm hoping she'll call me. If we can figure out who Candace visited that weekend, anyone can. She's going to realize that. Fear might convince her to talk when in the past it had her remain silent."

"You're smarter than average. Maybe no one else will put it together."

"We can't assume that no one else can figure it out, especially after the podcast tonight. And neither can Alexa. She knows what Candace planned to do when she disappeared. If we have that information, we might learn who had cause to kill her."

"How are you going to get Alexa to talk? To either call in or call you?"

"She needs to feel safe enough to trust me," Regan said. "Perhaps I could talk on the podcast tonight about witness protection or tells stories of people who stepped up to do the right thing even though it put them and their family in danger, and what the US Marshals Service does to help them."

"Like, put Alexa into witness protection?"

"I don't know if that would be an option. It depends on what she knows and how much physical danger she would be in if she were needed to testify."

Regan continued. "We lead with the Taylor James overdose. An article about it was published in the paper. It's brief, but we can start there. I'll call the sheriff's office, see if the Merritt name can get us more information. We shouldn't connect it directly to Candace or posit any theories about murder or suicide. I'm thinking something like how violence impacts people in different ways. How Taylor, Candace's good friend, former roommate, changed after Candace was killed, how she started doing drugs, barely passed her classes—violence affects more than the victim."

Lucas didn't say anything, but a cloud crossed his face, and his eyes watered.

"You okay?" she asked.

"Fine. Sorry. Just thinking."

Come on, Lucas. I know you're hiding something... What is it?

"Lucas, did you lose someone?"

He shook his head. "I didn't, not really, but my high-school girlfriend did. When we were sophomores in high school, her older sister went missing while driving back from college. They found her car but not her body. Her family doesn't know what happened to her."

"Let me guess. She was here, at NAU."

He nodded.

"Why didn't you tell me that at the beginning?" It made so much sense now why he was borderline obsessed with Candace Swain's disappearance. It was very similar to his sweetheart's sister.

"I didn't think it was important."

"Everything is important."

But he didn't say anything more about it. "We should go," he said. "It's nearly six."

Thirty-Three

Five minutes into Lucas's recap at the start of the podcast, Lizzy sent him a text that they had more than one thousand people streaming the show, more than twice as many as they had the last episode. They had also more than tripled the number of podcast subscribers.

After repeating the known facts of Candace's murder, Lucas said, "Tragedy struck the Sigma Rho sorority again this week. Taylor James, Candace's onetime roommate and sorority sister, died of an apparent drug overdose late Wednesday night." Lucas read the press report of Taylor's death, which didn't give much detail. "Regan, when we were talking earlier, you said that violence creates more than one victim. Can you expand on that?"

"Whenever someone is killed, they are not the only victim. Candace was a sister—to Chrissy Swain as well as to the Sigma Rho sorority. She was a daughter, a friend, a student, a colleague. When Candace was killed, others were hurt—grieving, in pain, unable to find solace that justice was served because Candace's killer was never caught.

"It's no secret that Taylor James suffered after Candace was killed. Losing a friend is always difficult. Losing a friend to violence can be worse. It's sudden, it's tragic, it's often emotionally painful. Taylor turned to alcohol and drugs. She went through rehab. She was putting her life together…and unfortunately, as with many people who suffer with addiction, she fell off the wagon."

Regan didn't know if that was true, but a friend of hers in the sheriff's department said they were ruling it an accidental overdose, pending investigation. "Her death is still being investigated," she continued. "The police will determine if it was accidental, on purpose, or if someone contributed to her overdose." She stopped short of saying *killed her.* "What often makes such a tragedy worse—for friends and family—is not knowing the truth. Of justice not being served. You have a personal experience with this, don't you, Lucas?"

Lucas stared at her, shocked that she had brought it up. What was he going to say?

"I think," she said, "that if you share why you are personally invested in Candace's disappearance and murder, your listeners will respond accordingly."

Lucas quickly recovered and said, "My girlfriend in high school—we were friends for years, since first grade. Anyway, her older sister disappeared driving back from NAU during winter break. It really tore up her family. You're right—not knowing what happened to Adele was worse for them in some ways. I mean, not worse than losing her, but there was no closure. They still don't know what happened to her."

"How long ago was that?"

"A little over six years."

"Why didn't you decide to do your podcast on that case?"

What did he say to that? "I don't know. I think maybe

because Adele had been a freshman and didn't know many people, and Candace was a senior, in a sorority, popular, friendly. I thought it might make for a more interesting podcast."

"I see your point," Regan said.

"I was also too close to that case, and to the family. Adele went missing while driving. Her car was found in New Mexico. Candace Swain went missing from campus, so it felt more immediate, relatable to students here. Candace was part of a sorority, but Adele hadn't made many friends. In addition, the circumstances of Candace's disappearance and murder were both different and compelling. There were no witnesses to Adele's disappearance, but there were several people who saw Candace the night she disappeared."

"That makes sense," Regan said.

Lucas was relieved he didn't have to expand further. He wasn't ready to talk about Adele. Just mentioning her and Candace in the same conversation had him squirming. He could practically feel the picture burning a hole through his backpack across the room—the physical proof that Candace and Taylor had known Adele. That they had been friends.

When Lucas had talked about Adele with Candace, she had flipped. Her reaction made Lucas suspicious. But until he found the photo, he didn't have any hard proof that they were friends. Now that he had it, he didn't know what to do with it.

Regan was staring at him. "Lucas," she said, "I think we have a caller."

He didn't realize that Regan had been talking about witness statements and reliability; he'd zoned out.

"Sorry. Brain freeze," he said and gave a little laugh. She looked at him oddly, so he turned away, glanced at Lizzy through the glass. She put up two fingers, and he pressed the second line on the studio phone.

"Hello, this is Lucas Vega with Regan Merritt talking about the reliability of witnesses. Do you have a comment?"

"Well, I'm sorry about your friend who went missing," a female voice of indeterminate age said. "But really, is bringing all this up again helpful? That poor girl overdosed. Don't you think that maybe your podcast had something to do with that? That you're dredging up this tragedy and reminding Candace's friends what happened? Maybe Ms. James couldn't take it. Depression and drugs don't mix."

"I don't know that Ms. James's personal problems can be connected to a true-crime podcast," Lucas said.

"Really? Well, if you think that, then maybe you're not all that sensitive to other people's situations. How do you think you'd feel if someone started dragging your friend's name through the mud? If they started talking about it and making you feel sad again? You're insensitive and sensational, throwing far-fetched theories out there. You have no idea what you're doing, other than hurting people. It's borderline evil."

The caller hung up.

Lucas had no idea what to say.

Fortunately, Regan intervened. "The police are currently investigating the death of Taylor James. Preliminarily, as the newspaper said this morning, she died of a drug overdose, but they will conduct a thorough investigation to ensure that it was accidental. Sometimes a tainted drug hits the streets and they'll want to track it to prevent more deaths. And we don't know Ms. James's state of mind. So that case needs to be left up to the authorities, as it's an active investigation.

"But Candace Swain is a cold case. Cold cases are notorious in that the police don't have the time and resources to continue an active investigation. Without evidence, the cases are put on the back burner, sometimes never solved. Sometimes a witness or piece of evidence surfaces, and an investigation finds new life. That's what I hope will happen with this podcast. We already have four viable witness statements that have been turned over to the authorities. The authorities are paying attention to this podcast and will likely follow up. I know there are more people out there, people who saw or talked to Candace the week she was missing, people who might have talked to her before she went missing that have an idea about her state of mind. What do you think, Lucas?"

"I agree. But Lizzy informs me we have another caller. Hello, you're on the air with Lucas Vega and Regan Merritt."

"I knew Candace," a voice said. The tone was disguised through a computer-generated program. Lucas glanced at the window at Lizzy, and she gave him a big grin and a thumbs-up.

This was Nicole Bergamo. He was positive.

"I have a question for Regan."

"Ask away," Regan said.

"You said the other day that if you don't tell the police something you won't get in trouble. I mean, if you're never asked and don't know that you might know something, right?"

"Yes, in most cases you're correct. Sometimes a potential witness might not know what's important to an investigation."

"What about hearsay? When, you know, someone tells you something?"

"Again, it depends. Hypotheticals are difficult to answer."

"I saw Candace on Tuesday morning. I mean, I thought I did, but when I mentioned it to someone, they said I had to be mistaken. And so...I just thought I was wrong."

"When did you mention it to someone? Then or recently?"

"Then. It was early. Between eight and eight thirty in the morning. I had just left my dorm to go to class. I saw her driving on University Street, heading to the main road. And I did a double take because she was driving a truck, and I wondered why."

"What kind of truck?"

"A truck truck. I don't know."

"Was it like a pickup truck? Small or large?"

"Yeah, a pickup, but not new. Kind of beat-up."

"Do you remember the color?"

"White. But dirty white, 'cause it was beat-up and old."

"Are you sure it was Candace driving?"

"I thought I was, then I was positive it wasn't. But after listening to the podcast and you wanting to know of any possible sighting, I felt I should call."

"Who did you mention it to three years ago?"

"I don't want to say. I don't want to get anyone in trouble."

"No one is going to get in trouble," Regan said.

Lucas wasn't so certain about that, but he didn't comment.

"Did you tell the police?" Regan asked.

"No, and no one asked me. And...well, I called in, and I really hope you find out what she was doing."

"One more thing," Regan said. "Was there anything about the truck itself that stood out? Such as was it a work truck or was there a logo on the side? Maybe a bumper sticker?"

"I don't know. It was just a basic truck. I have to go."

"Thank you for calling."

Regan caught Lucas's eye, and she nodded. She thought this was valuable, he did, too, but how could they prove it? No one had called saying they saw her after Tuesday...yet she was alive, somewhere, until Saturday night.

Lizzy was frantically waving her arms. Lucas grabbed the blinking light on the phone.

"Hello, caller—"

The caller interrupted him. "Lucas, this is Willa March. I know the truck the other caller mentioned. It belongs to Sunrise Center."

Thirty-Four

Regan leaned forward as the director of Sunrise Center spoke.

"I noticed the truck was missing that Tuesday evening, but I thought one of my clients borrowed it without permission. The exterior has seen better days, but it's in great working condition. I let my clients borrow it if they had a job interview out of the area, or to do errands. I never reported it, and I didn't think... Oh, God, I should have known."

"You never reported the truck stolen?"

"No. It showed up on Saturday. My weekend director called about it. He was taking out the trash after dinner and it was parked behind the facility, keys in the glove box, unlocked. I really thought it was one of our clients, and I didn't want anyone to get in trouble. I never put two and two together until now."

"Willa, this isn't your fault. You couldn't have known Candace borrowed the truck." Regan paused, considered. "Did Candace know the truck was often used by your clients?"

"Yes. She even drove it a couple of times to pick up supplies."

"You said you noticed it missing Tuesday evening. Before or after dinner?"

"Before. I just don't know when I last saw it. I wish I had known it was Candace who took it. I would have told the police, and they could have been looking for her."

"Just to clarify, do you know for a fact that the truck wasn't parked behind your facility before Saturday?"

"All I can say is that it wasn't there on Friday before I left after the dinner hour. I don't know when it showed up on Saturday, it could have been anytime from early in the morning until after dinner. They usually clean up and take out the trash between eight and nine at night."

"It gives us a window."

Regan glanced at Lucas and nodded, hoped he would pop in with something. He seemed surprised at the level of detail of the last two callers. But he quickly composed himself and said, "Willa, thank you for calling in."

"I'm calling Detective Young. He needs to know."

"Good idea," Lucas said. "I'm sure he's listening, but he will probably have more questions."

He ended the call and said, "Did anyone else see the old, beat-up, white truck with Candace behind the wheel the week she was missing? In or out of the area? If you did, please call. We have ten more minutes. Regan, do you have anything to add?"

Regan took the opportunity to try and entice Alexa to call in—or call her directly. "Early in my career, I worked in courtroom security. I did a lot of things in this capacity, including protecting the courthouse where I worked, a judge once who had been threatened, escorting prisoners to and from jail, and protecting witnesses who were testifying— different from the Witness Protection Program. There was one witness I was assigned for the duration of a high-profile trial. She had information about a hit-and-run involving a drunk driver. She wasn't a witness to the crime, she was an emergency-room nurse who heard a dying statement from one of the victims, identifying the driver of the car which was different than what was reported. The driver allegedly panicked and fled and drove immediately to a police station and turned himself in. Except he hadn't been the driver— he took his boss, a high-ranking government official, home first. So it was a complex case, but the nurse was impeccable in her memory, and it enabled the police to get a warrant they otherwise might not have gotten. The nurse did her civic duty, the lawyers got a conviction, and justice was served.

"Sometimes, we know something that we think can't help the police, either because we have no evidence or because it's hearsay. But sometimes, it's that information that can help the police most, give them a different direction to investigate."

"Like the white truck," Lucas said.

"Exactly. Candace Swain clearly had something weighing on her mind the week she was missing. A responsible, dedicated student doesn't just disappear. So the question is: Where was Candace after Tuesday? Where did she go, and who did she visit?"

There were no more calls, but Regan felt they had far more information than they could have hoped for. Lucas wrapped up the podcast and signed off, and Regan then said, "My dad left me a message. I'm going to call him back, then I'm happy to drive you home when you're done editing."

She left Lucas and Lizzy to do their thing, and she stepped into the hall and called her father. "You texted me. We just finished. Did you listen?"

"Yes. That was powerful stuff. The information about the truck—it sounds exactly like Willa March."

"I didn't know you knew her."

"Met her a few times at community events, you know all the things I was forced to do when I was sheriff that I detested."

"That you secretly enjoyed."

"We have different recollections. Anyway, yes, I can see her avoiding getting the police involved, and so the story sounds legit to me. She has a solid reputation. But that's not why I called. I may have found why Lucas is so involved with this case."

"Oh?"

"His high-school girlfriend's older sister, you mentioned her at the beginning of the podcast. Adele Overton."

"Yes. He said she went missing while driving home from NAU, to Phoenix, during winter break six years ago." She paused, did the math. "That would make her the same age as Candace."

"Yes, it would. They were in the same class."

"Do you have something on that case?" Regan had been happy that Lucas had finally come clean about his real motivation. It made sense to her, and having that weight off her mind—that he wasn't hiding something important—helped her focus on the podcast tonight.

"I have more of the story. Adele was reported missing by her parents to campus police the day after she was supposed to have arrived home for winter break and her parents couldn't reach her. When it was determined she wasn't in her dorm, the state troopers put out a statewide alert for her vehicle along with her description, and the next day her car was found in New Mexico, outside Gallup near Red Rock Park. There was a small amount of blood in the trunk matching Adele's blood type. Her blood was also found on the steering wheel. They believed she was the victim of foul play. There was front-end damage to the car, but no broken glass in the area where her car was found. And there were no prints in the car, no witnesses, no cameras, and her body was never found. Her roommate had already left campus because her finals were early, so no one can say for certain what time she left."

Gallup was not on the road to Phoenix.

"Do you know why she was in Gallup?"

"No. The troopers made an educated guess that someone intentionally caused an accident for the purpose of hurting her."

He didn't have to explain what could have happened to Adele.

"Do you have anything else?" Regan asked.

"Campus police have a report. I only have the troopers' report. You can read it when you get here. The case was turned over to the FBI as a possible kidnapping across state lines, but New Mexico troopers were taking the lead because her car was found there."

She wondered if she could get the campus-police report tonight. Because now, again, she wondered if Lucas had told her everything he knew.

Regan made a stop at the campus-police office and suggested Lucas stay in the car. Though the administrative office was closed, they had officers on duty 24/7. Friday and Saturday nights were their busiest.

The door was locked, but she rang a bell and was buzzed in. The desk sergeant asked, "How can I help you?"

"I'm Regan Merritt, an alumna and former US Marshal. I'm looking for a report your office wrote up about a student who disappeared after leaving campus for winter break six years ago. An Adele Overton, a freshman who didn't make it home."

"You're not the first person who has asked for that report, and I remember it. Tragic. I've been here for fifteen years."

"And they have you working nights and weekends?"

He smiled. "My son is in high school. He plays baseball, and his games are always during the week. I'd rather give up my weekends than miss even one of his games."

Regan's chest tightened thinking about how much her son had loved baseball. She had missed too many of his games because of work or had had to observe from the parking lot because she was in full uniform and on call and didn't want to disturb people in the stands. Taking a thirty-minute break to watch, feeling lucky if she saw the little guy at bat. It was time she would never get back and the greatest regret of her life.

Because he was gone.

She said, "You're a good dad. I'm looking at the Overton case—a fresh pair of eyes, so to speak, and I can write out a formal FOIA request but was hoping to just take a look at the file."

"It's public information. I have no problem sharing it with you." He typed on the computer. "Everything is digital now. Pain in the ass when you type as slow as molasses, but really nice when you want to print out a report. Can you hold tight a minute?" he asked as he stood.

"Of course."

The sergeant left his desk and went into another room. A moment later, he returned with a printout of the report. "I need you to fill out and sign this form, so we have a record." He pushed a clipboard toward her.

She wrote her name, address, and purpose for her request, then signed.

"Merritt—your dad wouldn't by chance be Sheriff Merritt?"

"He would."

"Thought the name was familiar."

"Do you have a record of who else pulled this report?"

"Sure." He sat back down at his computer and typed. A moment later he said, "Three people. The troopers pulled it from their system, a lawyer in Phoenix—that was probably for the family. And a criminology student."

She didn't have to ask who, but she did anyway.

"Name?"

"Lucas Vega."

"Do you know when he asked for the report?"

Click, click. "Three and a half years ago. First-year student, stated it was for a class."

Regan thanked the sergeant and stepped out. Lucas was staring at his phone in the passenger seat. Standing under the overhang outside the campus-police building to avoid the rain, she opened the report and read it under the outdoor light.

It was standard: the Overton family had called the campus police when they couldn't reach Adele, campus police followed up, learned she was supposed to have left for home. Adele's roommate had left before her, and Adele's car wasn't in her assigned parking lot. Someone in the dorm said she had left the evening of November 30—the last day of finals—but that witness didn't know if Adele was leaving campus or not.

The campus police had sent out an email to all students asking if they had seen Adele Overton on or after November 30 while also alerting the state troopers to be on the lookout for Adele and her vehicle.

On the last page of witness statements, one student had responded to the campus-police inquiry:

Taylor James.

Ms. James, a nursing student who was in two classes with Ms. Overton, said that she and another first-year student, Candace Swain, had lunch with Ms. Overton at the student union on November 30. Ms. James stated that Ms. Overton told her and Ms. Swain that she was leaving that evening for home and would see them after the break. Their lunch was around 1:30 p.m., which was confirmed through a review of the campus meal-plan log system. Ms. James, Ms. Overton, and Ms. Swain all used their meal-plan cards between 1:20 and 1:25 at the student union on November 30. Per student records, that was the last time Ms. Overton's student card was used.

From the Missing Journal of Candace Swain

In my philosophy class last year the professor had us consider a quote by Martin Luther King Jr. I had never heard it, though the sentiment has been expressed by many. "It's always the right time to do the right thing."

I've never been into politics, but I care about people. That's why I want to be a nurse. And at that moment I realized why I had never come forward before about what happened to Adele.

I was scared. Then I thought it was too late. And maybe the more time that passed, the more trouble I would be in. Then a year passed. Two years. Now three years, and Adele is still gone. What can I do to change it? Nothing. And if I say anything, my life will be ruined. My life and others. What would that accomplish? So I buried it, convinced myself it was okay.

But it wasn't okay.

Lucas walked into my life at the writing lab. Right away I felt uncomfortable around him. He personally knew Adele, and I thought, *Does he know what happened?* But of course he doesn't. I couldn't lie to him if he asked and say I didn't know her, because what if he found out that I lied? So I admitted that Adele and I had a biology class together and said it was so sad about what happened. I expected him to agree and move on, drop the conversation.

But he didn't.

I'll never forget what he said.

"Her mother is still looking for her. She barely sleeps, she barely eats, she wants to know what happened. Her dad didn't even want her younger sister Amanda—my girlfriend—to go to college at all because he feared something would happen to her."

Lucas told me all about the Overton family. How Amanda went to college anyway, out of state, against her father's wishes. He told me how what happened to Adele tormented her family. That all they wanted was the truth, peace, a body to bury. Well, his girlfriend wants to bury her body, but her mother still thinks she's alive.

All I could think of while he talked and talked was that Adele was dead. She was dead, and I knew it, and I could be the one to help give her family peace.

But I said nothing. Then I told Lucas I couldn't tutor him anymore, I was quitting the writing lab. But he kept showing up wherever I went. When I was at the library, he was there. At the dining hall, he was there. It felt like he was stalking and watching me. I knew he knew something, but what and how could he know? What did Lucas Vega know about Adele's last day? Why was he hounding me?

Guilt was eating away at me.

I was there, which maybe makes me an accessory? I stood there and did nothing, said nothing. I let others make her disappear. They lied, and I lied with them. This lie that has eaten me from the inside out.

And no matter how hard I try, nothing I do can right this terrible wrong. Except tell the truth.

I realize I've been waiting years for the right time,

but it's always the right time to tell the truth and do the right thing. Now is the time.

I will convince Taylor to come forward with me. There's strength in numbers, and she must be as conflicted as me. Because how can anyone live with this guilt?

Thirty-Five

Regan drove Lucas home, then turned off the ignition and hopped out of the truck with him, saying, "I'd like to check out your apartment to make sure it's safe."

"Sure. Thanks."

They jogged up the stairs because Regan hadn't grabbed her umbrella. The rain was falling steadily again, and by the time they stepped inside the apartment, they were wet. She took off her jacket and hung it on the doorknob because there wasn't a coatrack by the door.

She did a thorough check of the windows and locks. Nothing looked disturbed, just as it had been when she last looked.

Regan turned to face him, holding up the file she had gotten from campus police. "I have Adele Overton's missing-person report here."

He stared at her. Didn't say anything.

"I know you also have it. But you didn't share that with me. Do you remember three days ago when I agreed to go on your podcast? I asked to see all the information you had."

"That report has nothing to do with Candace."

314 Allison Brennan

"Taylor was interviewed by campus police about Adele's disappearance. She and Candace were the last people to see her before she disappeared off the face of the earth, and you don't think that's relevant?"

He didn't say anything.

"If I can't trust you, I am of no use here."

"Okay. Okay! I withheld the campus-police report because I was hoping to use it on the podcast as a bombshell once I had more… I mean, I needed a direct connection between Candace and Adele before I could make it public. Otherwise, it all just sounded like a nutty conspiracy theory."

"I don't know what your theory is, but you sure as hell haven't told me everything. I thought we were a team here, Lucas. I want to help you, but you intentionally withheld important information. What else have you been holding back?"

He seemed nervous, and she wasn't sure why. Because she was angry with him? She wasn't going to apologize or coddle him. He was a grown man, on the verge of graduating from college. He could come clean now, or she would walk away.

And investigate whatever was going on without him.

She tried to push back on her temper, to get to the heart of what was going on. "Adele is the missing sister of your ex-girlfriend. You knew her a long time."

"I've known Adele most of my life."

"Would you have done this podcast on Candace Swain if you didn't think that she was connected to Adele's disappearance?"

"Yes, of course, she was my tutor." Then he plopped down on the couch and said, "Maybe not."

Regan sat in the chair across from him.

When he didn't say anything, she prompted. "From the beginning, tell me what you did, what you thought, who you talked to. Leave nothing out."

He had tears in his eyes now, but he wiped them away and began.

"In my Intro to Criminal Justice class my first semester here, one of the lectures was about campus police and their role versus local police. One of the officers came in to explain what they did, and he brought up missing persons—how many college students go missing, why you need to tell someone where you're going even though you're an adult, et cetera. I thought of Adele, and after the lecture I asked him if it was possible to get a missing-person report. I told him why—that my girlfriend's sister had disappeared, and I wanted to know what they did, what the troopers did, that kind of stuff. I was polite, and he said it was public information and to come into the campus-police station and fill out a form. So I did. And in that report was Candace Swain's name."

"And Taylor James's."

He nodded. "Yeah, but Candace was more accessible, and Taylor was kind of a bitch. I know that's not nice to say, but I did try to reach out to her, and she ignored me as if I were a gnat. Candace was genuinely a nice person. She worked in the writing lab, and so I made an appointment. I could use the help, anyway. I didn't know how to approach her, so I went to her for several weeks before I worked up the courage to ask her about Adele. She went from friendly to blank."

"Blank?"

"Like, we'd chat about a lot of things, and she was nice. Not flirting or anything but just friendly. And at the time, I wasn't thinking she had anything to do with Adele going missing—I just wanted to know more about her friendship with Adele, to find out if maybe she'd said anything, if she'd been depressed or struggling, had a stalker, I don't know. Something that would explain why her car was found in New Mexico.

"But as soon as I mentioned Adele, Candace shut down. Went blank. She canceled our next session. Then said she didn't have time to tutor and recommended someone else. I tracked her down because I knew that it was me mentioning Adele that changed everything. She just said she was upset about what had happened and knew nothing about it, and she was sorry. It was just…weird."

He stared at his hands, and Regan let him take his time. The truth was coming out, but maybe he was still processing it because he hadn't told anyone.

Finally, he said, "I tracked her down right before winter break. I was angry because I didn't know why she had reacted that way, and I laid into her. I told her that Adele's parents had no idea what happened to her, they'd never found her body, that Mrs. Overton thought her daughter was still alive and she spent her days and nights on missing-person websites looking at pictures. She called hospitals monthly. Probably still does, even now, six years later. Amanda, my ex-girlfriend, couldn't stand it and never wanted to go home. She told me she might as well be dead because her parents remained so focused on Adele that they forgot all about her. Their lives were in limbo, and her parents didn't have money for a private investigator, so I asked Candace if Adele had said anything to her about her plans, why she was going to New Mexico, if there was a boyfriend, *anything* that would help find her or discover the truth. All she told me was that she barely knew Adele, they'd had a class together and sometimes had lunch together, and that was it, and to leave her alone."

"But you didn't leave her alone, did you?"

"At first, I did. I tried to talk to Taylor James, but I guess Candace had said something to her because Taylor wouldn't talk to me, either. That's when I started thinking something truly weird was going on. But between classes and working part-time, I couldn't follow up. Then, right after spring break, I had a memory pop up in my social media. It had been from four years before, when Adele had been a senior in high school. Me, Amanda, and Adele at a concert. And I cried because of everything I'd lost. I lost Amanda, I lost Adele, who was like a big sister to me, I lost friends because all I did in high school was try to help the Overton family. And then I got mad. I confronted Candace."

"At the party?"

"No. The Monday before the Spring Fling. I told her that if she knew anything about what had happened to Adele, she needed to come clean. That if she didn't, she was tormenting a good family for her own selfish reasons. I was cruel—I mean, I have never said anything like that to anyone. On Friday before the party, I went to apologize, because I hadn't meant to be so vicious. But my way of apologizing was to ask her to be my tutor again, and I just said I was sorry, I was out of line, and she told me no. Just, simply, no.

"And then she disappeared."

While Regan didn't think that Lucas was capable of cold-blooded murder, he had certainly landed himself on the suspect list with that confession—especially since he'd never told the police.

She asked, "What did you think would happen if you

solved Candace's murder? That you would find out what happened to Adele?"

"They're connected. I have nothing to base that on, except that when I finally confronted Candace, after she walked away, she turned back and looked right at me. She said, 'I'm really sorry.' I know, you probably think she said that because she couldn't help me or that she felt sorry for me, but it was *how* she said it. You had to be there. I decided to give her a little space, a couple weeks, then I planned to reach out to her again.

"I didn't know Candace had been missing until I found out she was dead. There wasn't a lot of public information about her murder, and the newspaper said the police were looking for a homeless guy who had harassed sorority girls. And I thought that was it, I would never know what happened to Adele. No one would know what happened to her. And I put it all aside, got on with my studies.

"When I took the internship at the morgue, I didn't do it with the purpose of investigating Candace's murder. I was filing reports for the ME, and I came across her file. Read it. That's when I learned she had been missing for over a week before she was killed, that she hadn't drowned in Hope Springs Lake, and that there was no physical evidence. I looked into the case as it stood. None of it made sense.

"Candace was popular and always went above and beyond. She volunteered everywhere. She built homes for homeless veterans through a program during the summers in Colorado. She worked at Sunrise Center downtown. I thought, *Is that maybe how her killer knew her?* But the manner of her death didn't make much sense, especially since she didn't drown in the lake where she was found. I read everything I could, and Joseph Abernathy seemed like a good suspect on the surface, but once I talked to Willa March and found out the seriousness of his alcoholism? It didn't make sense that he could kill her, then move her body and cover up the crime, then disappear on a train. So I came up with the podcast idea because I thought someone must have seen her during that week. Maybe they didn't know what they knew, but *someone* knew something. And that's everything. I swear, Regan."

"You thought when you started this podcast that Candace knew something more about Adele's disappearance," Regan said.

"Yes."

"Exactly what?"

He didn't answer. "I didn't have evidence. Just that Taylor and Candace had lunch with Adele the day she left campus. And then their reaction to me when I started asking questions. Taylor was angry and Candace was sad. That's it. She shut me out, but I just sensed she knew more. I didn't know how or why. Adele didn't belong to Sigma Rho or any sorority. But based on her schedule and digging around social media, I learned that the three of them had shared a class, then Adele and Taylor had had another class together. They'd all had lunch the last day of finals. It reasoned that they had done other things together. In the back of my mind, I thought that if I could figure out where Candace had been when she was missing, I might find out where Adele was—that maybe she'd gone missing for the same reason."

"Do you think she's alive?"

He shook his head. "She would never do that to her family. And if she was in an accident with a head injury or something, eventually authorities would have traced her to her family. And I realized my initial hypothesis just didn't work. It was based on some conspiracy theory that there was a serial killer who kept his victims alive before he killed them, or something stupid like that. None of the physical evidence held with anything bizarre like that. I think Adele's dead. And the troopers' theory—that someone created an accident and grabbed her—makes sense. It's plausible. But then why was Candace acting so odd, so sad, when I talked to her about Adele? Which led me to believe she knew more about Adele's disappearance."

Everything Lucas said answered Regan's questions and concerns. And opened up far more. According to both Candace's roommate Annie and Richie Traverton, she had changed at the end of her fall semester—just when Lucas was pushing her for more about information about Adele. She had acted out of character, like quitting the writing lab.

"I'm really sorry."

Guilt? Understanding? Empathy? What was Candace feeling at the time?

Regan wouldn't think twice about her reaction if Candace was simply empathetic about what Lucas was going through. Lucas overreacted. But Candace was now dead, Taylor was dead, and they were the last two people known to have seen Adele Overton before she left campus.

"I have some evidence," Lucas said and pulled something out of his pocket. He handed her a photo.

She recognized Taylor and Candace. "Is this Adele in the middle?"

"Yes."

She turned over the photo. On the back was written *Me with my BFFs, last day of classes before finals!*

"Where did you get this?"

"Taylor's house."

"You said you didn't go in the house."

"I went back."

"Dammit, Lucas."

"This was all I took, I swear." He paused. "I wore gloves."

That didn't make it better. Before she could admonish him further, he said, "I looked the last day of classes up from that year. November 20. Finals were the next week, then break started on November 30."

"Did you take anything else?"

"No. I swear. But I think her computer is missing. There were cords for a laptop, but no laptop."

"The police will have searched her house and made note of that," she said as she handed the photo back to him. "We'll keep this between you and me for now." She was concerned that his impulsive actions might have a permanently detrimental impact on his future career plans.

She wanted to turn all of this over to Detective Young. If she and Lucas could make a compelling case, maybe he would pursue it.

Yet…she didn't know if she trusted the cop. She wanted to. Nothing in his background said he was corrupt. But he was dating Rachel Wagner, which gave Regan pause.

Why? Because you didn't like her when you met her? Or because you think she had something to do with all this?

What would Rachel gain by helping Taylor cover up Candace's murder?

Until Regan could answer that definitively, she didn't know how much she should tell Young. She *wanted* to, because it was the right thing to do: it was his investigation. But maybe…she should bring in someone else, such as turn everything over to the sheriff's department. They technically didn't have jurisdiction, except for Taylor's death.

She wanted to run this all by her dad, see what he had

to say. He understood the potential problems and legal issues far better than she. For her, the most important thing was to make sure Lucas and Alexa were safe *now* while she and Lucas kept looking into Candace's disappearance and homicide through the podcast and follow-up.

Alexa definitely knew more about what had happened to Candace. And she might be the only person still alive who did—which put her in danger and which Regan might be able to use to get Detective Young to revisit the case sooner rather than later.

But none of Lucas's theories pointed to who might have killed Candace.

"Lucas, I'm going to try to convince Alexa Castillo to talk to me. Can you stay here? Don't leave the apartment. Don't answer the door."

"Okay."

"I'm serious," she said because he didn't sound convinced. "We opened up this hornets' nest tonight. You have been feeding details about Candace's death out, enticing listeners, implying you have more... What if the killer thinks you can implicate them?"

"But if Taylor killed Candace, why would anyone else come after me?"

"You can't assume that, not without more evidence. Let me work this out, and I'll call you as soon as I know something."

Thirty-Six

It was nearly nine thirty that night when Regan arrived at Alexa Castillo's house northeast of downtown, on a pine-lined street filled with small, well-maintained, single-story homes that were built in the early seventies. Jessie had lived not far from here when she first moved to Flagstaff with her mom; it was walking distance to their middle school for Jessie. Regan had lived too far out of town, so the bus had been her only option.

Even though the teacher didn't have an online presence, Regan knew how to locate almost anyone, so a few public database searches and some logical guesses gave her Alexa's address.

The lights were on, and Regan suspected that Alexa's daughter would be asleep, so now was the best time to talk to her.

She knocked on the door. The small porch was filled with potted plants, blossoms just now peeking out as winter was fading into spring. The rain had slowed, intermittent drops falling lightly to the earth. But it was cold, and she would have really enjoyed being home with the fire going.

But she needed answers, and Alexa Castillo had them.

A man answered. Early thirties, clean-cut, Hispanic. "May I help you?"

"I'm looking for Alexa Castillo. I'm Regan Merritt. I talked to her at her school earlier today."

His face darkened. "She doesn't want to talk to you."

"I have new information. Tell her it's about Adele Overton."

He closed the door. Two minutes later, he opened it. "Bella is sleeping. Do not raise your voice. And if you upset Alexa, you'll need to leave, understood?"

"Of course. And you are?"

"Mateo Sandoval. Her boyfriend."

He led her into the kitchen, where Alexa was sitting at a small round table, her head in her hands. She looked up at Regan, tears in her eyes. "I listened to the podcast. I'm scared."

Mateo sat down next to her, put his arm around her. "I'm not leaving you, baby. It's going to be okay. You don't want her here, she goes."

"I should never have written that letter."

Regan took a seat across from them. The kitchen was clean but cluttered, filled with cheerfully colorful dishes and tile work. The refrigerator door couldn't be seen through all the artwork attached to it with alphabet letter magnets.

"The anonymous letter where you witnessed the argument between Candace and Taylor."

She nodded. "Except I wasn't there. I heard about it, knew about it, but I wasn't there. I just thought I could do something."

"Was Kimberly Foster there?"

"Yes. I thought after I wrote it that someone would talk to Kim. I don't know, but I think she would have told the truth. I mean, she has a lot to lose, but at the same time, I don't think she would lie. But I don't know."

"Start at the beginning. You weren't at the Spring Fling party, but Candace came out to Kingman to see you."

She nodded. "She called late Friday night, told me she was coming. Got there at three in the morning. We talked until dawn, cried, slept, talked more. But that wasn't the beginning."

Regan took a leap. "Adele Overton. She was the beginning."

Tears formed in Alexa's eyes, and she nodded.

"Do you know what happened to her?"

"Candace knew, and she told me. I should have known."

When she didn't continue, Regan asked, "Did you know, before I mentioned Adele's name tonight on the podcast, that Lucas had known her?"

"Yes, because Candace told me. She told me about Lucas, that he'd been friends with Adele's family. That he said some things to her that had her questioning everything. And then, as I listened, I realized why he started this podcast in the first place."

"To solve Adele's disappearance."

She nodded. "It all made sense. I should have realized it sooner, but everything clicked tonight."

"What were Taylor and Candace really arguing about?" Regan asked.

"I'm scared. There were four people in that conversation, and two of them are dead."

"That will not happen to you," Mateo said firmly.

"But you didn't overhear the conversation," Regan said.

She shook her head. "I only said I was there in the letter because I didn't think you would take me seriously if I weren't."

Regan had suspected that. Good to know her instincts were still strong. "Go on."

"At the end of the Spring Fling, Candace asked Taylor to go to the police with her and tell them what had happened to Adele. She said it was the right thing to do because her family was still looking for her. Taylor said no, that they would all go to jail."

"And Kimberly Foster was there."

"Yes. And based on what Candace said, Kim was on the fence. She had already graduated, she had a good job, she had a lot to lose, but she reminded them that it had been an accident, and she thought they should get a lawyer to help with their statement. Kim was always practical like that. Candace didn't want to, she felt so guilty, but she said she would do it if that meant telling the truth. Then Rachel said no."

"Rachel Wagner was there?" Vicky had mentioned it this morning, but Rachel implied that she'd only been around for part of the discussion.

"Yes. Rachel insisted that they would all go to jail, she would lose her job, never attain full professor, that even if they got probation, it would cost time and money and they wouldn't be eligible for certain jobs. Rachel had a way of getting into your head, and she told Kim her life would be over—Kim was dating a ballplayer then, she was making nearly six figures two years out of college, she would lose her job and the condo she'd just bought, and everyone would talk about her. Kim was practical, but she was also vain, and she finally sided with Taylor and Rachel. Candace left. Then she called me."

"Why did she call you?"

"Because I was there when Adele died."

Alexa breathed in deeply, let it out, asked Mateo for

water. Then, finally, she started to talk. "It was over six years ago. I was a sophomore, Adele was a freshman. The last night of finals, we all went to Rachel's apartment."

"Your advisor."

"She wasn't our advisor then. It was her first year teaching on her own. She was friends with Kim and a bunch of other girls. She liked to hang out with us."

"Who was there?"

"Me, Kim, Candace, Taylor, and Adele. And, of course, Rachel."

"What happened?"

"I don't know."

"What do you mean you don't know? Were you there or weren't you?"

"Hey," Mateo interrupted. "Don't badger her. This is hard enough."

She hadn't thought she was badgering, but Alexa contradicted herself and Regan needed clarity.

"I don't remember much of anything about that night," Alexa said. "I'm telling you the truth. We had homemade wine coolers and drank a lot. Then Taylor brought out joints. I remember that much, I wasn't so drunk I was passing out, but I was definitely intoxicated. Rachel didn't want anyone smoking in her apartment, so the six of us walked to the preserve next to the country club. It wasn't far—just on the other side of her complex. It was dark, and there was a steep hill to get up there. We sat down and smoked, and then…I remember absolutely nothing after that. I don't even remember smoking. I don't remember how I got back to Rachel's. I don't know how long we were out there. I don't remember *anything* until I woke up the next morning with the worst hangover in the world. I was so sick. I don't drink a lot, and so I thought this was normal. I still can't drink alcohol after that night, I don't even like the smell.

"When I woke up in Rachel's apartment, Candace was the only one there. She was on the phone with someone, yelling at them, which is what woke me up. She hung up and threw her phone across the room. She looked angry, and she'd been crying. I asked her what was wrong, and she wouldn't talk to me. Then I asked where everyone was, and Candace said she didn't know. Later—I don't know how long because I fell asleep again—Kim, Rachel, and Taylor came in. I still felt awful, and Candace was making me drink a lot of water and eat crackers. I asked where Adele was—or Candace did, I don't remember. Rachel said she hadn't come to the party last night. She turned to me, said didn't I remember that Adele had decided to go home? I remembered precisely nothing. I *thought* Adele had been at the apartment, but everything was a jumble, and when Rachel said she wasn't there, it was like I erased any memories of her. I looked at Candace, and she didn't say anything. Then I just assumed I remembered wrong. I was really sick and out of it."

They had basically gaslighted Alexa. Candace knew the truth, but she remained silent.

Until her conscience couldn't take it anymore.

"What happened to Adele?" Regan asked.

"I didn't know until Candace came to me after the Spring Fling. I didn't even make the connection, even though I knew that Adele had gone missing after winter break."

Alexa drank her water; her hand was shaking.

"I was living with my parents in Kingman, single and six months pregnant. I was a student teacher and trying to figure out what I was going to do about my life as a single mom. That's when she told me the truth."

"The truth about Adele," Regan prompted.

"The pot was laced. Taylor brought it, swore that she hadn't known, but it was either LSD or PCP or something really bad. Adele freaked out the worst and ran into the woods. Candace was the only one who wasn't impaired, and she tried to catch up to her, but Adele turned, knocked her down. Then Adele jumped up, took off, and ran into a tree. She stumbled and fell down a short cliff. Her head split open on a rock. It was an accident, but Candace said everyone panicked. Even her—and Candace is pretty unflappable. But Rachel convinced us—I guess me, too, though I don't remember—that we couldn't say anything because our lives would be ruined. Rachel was hysterical. Said she would go to jail and lose everything—her job, her life—because she had given us the alcohol and let us get stoned. This was before pot was legal and we were all under twenty-one. She was an associate professor, so she'd be doubly punished, and we'd all be expelled. Rachel said it was an accident, and our lives shouldn't be ruined because of an accident.

"That night Candace stayed at my side because I guess I was really out of it, and she thought I might need to go to the hospital. Rachel, Kim, and Taylor went to move Adele's body. Candace said that she had always felt guilty, but that she'd met someone who knew Adele and now she had to tell the truth. She told me about the argument at the Spring Fling.

"Taylor told Candace what they did with Adele's body. Kim's family owns hundreds of acres in Payson. There's an abandoned gold mine near her property, and they put her body in the mine." Tears were rolling down Alexa's face. "Candace wanted to find her, take pictures, and go to the police. But she didn't know where the property was or how to find it. I gave her some ideas on how to track it down, and she went back to campus to use the library. She was going to inspect all the mines near Kim's property to find the right one and then get the evidence and go to the police. She wanted to put Adele's body to rest and give peace to her family."

Mateo got up and brought back tissues for Alexa. She blew her nose, then wiped her face. He kissed the top of her head.

"I would have gone with her to Payson, but I was having a difficult time with the pregnancy, and I was also working. I couldn't leave. She went back to campus to access the library and find old maps of Payson to locate the right mine. She said she was going to try to be incognito because if Rachel and Taylor knew what she was doing, they might stop her. And that's the last I heard from her."

"Why did she steal the Sunrise Center truck? Why not take her car?"

"I don't know. Maybe because she didn't think her little VW Bug could get up into the mountains. Some of those mines are really remote. She would have to park and hike in."

That made sense. Regan asked, "What about Adele's car in New Mexico?"

"After they put her body in the mine, they drove to Gallup and left her car there, making it seem like she'd gotten into an accident. Came back to campus as if nothing happened and left for winter break. When they heard that Adele was missing, they pretended to be shocked. I'm so sorry I never said anything before, but when Candace was killed, I was terrified that if I said anything, I would be next. I didn't have any firsthand information or proof, and I couldn't even swear that Adele was at Rachel's apartment because I don't remember anything from that night. When Candace died, I was six months pregnant, and all I could think about was my daughter being raised without me. Am I going to jail? Are they going to arrest me?"

"No," Regan said. She highly doubted that anyone would prosecute Alexa. First, there was no proof that she had been involved, and her story was credible. She didn't remember anything from that night and only knew about it because Candace told her three years later. Unless the police could catch Alexa in a lie, Regan didn't think any DA would take the case.

And now, Regan knew where Candace had gone on Tuesday after she had left the library. She'd "borrowed" the Sunrise Center truck and driven to Payson. It was nearly a three-hour drive from campus. It could have taken her days to inspect all the mines in the area. Then she returned, either because she'd found proof or...didn't find anything.

Alexa said, "She documented everything."

"What do you mean, *documented*?"

"In her journal. She wrote down everything that she remembered about the night Adele died, and she wrote down everything that happened at the Spring Fling."

"Her roommate told me about her journal, but the police never found it, and her family doesn't have it."

"She hid it. Rachel Wagner had become the Sigma Rho advisor that year, the year after I graduated, and Candace didn't trust her because of what had happened to Adele. So she bought one of those prepaid flip phones, and she kept her journal in the library where no one would find it."

Hope grew, just a little bit. "Do you know where?"

Alexa shook her head. "She never told me. Only that the

chances of anyone checking out the book she had hollowed out to hide the journal were next to zero."

Mateo spoke up. "Do these people at the sorority, the ones responsible for Adele's death, know that Candace sought Alexa's help? Do they know who she is? Are they going to come after her?"

"No, but they do know that Alexa was there when Adele died, and they might think she knows what happened."

Alexa turned her head, buried it in her boyfriend's shoulder. Mateo said, "I'm not going to let anything happen to you or Bella, honey. I promise."

"I'd suggest that if there is a way to leave town for a couple of days, you do it. Just as a precaution." But Regan was torn about what to do. Talk to Detective Young...or find the answers herself.

"You can't tell anyone about me," Alexa said. "Please don't. I haven't participated in Sigma Rho alumnae events since I graduated. I don't fill out surveys. I never told them where I was working or living. If Rachel finds out..."

"Right now, I can keep your confidence, but you may need to talk to the police later. I can help with the process. I've worked with a lot of witnesses, and I haven't lost one."

"But you're no longer a marshal," Mateo said pointedly.

"I have lots of friends who are. I won't reveal your name without talking to you first, okay? But I am going to look for Candace's journal. Your name might be in it." After tonight, Regan absolutely didn't believe that Taylor had died of an accidental overdose. Either she killed herself out of guilt, or Rachel Wagner killed her to keep her quiet.

Maybe Rachel thought Taylor was Lucas's anonymous letter writer, which would explain why she felt the need to kill her and why Taylor's computer was missing.

Mateo said, "Baby, I'll take you and Bella to my parents' house this weekend. We'll be safe there, and we can stay as long as we need to." He turned to Regan. "You'll call when you know anything, okay?"

"I will."

Thirty-Seven

Vicky spent the entire evening trying to keep her sorority sisters happy. Now she finally understood what her mother always used to tell her: "You can't make all the people happy all the time."

She never liked that adage because she'd worked so hard for years to make sure that everyone was listened to, that everyone had a voice, that people *were* happy. And she'd done a terrific job of it.

But now people were complaining or worried.

Why would someone in the sorority disguise their voice and call in to the podcast? Why wouldn't they bring the information to the council and let them decide as a group?

Vicky just felt sick about the whole thing. Maybe she was wrong, and she should have let Sigma Rho participate in the podcast. But she was so certain that creep had killed Candace. It made sense at the time, and it had really freaked everyone out—as well as Vicky. No one wants to see an old drunk pull out his junk and take a leak. And that's what the police thought, too. They just couldn't find him.

But what if they were wrong? What if the police had gotten it wrong? Or…maybe Candace really did take the truck and then the creep killed her.

She frowned, rubbed her eyes, and flopped down on the couch in their lounge. She just wanted this all to be over. The podcast was ruining her last year in college. It overshadowed everything she was doing. They were planning this year's Spring Fling, which was still five weeks away, and all people could talk about was Candace and the podcast.

Nia Perez walked into the lounge, looked around. "Hey, have you seen Nicole?"

Nia was on Vicky's shit list for contacting the podcast about Candace driving on Sunday. They'd figured out it was her real quick. If they did nothing when someone violated the rules, then everyone would break the rules. They hadn't expelled her, so why was everyone upset?

"She's around," Vicky said. That was another thing. Her best friend didn't agree with her on this. Nicole said she understood, but she'd been spending less and less time with Vicky and more time with the troublemakers, which was how Vicky saw the minority of sisters who wanted to help Lucas Vega.

"Okay. I'll check the quad."

"Did you call her?"

"I texted her. She didn't respond."

"Try our room. She's probably studying." Vicky had to remember that she was the president: she had to be accessible and friendly to everyone, even the rule-breakers.

"I knocked. She didn't answer. It's not a big deal. I'll call her later."

Nia hurried away. Probably still felt guilty for betraying the sisterhood. Vicky *hoped* she did.

Vicky got up from the couch and finished organizing their lounge. She liked things in their place and having a cheery environment to hang out in. Usually Nicole helped her, but she hadn't been around most of the evening. Probably because she had betrayed the sorority. Betrayed *her*.

The more Vicky thought about it, the more she thought it was Nicole who'd called in to the podcast and disguised her voice. Why hadn't she come to her first? Vicky would have listened.

Honestly, she was hurt. Ever since the podcast started, she and Nicole had been arguing. Vicky hated conflict. She needed to figure it out. She didn't want to lose her best friend. They had done everything together for four years. They'd planned to move close to each other, maybe even share an apartment, depending on where they ended up working.

This whole thing was making her half-crazy. She didn't know what she was supposed to do. Rachel had been the only one she could talk to. She'd been solid through this whole ordeal.

Vicky turned off the lights and went up to her room. She unlocked the door; the room was dark. It was eleven, maybe Nicole had gone to sleep, but you'd think she would have left a light on.

Vicky turned on the small light over her desk. Nicole was lying on her bed, fully clothed. "Nicole," she said. "We really need to talk."

Nicole ignored her. Was she that upset? Vicky was the one who had a right to be angry about everything that had happened the last two weeks, ever since that stupid podcast started and split the sorority in half.

"Nicole, come on, this is important."

Vicky sat at the end of Nicole's bed. She didn't move. Maybe she had fallen asleep.

"Nicole," Vicky said, shaking her lightly. "I'm sorry, okay? Please forgive me." She didn't know why she was apologizing, this was mostly Nicole's fault, except that Vicky felt bad and she couldn't lose her best friend over this.

Nicole didn't respond.

"Are you okay?"

Vicky got up and shook her by the shoulders. Rolled her over. Her arm flopped over the edge.

She wasn't breathing.

Thirty-Eight

Saturday

Both Regan and her dad were early risers, so she wasn't surprised to find him drinking coffee in the nook when she came downstairs at five thirty. She poured her own coffee and sat next to him. The sun was just rising, but they couldn't see any colors in the sky, telling her that it was overcast, even though it wasn't raining. At least not yet.

"What happened with Lucas?" he asked.

She told him everything she'd learned from Lucas and Alexa. "I want to pass this over to Detective Young, but he's involved with Rachel Wagner. They're dating."

"The advisor? The one you think may have covered up Adele Overton's death?"

She nodded. "I believe Alexa. If you talked to her, you'd believe her, too. Everything she's said has been substantiated by the information we have. She could have ignored the podcast and not written that letter. She wants to do the right thing but is legitimately scared. Plus, she has a young daughter. Her boyfriend is taking her out of town, and I have their contact information."

"Young has a conflict of interest. You should bring this to his boss."

"Taylor was killed—"

"There's no evidence she was murdered. You said it was considered an accidental overdose, pending investigation."

"This is part of that investigation."

"But Candace Swain is Young's case, and while NAU has their own police department, they would immediately pass a capital case to FPD, so going to them would just delay the investigation. Like I said, go to Young's boss, let her figure out whether to reassign or pull Young in." He paused. "You don't have enough, do you?"

"Alexa's statement. She has no firsthand knowledge except that Candace was with her from late Friday night until Sunday afternoon. She can swear to what Candace told her, but that's it. A defense attorney would tear her statements apart without additional evidence. Lucas and I traced Candace's whereabouts up through Tuesday, when she was seen in the Sunrise Center truck, and then we have Alexa's statement that she planned to go to Payson. I want her journal. Alexa said she hid it in the library, so that's where Lucas and I are going as soon as they open."

"And then?"

"I'll go to Young's boss. I want to warn Young about Rachel, but then I'd have to spill everything, so it needs to go up the food chain."

"I know the chief well. I'm happy to help facilitate this."

"Thanks. I may call on you."

"I'll be at the golf course with Henry. Nine holes and then lunch."

"It's not raining now, but it doesn't look promising for this afternoon."

"We'll get in as many holes as we can," her dad said. "Can I share this with him?"

"I don't see why not. If he has any advice, let me know."

Regan left to pick up Lucas. They would need to put their heads together to find Candace's journal.

As soon as he got in her truck, he said, "Lizzy is meeting us there. It's okay that I told her what's going on, right?"

"We need help, but let's keep this between the three of us for now. If the killer knows that Candace hid her journal in the library, they might find it first."

"Unless they already have."

"Hey, no pessimism," she said. "You were far more optimistic than I was at the beginning."

"Until I realized what happened to Adele. My faith in people is nonexistent right now."

"Her death is an apparent accident. Covering up an accidental death? That's a crime, but it's rarely prosecuted and often with minimal penalties. Candace? She was murdered because she wanted to tell the truth about what happened to Adele, and that's because of you. Even if you didn't know it, you brought Candace's humanity to the surface, and she wanted to do the right thing. It's easy to go along with the crowd, but we all have a conscience."

She glanced over at Lucas. He still seemed disillusioned. "I think we should call Chrissy Swain. She knew Candace better than anyone."

"She's going to be heartbroken when she finds out what Candace did to Adele."

"Maybe. But she also wants the truth."

"Do we have to tell her now? She should know, but I don't want to tell her. I wouldn't know where to begin."

"We don't have evidence, and we don't need to say anything until we do, but Chrissy will learn the truth."

"Okay. Good. Just—let's be careful here."

Regan understood Lucas's conflict. Sometimes, the truth wasn't pretty. But it was real, and she had to show him it was better than keeping secrets.

Secrets got Candace killed.

They arrived at the library just after it opened. Lizzy wasn't there, but Lucas texted her where they would be.

Regan closed the study-room door and Lucas called Chrissy. He put the phone on speaker.

When she answered, he said, "Hi, Chrissy, it's Lucas Vega. I'm here with Regan Merritt, who's been helping me with the podcast."

"Lucas, hey. I just finished listening to the podcast from last night. You really are doing it. You're going to find out what happened to my sister. Thank you so much."

"We're close," he said. "But we need some help."

"Anything."

"A friend of Candace told us that she may have hidden her journal in the library, in a hollowed-out book."

Chrissy said, "You think it's still there, after three years?"

"Yes. If someone found it, they would have turned it in to the librarian, who would have turned it in to the police," Regan said.

"Unless the person who killed her found it."

"It's possible but I think unlikely," Regan said. "Lucas has received two threatening notes, and you know what happened to Taylor."

"Was she killed, too?"

"That's still being investigated. But I think if Candace's killer found the journal, they wouldn't care about the podcast. That journal is, potentially, the only evidence we have about what Candace was doing and might give us a motive for her death."

"You've lost me."

Regan couldn't betray Alexa's confidence, but she felt she should share part of what they'd learned with Candace's sister. Lucas didn't want to say anything, so Regan spoke vaguely of their theory. "We believe that Candace was aware of a crime and wrote in her journal about it. She wanted to go to the police, her friends didn't, and that may have been the reason she was killed."

"Oh, God, that…that would be awful. You think someone she knew killed her? Someone she trusted?"

"It's possible. So if the journal is here, we need to find it," Regan said.

"What do you need from me?" Chrissy asked.

"You knew Candace better than anyone. We need to make a list of her interests, favorite books, anything that we can use to narrow down our search. I'll start," Regan said. "My contact said that Candace was in the library researching gold mines in Payson. So books about Payson, Payson history, and gold mines should be on the list."

"Right. Okay," Chrissy said, "her favorite book in high school was *To Kill a Mockingbird*. She read it like a hundred times."

Regan thought that book would be too small to hide a journal in, plus it could easily be checked out for a class or used in research. But she wrote it down. "What were some of her other favorite books?"

Chrissy gave them a list of popular YA fiction. "She was a nursing student, so anything related to that."

Together, they brainstormed and came up with a detailed list of possible books Candace would have used to hide her journal.

Lucas promised to let Chrissy know if they found it, and they ended the call. Lizzy ran in. "Oh my God, Lucas, Nicole Bergamo is in the hospital. In a coma."

"What happened?"

"I don't know. Someone posted it on social media. Last night her roommate, Vicky Ryan, found her unconscious and not breathing. People are speculating an attempted suicide. Her parents are coming in from Washington, and Vicky is at the hospital with her."

Suicide seemed unlikely. Regan asked Lizzy, "When you talked to her, did she say anything that made you think she was suicidal?"

"No. Nicole is one of the nicest, happiest people I know."

That didn't necessarily mean she didn't have problems, and mental-health issues were sometimes not easy to identify.

Lizzy continued. "Nicole is the one who called in last night. I disguised her voice like I promised. What if she knows more? And she never identified the person who told her not to go to the police, who told her she was wrong about the truck."

"Lucas, you and Lizzy start looking for the journal. I'm going to make a call."

They left the room, and Regan called her dad. He hadn't started his golf game yet.

"Dad, I need a favor."

"Anything."

"One of the Sigma Rho sorority girls is in the hospital, in a coma, found unconscious last night. She was the disguised voice on the podcast. I'm worried about her safety."

"I'll talk to the hospital, get security on the door, at least for twenty-four hours. Is that good?"

"Yes, thank you." She ended the call.

Ten minutes later, as Regan was looking through the Payson history books, Lucas texted her.

I found it.

The three of them met back in the study room. Lucas had found Candace's journal in the middle of a hollowed-out book about Fanny Durack, the first female Olympic swimming champion.

Heads together, they read through the journal, and Regan immediately identified the tipping point. It started with Lucas, but it ended with indifference.

From the Journal of Candace Swain

Kim and Taylor were laughing Friday night.

Kim is doing great. She has an amazing new job as media rep for a pharmaceutical company. Taylor always admired her. And all I could think about was that Adele wanted a future, too. That she wanted to be a nurse and help people. And she was dead. And her family hurt. And they should know the truth.

I thought about how I would feel if it were Chrissy. If she disappeared and I didn't know what had happened to her. I don't think I could function. I would demand that someone do something. I would search everywhere for her. I wouldn't rest until I knew the truth. But if Chrissy were Adele? No one would find her body. And that was it. I would be lost. Broken. And at that moment, I knew what I had to do.

I went to Kim and Taylor and told them we had to tell the truth. We had to at least tell Adele's family. If they didn't want to go to the police, maybe an anonymous letter—tell them where she was buried. Kim said no, but then we talked, and she said she would consider it if we went to a lawyer first, to protect us. I didn't care about that! But I wanted Kim on my side, so I agreed. Taylor wanted none of it, and then Rachel came over and Taylor told her everything we'd discussed. Rachel was livid, told us we would be in serious trouble but she would be the one in jail. And if we wanted her in prison, go ahead.

Then Kim faltered. We had to remain silent. No anonymous letter, no going to the police, no anything. It had been an accident, she didn't want anyone to get in trouble, or worse.

I'd once admired Kim. I'd once loved Taylor like a sister. And they both turned on me, because of Rachel. For the first time I saw Rachel's true face.

She gloated. I could see it in her expression, the way her eyes looked into mine silently saying, *I won.* She didn't care about any of us. She only cared about herself. How could I have not seen the truth for the last three and a half years? How could I have trusted Rachel and not realized she is a monster?

I have to find answers.

But I'm scared, too.

I'm on my own.

No one wants to tell the truth.

I'm heartbroken.

I hate myself. I hate my sisters. What is loyalty when they want you to do the wrong thing?

I don't blame Alexa. She was so out of it that night, and she has someone more important to worry about. She would have come with me to Payson if she weren't so pregnant and throwing up every morning. She's scared about the baby, about being a single mom, and I don't want to add to that. None of this was her fault. She said when I had proof she would back me up. But how can she when she doesn't remember anything that happened the night Adele died?

I can't live like this anymore. Damn Lucas Vega for reminding me that there are people out there who loved Adele.

Maybe it was spending winter break with my baby

sister who has always, 100% of the time, done the right thing. She would be the first to say she's not perfect, but I don't see it. She is kind, she is truthful, she is sweet and loving and smart and helpful. I was going to tell her what happened to Adele and seek her advice, but I didn't have the courage. And I knew exactly what she would have said.

She'd have told me to come forward. Because it is the right thing to do. I can practically hear her voice: "Better late than never, Candy Cane." She's the only person I ever allow to call me Candy, a nickname I hate. But Chrissy says it with love. I miss her so much.

I hate that I'm going to disappoint her. My parents, sure, but mostly my little sister who always looked up to me, when truthfully, I looked up to her because she is a better person than I could ever hope to be.

I'm really scared. When I came back after talking to Alexa, Taylor saw me. Asked me where I was and what I was doing. I lied, of course. I will never risk Alexa, not after everything she's done for me. But I couldn't stay in the dorm anymore. Taylor wasn't herself, she seemed…cold. Different. She gave off a weird vibe. I think she's the one who searched my dorm room over the weekend. Things were moved and my plant was knocked over. It was her or Rachel. I just think Rachel would have been sneakier and have cleaned up the mess.

I can't believe Taylor would try to hurt me, but I also can't believe what we all did three years ago, and that she's okay with it.

I think I've finally figured out where they took Adele's body. I narrowed it down to three possible places. I'm going to find proof. Taylor can't know what I'm doing. I can't let her or Rachel stop me. I have to just do it. Like Chrissy always says: Do, or do not.

I don't trust Taylor anymore. She knows I write everything in this journal. But in case something happens, I'm writing a letter to Adele's family to explain what happened and ask for forgiveness.

But mostly, to give them the closure they need. Because if I can't forgive myself, I don't expect anyone else to.

Thirty-Nine

Regan realized that what they had discovered was in a sense Candace Swain's deathbed confession. There was a good chance that a judge would consider it as testimony, but Regan was unsure about the legal aspects of what was admissible or not.

That was Candace's last entry; she'd never come back to the library after Tuesday. But she'd included her notes on how she picked the places to look for Adele's body, and copies of maps.

There was also a sealed letter, addressed to *Mr. & Mrs. Overton*. Lucas couldn't stop staring at it.

She had to get this diary somewhere safe. It should convince Young that his girlfriend was at best an irresponsible bitch and at worst a killer. But first, she needed to make a copy. Better, she should make a copy to give to the police and give the original to Henry Clarkson. She trusted him, and he was still a registered lawyer, still part of the legal system, even though he didn't practice.

Until she knew exactly who else she could trust, this was the most valuable piece of evidence they had about what had happened to Adele Overton—and what might have happened to Candace.

"What do we do now?" Lizzy asked. "This is—I mean, I don't think we expected this when we started the podcast. Did you, Lucas?"

"I don't know what I expected. I just wanted the truth."

Regan said, "Stay put. I'm going to copy this."

Regan went to the library media center and carefully made two Xerox copies of the journal. It started at the beginning of her senior year and was labeled on the first page *Candace Swain's Journal, #6* and ended the Monday before she was killed, based on the dates. She had somehow been in the library that night, presumably to add this last journal entry and research Payson. Why spend the night in the library? Was she scared to go back to her dorm?

Regan felt the pain in Candace's writing. Her soul-searching and her guilt and her desire to do the right thing, even if she got in trouble, was clear on every page. She was a good person at heart. Torn and alone, wanting to fix everything.

Regan was pretty certain that Rachel had killed Candace to keep her from going to the police. Rachel had made one big mistake: she had moved the body. Did she do that because of *who* would be investigating? Or because she had been seen near the aquatic center? Perhaps she moved the body to destroy evidence or delay the investigation. Did she have help? There were external security cameras. How had she avoided them?

And why didn't she take Candace's body to the Payson mine where she'd dumped Adele?

She had only part of the picture, but she was now certain that it was Rachel who'd told Nicole Bergamo not to tell anyone she saw Candace in the truck. Why, Regan could only speculate. Maybe Rachel thought if Candace were found by the police first, she would tell them about Adele. Then, when Nicole went on the podcast, whoever she told—Rachel or someone else—had known it was Nicole sharing the story, even with the disguised voice.

And now Nicole was in the hospital, in a coma.

Abernathy either had seen something suspicious and was killed because of it, or he was killed to frame him for Candace's murder.

That wasn't the work of selfish Taylor James or needy Vicky Ryan or conceited Kimberly Foster. That was the work of a sociopath, someone who would do or say anything to avoid getting in trouble for her actions.

It was the work of Rachel Wagner. Regan would bet her life on it.

When she was done copying the journal, she went back to the study room and said to Lucas and Lizzy, "I'm going to take the original to Henry Clarkson for safekeeping and bring the copy to the chief of police. Young has a conflict, but he might be able to fill in blanks. And I can't see him defending Rachel, not when confronted with overwhelming circumstantial evidence of her guilt."

They were on the clock: if Nicole regained consciousness, she might identify Rachel. Rachel could run. If she hadn't already.

If she ran, Regan would find her.

"What about the letter to the Overtons?" Lucas asked.

"I didn't open it. I kept it in the journal. The police have to make that decision as part of their investigation. Eventually, the family will get it."

Lizzy said, "I'm leading a study group with my math dummies after lunch, but I can cancel if you need me."

"Go," Lucas said.

"You're sure?"

"Yeah."

"I'll call you and maybe come over after, okay?"

"That'd be great."

Lizzy gave him a quick kiss, waved to Regan, and left. He looked after her. "Is she in danger?"

"I think she's fine. It's you I'm worried about. You started this, and if Rachel sees her carefully constructed lies crumbling around her, she might lash out."

Regan had majored in psychology, but she hadn't spent enough time with Rachel to fully assess her. She was smart—as evidenced by her career path. She was articulate and cultured. She looked younger than her age and envisioned herself as the friend and protector of the Sigma Rho sorority. She wanted to be their confidante, their best friend. Regan would bet her savings that Rachel loved when the girls came to her with their problems so she could "guide" them. She wanted to *be* back in the sorority. She didn't want to grow older—she was Regan's age, thirty-five, but spent her entire life with college students. Not married. She dated a cop of the same age, but for how long? Was it serious? Had she started dating him because of his investigation? Had she misled him?

Regan remembered that Rachel's office was filled with mementos of her own college years. Of her sorority and cheerleading and other activities. Nothing about NAU or what she'd done here for nearly seven years. Interesting... and telling. She missed it. Whatever she'd had in Tucson, she wanted it back.

And then the odd conversation yesterday. Rachel had implied that Taylor might be guilty of *hurting* Candace. That was the word she'd used. In hindsight, it felt like she had been planting seeds.

Taylor was now dead, unable to defend herself—or accuse Rachel.

So many questions; Regan needed answers. At this point, she believed that Rachel valued her position, craved youth, worked with college students not to guide or educate them but because she wanted to be one of them again.

She called Henry, who informed her that he was at the hospital with her dad, and then he put her father on.

"Lucas and I are heading there now," she told him. "We found Candace's journal, and I want to give it to Henry for safekeeping. How's Nicole?"

"She's still unconscious. They believe she was poisoned with a depressant, they're still running tests. Her central nervous system was compromised, and she hasn't come out of the coma. They are doing everything they can—because she was found quickly and her roommate administered CPR, they think she'll make it, but it's iffy right now."

"I'm going to give Henry the journal, then give a copy to the chief and Detective Young. He needs to see what's in it. It implicates Rachel Wagner."

"If you need my help, holler."

"Don't let Rachel anywhere near Nicole. I don't think Vicky is involved, but keep an eye on her because she trusts Rachel."

Henry met her in the hospital lobby. She gave him the original journal, then she and Lucas drove to the police station. Lucas was unusually quiet.

The chief of detectives wasn't on duty, but the shift commander, Olivia Gomez, met with Regan and Lucas in her small office.

Regan closed the door because she didn't need anyone overhearing what she needed to say.

After introductions, Olivia said, "I listened to the podcast. A lot of people are talking about it."

"Did you listen to last night's episode?"

"Not yet, but Steven sent me a note that there is a potential witness who saw Candace in a truck the week she was missing—a truck that belonged to Sunrise Center."

"Yes. The person who made that call asked that her voice be disguised. She's now in the hospital, in a coma, with a suspected poisoning."

"I haven't seen that report."

"It happened late last night. I don't know the details, but I asked John Merritt to keep an eye out."

"The former sheriff?"

"My father."

"I figured."

Regan handed Olivia the copy she'd made of the journal. "This is a copy of Candace Swain's journal. Lucas found it in the library, hidden in a hollowed-out book. We knew to look there because Candace had told a friend that she needed to hide her journal because she was afraid it would be destroyed. I wanted to talk to Detective Young, but not alone. I learned this week that he's involved with Rachel Wagner, the advisor to Sigma Rho and a professor at the university."

"I'm aware. I don't generally involve myself in the private lives of my colleagues."

"This time, you might. I wanted to share with him some information that came to light after one of Lucas's episodes, but because of his relationship I didn't. That journal details allegedly criminal activities by Ms. Wagner, including covering up the accidental death of another student, Adele Overton. Candace disappeared three years ago in an attempt to find Adele's body. When she failed, she returned to campus and was murdered."

Olivia flipped through the copy. "Where is the original?"

"Safe."

"You understand that chain of custody is compromised."

"It's already been compromised because the journal was hidden in the library for three years. But I'm certain that a handwriting expert would be able to confirm the journal is Candace's."

"This is a complex case with no physical evidence."

"I have a witness who is willing to come forward who can offer some testimony about the events that led to Adele's death, and who saw Candace after the Spring Fling party."

"Why didn't she come forward earlier?"

"She didn't live in Flagstaff at the time and didn't know that Candace had been missing. She only heard about her death later. She is fearful for her life because she believes that Taylor James was killed because of what she knew about Candace's murder."

"You think that Rachel Wagner killed her?"

"Yes. I can't prove it." *Yet.*

"Steven thoroughly investigated Swain's murder. There were a lot of issues—contamination of the evidence because of the lake, and the fact that the body was moved, but we didn't know it until more than a month later because of a backlog in the state lab. Time was not with us on this. The suspect was known to have harassed Ms. Swain and had been seen on campus multiple times. She knew him from Sunrise Center, and he had a record of being belligerent when intoxicated."

"And a witness allegedly saw him jump on a train, and

he has never come back," Lucas said. Regan was glad he spoke up; she wanted to see him engaged. "I talked to Willa March; he rode the rails frequently, but he always returned to Flagstaff. He hasn't been seen in three years."

"Possibly because he's wanted for questioning in a murder investigation."

"Did you have any other suspects?" Lucas asked.

"Normally, I would tell you I can't say, but in light of the information you already have—and the fact that I don't want this department adversely represented on your podcast—the answer is no. We cleared the two boyfriends. No interview pointed to anyone having a problem with Ms. Swain, other than Mr. Abernathy. Steven has been looking at the case again, in light of the people who have come forward through your podcast."

"I wanted to interview Detective Young," Lucas said. "He refused to help."

"He wouldn't generally be allowed to speak to the media, not on an open case like this," Olivia said. "Now, he has a clear conflict of interest. I'm going to have to reassign the case." She looked at her computer, typed, read something. "I'm passing this on to Detective Brian Hernandez. He'll contact both of you for statements. He'll have to get up to speed."

"That's all I can ask," Regan said. "Thank you."

Regan and Lucas left their contact information with the commander and exited the building.

"What now?" Lucas said.

"We wait. I'll take you home."

Lucas didn't look happy. She was more optimistic. The wheels of justice moved slow, but they worked more often than not.

Still, Regan knew how he felt. So she said, "We have a podcast on Tuesday, and if Rachel Wagner is still walking free, we're going to make her life a living hell."

Forty

Rachel Wagner needed to know *exactly* what Lucas Vega knew. Steven had listened to the podcast last night and called her, told her to listen and share with him any insight she had.

She'd already listened to the damn thing and knew that Nicole Bergamo was going to cause her huge problems. If she told the police that *Rachel* had told her not to share the information about Candace and the truck, Steven would become suspicious. Rachel had been relieved that Nicole hadn't shared her name on air—until Steven called her. He was obsessed with the podcast, even though he thought Lucas Vega was a novice. Even when Rachel had told him how much the podcast upset her girls, he still thought it was an interesting approach.

"It's a cold case. I look at it from time to time, mostly sending notices to homeless shelters and hospitals looking for Abernathy. But maybe I need to be looking at the case in a different way."

That was a problem. A *huge* problem. Abernathy had to be guilty in Steven's mind, because that was the only way he wouldn't look at other possibilities.

Rachel didn't want to lose everything she had. How could she rebuild again? Rebuilding after everything that had happened in Tucson had been difficult and mentally exhausting. She didn't want to go through that again.

Rachel waited until first Lucas, then his roommate, left their apartment. She'd parked down the street. His roommate had an overnight bag, and Lucas left with Regan Merritt.

Rachel did *not* like Regan. She was nosy and trouble, acting like some sort of investigator when she was nothing but a failed cop. Yet, Lucas couldn't have gotten half this far with his stupid podcast without her. She was just as much to blame as Lucas if Rachel's carefully built world disintegrated.

Rachel had dressed like a college student, had a jacket with a hoodie—just in case someone saw her, she didn't want to be recognized. She easily opened the door—the lock was quite simple, and this wasn't her first rodeo.

In his apartment, she went through Vega's files. The more she read, the more upset she became. He had made the connection between Candace, Taylor, and Adele. He had a timeline on his wall, and he'd written that Candace had been at *"Payson Mine"* from Tuesday to Saturday.

How the hell did he figure it out?

Kim was the only person still alive who knew where they had gone and what they had done. Rachel couldn't imagine that she would have said anything, but what if she had? What if she'd hinted? Was Vega smart enough to figure it out?

Doubtful. But maybe the ex-marshal had.

She didn't think so, but she couldn't be certain. Taylor might have told Candace, even though Taylor swore up and down she hadn't, but if Candace had said anything to Lucas three years ago, why had he waited until now?

On a sticky note on the wall, Lucas had written *Was Taylor's overdose accidental or suicide?*

Good. He was thinking what she wanted him to think, that Taylor had killed herself out of guilt for killing Candace. That kept Rachel out of it, exactly as she wanted. If these people needed a guilty party and wouldn't be satisfied with the drunk, then Taylor was the next best to blame. She'd already laid the groundwork with Steven and with Regan Merritt.

Taylor killed Candace, then killed herself out of guilt because of Lucas's podcast. Case closed.

Rachel breathed a bit easier, but she still had more to go through.

Lucas's backpack had notes, a copy of the notes she herself had sent in the hopes that he would drop the podcast— not smart in hindsight, she realized, because Regan had barely left his side since.

Then, she found the photo of Taylor, Candace, and Adele.

Well, fuck.

Rachel had taken this photo. It was the last day of her Intro to Bio class where the girls had met and befriended each other. She had caught them on the way out. They were happy because they had all gotten an A, and no matter how well they did on the final, their grades would be nothing less than an A minus. Rachel had hoped they would be her friends, girls she could mold and help develop. That's what she wanted, to be a good mentor to her Sigma Rho sisters, to build friendships, to be liked and appreciated. Was that so much to ask?

Now it was on the verge of slipping away.

Where had Lucas gotten this photo? She'd had four copies made, given one to each of the girls, kept one for her own album. After Adele died, she'd used a master key she'd "borrowed" from Housing to access Adele's room and take the picture, just so no one would question Candace and Taylor. She also looked for anything else that might give people the idea that Adele had been to her apartment. Had Candace given it to him three years ago? Or Taylor? Rachel had taken her computer, but she hadn't searched that disgusting hovel Taylor had lived in.

Shit, shit, shit.

No, it wasn't a problem. No one alive knew *she'd* taken the picture, and her copy was in her album, and no one had cause to look at it. And even if they did, it meant nothing: she was their professor; they gave her the photo. Simple as that.

She would have to destroy the picture. Just in case.

But Lucas had it.

She pocketed the picture.

Now he didn't. One problem solved.

She read through the messages, finally found the anonymous letter that Regan Merritt had talked about on last night's podcast. She read it. Once, twice, three times. Dammit!

Who was at the party who'd overheard Kim, Taylor, and Candace arguing? Who would do something like this, writing and sending Lucas this...this ridiculous diatribe? Kim? Maybe Kim thought she could throw Rachel under the bus.

That would be a mistake. Rachel had a lot of dirt on Kim, and maybe it was time to remind that bitch everything Rachel had done for her. Kim owed Rachel.

Could it have been Vicky?

Vicky had been new back then, she didn't know anything about anything, and she worshipped Rachel. Rachel couldn't imagine Vicky being so deceptive, going along with everything Rachel suggested about ignoring the podcast while writing secret notes on the side. Vicky wasn't smart enough to pull off that kind of duplicity. In fact, Rachel had worked Vicky carefully, so that in the end she thought it was her own idea to forbid anyone in the sorority from talking to Vega or supporting the podcast.

Dammit, someone was playing games.

She didn't know how long she had been in Lucas's apartment. She took pictures of everything she saw, then slipped out.

She had a lot of thinking to do, to figure out how to proceed.

Rachel would fix this. There was no evidence that she had done anything to anyone. And as long as she stuck by her original story, all would be well.

It had to be.

Forty-One

Three Years Ago
Saturday, April 18

Candace Swain wanted to do the right thing.

Silence was complicity, she'd come to realize. She'd tried to convince herself that she shouldn't feel guilty because she hadn't killed Adele. But her guilt didn't fade. In fact, the opposite. From the day Candace had chosen to remain silent over three years ago, it had grown like a cancer, shredding her soul.

By telling the truth, she probably wouldn't graduate, even though she was only one month away from earning her nursing degree. She would certainly lose her friends in the sorority. She might even lose her family. Her future would be forever changed.

But her guilt would be gone. Even if she was sent to prison, the truth would set her free. It *had* to. She'd beg for forgiveness and take whatever punishment the system meted out because she deserved it. She didn't want to go to jail, but if that was the result, she would take it.

Candace wouldn't be alone. Taylor had finally agreed

to join her. Candace had been alone in her grief and guilt for so long, that having someone by her side gave her hope that they would, eventually, get through this. Together.

That meant the world to her.

Once upon a time, they'd been best friends. She and Taylor had met the first day of college in a biology class and became immediate friends. They rushed Sigma Rho together, ate lunch together most every day, went on double dates. With Taylor, she had another sister. She missed her real sister, Chrissy, but with Taylor she wasn't so homesick and miserable.

The choices they'd each made that first year had, ultimately, torn them apart. But now, maybe, from the ashes of their lives, they could reclaim the friendship they'd once had. They would endure this together. United.

Candace had been waiting at the aquatic center for an hour. She'd slipped in right before closing, hidden in the locker room, and when everyone had left, texted Taylor where she was.

It had taken her time to drive down the winding mountain highway from Payson, then return the truck she'd taken. She felt bad about it, but she didn't want to get anyone else involved with the mess she'd helped create. She'd filled it up with gas with the remainder of the cash she had, and she'd explain to Willa when she had a chance.

Because maybe—maybe—she wouldn't be arrested. Maybe she could ask for mercy or community service. All she really wanted was to give Adele's parents the truth.

Candace sat on the bleachers running alongside the pool. Her eyes had become adjusted to the near-dark security lighting under the bleacher stairs and over each door casting odd shadows everywhere. The water was still, the

Olympic-size pool ominous even with waterproof lights under the cement lip.

Candace had propped the side door of the locker room open with a small block. They'd done the same thing many times over the years, when the sorority wanted to have a midnight swim party. Totally against the rules, but so much fun. There were security cameras on the outside of the building, but not in the locker room or inside, so the sorority took advantage of that once a year.

The pervasive chlorine smell and humidity of the enclosed swimming pool almost made Candace believe that everything was going to be okay. That her conscience would finally be clean once she told the truth. Over the years, she had spent many hours sitting on bleachers next to pools. Candace was a good swimmer, but her sister, Chrissy, was amazing. Candace had gone to most of her kid sister's meets, even after Candace had gone away to college. Chrissy had won so many championships in high school and was now swimming for the University of South Carolina.

She'd almost called Chrissy today, now that she'd finally made her decision, but what would she say?

"I'm not the good sister you thought I was."

Candace would rather tell her after she better understood what was going to happen. Such a conversation would be better in person, face-to-face. She would ask for Chrissy's forgiveness, for her love, for her support. And in her heart, she believed Chrissy would give it. Because that's who she was.

She heard the door to the aquatic center open, a faint echo in the cavernous hall.

Candace watched a shadowy figure walk toward her. For a split second, she was frightened, then as the figure came closer and started up the few stairs to her level, Candace breathed easier.

Taylor.

"Hey," Candace said quietly.

Taylor James stopped about ten feet away, sat down on the bench, glanced at her, then looked out at the pool. "Where have you been?"

"Looking for the evidence," said Candace. "I can't get to it. The only option now is going to the police. They have the tools and resources to find her body."

"That's what you were doing? I thought you were just saying that. I didn't think you would actually go up there. Oh, God…Candace. That's…shit."

"It's the right thing to do."

"Are you sure?"

"Yes," Candace said. "It's the only way I can live with myself. I thought you agreed with me."

"You don't have to do this," Taylor said.

"Yes, I do. *We* do. Remember? We agreed that it was for the best." This afternoon, only hours ago, Candace had talked to Taylor. "Remember?" she repeated, now becoming confused. She'd been alone all week; maybe she had heard wrong.

You heard right. Someone talked Taylor out of going to the police. Taylor has always changed her mind based on the last person who talked to her.

"What happened?" Candace demanded. "Have you changed your mind? Please…Taylor…together we're stronger. You *know* that."

Taylor wouldn't look at her. Then her old friend got up and walked back the way she'd come.

Candace jumped up and ran after her, tripping down the

bleachers stairs but then catching herself. "Taylor, stop! Listen to *me* for a change."

Her voice echoed and Taylor kept walking toward the locker room.

Candace followed.

As soon as Taylor stepped into the locker room, another person came out and shined a light directly in Candace's face.

Security?

"I'm sorry. I'm leaving."

"No," a familiar female voice said, but Candace couldn't immediately place it. There was so much rage in the one word.

The light turned off, but Candace was temporarily blinded.

"You will ruin my life, you fucking bitch," the woman said.

Fear gripped her. She turned to get away and tried to scream, but the woman behind her grabbed her by the throat and squeezed.

Candace spun her arms around and elbowed her attacker. She felt the hands loosen just a bit. She tried to take in a breath so she could scream, but the fingers dug into her neck, pushing into her trachea. She started to choke.

She flailed. Candace realized that if she didn't break free, she'd be dead.

"Help! Tay…lor!!" Candace choked out, then couldn't say anything else. She tried to scream for help, but she couldn't catch her breath.

You're an idiot, Candace.

She had never thought that one of her sorority sisters would betray her.

She'd never thought one of them would want her dead.

Candace felt herself being pulled backward. Her eyesight started to return as the temporary blindness faded and she could see shadows from the security lighting. Her head was spinning; her neck ached. All she had left to fight with were her arms and legs, but her strength was waning.

She was going to die.

With renewed vigor born from adrenaline and fear, she kicked back as hard as she could, her shoe connecting with a bony shin.

A grunt told her that her kick had hurt. Candace reached up and grabbed the hands that held her neck, squeezed the wrists as hard as she could, trying to wrench herself free from the tight grasp.

And suddenly, she was free! Candace stumbled, fell to her knees, coughing, knowing she had to get up and run again. Run away as fast as she could…but her body wasn't responding as quickly as she wanted.

She crawled on the hard pool deck, then took a kick to her stomach, as if she were a soccer ball and her attacker was trying to drop-kick her across the field.

She fell into the pool, its shocking cold water giving her renewed energy. But she still struggled to swim away, gasping for breath, sputtering, spitting out water as it filled her mouth. Her throat hurt when she drew in a deep breath. She tried to scream, but it came out a squeak. Her throat was so bruised she could barely make a sound.

She heard the splash behind her. Candace tried to push herself through the water, but her limbs were like Jell-O, and she made little progress.

She spun her head to see how close behind her attacker was.

No.

"I can't let you tell anyone. I have too much to lose."

Candace recognized the woman who wanted her dead. Her friend, her teacher.

Rachel.

As the truth hit her, that Taylor had betrayed her, that Taylor knew that Rachel had planned to kill her, Rachel shoved Candace's head underwater. She fought back, but weakly this time as water filled her lungs. Her arms and legs kicked futilely. Candace's vision went black. Her mind and body became numb.

Her pain disappeared.

Forty-Two

After their morning at the library, Regan left Lucas at his apartment after asking if he would rather stay with her. He said he was fine, that Lizzy was coming over after lunch, and he wanted to prepare for Tuesday's podcast. She reminded him to stay put, trust his instincts, and call if anything out of the ordinary happened.

Regan headed over to the hospital again, this time to check on Nicole Bergamo. She called her dad when she got there; he didn't answer.

No one would give her information about Nicole's status, so she tried Vicky Ryan's number. She didn't answer, either.

Something wasn't right. She texted her dad and said she was in the hospital and then sat in the lobby. After thirty seconds she got up and paced, reading every plaque under the pictures of people she didn't know—former administrators, heads of departments, benefactors.

A few minutes later, out of the corner of her eye Regan watched a group of young women enter. Four of them, carrying flowers and balloons. Two wore NAU sweatshirts, two wore the Greek letters that signaled they were members of Sigma Rho. They approached the information desk across from where Regan was standing. "We're here to see Nicole Bergamo," one of the girls said.

The receptionist typed. "I'm sorry, she can't have visitors right now. You can take the flowers to the third-floor nurses' station, and we'll bring them to her."

"But she's okay, right?"

"I don't have that information. All I can confirm is that she's a patient here."

Third floor. Regan let the girls go in the elevator; she took the stairs. As soon as she exited on the third floor, she heard an argument at the end of the hall. Rachel was there talking to a uniformed deputy about being allowed into Nicole's room.

The four sorority girls were at the nurses' station, watching Rachel cause a scene.

Two hospital security came out of the staff elevator and walked down the hall. Regan still didn't know where her dad was, and Vicky was nowhere to be seen, either.

Rachel glanced at the two security officers, but she locked eyes with Regan.

"You need to leave, or we will place you under arrest," one of the guards said.

Rachel turned on her heel and walked straight down the hall toward Regan. She almost welcomed a confrontation: she'd found that criminals were more likely to talk when they were angry or felt trapped.

But Rachel just glared at her, then turned to the group of girls only a few feet away. "No one is allowed to see Nicole. I'm responsible for her until her parents arrive, and no one will help me."

Regan didn't know if that was true. She supposed that

there could be a medical release form that Nicole, as an adult, might have signed when she joined the sorority. Regan hoped if that was the case, her dad had found a way around it.

"I'm heartbroken. They won't tell me anything about her, and I haven't been able to find Vicky. I'm worried about her."

"She's with Nicole now," one of the girls said. "I texted her, and she said she's not leaving until Nicole wakes up."

The nurse said, "Girls, there are too many of you on the floor. You can leave your gifts here, I'll make sure that Ms. Bergamo receives them."

Rachel turned to Regan and said, "What are you doing here? You and Lucas Vega did this. You *know* you're responsible."

Regan didn't say anything. There was nothing for her to say. She was happy to let Rachel dig her own grave.

Her silence angered Rachel, but the advisor had enough self-control not to lash out. She turned to the girls and said, "Let's go. I'll take you all to lunch."

The girls left their gifts with the nurse. Rachel let them enter the elevator first, then as she passed Regan, the former marshal said quietly, "I will prove you killed Candace."

One of the girls heard what Regan said and did a double take.

Regan watched the five of them leave together. If looks could kill, Regan would be dead. Rachel was losing control. That could be good, because she might make a serious mistake—or it could be trouble, if she thought she could get rid of potential witnesses. Regan texted Lucas and Lizzy both and reminded them to be careful, stick together, and let her know if they left the apartment.

Then she went down the hall to where the deputy stood.

Nicole was in a room with windows, but blinds offered complete privacy. She said, "I'm looking for my dad, John Merritt."

"He's in with the patient. I'll get him for you."

The deputy opened the door. Regan peered inside. Nicole was in the bed, hooked to monitors. Vicky was sitting next to her, her head on the bed, her pale hand holding Nicole's darker hand. John was keeping watch. When he saw her at the door, he came out.

"You didn't answer my text," she said.

"I missed it, sorry. I was talking to Nicole's parents on the phone. They are boarding a plane right now, and I explained to them who I was, what my interest in their daughter is, and about my concern for her safety. They asked the doctor to include me in discussions, which helped me get some information. She was poisoned with haloperidol or a similar depressant. The doctors claim they don't know if it was intentional, but according to Vicky, Nicole isn't suicidal, and she doesn't know where she'd have gotten any antipsychotic drug. But now that they know, they have a process to reverse the effects, then they'll be able to treat any potential issues as they come up. Vicky saved her life. Nicole would have died without CPR."

"Does Vicky know about Rachel?"

"I told her. I figured it was safer for her to know what's going on."

"Did she say anything?"

"She was—still is, I think—in shock. She said she trusted Rachel. But then started talking, and I figured out that Rachel was the one who didn't want the podcast to air. She tried to stop it every way she could—going to the administration, to Henry, even her boyfriend, Detective Young. When nothing worked, she convinced Vicky the podcast would be bad for the sorority. Vicky would do anything to protect the institution, because she felt it was her duty. Rachel pushed duty and honor, loyalty and sisterhood. Now, Vicky thinks that Rachel manipulated her."

"Can you do me a favor? I'd like to borrow Vicky's phone to call Kimberly Foster. She isn't returning my calls, but she may answer Vicky."

"I'll get her phone."

"And, Dad? Thank you for being here for her."

Her dad squeezed her arm. "I'd do it for anyone."

Ten minutes later, Regan had Vicky's cell phone, and she stood outside the hospital entrance. She wasn't surprised to find Kimberly's contact information in Vicky's phone, which made this even easier: Kim would see Vicky's name pop up.

Regan was right. Kim answered on the second ring.

"Hello, Vicky?"

"Vicky is in the hospital."

"Who is this? What happened to Vicky?"

"My name is Regan Merritt. I left several messages for you this week. Vicky's roommate, Nicole Bergamo, was poisoned and is clinging to life, and Vicky won't leave her side. I'm calling you because you are in danger. You know what Rachel Wagner is capable of, and apparently, you're the last living person who knows the truth about Adele Overton."

She laid it all out, hoping to shock Kim into talking.

"Hold on."

Regan feared she'd hung up on her, but a minute later Kim came back on the phone. "I needed privacy. What is it you think I know? Why am I in danger?"

"I read Candace Swain's journal. I know what happened

to Adele. The police now have the journal and they will be calling you. You told Candace at the Spring Fling that you were willing to come forward about what happened to Adele but wanted to get a lawyer to protect yourself and the others. It was an accident. I think you're smart enough to know that you wouldn't have been prosecuted for a crime, maybe get a slap on the wrist. Rachel talked you out of it. Now, you have no choice. If you don't speak up and tell the truth, Rachel *will* come after you. She killed Candace, she killed Taylor, and she poisoned Nicole."

"Killed? You think Rachel killed *Candace*? No, she wouldn't. That homeless drunk killed Candace. That's what the police said."

"That's what Rachel told you the police said, and I think she steered the police in that direction. She's dating the lead detective."

"Do you have proof of any of this?"

"Candace's journal is proof of what happened to Adele. Rachel's not walking away from that. She'll lose her job, at the minimum. But I want to get her on murder. I want to give Candace's family answers. And if Nicole Bergamo dies, that's another murder charge."

"You're not a cop."

"No, which gives me a lot more leeway in finding the proof I need to put that woman away for a long, long time. I have enough circumstantial evidence that the police are going to revisit Candace's homicide and go back to Adele's disappearance. If you don't come forward now, Rachel could consider you the only loose end. You need to do the right thing."

"You're saying because Candace was going to come forward about Adele that Rachel killed her. God, that's insane."

Regan couldn't tell whether Kim believed her or was dismissing her.

"I can give you the name and number of the detective in charge—the detective who replaced Rachel's boyfriend. He'll tell you exactly what I'm saying." A slight exaggeration, no cop would share such theories, especially over the phone, but maybe Kim didn't know that.

"Okay."

"Okay what?"

"I'm calling my lawyer," Kim said, "then I'll have him contact Flagstaff police. Is that good enough?"

"For now, but you need to do it sooner rather than later."

Kim hung up without another comment.

Forty-Three

Rachel was angry. A slow boil that had been percolating for weeks was now about to explode.

Steven kept declining her calls.

They'd had plans for tonight because his daughter had a sleepover at a friend's house, but he only responded to one of the many text messages she'd sent today.

Sorry, busy, important case, talk to you later.

No kiss emoji or frown emoji or anything.

She drove slowly past his house. It was Saturday, and the weekends he had to work he usually had a babysitter for Wendy or took her to her friend's house for a sleepover. Today maybe he took her there early. No one was home.

Feeling bold, she went inside. She had a key—he'd given her one more than a year ago—and looked around. Nothing seemed out of place. Yet…

She walked into Wendy's room. She had a purple suitcase she kept under her bed for when she went to visit her bitch of a mother, visits that Wendy's mom canceled more often than not.

The suitcase was gone.

Something was wrong.

Not necessarily. She could have brought the suitcase to the sleepover.

She sat on Wendy's bed and dialed the kid's cell phone. Wendy answered. Okay, that was good. If Steven had said anything to his daughter, she wouldn't have answered Rachel's call.

"Hey, Wendy, I came by the house to take you for ice cream, but you're not here. Are you at Ginger's?" Ginger was her weekend babysitter. "Maybe you can call your dad and ask if I can pick you up?"

"Oh, no! I love ice cream. But I'm at my grandparents' house. My grandpa came to pick me up because Daddy has to work all weekend, and Grandpa got tickets to a baseball game, and I love baseball so I get to stay the whole weekend."

"That sounds like fun." Rachel forced her voice to be light and happy when she was awash with dread. Steven was never spontaneous. His life was orderly, and he kept Wendy's life ordered as well because of her unstable mother. If Steven's dad wanted to take Wendy to a ball game, he would have planned it days, or weeks, in advance. Something had happened... Something had forced Steven to change his habits. That couldn't be good.

Rachel's life was crumbling around her. She could practically see the pieces at her feet.

"Next weekend, okay?" Wendy said.

"Sure, we'll make it a date. Bye."

Rachel sat on Wendy's bed for a long minute. She had to get in front of this. Fix it.

First, Steven *couldn't* have any evidence. If he did, he would have already arrested her. Also, he couldn't have evidence because she was too smart. There was *no* evidence for him to find.

Plus, conflict of interest. They had been dating for nearly three years. She could claim—and she would make it believable—that he was persecuting her because she'd broken up with him. She could easily lay an electronic trail. She'd have to be careful, though. Tell one person, maybe, that Steven wasn't the upstanding citizen everyone thought he was. Plant doubts. Create conflict. It had worked for her in the past, it could work this time—but she had to be doubly careful because Steven wasn't stupid.

Plus, she had to deal with Regan Merritt and that asshole podcaster.

Everything they said about Candace was theory and conjecture. But on the subject of Adele, that was something Kim Foster *would* be able to speak to. And no doubt Kim would throw her under the bus to save herself, if the police talked to her.

After everything Rachel had done for her, Kim would betray her—of that, Rachel was certain. Rachel would lose her job, her beautiful condo, her life at Sigma Rho. She could destroy Kim, but mutually assured destruction would still mean Rachel lost everything.

She might go to jail. That was not okay. She should *not* go to jail for an *accident*.

First, she had to start laying the groundwork to discredit anything Steven claimed to find about her. Then she would figure out what to do about Kim.

She walked into Steven's small den and logged in to his computer. For a cop, he wasn't all that security conscious. Rachel had learned all his passwords just by watching him. She would simply send herself a couple messages from his email, then respond, then have him threaten her, something like that.

She sat there and thought about how best to do it. Maybe she should have the supposed Steven send emails to a few people that would help discredit him, not just to her. Inappropriate emails, to divide and conquer.

As she was about to execute her plan, she realized his work email could also be accessed from his home computer. This was even better: she could find out exactly what he knew about Candace's death.

She opened his work email.

As she read, her stomach tightened.

Steven had been removed from the case.

His boss had sent him an email this morning.

Effective immediately, you are removed from the Candace Swain homicide investigation. Please turn over all notes and files to Senior Detective Brian Hernandez as soon as possible, and call me to schedule a meeting to discuss, today if possible.

Her stomach flipped.

Why was Steven being removed?

Her face heated. Regan-Fucking-Merritt.

That bitch must have talked to someone higher than him, had him removed from the case. The whole conflict-of-interest bullshit that was supposed to protect Rachel was now a problem.

How did she become a suspect so fast? No one knew anything about Candace!

She rubbed her eyes and tried to figure a way out of this mess.

Maybe she was overthinking it.

She continued reading through his emails. They were meeting at the station today at four. That was in ten minutes.

Only one other email jumped out at her. It was from Detective Hernandez.

I asked Regan Merritt to sit in on the meeting since she found the journal; CCSD put a hospitalized student in protective custody as a possible witness. Student is in coma. Prognosis 50/50.

Journal? What journal? Taylor said she had destroyed Candace's journal... Had she lied? Did she have it? Had she given it to Lucas Vega? To Regan Merritt?

And how did Regan know that Nicole was the caller about the truck? Dammit, Nicole should have died. If she regained consciousness, she could implicate Rachel.

Rachel could feel the noose tightening around her neck. Nicole could destroy her. She should have died! If she'd died, none of this would be happening... Damn damn damn! How could she have survived that dosage?

All thoughts of creating problems for Steven vanished. She had more important things to address. Rachel left the cop's house, drove directly to her condo.

She recognized when her time was up. If Nicole survived, Rachel wouldn't be able to mitigate the damage.

For now? She had enough time to execute her backup plan. Escape. Disappear and rebuild.

She wanted to scream. She had everything she wanted *right here*! She didn't want to leave, but she had no choice.

Survival would always win.

Rachel packed two suitcases and put them in her Jeep. She grabbed her emergency fund: five thousand dollars.

She'd close her account on Monday once she knew where she was going; she had another six thousand in her savings. Not a lot of money, but for now it would be sufficient.

She had places she could go for a while. Friends across the country she could stay with.

Rachel also still had access to the university lab. She needed a few things. She might be forced to leave town and disappear, but dammit, she was going to punish the little asshole who'd started this disaster.

You ruined my life, Lucas Vega.

I am going to kill you.

Forty-Four

The meeting at the station went as well as Regan could expect, and she was happy that they included her so she could share her perspective. Brian Hernandez seemed like a solid detective, and Steven Young willingly handed over all his notes and evidence and answered questions. She had suggested that Lucas come down, but Brian said he'd reach out to Lucas if he needed more information.

Steven was professional but clearly upset that his girlfriend was a murder suspect. He didn't question the journal, however. On the advice of the DA, they opened the letter to the Overton family and made a copy.

The letter was a clear explanation of what had happened the night Adele died. Candace asked for their forgiveness.

Steven read the letter twice and, after, seemed hardened.

Brian said, "Going back to Joseph Abernathy. I remember the BOLO at the time. There were—" he skimmed through a file "—six sightings of him on campus, and twice the police escorted him off."

"Correct," Steven said. "Sigma Rho wasn't the only complaint. The cheerleading coach, another sorority, other students. At the Spring Fling, four different people stated that they saw Candace talking to Abernathy before the party began. Those statements are in the file. I also have statements from Taylor James and Kimberly Foster that Taylor had wanted to call the police that night but Candace didn't. She wanted to handle it herself, fearing that Abernathy would be imprisoned for continuing to violate the order to stay off campus. That was consistent with other statements from her boyfriends and Willa March, the director of Sunrise Center."

"And he was spotted at the homeless camp near the tracks, according to a caller on Vega's podcast," Brian said.

"I was not aware of that, though we regularly patrolled the camp looking for him."

Regan said, "Willa March confirmed that one of her other clients contacted her about Joseph, and she went down to talk to him, but by the time she got there, he was gone."

Steven said, "I worked with Ms. March during that time. She seemed to be forthcoming, and while she was protective of the people she helped, she also recognized that Abernathy wasn't always aware of his actions and could lash out. It's why he was no longer allowed shelter but could come for meals. I don't know why she didn't mention the sighting to me."

"Maybe because he was no longer there," Regan suggested.

"She should have come forward. Same with the information about her truck. She knew we were looking for Abernathy, the truck was missing, Candace was missing, and both of them knew the truck was available to use."

It was a valid point, Regan thought. Perhaps Willa, in her desire to help those in her care, had let her ministry cloud her judgment.

"What about the witness who saw him boarding a freight train?" Regan asked.

"It fit with what we knew about him," Steven said. "Abernathy was known to ride the rails, had been doing it for years. We knew which train, but by the time we were told and contacted the railroad, the train had made three stops. At the fourth, in Oklahoma, authorities searched all cars and didn't find him. He could have gotten off anyplace in between here and there."

Brian flipped to the next page. "Is this right? The witness was Nicole Bergamo, the same person who is in a coma now?"

Regan straightened. "Nicole saw Abernathy?"

Steven hesitated, realizing the potential problem, then said, "Yes, she said she was at breakfast that morning with friends and saw him jumping into the car as the train started to move. No one else saw him."

"Hmm."

Regan said, "When Nicole called in to the podcast, she insisted that her voice be disguised because she didn't want anyone in the sorority to know that she was calling. Specifically, someone in the sorority had told her three years ago *not* to tell the police about seeing Candace in the truck, that person convinced her that she had been mistaken. I believe that person was Rachel Wagner and that, when Nicole is out of her coma, she'll state that. What if Rachel also convinced her to be the official witness to Abernathy's last sighting? Who was she with that day?"

Steven didn't even wait for Brian to read the notes. "Vicky Ryan, Rachel Wagner, and Taylor James. None of them saw Abernathy, but why would Nicole lie?"

"Rachel is manipulative. She could have convinced Nicole that the man was Abernathy, to the extent that Nicole believed it. Just like she had been convinced it wasn't Candace in the truck. Remember, she was a freshman then, away from home, new to the sorority, and Rachel was in a position of authority. And now, three years later, listening to the podcast, she's rethinking what she knew then."

"I can't arrest Rachel for the information in the journal or on conjecture," Brian said. "I can ask her about the journal. Get her on record either confirming or denying, which could help us if we catch her in a lie. But I would really like Nicole's statement first. She's still in a coma, and I have no idea when she'll be ready to give a statement once she wakes up. Steven, I'm sorry to take the case, but I'll keep you in the loop as much as you want. You did say you were breaking it off with her, right?"

"I've been ignoring her calls all day," he said.

"She's going to know something is up," Regan said.

"What am I supposed to do?" Steven said, showing the first outward sign of frustration and anger. "Pretend nothing is wrong? Pretend she didn't cover up the death of a college student? Pretend she had nothing to do with poisoning a young woman?"

"We don't know for certain that she did," Brian said.

"She did it," Steven said. "Everything is coming clear to me. I honestly believed that Joseph Abernathy was involved in Candace's death. Everything pointed to him, but there were a couple of things that didn't quite fit. When he was seen leaving town, it made him seem a more likely suspect, but I should have looked harder at the sorority. Rachel convinced me not to."

"How so?" Brian asked.

"Because she made it so compelling that Abernathy was guilty. And the girls who spoke to me were genuine about their concerns about him. The campus police had numerous reports. I guess I wanted to believe it was him and he ran because of what he did. But I listened to Lucas's podcast, and he brought up some good questions that I shouldn't have easily dismissed—like how Abernathy, a known alcoholic, could have killed her and moved her body without being seen, without leaving evidence. That takes more planning than luck."

"Did you grab the security cameras from the college?"

"By the time we knew she'd drowned in chlorinated water, the tapes were worthless. The college keeps tapes only thirty days. We had requested the tapes from the weekend of the party and still have those—I've gone over them several times. But there is not full coverage. Very few indoor cameras for privacy reasons. Had I known she was seen in the library, I would have requested those tapes, but no one came forward, until now."

"Buddy, you did what you could with what you had to work with," Brian said.

"I feel used and manipulated. I met Rachel during the murder investigation."

Regan had been wondering about that, but didn't comment.

"I liked her," Steven said. "She seemed genuine, smart, kind—and I was wrong. If I can date a woman for nearly three years and not know who she really is, that doesn't make me a good cop."

"It makes you human," Regan said.

He frowned.

"Three years is a long time," Regan said. "Most people get married, move in together, or call it quits."

"I have a nine-year-old daughter. She comes first in my life, and Rachel understood that. She said she wasn't ready for a lifetime commitment because she was working on a full professorship and she devoted so much of her time to the sorority, as their advisor. And looking back on it now, it was convenient for me, because I didn't want a serious relationship, and I enjoyed her company. We were both happy with the arrangement. I admired her career, that she had a life separate from me, and respected my time with Wendy. But she used me. Clear as day now."

"Where is your daughter?" Regan asked.

"After I talked to my boss this morning, I called my dad and asked if he could take her for the weekend, and I would explain everything later. I didn't want to call in my regular babysitter, not knowing what was going on with Rachel or what she might do. I can't see her going after me or my daughter, but as a precaution I didn't want Wendy in town."

"I get that," she said.

She understood more than Steven could possibly know. If she'd had advance knowledge that one of her enemies was in town, she would have done more to protect her son.

Don't think about it. Don't think about it.

She didn't know how not to think about it, but she pushed her guilt aside for now.

Brian said, "I need to talk to the DA and the hospital to check on the status of Bergamo. I might have more questions. I have your contact information, Regan. I'll reach out if I need anything else."

"If you don't mind," she said, "I'm going to head to the hospital now. If I hear something first, I'll call you."

"Appreciate it."

After Regan dropped him off, Lucas spent the rest of the morning and early afternoon digging into the life of Rachel Wagner. By the time Lizzy came by at one thirty, he had a headache from reading so much material online, but he was beginning to think he might be onto something.

Candace Swain wasn't the first person Rachel killed.

"What's all this?" Lizzy asked, waving her arm toward the coffee table where he had spread out a hundred sticky notes and his laptop was open, its charger draped across the room, attached to an extension cord. Four Coke cans and an empty bag of chips littered the floor.

He quickly picked up. "I'm not this messy, really."

"I know you're not. What are you doing?"

"Trying to figure out something."

"Let me help."

"I thought we weren't going to talk about the podcast."

"Do you think you can put all this aside right now?"

He shook his head.

"Then, spill it. Tell me what you've been doing."

She plopped down on the couch, waiting.

He sat down next to her. "Regan told me that Rachel had a lot of stuff in her office about her time in college. She was a cheerleader, in the Sigma Rho sorority, all that stuff. She graduated the same year as Regan, so that gave me a starting point. I went through the Sigma Rho archives from U of A, I looked through local press reports, blogs, things like that. When Rachel was a sophomore, another sorority sister—Brittney Posner—disappeared. It was at the end of the school year, and like Adele, Brittney was expected home but never showed.

"Rachel was quoted in the newspaper, along with two other girls, about Brittney. The police told the press that Brittney had been at an end-of-year cleanup party at the sorority house and planned to leave early in the morning for her parents' house in Santa Fe. Like Adele, she didn't show up, but this time, the police had more information.

Brittney's car was still on campus, so they knew she hadn't left. They tracked down everyone who was at the cleanup party. Two said she left a note that she went running early in the morning. One of those people was Rachel."

"The police told you that?"

"No. The reporter tracked Rachel down for an article that came out at the beginning of the next school year. He interviewed several of the girls who had known Brittney. Here." He turned his laptop around to face Lizzy. "I already sent this to Regan. Her dad probably has a lot of law-enforcement contacts all over the state. Maybe he can learn more."

Lizzy skimmed the article. "Party, drinking, yada yada. Oh, here. *Rachel Wagner, a third-year student from Scottsdale, was one of the last people to have seen Brittney. 'We were cleaning the kitchen together, talking and drinking mimosas. Brittney had just broken up with her boyfriend and was looking forward to going home and forgetting about him. I am just so upset that she practically disappeared off the face of the earth.'* Then the reporter goes on about how Doug Harrison was a person of interest in the disappearance because a witness saw him and Brittney arguing the day before her disappearance. Wow. Well, boyfriends are usually the first people cops look at."

"And maybe he had something to do with it, I don't know. Another article, which doesn't mention Rachel, came out in July. Brittney had been missing thirteen months when her body—what was left of it—was found at the bottom of a cliff, near a trail on Mount Lemmon. But cause of death was inconclusive, and nothing has been written about her since."

"Which is why you want former Sheriff Merritt's help."

"Yeah. I guess. It just seems coincidental that someone from Rachel's sorority disappeared while she was there."

"But it *could* be a coincidence."

He agreed. "The case is still open. At least, I couldn't find any resolution online. But one interesting thing— Rachel hasn't been mentioned in any alumni articles. I spent hours going over them. If she was so rah-rah college, why isn't she still involved?"

He rubbed his eyes. He shouldn't have had so much caffeine and sugar.

Lizzy kissed him. "Let's put this all aside, okay? You've done everything you can. It's dreary outside, your roommate is gone for the weekend, let's binge-watch something and put mean girls and murder and everything on the back burner."

An hour later, Lucas was grateful that Lizzy had distracted him. His headache had disappeared, and he was laughing for the first time in a long time.

A night off was just what he needed.

Forty-Five

Sunday

Lucas jumped at the sound of the smoke alarm in the middle of the night. It came from downstairs, the shrill *beep! beep! beep!* that used to drive his dog crazy when he was a kid and the smoke alarm batteries went out.

But this wasn't dead batteries, this was an actual fire.

Lizzy groaned, and Lucas shook her awake. They'd fallen asleep on the couch. "Hey, it's a fire alarm. It's downstairs."

She sat up and rubbed her eyes.

Lucas heard shouting. It was dark, so it was late—or early. He looked at his phone. Four forty-five.

He ran over to the small front window and looked out. Lizzy came up behind him. "That's smoke!" she said.

He saw it, too, coming from the apartment right below him, he thought. But it looked odd in the streetlights, and he didn't see any flames, which should be good, right? An odd smell accompanied the smoke. Something toxic might be burning, though he couldn't imagine what.

"We have to make sure everyone gets out," he said.

"I'm calling 9-1-1." Lizzy already had her phone in hand as she slipped on her shoes.

Lucas left his apartment and started knocking on his neighbors' doors. Dogs were barking. He glanced over the railing and saw Mrs. Levitz, his landlady, coming from her apartment, two cats in her arms, the other two running in front of her. One of the cats scratched her in his furry panic and jumped from her grasp. She followed the cats across the street.

His neighbor on the left came out to the balcony. "Where's Troy? He okay?" the guy asked. He, too, was a student.

"He's out of town."

Lizzy stepped through the door. "Emergency services said the fire department is already on their way."

"I need my backpack," he said. "Go, Lizzy. I'll be right out."

"You'd better," she said.

"That's my landlady down there, in the pink bathrobe. Go help her. She's very nice, and her cats are all outside."

"One minute, Lucas. I mean it!" Lizzy said and ran down the stairs.

There was no smoke in his apartment, but outside it smelled awful, like sulfur. His eyes burned and watered, making him think this was a reaction to a chemical.

He ran to his bedroom and stuffed his laptop into his backpack, then ripped all his notes off the wall and shoved them inside. He was about to leave when he remembered what Troy valued more than anything—his collection of football trading cards, many of which were signed or rare. He grabbed that out of Troy's bedroom and ran out the door coughing as the thick smoke increased.

Lucas stumbled down the stairs, and one of his neighbors grabbed him before he tumbled and did serious damage like breaking a leg.

"Let me get this for you. Is this Troy's football-card collection?"

"Yeah, he'd be destroyed if something happened to it. Is there anyone else inside?" asked Lucas.

"I think everyone is accounted for." They both looked across the street, counting heads. The apartment complex was small, only eight units with nineteen total people, including Mrs. Levitz.

The two yap-yap dogs who lived downstairs next to her were barking at the commotion. All the downstairs apartments were filled with smoke, there was smoke practically surrounding the building outside, but Lucas didn't see any flames. Were they in the back?

A fire truck could be heard in the distance. This whole thing was weird. Lizzy ran up to him. "That smoke—it's toxic. Everyone's eyes are burning. But there's no flames. What is this?"

"I don't know," Lucas said. His own eyes were watering so much it looked like he was crying. They walked across the street, and Lucas put his backpack on the lawn.

He called Regan. Her phone rang and rang, she was probably sleeping. Lizzy ran to help the owner of the dogs when one of them got away.

Regan answered. "Hey."

"There's a fire at my apartment."

"Where are you?" She now sounded more alert.

"Outside, with my neighbors."

"Do I hear fire trucks?"

"Yes, I can see the lights, a couple blocks away."

"Stay put. I'm on my way."

He ended the call and was about to walk over to where

his neighbors had gathered when someone came up behind him.

A hand fell onto his left shoulder, and another came around his front. "Say one word and I will kill you." He felt a sharp jab in his right side, then excruciating pain. He could feel blood dripping down his skin.

"Whoops," the woman said.

He turned and saw a black Jeep Wrangler on the street. Its rear door was open. A rag came down over his face, and it smelled sweet. He looked at the woman, as he clutched his side. Everything looked fuzzy and unfocused.

Rachel Wagner?

Rachel pushed him into the back seat as he grew woozy, and then he couldn't think straight. He heard Lizzy scream his name. She sounded far, far away…then the car, with him in it, was moving.

He lost consciousness before the first turn.

Forty-Six

Regan jumped into her truck not five minutes after Lucas called—she'd simply pulled on the clothes she wore yesterday. She was twenty minutes out of town, but this early in the morning, she punched it, figured she could make it to Lucas's in fifteen minutes.

Her phone rang as soon as she got on the highway.

"Regan Merritt," she answered.

"It's Lizzy Choi. Rachel took Lucas! I called the police. I don't know what else to do."

"Tell me what happened."

"The smoke alarm went off, and we were helping people get out of the apartment, and I went to catch this woman's dog, and Lucas was just standing there. He was going to call you."

"He did."

"I don't know what happened, he was right there, but I saw her and did a double take. She pushed him into her Jeep, just pushed him in! I ran after her, but she drove away, nearly hit me with her Jeep."

"Did you get a license?"

"Partial. The smoke really burns and everything is

blurry." She rattled off three numbers. "I told the police, too. Why would she do that?"

Last night, Nicole Bergamo had come out of her coma but wasn't communicative. Her doctor told Detective Hernandez that he could try to interview her this morning. While the hospital knew not to release the information to anyone, and Vicky was completely on board with keeping the information to herself, it wasn't unreasonable to assume that Rachel had a way of finding out her status, maybe through another sorority sister. Even if she didn't know for certain, Nicole wasn't dead, and that meant Rachel's time as a free woman—if Regan was right about everything—was limited.

"I'll be there in fifteen minutes. Stay with people."

Regan made it in fourteen—relieved she didn't get pulled over on the way. The fire trucks were there; she parked as close as she could. As soon as she got out of her truck, her eyes started to water. She saw no flames, only lots of smoke. Maybe the fire was already extinguished?

She found Lizzy standing with an older woman holding a black-and-white cat. "Regan," Lizzy said, relieved. "You have to find him."

"I will. What happened here?" If Rachel was here waiting to grab Lucas, it reasoned that she had started the fire in the first place.

"I don't know. They haven't said yet."

Regan sought out a uniformed officer, introduced herself and Lizzy. "Lizzy called in a possible kidnapping. Lucas Vega."

"I'm aware. We put out a BOLO on the Jeep and a description of the suspect and the victim."

"The suspect is Rachel Wagner," Regan said. "She's currently under investigation by your department."

The fire chief approached. "I need you all to move farther back."

Regan asked, "What was this? It doesn't look like a fire."

"An unidentified chemical created toxic smoke. The hazmat unit is on its way. We need to neutralize it, but people have to move to a safe distance."

"What about Lucas?" Lizzy demanded.

"I'll find him," Regan said.

"How?"

Regan motioned for Lizzy to follow her back to her truck. She tried to think like Rachel, figure out what she would do to Lucas. If she wanted him dead, she could have killed him here during the commotion.

She does want him dead, but she also wants to get away. She's a sociopath, not stupid.

"Rachel is smart and determined," Regan said. "She advanced quickly through the ranks, but she still wants to hang out with college-aged kids at Sigma Rho. Be their advisor, their mentor, their friend."

"What?" Lizzy said. "Why does that matter?"

"I'm trying to get in her head, figure out what she will do."

"She's going to hurt him!"

"Lizzy, you need to calm down. Rachel is predictable. Anything that happens that might jeopardize her goals, she mitigates. I don't think Adele's accidental death was the first time she found herself in such a situation. She didn't panic, she came up with a plan almost immediately to protect herself but convinced Candace and the others that she did it to protect *them*. Smart...but predictable," Regan muttered. "Narcissistic personality, at the very least needs to be liked, craves admiration. She was a cheerleader, check the popular box. She's in the sciences, check the smart box. Rachel is exactly who and what she needs to be… She reads people well. Manipulates them in order to advance her goals. It's all about *her*."

"The podcast," Lizzy said. "It uprooted her perfect life, didn't it?"

"Yes, and that's the sole reason she went after Lucas. He pushed and pushed until people started talking. Nia, the first caller, went to break the dam and was punished for it. But the dam still broke, and Nicole came forward. She has a lot more to say. Once that happened, Rachel knew she had to do something. She tried to kill Nicole, failed."

"She's going to kill him! Why are we standing here doing nothing?"

"Where do we look, Lizzy? She didn't take Lucas because of what he knows that could hurt her, she took Lucas out of anger, as payback. But her ultimate goal is to avoid being arrested."

Regan snapped her fingers. She pulled out her copy of Candace's journal. "I know where she's going—where she's already been successful in getting rid of people."

"I don't follow."

"Payson. From Payson she can go in four or five different directions, making it harder to track her. We need to study Candace's maps. Lizzy, help me. When Lucas and I were looking at these yesterday, we really didn't know what Candace was seeing. The maps aren't traditional maps. Where is the mine? Where would Rachel take Lucas? Where did she take Adele's body?"

Candace had highlighted two abandoned mines in Payson, then put a question mark on a third.

Lizzy looked, then she pulled out her phone and looked up Google Earth maps. "Okay, a mine, abandoned because no one found Adele's body, remote, but accessible by car because you can't really carry a body a great distance, right?"

Now she was thinking. "Exactly," Regan said.

"Candace was off. This mark?" Lizzy pointed. "That's an emergency exit to the mine." She flipped through her phone and showed Regan an article about the history of mines in Payson. "I was reading this last night when I fell asleep. The entrance was barricaded after a kid got lost in the mine more than ten years ago. But I'll bet that's where she went. This one gets too much traffic. Not the mine itself, but there's a road too close to it. And the one down here? That's impossible to access except maybe on horses. The road that used to go down there got washed away in a storm more than six years ago."

"If she dropped Candace in the mine, we'd never have figured this out," Regan said.

"Or maybe someone would have come forward because they didn't have the scapegoat in Joseph Abernathy."

"Good point. Let's go."

"Go?"

"Yes. I'll call the police on the way, but I don't want to wait for them. Rachel certainly isn't going to wait. As soon as she gets there, Lucas is going to die. I'm a great driver, I'll gain on her. How long ago did she get him?"

Lizzy looked at her phone. "I called you, like, one minute after. That was at four fifty-six."

It was five twenty-five now. Rachel had thirty minutes on them.

"It's nearly a three-hour drive. We're going to punch it. I hope you don't get carsick."

Forty-Seven

Regan called Detective Hernandez as she drove and laid everything out, including what she was doing. He would contact the Gila County Sheriff's Department and the Payson Police Department. Regan told him which mine they were going to first but gave him all three locations. When he suggested she stand down and let the authorities handle it, she hung up.

She was not standing down. Lucas was in danger. If the police could set up a command center first and find him, great; if not, she wasn't going to take the chance that he might die.

They drove in silence for a long time, which was fine by Regan. South Lake Mary Road wound through Coconino National Forest, but she knew it well. Eventually, it would hit Highway 87, which was just as winding but smoother.

There were better roads, but this was the fastest way. She assumed that Rachel had gone this way as well—less chance of being seen by law enforcement than on the interstate, and Rachel would assume that they'd be looking for her car. Rachel would also be following the speed limit to avoid being pulled over; Regan didn't care. She'd gone through extensive road training at FLET-C and took every advanced driving class that she could because she enjoyed it. So while she was breaking a lot of traffic laws as she drove, she was gaining on Rachel.

She wasn't going to lose Lucas. She should have insisted he stay at her dad's.

She hadn't seen who Rachel really was. She'd suspected that once Rachel knew that Nicole was going to make a full recovery, she'd bolt. That self-preservation was more important to her than revenge. Clearly, Rachel was far more devious and unbalanced than Regan had seen from her actions.

"Your driving is scaring the hell out of me," Lizzy said.

That's what her older brother used to say, and that was before she had offensive driver's training.

"Are you going to puke?"

"No."

"Just navigate for me once we hit Payson. We're still an hour out. Hold on."

Rachel mentally went through her checklist.

She had money, but it wouldn't last forever. Once she dumped Lucas she would head down to Fountain Hills. One of her sorority sisters lived there, and she had done Donna a *huge* favor…namely, helped her get her dream job. She'd stay there one night, trade her Jeep in for another car, then leave and head east. She wanted to go to Tucson—she knew that area well—but being smart meant avoiding familiar places.

She had another friend who lived in Las Cruces, and Rachel could make that drive in a day. She'd close out her bank account and continue heading east. Or north. A big city where she could disappear, get another identity, rebuild her life. Dye her hair, get a stylish new cut, find a way to lie low.

She needed a better long-term plan, but she'd work on it along the way. She'd never thought she'd have to leave Flagstaff. She'd built something really amazing there, and now it was gone, thanks to the drooling dope in the back seat.

Rachel would be okay for a while. She emailed the department head, saying she had a personal crisis and was going to stay with her aunt in Oregon. She apologized but sent along the rest of her semester plans for her classes and said her assistants could handle everything. She didn't want to leave anyone in the lurch.

It infuriated her that she had to do it in the first place.

Because of Lucas Vega.

She did have the wherewithal to switch out her phone. She couldn't have the police tracking her.

She would have to dye her hair. Dammit, she wasn't as cute as a brunette. Maybe…red? A nice strawberry blonde. That: she'd still be cute.

Still didn't make her happy.

She should have had at the ready a better escape plan, except that Rachel had never actually thought she'd have to leave.

"I hate you," she said out loud.

Lucas was still unconscious. The chloroform had worked well. Might even kill him, which would make things easier.

Though, bodies seemed heavier when they were dead.

She couldn't believe how easy it was to create a chemical smoke bomb that cleared out that apartment building so quickly. First, because it was small, and second, because she was smart. A little potassium nitrate, a lot of sulfur, sugar to keep it going, and add the special ingredient of chlorine powder and voilà! Everyone thought it was a fire.

Just enough chaos to grab Lucas and leave.

She waited until she was on a stretch of the highway where she could call Donna without fear of losing her.

"Donna! It's Rachel Wagner. I hope it's not too early to call."

"Oh my God! Rachel! No, you know me, I'm an early riser. It's so good to hear from you."

"You sound great. How are you?"

Donna rambled about her husband and two little kids and how happy she was at her amazing job at the casino—the job that Rachel had given her a stellar recommendation for.

"Tell me you're coming down."

"Yes, I am! I have a hotel reservation at the Biltmore, but then I thought as I was driving that I haven't seen you in forever. I have a great bottle of wine in exchange for your guest room."

"Fabulous! I would love to see you. I can't wait for you to see how the kids have grown. I can hardly believe Josh Junior is going to be starting first grade next year. What time will you be here?"

"Not too late." It was seven in the morning now: she'd dump his body by eight thirty, maybe nine, head down the mountain… "Is eleven this morning good? We can go for brunch."

"Perfect! I know the best place, with the best mimosas. We'll catch up. Josh will be happy to watch the kids for us."

"Sold."

Rachel smiled. Yes, she was going to be just fine.

Regan pulled over to the side of the road when they got into Payson to check Candace's map. She trusted Lizzy, but she knew the area better. She also took the opportunity to call Brian Hernandez. He was on his way and said the sheriff was aware of her presence and was putting together a team, but he didn't have an ETA yet.

"Give him my cell number, though reception out here is going to be spotty."

"Nicole Bergamo is out of her coma. Your dad is already there, and her doctor says I can interview her this afternoon."

"He's an early riser, and he was worried when I woke him up this morning and told him Rachel had Lucas. He wanted to make sure Nicole was safe."

"We have a police officer on her door."

"Yeah, but I'm not going to tell former Sheriff Merritt no." She loved how her dad always stepped up. He was everything she wanted to be and hoped she was worthy of the Merritt name. "Let me know when you get here," she said to Brian, then ended the call before he asked her any more questions about her plan. She said to Lizzy, "What if we go this way?" She pointed along a narrow road.

Lizzy looked it up on her Google Earth map. "Yeah, it's going to be rough, but it looks clear."

"Let's go."

Her phone beeped. It was a text from Brian that said the Gila County sheriff would have a team at the mine in twenty-three minutes. She gave him a thumbs-up and typed I'll be there in fifteen.

And she hoped they had picked the right mine, otherwise Lucas would be dead before they caught up to Rachel.

"He's going to be fine," Lizzy said. "I know it."

"Yes."

"You don't sound like you believe it."

Regan wanted Lucas to be alive and well, but hoping for something didn't make it true.

She learned that the hardest way possible.

"Please, tell me no one else is going to die."

"I'll do everything in my power." Her voice cracked. Her best wasn't good enough.

It hadn't been good enough to save her son.

"What's wrong?" Lizzy asked.

Regan didn't look at her as she drove over the rough terrain of the fire road. It was muddy from the recent rain, but she trusted her truck and tires to do the job she had paid for.

They bounced heavily on the suspension. Another vehicle had very recently come through here, based on the tracks. That gave Regan hope that they were right about the location.

"Regan?"

"My son. Chase. He was killed."

Each word hurt coming out of her mouth.

"That's awful. I—"

"You knew. I know Henry told Lucas."

"He didn't. I mean, he didn't say anything other than you lost your son. Lucas didn't want to pry."

Regan had appreciated that. Yet…she'd been thinking a lot about her son this week. Maybe because her divorce was final. Maybe because Chase's birthday was coming up. Or maybe because he was her son and she would always think about him.

"I had tracked a fugitive, found him, put him back in prison. Two years later he was released—that's another long story. He should never have been released, but someone screwed up in court and he got out." She took a deep breath. "He came for my family. Later, he said he wanted to kill my husband. Instead, he shot and killed my son."

Lizzy, thankfully, didn't say anything.

"I didn't believe him. Nothing added up. I was a marshal. I hadn't arrested him in the first place, I just tracked him when he escaped from a minimum security facility. I didn't prosecute him or testify against him. I couldn't see where he had a beef with me. And yet—he stole from me the only thing I loved more than my life."

Regan blinked away her emotions. She had to focus on the task at hand.

It was the only way she could make it through the day. As Tripp said, one day at a time.

"What happened to him? The man who killed your son?"

"He was killed in prison. And I never got answers. And that's been hard to accept. Not knowing the *why* is more than a little difficult to live with."

"You understand Lucas. And the Overtons. And Chrissy Swain."

"I do. Someday I will know why Chase was killed. Not today. Maybe not tomorrow."

But someday.

"I'm not going to let Lucas die," she said.

Out of the corner of her eye, Regan saw something. She immediately stopped, causing Lizzy to almost hit her head on the window.

"Sorry," Regan muttered and glanced out her side window.

Below her, around the bend in the fire road, through the pine trees, she saw a flash of black and chrome.

A Jeep.

She took a deep breath.

"Lizzy," she said.

"Are we stuck?"

"No. But I want to get out here."

"What? Why?"

"The mine is around this bend. I'm afraid if she sees the

truck, she'll panic. I'm going to sneak down the mountainside, using the trees for coverage, and come at her from the other side." She pulled the truck over to the side so that the sheriff's vehicles could get by when they arrived. "Stay in the truck, okay? I can't protect you and save Lucas at the same time."

"Just save him. Please."

She didn't answer that because she was thinking about Chase. She hadn't been able to save her son. With all her training, all her street smarts, her son had still died.

She didn't want Lucas's mother to suffer the same pain. She had to save Lucas, her friend, a smart, compassionate kid with a future.

She got out of the truck and grabbed an extra magazine of bullets for her .45 that she secured in its holster. She also retrieved her Kevlar vest. It wasn't the protection issued by the US Marshals, but it was one of the best you could buy on the civilian market. She strapped it on and hoped she didn't have to draw. She wanted to resolve this peaceably, but she feared Rachel wouldn't allow it.

Regan came down the mountainside at an angle so she could control her descent. It was damp, but not too steep. She used the trees for both support and to hide her approach, glancing down into the valley to gauge where she was in relation to the mine and what Rachel was doing.

She was two-thirds down the hill when she heard a car door shut. She paused, leaned against a tree, and looked down. The Jeep was there, close to the entrance of the mine.

The mine was cut into the mountainside and had long been closed, like most of the mines in the area. Regan didn't know the history of this particular mine, but either they had shut down because of the danger it posed to the miners, or they had gotten everything out they could.

An old federal sign, tarnished with age, warned that the mine was dangerous and to keep out. The area in front of it was overgrown with weeds and shrubs, and trees grew around, so high and thick that if you didn't know the mine was there, you wouldn't see it from any road or even the air.

Regan needed to give big kudos to Lizzy for identifying this based on very limited data.

It was cold, even though the sun had crept up ninety minutes ago. Partly cloudy with a wind that benefited Regan because it masked any sound she made.

Rachel was out of the Jeep and had a confused Lucas staggering in front of her. She held his arm tight, and she had a knife.

A knife could easily kill Lucas. Regan saw some blood on his shirt, but not enough to suggest that he'd been fatally stabbed.

Yet, if Rachel felt trapped, she would kill him just out of spite.

Regan half slid, half ran down the mountain as Rachel pushed Lucas toward the mine entrance. Regan hoped she made it to the Jeep before Rachel saw her, but no such luck. As soon as she emerged from the trees into the flat valley that fronted the mine, Rachel spun around, keeping Lucas between her and Regan.

"Leave," Rachel said. She sounded more angry than scared. Her grip on Lucas was firm. She might not have a gun visible, but that didn't mean she didn't have one, in addition to the knife that Regan saw in her hand.

Regan kept her hands visible, not wanting to spook Rachel, but out of habit, her right hand rested on the butt of her holstered gun, ready to draw.

"Don't come any closer," Rachel said, holding the knife under Lucas's armpit, against his rib cage. One thrust sideways and it would cut into his chest, slicing his lungs. He would likely not survive.

Regan stopped.

"Let him go."

"You don't understand."

"Explain to me." Regan knew that getting a suspect talking was the best way to defuse a situation. But as with any sociopath, she had to be careful. They could be unpredictable because they needed to win. To feel superior and justified in their actions. At the same time, Regan could use that against her. Let her talk. The more that she talked, the greater chance they could get Lucas out of this alive. Her mental clock said she had five to six minutes before the sheriff arrived. She just needed to drag this out a little longer.

"You turned Steven against me. You turned everyone against me," Rachel said.

Rachel was slowly moving backward, toward the mine entrance.

"No, I did not."

"You did! I don't know what you said. But you somehow convinced him that I did something wrong."

"You did that yourself, Rachel. We found Candace's journal, and what she wrote was very believable. You could blame her, I suppose, but you already killed her."

"Where?"

Not what was in it, or denying that she killed Candace, but where had they found the journal?

"She hid it in the library."

"Cline Library?"

"Yes. It's been there for nearly three years. She detailed what happened to Adele, that she wanted to go to the police, that you argued against it out of fear of being fired or imprisoned. Hiding the truth from Adele's family really got to her. So she came here, to look for Adele's body, as evidence of what you did."

"She never found anything. Because there's nothing to find."

Her first denial. Regan didn't believe her.

"Rachel, look at yourself. You're holding a knife on a young man. Practically a kid. Lucas didn't do anything to you."

"He destroyed everything I built! I had the perfect life. It's gone. All because he couldn't let the past stay in the past. Adele's death was an accident. If you really have Candace's journal, you know that."

"I know her death was an accident. But you covered it up. You staged it to look like she was kidnapped on the road. Her family is still looking for her."

"I don't care! I didn't kill her."

"But you killed Candace. And you killed Taylor. And you almost killed Nicole, but right now, as we stand here, Nicole is talking to the police. She's telling them everything."

Where are the damn deputies? They should be here by now.

Regan spared a brief glance toward where she'd parked, up the mountainside, but didn't see another vehicle or hear a helicopter.

"Nicole knows nothing."

"She knows that you're the one who told her not to tell the police she'd seen Candace on campus. And she was the witness who said she saw Joseph Abernathy hopping onto a train. But you and I both know she didn't see anything like that."

"Then *she* lied to the police."

"My guess is that you said *you* saw him. Maybe she did see something, because the homeless had an encampment down there. But you are manipulative and smart, Rachel. You could have easily convinced her that she *did* see Abernathy, maybe even said you saw him, too, but you were too close to Candace, or maybe by that time you were already involved with Young and it would create a conflict. You needed him in charge of the case so you would know what was going on, to ensure that you were in the clear."

"I love Steven. And you messed it all up."

"I don't think you're capable of loving anyone but yourself, Rachel. People are tools for you to use. You seduced Steven to get close to the case, make sure you weren't implicated. You befriend the sorority girls because you miss college life. I saw your office. The pictures of you. Not one picture of you with anyone outside of the sorority or cheerleading. You miss your youth. You're my age, Rachel. We're thirty-five. I'll be thirty-six in September and it doesn't bother me. My guess is every year you see your youth getting farther away. You never grew up. You *wish* you were in college again, so you made your career *at* a college."

The wind was howling through the trees, which might mask the sound of approaching police. Regan inched forward at the same pace Rachel was inching toward the mine.

"You're sick," Rachel said to Regan.

She laughed. "Me? You have a knife on a kid and *I'm* sick? You poisoned Nicole. All because she figured out that you were using her."

"I am going to reclaim my life."

"You can't. You're wanted for murder. If the warrant hasn't already been issued, it will be by the end of the day.

The police are on their way. I'm just waiting for them to get here."

She wished they would drive faster. Was she the only one with a lead foot?

Rachel scowled. She was now only ten feet from the slight rise that led to the mine. It was mostly boarded up, but from this angle it was clear that one of the boards was loose.

"Stop," Regan said. She was trying to avoid looking at Lucas's face because his fear was real, palpable. She couldn't let his panic direct her actions. She would have to take Rachel down. But she had to get her in a position where Lucas had a minimal chance of serious injury. Right now, she was most concerned about their proximity to the mine entrance. The mine was dangerous, and Rachel knew it. Worse, Rachel had been here before and might be able to disappear into the mine—with Lucas in tow.

Regan couldn't let that happen.

She said, "You stab him, I shoot you."

"You don't even have a gun in your hand."

"I can draw faster than you can blink."

Rachel looked at her, skeptical, but also worried.

"Rachel, this ends one of two ways. Either you live or you die. It's your choice."

"He ruined everything!"

Now Rachel was in the explanation-and-denial phase. Regan waited for her to continue.

She didn't have to wait long.

"I was protecting Sigma Rho from those who would destroy it. You don't understand how hard it is to build something good, something worthwhile. Something that lasts."

"And you do?" Regan countered. She kept a close watch on Rachel's hand, the one with the knife against Lucas. As

Rachel moved backward, Regan moved forward. "Let me tell you what I know. You got a bunch of underage sorority girls drunk and stoned. One of the girls freaked out and died in an accident. You couldn't stand the thought that you might have to take responsibility for your actions, so you disposed of the body and threatened the girls to keep quiet."

"Adele's death was an accident."

"Yes. And if you had reported it you might have been fired, or maybe not, but none of those girls would have suffered. None of them would have died. But you couldn't do that. You couldn't take responsibility, and when Candace couldn't live with the guilt of what you all did, you killed her. You strangled her and drowned her at the aquatics center, then moved her body in an attempt to thwart the investigation."

Rachel scowled. "Taylor killed her."

"I don't think so."

"You can't prove anything."

"Convenient, because Taylor is dead."

"She killed herself out of guilt."

"The police are looking at Taylor's death as a possible homicide."

"No one can prove anything."

"Then, why are you running? Why did you kidnap Lucas if no one can prove anything?"

Rachel hesitated. Then she said, "People lie. And some people want to hurt me. They *lie* about me because they're jealous. I have to protect myself!"

"Let him go."

"That stupid, stupid podcast. He needs to pay for stirring up all that shit."

"If there's no evidence that you killed anyone, then all we have on you is kidnapping. You might be able to plead down. You let him go, the courts will go easy on you. You're a smart, attractive young woman without a record."

Her eyes flickered, and Regan wondered if there was more about Rachel's past that they didn't know. Something that might make the courts not go easy on her.

Also, Regan had already mentioned Nicole, and Rachel hadn't denied Regan's theory. Rachel was weighing everything, who knew what and how she could get out of this situation. Regan could practically see the wheels turning in her head.

She wished Rachel wasn't holding Lucas so close, plus Lucas was injured. She needed to find a way to signal Lucas when to run. He kept looking right and left, as if he wanted to bolt, but didn't move out of fear or because he was injured worse than it appeared.

"Stop moving toward the mine," Regan ordered. "Is this how you want to be remembered? A fugitive, kidnapping a college kid, fleeing police, dying in the middle of nowhere?"

"I'm not going to die! I'm not going to prison."

"Let Lucas go, and I'll let you leave."

"I'm not an idiot, Regan."

"Walk with Lucas to your Jeep, get in, and leave. I'm not a cop. I can't arrest you."

"You're not going to let me go."

"I will, as long as you don't hurt Lucas."

"I don't believe you."

Rachel was now at the mine entrance. Her knife cut into Lucas; blood seeped through his white shirt. Regan didn't like this. It didn't seem that Rachel even realized what she was doing.

"I know who's down in the mine," said Regan. "Adele

Overton and Joseph Abernathy. You killed him, made it seem like he left town after he supposedly killed Candace."

Rachel stared at her as if Regan had read her mind.

Regan continued. "You thought you could kill Lucas and add his body to the collection. But if you kill Lucas, I will kill you. You have until the count of three. Drop the knife, or I take you down. One."

"You can't shoot me. I'm unarmed."

"Two."

Rachel pulled Lucas with her into the mine. But as she did so, her hand hit the wood planks, and the knife fell to the ground.

Regan ran toward them. Rachel looked like she wanted to pick up the knife but saw Regan coming and disappeared into the mine, still holding Lucas.

Regan followed. "Lucas!"

She couldn't see anything at first, completely blind in the dark, only a thin beam of light coming through the opening.

To her right was movement, but she couldn't tell if it was Rachel or Lucas, so she couldn't shoot.

At the last minute, she saw a rock coming at her. She ducked just in time, but then a second rock hit her head, and a third pummeled on her shoulder. She winced, barely keeping herself from crying out. She wouldn't give Rachel the satisfaction.

"Lucas!" she called.

"Here."

His voice was faint, but he was somewhere on the ground.

Rachel rushed her from the right, a small boulder in her upraised hands. Regan had been expecting it, based on the trajectory of the rock that hit her. Regan could barely see, but she had her gun out and fired three times.

Rachel fell to the ground.

"Lucas! Give me your hand."

She saw a hand come up in the dim light, and she grabbed it, pulled him up. She saw Rachel's body in the shadows, prone on the ground, and while she was certain she was dead, Regan needed to get Lucas to safety before she could be sure. She immediately left the mine, holding Lucas up.

"Are you okay?" she asked.

He didn't answer.

Four deputy sheriff's vehicles pulled into the clearing.

"Gun down!" one of them called out.

She immediately holstered her weapon. "I'm Regan Merritt. My identification is in my truck on the ridge. I'm working with Brian Hernandez from Flagstaff. The kidnapper is in the mine. I shot her. Be careful, I don't know if she's dead, and I don't know if she has another weapon. Her knife is on the ground near the entrance."

She sat Lucas down behind the Jeep and he leaned against the rear, his head resting on the bumper. "Are you okay?" she asked again. "You're bleeding."

He was out of breath, perhaps drugged, but he was alive.

"Talk to me, Lucas."

"I'm okay. It hurts, but I'm okay."

Thank God, she thought.

He hugged her. "Thank you. Thank you for coming for me."

An ambulance came and took Lucas to the hospital for stitches and to make sure there were no other injuries. Lizzy went with him. The coroner had left with Rachel's body. The sheriffs were already on-site, along with the fire department, and the US Forest Service that was responsible for the mine.

Lucas had given his statement before he was transported, and Regan gave her statement and turned over her gun for ballistics, knowing she'd get it back. It was a justified shooting. Though she wasn't a marshal anymore—and would never be one again—she had the credentials to withstand an investigation. Clearly, she fired in self-defense.

A team of two had gone into the mine more than an hour ago. Regan wasn't leaving until she knew if she was right.

You know that you're right.

Brian Hernandez showed up shortly after the ambulance left. He talked to the assistant sheriff, who was in charge of the situation, then walked over to where Regan was sitting in the front seat of one of the deputies trucks. Alone. She wasn't good company right now, and she just wanted to know if there were bodies in the mine so she could go home.

Brian put his hand on the roof of the truck, standing by the open door. "It looks like a clean shoot."

"It is."

"The kid's going to be okay."

"He will be."

"You okay?"

"Yep."

"That cut over your eye is going to leave you with a nice shiner."

She shrugged. "It'll heal." The paramedics had cleaned out the wound and bandaged it. Her shoulder hurt a lot more.

"The chief is going to want to talk to you. You're a civilian now."

"I know."

"Well, I guess that's it. You can go."

"I'm waiting."

"They said it could be a couple hours."

"I have nowhere else to be." She wanted to talk to her dad. Shower. Sleep. Visit Lucas, make sure he was going to be okay. Physically? Yes. But he went through a trauma and she wanted to be there for him when and if he wanted to talk.

Brian sensed she wasn't in the mood to talk, but he stood with her silently, and she appreciated it.

The team emerged nearly an hour later and walked over to the assistant sheriff. Regan jumped out of the truck and strode over to them, Brian right behind her.

"We found two skeletons in a pit about sixty yards down one corridor. It's going to take some work getting them out," one of the men said. He glanced at Regan.

"Go ahead," the assistant sheriff said. "She's going to hear sooner or later. You found two skeletons?"

"Yes. Based on the pelvic bones, one male, one female. We'll know more after the autopsy. We'll have them out before dark. I called in another team to search deeper in the mine, but that won't be today."

"Adele Overton and Joseph Abernathy," Regan said. "Those are the two victims. Of course, you'll want to confirm. But I'm right."

She turned to the sheriff. "I'm going to check on Lucas, see if I can take him back to Flagstaff. You have my contact information."

"How'd you know there were two bodies?" Brian asked. "Why'd you think Abernathy was here?"

"Because she framed him for Candace's murder. I just can't figure out why she didn't bring Candace's body here as well. It worked for her before. We may never know."

"It's a good question," Brian said. "I still have a lot of work to do on this case, maybe I'll figure it out."

"If you do, let me know. I'm curious." She thanked the assistant sheriff, and Brian, and walked up the hill to where she'd left her truck. She took a final look down into the clearing at the mine, thinking about the senseless loss of life. Adele. Candace. Joseph. Taylor. Even Rachel, though Regan had to really dig down to dredge up sympathy for her.

A pathetic, selfish, sociopath.

Maybe she didn't have any sympathy.

Letter Found in the Journal of Candace Swain

Dear Mr. & Mrs. Overton,

My name is Candace Swain, and I want you to know what happened to your daughter Adele. This isn't going to make you feel better, but maybe knowing the truth will give you some peace. If not peace, then understanding.

Adele was my friend. Taylor James, Adele, and I would hang out together, study at the library, eat at the student union. I really liked her and wanted her to rush the sorority Sigma Rho with us, but she said she wasn't into sororities. Even so, we became friends, and it helped that we all had the same major.

Finals were over, and we were celebrating. One of the new professors had invited us over to her apartment. Rachel Wagner taught our biology class. She'd only been at NAU for a year. She was twenty-nine and acted more like us than other professors, so we all loved her. She had wine, and we made homemade wine coolers. Me, Taylor, Kim Foster, Alexa Castillo, and Adele. Adele was the only one not in Sigma Rho, but everyone liked her because she was funny and always willing to help when we were stuck on something. She was so smart.

Taylor had a couple joints, but Rachel didn't want to smoke in her apartment. So we walked through the woods outside her complex. We climbed up a hill for the view and quiet. Everyone took a couple drags, except me. I have asthma and didn't want to smoke anything.

But something was wrong. I think—everyone thought, after the fact—that a hallucinogen was mixed in with the marijuana. Taylor never told us where she got it.

Adele flipped out. She ran, terrified of something. No one moved to help her. Everyone was acting... off. I tried to follow Adele because we were in the middle of the woods and it was dark. She pushed me down and ran. I couldn't see much, and I was drunk and not really thinking all that straight, and then I heard her scream.

Then silence.

By the time I could get everyone else with it enough to help me look for her, it was an hour later. We used our cell phones to guide our way.

When we found Adele, she was dead. She'd fallen down a cliff and hit her head on a boulder. It was awful.

Because of the drugs and drinking or maybe because we were all just awful people, we left her there. No one called the police or an ambulance.

The next morning, I woke up on the couch in Rachel's apartment. Only Alexa was there. I called everyone, trying to figure out what happened. That's when Taylor told me, over the phone, that they were "taking care of it."

Alexa didn't remember anything about the night before and kept asking where Adele was. I didn't know what to tell her.

Two hours later, they all returned. Taylor, Kim,

Rachel. I realized then that they hadn't slept at all. They had gone back to find Adele's body almost immediately. Kim made it clear to everyone that no one could say a word. That we would all be kicked out of school, Rachel would lose her job and be prosecuted, we could go to jail. Our futures would be over. Alexa asked, "But where is Adele?"

That's when the story changed. Alexa really didn't remember, and Rachel used that. She said, "She went home last night, don't you remember?"

And Alexa didn't remember anything, but she trusted us.

Rachel took me outside. She told me that Adele's death was an accident and our lives would be ruined if anyone found out the truth.

"It's better this way," she told me. I believed her. I am so sorry, but I believed her.

Rachel and Kim came up with a story that was partly true. That Taylor, Adele, and I had lunch with Adele, and she told us she was leaving that evening for home. We were to all go home and if anyone asked us, we didn't see her after lunch.

Taylor, who'd spent all night with them, had already bought into the story. She had been my best friend, she was scared about getting in trouble, she believed everything Rachel told her—that she would lose her scholarship, her future, her freedom. I was the only one who objected. And…I ended up going along with it.

I let them convince me. For three long years, I let them convince me that we had done the only thing we could have done.

I was wrong. I regret not coming forward three

years ago. I hate myself for hurting you, because you didn't know the truth about your daughter. And if Lucas Vega hadn't told me how you were suffering, I might never have said a word.

I didn't know until later that they staged the car accident in New Mexico, or that they had left her body in a mine in Payson. That doesn't justify anything that we did, but I'm hoping you can find her and give her a proper burial.

I am sorry. I don't deserve your forgiveness, but I hope that now you can have some peace.

Candace Swain

Forty-Eight

Tuesday

Regan met Jessie for breakfast Tuesday morning. Regan filled her in on everything that had happened. "But listen to the podcast tonight."

"You going on it again?"

"No, I'm going to listen with my dad. Lucas is going solo, and I think he has several interviews lined up. I can't tell you how relieved I am that this is over and Lucas is okay."

"And the girl? The one in the hospital? Don't tell me to wait until tonight."

"She'll be fine. I heard she's being released this morning. Everything else? You'll have to listen."

"You're a bitch," Jessie said with a grin. "Now, important things. Next Saturday, no canceling on me. We hike, rain or shine."

"Next week we might be able to tackle Humphreys," Regan said.

"You're so fucking out of shape I don't think you can get halfway up the mountain."

"I am not out of shape."

Jessie snorted. "Sedona first, then Humphreys next month. We'll hike to the top, camp overnight."

"Sounds like a good plan." Regan would love to get away for a weekend. Camping was just the ticket.

"Are you looking for a place to live?"

"Found one," she said. "I'm going to remodel the apartment over the barn where my granddad lived when I was a kid. It's private, plenty big enough. I'm meeting with an architect later this week. I'll probably gut the place, make it my own. I love Flagstaff, I miss you and my dad, and I'm not far from my brothers and sister. It'll work." For now. But that's all Regan could do: focus on the present.

"And then you can bring home a hot guy to jump on."

"I'm not looking to jump on any guys right now."

"Really? Not even Tripp Garza?"

"Oh dear Lord, Jessie, he's JT's best friend."

"Still hot. And I think he's always had a crush on you."

"Does not."

"Then, why does he keep staring at you?"

She glanced over to the counter, and Tripp was there, held up his coffee mug to her, then walked over. "How'd you get that shiner?" He gestured to the bandaged cut above her eye, which had also caused a bruise to form over half her face.

"Maybe I'll tell you someday."

He sat down with them. "Jess, good to see you."

Jessie snorted. "Right." She finished her coffee. "Gotta go to work to pay the bills. Later, gators."

She walked away.

"I've come in nearly every morning, hoping to see you," he said.

"Why?"

"I want to take you to dinner."

"You can come over for dinner anytime. My dad loves you."

"You can't possibly be that obtuse, Regan."

Her stomach fluttered. Jessie was right. She'd always had a crush on Tripp. But she would never act on it.

Never say never.

"You're JT's best friend."

"He's not going to beat me up because I want to kiss you."

"Stop."

"No."

"Really?"

He smiled. "Come on, you want to go out with me."

"Arrogant and cocky, just like always."

He reached out and touched her hair, dropped his hand. "Maybe I just want a friend."

"Yeah?"

"No. I want to go out with you. How about we start at breakfast tomorrow and work our way up from there?"

"Breakfast?"

"On one condition."

"I don't do conditions."

He laughed. "Fair enough. Okay, how about this? If you enjoy my company tomorrow over breakfast, without once mentioning that I'm your brother's best friend, you can then join me for some off-roading. I just fixed up my quad and want to take it for a spin."

"Wait—I don't even want to go out with you and you're putting a condition on it?" She laughed because she couldn't help it. "You're a piece of work, Tripp Garza."

"So?"

"Breakfast is fine."

"Tomorrow. Seven."

She got up. "I'll see you then."

She walked out, not sure what was going on with Tripp, but it would be good to catch up. She didn't plan on taking the flirting any further than that, but he had been a good friend to JT...and had been a good friend to her, back in the day.

And good friends were hard to come by.

One day at a time, she thought. But Regan was looking forward to tomorrow for the first time in a very long time.

Lucas sat in the studio alone. He'd come in early because he wanted to get his head together.

This was going to be a lot harder than he'd thought.

He had all the answers he wanted, but it didn't seem to satisfy him. Sure, he was glad he had found the truth for Adele's family. He'd spoken to her dad last night. He had cried. Her dad cried, and Lucas felt miserable, even though Mr. Overton said thank you over and over.

Thank you.

He didn't want thanks, he wanted Adele and Candace to be alive. They were dead, and he still didn't quite feel like justice had been served because Rachel Wagner was dead: she wasn't going to prison.

Regan had saved his life, but he still wished he could have confronted Rachel, testified against her, made her live the rest of her life in prison.

He still had questions. Maybe it would take a psychology degree for him to understand why Rachel went to these lengths. Regan had explained that everything Rachel had done was to protect her image. And the more her carefully built life began to fall apart, the more violent she became.

He had more information today than they'd had this

weekend, and he had spent the afternoon recording interviews with key people—people who had refused to talk
to him before. They might have refused today, except that
Regan went to bat for him.

There was a knock on the studio door, and he jumped.
He saw Henry Clarkson through the glass and waved him
in.

"How are you doing?" Clarkson asked.

"Okay."

"You don't sound confident."

"Sad. I don't know why."

"Because murder is senseless. You either get angry
or you get sad. Sometimes, a combination of both." He
sat down. "You did a good thing here, Lucas. Don't start
second-guessing yourself."

"Taylor James is dead because I did this podcast. Nicole
Bergamo was poisoned. She almost died. I could have died.
I'm not ready to die. That sounds lame."

"No. It does not sound lame. If anything, it should remind you that every day is a gift. If you're religious, you
might say every day is gift from God. If you're not, you
might just call it living in the moment. You are going to
go far, Lucas. You have compassion and intelligence, and
you'll use both in your chosen field."

"There were so many mistakes in the investigation, but
not on purpose. Just little things—like the delay from the
lab on Candace's lungs. I don't want to make mistakes that
might let a killer go free."

"We all make mistakes, Lucas. It's a part of life, a part
of growing up. It's owning those mistakes, of trying to
not make the same mistake twice. Of learning each and
every day."

Lizzy burst in. "Oh. Sorry. Didn't see you, Professor."

Clarkson smiled and stood. "Good to see you, Ms. Choi. I'm going. I'll be listening live tonight. I'm going over to John Merritt's house to listen with him and Regan." He glanced at his watch. "I'd better hurry."

"You have time. Lizzy and I have a lot of work to do first. And, Professor, thank you. I'll be okay. I'm just working through things."

"I know you'll be fine. But I'm always here if you need someone to listen."

Clarkson left, and Lizzy kissed Lucas. "I wish you'd have waited for me."

"Stop worrying."

"I came from your apartment. I helped Mrs. Levitz find her last missing cat. She's much happier to have them all together again."

The fire department had cleared the apartment for residents to move back in today. Troy had gotten him and Lucas an Airbnb for the week, said he was touched that Lucas had thought to save his football-card collection, even though there was no fire. And even though they could move back in now, the place still reeked of sulfur and smoke. Mrs. Levitz brought in industrial fans to help air everything out.

They had already mapped out the show, and Lizzy had edited and prepped the interviews he'd done. He also had someone calling in for a live interview. When they were done with the preliminary work, Lizzy asked, "Are you ready to do this?"

"Yes."

"Then, let's do it." She went into the producer's side of the studio and gave him a thumbs-up, then blew him a kiss. He smiled. He was ready.

"This is Lucas Vega, and I'm here talking about the Sorority Murder. A lot has happened since our last episode."

He summarized the purpose of the podcast and said, "I wasn't completely honest with you, my audience, about why I decided to air this podcast. I did, in fact, have another motive. I wanted to find out what happened to Adele Overton, the older sister of my high-school girlfriend. And I believed that if I solved Candace Swain's murder, I would learn what happened to Adele.

"Adele disappeared from NAU over six years ago. She allegedly left campus at the beginning of winter break, heading for home in Phoenix. She never arrived. Her car was found in Gallup, New Mexico. Based on the evidence—a broken headlight and a small amount of blood found on the steering wheel—troopers believed that someone caused an accident for the purposes of hurting Adele. Her body was never found.

"When I came to NAU, I started thinking about Adele again. I learned that she had had classes with Candace Swain and Taylor James. So I reached out to Candace— probably not the best way to do it, but by scheduling a tutoring appointment through the writing lab. She was very nice, smart, helpful. And after a couple sessions, I asked questions about Adele. Did she remember her, did she have any idea what might have happened? Candace stopped talking to me. At first I thought maybe I was too pushy or she was sad, but then I thought maybe she knew something more.

"I was right.

"Candace Swain was with Adele the night she died. Adele's death was an accident with drugs and alcohol as contributing factors, but the decision of four women to cover up the accident was a crime. They conspired to make it appear that Adele left campus for home and pretended when questioned by campus police that she told them she was leaving campus on November 30.

"Instead, they took her car to Gallup and made it appear she had been in an accident. They took her body to Payson and left it in the bottom of a mine shaft. Then they pretended to know nothing. Candace Swain's journal documents this."

He read a passage from the journal that verified what he'd said.

"But you don't have to take a dead woman's word for it. Earlier today, I interviewed another woman who was present. She has asked to remain anonymous, and because she didn't participate in the cover-up, I agreed."

He motioned to Lizzy to start the clip they had from his interview with Alexa Castillo. "We all went to Rachel Wagner's apartment the night of November 30. Me, Adele, Candace, Taylor, and Kim. We drank too much, and Taylor handed out joints. This was before pot was legal, but we all knew that was only a matter of time, and no one really cared.

"I don't remember anything after we smoked. I remember that Candace didn't, because she had asthma and didn't want to smoke at all. Later, I learned that there was something in the pot, something dangerous. Adele ran away from us, fell, and cracked her head open. I don't remember this, but Candace told me later. The next morning, I was told that Adele wasn't at the party, that she'd gone home. It was repeated over and over, and eventually I believed it. But I had dreams about that night—nightmares—and never knew why.

"Three years later, Candace came to me. I had already graduated. She told me she was going to find Adele's body and tell the police what happened. She felt guilty because Adele's family didn't know the truth, and she wanted to give them peace. That's when she told me the whole truth. When she died, I was scared that I would be next, so I didn't say anything. I'm sorry I kept quiet, but I truly feared not just for me, but for my family. I was six months pregnant."

Lucas said, "What happened to Adele never sat right with Candace, but she allowed herself to be convinced that it was an accident that they could get in serious trouble for. Over three years, Candace changed her mind. She felt increasingly guilty about what happened. I've read Candace Swain's journal and, with her family's permission, I'm sharing this brief excerpt."

He cleared his throat and read. *"We always listen to what we want to hear and disregard the rest. I pushed aside my doubts, allowed my fears to rule me. My fear of losing friends, of getting in trouble, of betraying those closest to me. I let Rachel play on those fears. I let her manipulate me. And finally, I said, no more. I had to come forward. I had to do the right thing. Not because of me but because Adele's family was suffering, and I could no longer live with my actions."*

Lucas continued. "Chrissy Swain spoke to me this morning."

Chrissy's voice came over the radio. "The pain Candace suffered is evident on every page of her journal that last year of college. It hurts that she didn't come to me, talk to me, that she put me on a pedestal and thought I would think less of her. I have never been so proud of Candace as I am today."

Lucas continued. "Candace wanted to come clean. But her friends did not. The argument I talked about in previous episodes is only partly accurate.

"Joseph Abernathy *did* walk on campus the night of the Spring Fling three years ago. Candace *did* confront him and ask him to leave. There *had* been multiple complaints about the homeless man, and Taylor James did want to call the police, something Candace was opposed to.

"But their argument wasn't about Abernathy, not that

night. Candace wanted Taylor and Kimberly Foster, an alumna, to join her in going to the police. And according to Candace's journal, Rachel Wagner convinced them not to. So Candace took it upon herself to look for Adele's body, based on limited evidence.

"You, the listeners to my podcast, helped us piece together what Candace did during the time she was missing.

"The brave sorority sister who faced expulsion because she called in and said she saw Candace on Sunday night, driving into the Mountain View parking lot.

"The student who called, telling us that she saw Candace exiting the library early Tuesday morning, and the male student who called stating that he saw her late Monday night in the library. Because of that information, Regan Merritt and I were able to locate Candace's journal, which gave us valuable information about what really happened to her.

"Candace spent the night in the library. You might think that would be difficult, but security cameras only capture part of the interior. You *can* be locked in the library, as long as you don't attempt to use any of the exterior doors. We found her journal, hidden in a hollowed-out book, on the third floor near a study room where she could have easily spent the night.

"But the most valuable piece of information came from a sorority sister who has agreed to come forward. Nicole Bergamo nearly died because of the information she shared on this podcast."

Nicole's voice came through. "I called because I had information, but I had been convinced that I didn't remember it correctly. Three years ago, I saw Candace in a beat-up white truck driving through campus on Tuesday morning. I knew she was missing, and I thought it was odd. I went to our advisor, Rachel Wagner, and she told me I was mistaken. I don't remember exactly what she said, but she made me feel stupid, and I began to believe I was wrong. Then on Sunday morning, we went out to brunch, and something caught my eye. Rachel was with us, and I said I thought I saw a guy getting on the freight train. You know the place, the Rail Yard Café. Rachel said it was Joseph Abernathy. She told me I had to call the police. So I did. But I don't know that it was Abernathy. I didn't recognize him, I only caught a glimpse. Rachel has a way of making you think you knew something when you didn't or believe you didn't know something when you did. It's subtle psychological manipulation, but you have to understand how much we looked up to her. She was our mentor, our friend, and I never thought in a million years that she would lie to me. Until she tried to kill me."

Lucas said, "Nicole didn't realize when she called in to the show that Rachel knew who she was—she had disguised her voice. But by her statement, Rachel worried that Nicole would tell the police that it was actually Rachel who identified Abernathy—the perfect scapegoat for the murder of Candace Swain. Rachel wanted to silence her, so poisoned her with a dangerous depressant she'd stolen from another sorority girl who had a prescription. If Nicole's roommate, Vicky Ryan, hadn't come into their room right then and recognized that Nicole wasn't breathing, Nicole would have died."

Vicky's voice came on. "I thought Nicole was angry with me, ignoring me, so I touched her and realized she wasn't breathing. I called 9-1-1 and immediately began CPR. My instincts took over. By the time the paramedics got there, she had a pulse. Faint, but it was there."

Lucas said, "Nicole was in a coma for twenty-four hours

and was released from the hospital this morning. She is expected to make a full recovery.

"Knowing that if Nicole survived, she would be exposed, Rachel Wagner created a chemical smoke bomb around my apartment, and as my neighbors and I fled early Sunday morning, Rachel stabbed me and took me hostage. She drove me to Payson, a small former mining town in the mountains, and planned to leave me at the bottom of a mine—with the skeletons of Adele Overton and Joseph Abernathy. If it wasn't for the quick thinking of former US Marshal Regan Merritt, no one would know what had happened to me.

"Rachel was shot and killed, and the truth is finally out. She killed Candace Swain. She then killed Joseph Abernathy—we don't know how, the coroner is still conducting the autopsy—and dropped his body where she left Adele. For no other reason than to make him disappear so it appeared he had killed Candace and fled.

"So where was Candace Swain the rest of the week she was missing? She was in Payson looking for the mine that had become Adele's grave. We don't believe she found it. But her extensive notes and maps helped Regan Merritt find me, and I owe both Regan *and* Candace my life.

"If anyone saw Candace in Payson the week of April 12, three years ago, call in or email me. But chances are she was keeping a low profile. We don't know if she knew that she'd been reported missing and people were looking for her. According to her journal, she ran into Taylor James on Monday, and yet Taylor never reported the encounter to the police. Today, Taylor is dead of a drug overdose. It's a suspected homicide—Taylor was the only person who could have known that Rachel killed Candace. According to Regan Merritt, it was Rachel who first floated the idea that Taylor had killed her onetime best friend."

Regan said in her recording, "I spoke with Rachel Wagner twice. Each time, she tried to convince me to encourage Lucas to drop his podcast. The second time, after Taylor was found dead of a drug overdose—after being clean and sober for over a year—she implied that Taylor might have killed herself out of guilt, that her drug habit had begun after Candace was murdered. Rachel wanted to push that narrative because it helped keep her name out of the investigation. I don't know if we'll be able to prove Rachel killed Taylor—the police are conducting a full investigation—but I learned from a friend of mine in the police department that Taylor's laptop was found in Rachel's suitcase."

Lucas said, "Tonight, I have Senior Detective Brian Hernandez on the phone. He has agreed to grant a rare interview. Thank you for joining me tonight, Detective. Can you please tell my audience how you came to be in charge of this case?"

"Of course, Lucas. I'm happy to. On Saturday morning, it became clear that there was a potential conflict of interest in the Candace Swain murder investigation. The detective who had been in charge cooperated and provided all documentation to me, and Ms. Merritt provided me with a copy of Candace Swain's journal, which has since been authenticated by a handwriting expert. The journal provided some verifiable evidence that Candace had been involved in the cover-up of an accidental death at Associate Professor Rachel Wagner's apartment. The journal also documented other parties and Candace's efforts to come forward to authorities with the information.

"Ms. Merritt also had compelling evidence that Nicole Bergamo, who was at that time in a coma, might have eyewitness evidence to Ms. Wagner's guilt in her poisoning as well as witness intimidation. When I interviewed Ms.

Bergamo on Sunday afternoon, I was able to confirm that, as well as gather other evidence from the sorority, witness statements, and at Ms. Wagner's residence."

"But it was when Ms. Wagner kidnapped me that you had what you really needed for a warrant."

"Correct," Brian said. "She made statements to both you and Ms. Merritt that implicated her in multiple felonies. Unfortunately, she was shot and killed while attempting to kill you and Ms. Merritt."

"I'm a forensics student," Lucas said, "and I am more comfortable with the science than with other investigative techniques. Would you have been able to get a warrant to search Wagner's house without her decision to kidnap me?"

"Yes, based on Ms. Bergamo's statement, I would have been able to get a warrant. Even before then, the DA was looking at precedents to admit Candace's journal into evidence for the purpose of a warrant. That was in the works when Ms. Wagner decided to set the chemical bomb and kidnap you."

"There is some question that the initial police investigation was compromised because Ms. Wagner was dating the detective in charge. A media report—which I didn't comment on—wrote about it this morning."

"The official statement of Flagstaff Police Department is that the Candace Swain investigation is being reviewed for compliance with departmental policy, but to date, all procedures were followed. But my own unofficial analysis is that the detective who was in charge had done everything he could with the evidence he had available to him. An investigation is only as good as the evidence we can find, and in this case the delay in the state lab coupled with false statements by Ms. Wagner and Ms. James contributed to the faulty investigation. We are currently reviewing our process of working with NAUPD and the state lab on any future investigations, including how we retain and use security footage."

"One more question, Detective Hernandez. You have been looking into the past of Rachel Wagner and the death of another Sigma Rho college student, some years ago, at the University of Arizona. Can you share what you know?"

"We're working with the Tucson Police Department in a joint investigation, but a sorority sister went missing near the end of her sophomore year of college. Her name was Brittney Posner. Her body was found off campus over a year later, at the bottom of a cliff near a trail on Mount Lemmon. The Tucson police investigated the disappearance and interviewed several people in the sorority, including Rachel Wagner—the victim's roommate. Ms. Wagner gave conflicting statements, but the police found no physical evidence tying her to the victim's disappearance. When her body was found, they again questioned Ms. Wagner and again found no probable cause—but she remained a person of interest. The main issue was that two autopsies conflicted. The first said cause of death was indeterminate, that they couldn't confirm whether she'd died from the fall or was already dead when she fell. A second autopsy suggested that she died from the fall itself. Tox screens were done, but many drugs don't last in the body over time, and when found the body was in such an advanced state of decomposition, many of the tests were inconclusive.

"We're now helping to revisit the case, and based on some documents we found in Ms. Wagner's residence, we believe she may have been involved. I can't say more right now but hope to have a full report shortly."

"Maybe you'll be able to share that report with my listeners on my final podcast episode in two weeks."

"If I can, I will."

"Thank you for your time, Detective."

Lucas cut off the call and said, "One accidental death six and a half years ago spiraled out of control, resulting in the deaths of three other people—and the attempted murder of three more. Why? Why did Rachel Wagner go to these lengths to protect her reputation? How did she manipulate people into helping her? Those are answers I don't have. On Friday, I'll be interviewing Professor Henry Clarkson of the Criminology and Criminal Justice Department and Dr. Edith Vlansky, a forensic psychiatrist and honorary professor here at NAU. Maybe between them, we'll find answers.

"But even if we have answers as to why, that doesn't discount the lives lost. We have answers, and we might have justice, even though Rachel Wagner was killed and families won't be able to face her in court. But do we have closure?

"I don't know. What is closure, anyway? People we care about are still gone. Justice may be served, but justice doesn't fill the hole in the hearts of those who loved Candace and Adele.

"The Swain family and the Overton family know what happened to their daughters, but they may not be at peace. Yet, this is all that we can do. Sometimes, it has to be enough."

Lucas caught Lizzy's eye. She nodded to him, and he nodded back. "I'm going to end with one final thought. In her journal, Candace quoted Martin Luther King Jr. He said, 'It's always the right time to do the right thing.' Candace died by that motto, but she didn't die in vain."

* * * * *

Acknowledgments

Sixteen years ago, my first book was released into the world. Now, forty books later, I feel so blessed that I can continue to do what I love—write stories that entertain.

My early books I wrote without much thought about research—largely because when I asked questions, people would look at me oddly (i.e., How can I disable a car? What poison will immobilize a person but not kill them?) Everything I learned then I learned from books.

Over time, I've been lucky to find people who can answer questions and don't think I'm plotting a real-life murder. It started with friends and neighbors, and now I'm comfortable reaching out to people I don't know. I still do most of my research by reading, such as the history of Flagstaff, a memoir about growing up on the Navajo reservation, and my well-used Writer's Digest *Book of Poisons*. But I still had questions that couldn't be found in a book or on the internet.

So a special shout-out to Dr. Luis Fernandez, the chair of the Criminology and Criminal Justice Department at Northern Arizona University. He answered numerous questions about their program, the capstone project all seniors are required to complete and general questions about the university. I'm sure I got some things wrong, and I took a few liberties for story purposes, but his information was invaluable in helping me create a plausible background for my character Lucas Vega.

I also reached out to the NAU Police Department, and Officer Tanner Carson, community relations officer, was gracious enough to answer questions about security, how they approach missing-persons cases and the general role of campus police. Again, some liberties needed to be taken, but I tried to get the details right!

Finally, fellow author Martin Roy Hill bailed me out for some much-needed medical information that I needed immediately. I can't tell you how grateful I am to him and other experts at the Crime Scene Writers loop. They are always there to help me not look bad. Thank you!

The writer's life is often solitary, but there are many people involved in bringing a book to publication. First is my agent, Dan Conaway, who has guided me for coming on twelve years (I don't think he even knows we've been together that long!). He's been a rock and much-needed sounding board. Dan's superorganized assistant, Lauren Carsley, has made the administrative end of my business seamless, even when she had no office to go into. She's a saint!

The team at MIRA is fabulous. My covers have been among my favorite in my career, the editing has been stellar, and their enthusiasm for my stories keeps me well-motivated! Kathy Sagan is an editor who loves editing, which helps me craft the best book I can write. I cannot underscore enough the need for an author to have a good editor. It makes all the difference in the world. Nicole Brebner and Margaret Marbury steer the ship with insight and big-picture guidance. The entire design, sales, and marketing teams are amazing, but a special shout-out to Justine Sha, who keeps me up to date on reviews, social media activities, book signings, and more. If she doesn't have an answer, she finds who does. She is enthusiastic and genuinely loves her job, which I can tell by her liberal use of exclamation points in her emails to me!

A thread that runs through *The Sorority Murder* is friendship: what makes a true friend, who you can count on, and who is going to bail on you when you need them most. Lucas has Lizzy, and Regan has Jessie, and in the sorority some friendships fail while others are strengthened. Real-life friendships often travel the same course—and you really know who your friends are when you are moving! As Dan and I juggled selling our house in California and moving the family to Arizona, some of our friends really stepped up to help. Tim Simonsma in particular helped Dan in more ways than I can count—and took him fishing when he needed a break. That is the mark of a true friend. Thanks, Tim, for helping keep my husband sane during the most stressful time in his life.